FRAGILE DREAMS

DREAMS

& Old Photographs

FRAGILE DREAMS

& Old Photographs

Elizabeth Gibson

BETHANY HOUSE PUBLISHERS
MINNEAPOLIS, MINNESOTA 55438

Originally published as *Old Photographs* in England by Lion Publishing in 1990.

The poems "Old Photographs" and "Negatives" are by Elizabeth Gibson © 1990.

Lines from "Poem on Her Death" by Elizabeth Gibson © 1981 appear here with acknowledments to the Vineyard Arts Fellowship, Atlanta, Ga., where the poem first appeared in *Motif* magazine.

Published by Bethany House Publishers
A Ministry of Bethany Fellowship, Inc.
6820 Auto Club Road, Minneapolis, Minnesota 55438

Printed in the United States of America

Library of Congress Cataloging-in-Publication Data

Gibson, Elizabeth, 1949–
  [Old photographs]
    p.   cm.
  Original title: Old photographs.

  1. Title.
PR6057.I246042   1991
823'.914—dc20   91–4146
ISBN 1–55661–230–3   CIP

For Johnny and Joan,

with love as ever,

and in loving memory of

Helen and Clem Archer—

friends where I had none

and family when I needed one

ELIZABETH GIBSON is an award-winning British novelist married to an American, and living in Kent, England with their two children. A previous novel, *The Water Is Wide*, won the ECPA Gold Medallion Award in 1985. This new novel, first published in 1990 in Britain, won the prestigious Deo Gloria Award, given for a novel, secular or religious, that singularly traces a spiritual path with dignity and insight.

Preface

I first met Elizabeth Gibson at a publishing convention in England. Warm, friendly, eager to "*talk shop*," she introduced herself as *Lizzie*. It took me a while to make the connection between Lizzie and the remarkably talented novelist I had known and admired for years as *Elizabeth Gibson*! (Her first American novel, *The Water Is Wide*, is crafted with such beauty and power that it ranks a place of honor on the bookshelf above my desk!) Once that connection exploded in my brain, I waited in a long line in order to get my own autographed copy of her new book, *Fragile Dreams & Old Photographs*! We laughed and hugged each other. Like school girls at summer camp, we exchanged addresses and vowed to write one another our life stories! I read my copy of her novel non-stop on the flight back home and page after page found myself in awe of her talent. *This is the stuff of which great literature is made!* The story lingers in my heart even today.

Elizabeth Gibson is *dear Lizzie* to me now, but that friendship does not dilute the admiration I have for one of the finest novelists of our time.

Bodie Thoene

Contents

The First Photograph
1962

Cameras clicked, popped and whirred as the players took their bows, and Eleanor McEnroe was preserved like the crystal swan on her parents' dining-room sideboard: iridescent, white, and dead still.

In the audience, Margaret sat enraptured. She was not with her own family. Just a week ago her father had left home without explanation, and her mother had taken her brother David and gone away to stay with her grandparents for a while. For the first time she could remember, she had stood up to her mother and refused to go. So, instead, she sat between Eleanor's parents: Marianne, perfumed and bright as tinsel, and McEnroe himself, smelling comfortably of cigars and the outdoors. "I got in one last round of golf, since we've no snow yet," he'd confided, as if she were twenty-six, not sixteen.

Margaret was suspended in a magical web, the McEnroes beside her and Ellie triumphing on the stage, sweeping white wings before her. Ellie was the girl the teachers despaired of until she won the role of Gabriel in the high school pageant, far outshining Mary or the tarnished star above the crudely carpentered stable. The girl who had cared enough about Margaret's father disappearing to ask her to come for Christmas. The girl everyone in Bishop O'Rourke's Academy envied and adored (except the teachers) because she sang like a thrush and danced like a lithe ballerina. High cheekbones, watchful eyes vivid and candid as a cat's, and a cloud of red hair about her face.

A few days later, Margaret stood under the McEnroes' tree. Brilliantly wrapped presents tumbled over each other at her feet. Red-wine velvet bows hung on every branch, dipping slightly in the currents of warm air. Silver bells and golden candles winked among the rain of tinsel that glittered and stirred on the tree. Nowhere had she seen a Christmas tree decorated so lavishly. Rising above the mezzanine banisters, it dwarfed her. But she was already dwarfed—a small, rounded person—by the expanse of the McEnroes' foyer.

"Kick your shoes off," Ellie hissed, coming up behind her. "McEnroe keeps this place like a hothouse."

Without answering, Margaret bent and unlaced her school shoes. She caught sight of Ellie's black patents discarded among the presents—outlawed by the teachers, but elegant and shining all the same—then the thick pile of the Persian carpet pushed up between her toes.

"Isn't it gorgeous?"

Margaret looked down at the patterns under her feet. "Yes, it sure is."

"No, not that, you loon! The tree, I mean."

"Oh, yes." The tree towered above her, smelling at once of the woods and of money. The words she wanted wouldn't come out.

Ellie grabbed her by the sleeve and steered her up the stairs. "Just you wait till you meet my brother. He's a pain. Talks all the time about cows and herd averages, whatever they are. But he's quite cute. You'll like him."

"Where is he, then?" She looked around at all the doors on the landing, some open, some shut. She said in a straight voice, "Where is this nature-loving paragon of a brother? Will he appear any moment in his natural state?"

Ellie punched her. "I see you got your sense of humor back at last. That's good. Don't let the McEnroes get to you, not at all."

"Not even your brother?" She was curious now. "Well, where is he? I can't wait."

"On his way home from the tech, I guess. Unless he's been sidetracked talking to a farmer. He always drives on the backroads. Says he hates to miss the rural scene. Quite a loon. Worse than you, in fact."

And there he was at the table when the family sat down for dinner: *Donald McEnroe*. About the same age as her brother, perhaps, but nothing like David, who was wiry and intense. Not that Don was elegant like his mother or sister, or expansive and shrewd like his father; but light shone from his eyes when he talked about ag school and about his dreams for a farm. Margaret stared, fascinated, at his wind-burned face, grained hands and untidy black hair. She stared and went on staring until Ellie kicked her under the table and she blushed hot as a red pepper.

"Sure are happy to have you with us, Margaret," McEnroe said when the presents were opened on Christmas Day. "Stand over there, now, next to Ellie. Let Marianne get your picture. Attagirl! Now you, Don. That's right, put your arm around her. You gotta treat her like the little lady she is."

Don's arm went around her shoulders with a powerful squeeze. He made a face at his sister before Marianne aimed the camera, and Ellie pealed with laughter. Margaret had never stood more still, leaning slightly against him.

The flashbulb exploded across her retinas. Her eyes

were blinded, and her shoulder ached from the contact with him. She might have lost her father for a while, but she had found a place where she did belong. *That's it*, she said to herself, falling asleep in the guest room that night. *Ellie McEnroe, it's all your fault. Donald McEnroe.* She said his name over and over to herself in the dark and saw also in the dark the blue depth of his eyes. *Donald McEnroe.*

PART I

Old Photographs
March 1971

Sepia sunsets curl away, embarrassed,
   from the light;
   from the keen-eyed grandchild's smirk.

They are faded now, innocent
   of crystal-sharp lens,
   of snapping shutter.

Look, I will box and blue-ribbon all
   and hang instead
   a gallery of you.

Of you shooting pointblank as the sun
   into my dazed,
   my aching eyes.
You—on the hard wall of weeping.

Highway 100 fell away down the final slope to the Hammond farm. The last curve in the road. She glanced in the rear-view mirror. Behind her was a kind of nothingness: wind rattling in the trees out of a slate-like sky empty of everything except a crow fronting the gusts. Wind; ridged clouds; crystalline sleet; big, rounded hills—wooded except at their granite tops.

Before her in the narrow valley lay all she hoped for. She flicked her eyes forward again and hardly heard her own small sound of happiness.

The barn always appeared first. At this time of day— late afternoon with no sunlight—the buildings made a red beacon in the drab landscape. She watched them grow into sharper focus as the Buick pressed downhill, faster and faster. First the buildings and then the wooden fenceposts separated and became distinct; the boards on the side of the milking parlor divided them-selves between weathered cracks, grain lines and knotholes. And then she was there, slowing, pulling into the muddy area in front of the farmhouse. The dogs were yelping, running round the car, leaping up at the windows.

Turning off the ignition she sat still briefly and tried to gather herself. No one came into the yard; she didn't have to face him yet. She shoved the door into the wind and stepped out. Cold air slapped her face and whirled her coat around.

Then one of Hammond's young sons came out and pulled the dogs away. "Down! Yah! Get down, you stupid animals." He looked at her without curiosity and shouted over the wind, "Don? I don't know. Shall I get my dad?"

"You don't need to. Don's expecting me. May I walk around a bit?"

"Go right ahead." The boy was looking at her with puzzled half-recognition. He said cautiously, "At least I guess you can—if he knows you're coming." He stood there as if waiting for more from her. "Sorry about the dogs. This wind's under their tails."

"It doesn't matter." She was used to children, but she hesitated all the same. "You don't remember me . . . I'm sure."

"Nope."

"Margaret Fuller. I used to come up, summers—with Don's sister, Ellie."

He looked blank, hovering on the edge of politeness. "Oh, a while ago, you mean?"

"Yes." She scanned the buildings. "Hey—I think I'll walk around." She went back out to the edge of the highway and searched with her eyes the sleet-whitened pastures for even a sign of him. She was hungry now to see him, her stomach hollow with anticipation.

Was that Don? Someone in a jacket that ballooned out below the shoulders was moving a section of electric fence. He passed the cows, slapped a few of them on the rump and trudged on to the next stake. The animals stood still, backs to the wind, their uneasy lowing drifting faintly up to where she stood. She watched him closely, the deliberate slowness of his movements, the way he stopped periodically and looked up at the crows diving through the wind, the contours of his body each time he bent down. Yes, that was Don.

Shivering, she turned back into the yard again, to where the boy still waited with a dog on either side. "I saw him down in that bottom pasture."

"Then he'll be up again in a minute, very likely."

"Are you busy?"

"Nope. I just finished some chores. Want me to run down and tell him you're here?"

"Please. That'd be great."

————

The din of the wind drowned almost everything. It thickened his ears and forced his eyes shut. He bent his head and went on as it died down for a moment. Then, just as he reached the upper gate of the pasture, he met Hammond's youngest boy running down the track, mouth open in a shout, and the dogs barking behind him. The wind came up again with a crash, and he had to bend to hear him.

"A woman's up there for you," the boy shouted.

"Right now?"

"Said you were looking for her."

He frowned and followed the youngster to the yard. Inside his boots, his feet were bloodless and aching with cold. Who would have come now, at the start of a storm? Then, remembering, he stopped in the middle of the track. Ellie: his sister was here. March 25, and he hadn't laid a hand to the cottage since . . . before Christmas. Ray Hammond had kept him busy, not just with chores but with extra work. He'd wanted the sheds rearranged. The silo unloader had broken down, and he'd made several trips before finding the right parts to repair the motor. Then one of the tractors froze and wouldn't run; he'd spent three days on that. No wonder Ellie had scarcely entered his mind since he'd seen her at home on Christmas Day.

As they rounded the corner, there she was, too, her old car awkwardly straddling a bank by the farmyard wall. If it snowed tonight, she'd never get out, he thought. Standing beside the car, her hair blown over her face by the wind, she raised her arm in a wave. He noticed the new coat she wore. No, it was an old coat, not a coat of Ellie's at all. And that was not Ellie. He blinked to clear his eyes; the gale had dried them to a gritty scratchiness. Yet it was his sister's car. He waved hesitantly.

It was Ellie's friend waving at him, he realized. Ellie must still be in the car. As he approached the car, he narrowed his eyes and squinted into the splattered, back-reflecting glass of the windshield. No, Ellie had not come.

Disappointed and puzzled, he motioned the other woman into the milking parlor.

When he'd rolled the door shut, he found the quiet inside overwhelming. It was hard not to shout. "Whatever's happened to Ellie? Why isn't she here?" He looked past Margaret and out of the small, high window behind her, half-expecting to see Ellie come sauntering in her laughing way across the farmyard. *Silly old Don! Fooled you! We traded cars. Surprise! Of course I came . . ."*

Margaret was smiling at him, pushing back her thick, smooth hair. "She couldn't come."

"Seriously?" He noticed minute beads of the first snow melting on her hair. Tiny, like little pieces of glass.

"Absolutely. She's got a meeting on Monday that she can't miss. Some kind of change in the agency . . . she didn't tell me. But she'd talked about coming, ever since Christmas."

"Typical!"

"She'd said I should go with her. We've all talked about a weekend together for so long, and I took an extra day off this weekend."

"And came alone. She might have called."

"She thought I should come anyway."

He laughed and pushed his hands into his overall pockets. The wind and cold metal stakes had numbed them into clumsy blocks. "Typical again." He heard the irritation in his own voice, but went on, "You sure picked the lousiest weekend possible. A north-easter's blowing in again. You'll get stuck."

She shrugged. "I needed to get away."

"Well, you did—more than you bargained for. Maybe you'd better jump right back in Ellie's old scrap heap and get going again—before you're caught." He made sure that he had her eye. "You might make it if you start now."

She raised her chin slightly, but he could see that he had scored a hit; she paled a little, but the determination never left her eyes. "It took me long enough to get here. And anyway, I really wanted . . . it's been three years . . ."

He sighed. Why was she always so persistent? Wasn't it enough that she kept writing him letters? Why did she have to spring herself on him now? "Oh, Margaret," he shook his head. "I completely forgot she was coming. Things aren't fit for a woman out at the cottage. I can cope . . . but I'm not sure about you." He looked down at her leather boots. "You're a doll coming all this way, but I don't know if you should take the chance . . ."

She turned, craning her neck to look out of the window. "But if the storm's going to be as bad as you say, then I'd never make it back in time anyhow. Couldn't I just stay at Hammonds', if your place is a pigpen?"

"No way!" he snorted. "It's not that bad, Margaret."

"Then what do you suggest?" She sounded only mildly ironic.

Annoyed at her teasing insistence, he murmured, "I don't know."

"Just look at that sky. There's no way I can go back now."

He found himself smiling unaccountably. "All right. You win. If you can put up with the rough rural primitive for a few days—"

"You? Or the cottage?" she asked, deadpan.

He ignored that. "Then let it be chez McEnroe. But just remember, this is McEnroe North, not McEnroe East. No mansion, okay?" His voice sounded hollow in the parlor empty of all animals now but Hammonds' white cat curled in a loose pile of hay. "For the life of me, I can't see what you and Ellie like so much about this place. Not exactly a pastoral idyll here."

"Don," she said quickly, "Ellie and I weren't planning to come up here to be entertained, you know." She lightly touched his folded arm.

He backed off. Why did she always press herself on him? "Huh! Ellie comes out here to do what she calls a clean-up and turns everything topsy-turvy. Then she has the nerve to stand in the middle of all the mess *she's* made and tell me what a hayseed I am."

Margaret laughed, "She can talk! You should see *her* room!"

He let his arms drop. "Shall we go, then?"

He began an internal debate about the cows. *Should they be in, or shall I chance it?* "I could probably quit now for the day."

————

They left the milking parlor for the roar of the wind again. Cold in her old plaid coat and thin leather boots, she shivered as he made her stand in the yard while he moved the Buick out of the road. Then they transferred her bag into his jeep and drove the two miles to the cottage. The jeep jolted, bounced and slid where the wind had molded the muddy ruts into treacherously unyielding grooves.

The stove fire had gone out, so the cottage lay chilled and still. Margaret looked around, remembering other times—always in the summertime, before—when she and Ellie had come to visit. Not for a long time, though, and things weren't quite as she remembered them. No curtains hung at the windows; the kitchen smelled of manure and rancid fat; the living room sofa disgorged stuffing onto the scuffed floor; and with no fire in either room, even the thick stone walls and clapboard didn't keep out the cold.

Don made a log fire in the living room grate. It burned brightly but heated only the one room. She sat in front of it with her hands outstretched and her teeth chattering, but then, feeling uneasy, offered to help make supper.

"Nah—just rest up," he called back. "Pour yourself a drink if you want one . . . I guess you're old enough that I can legally offer you one."

Clenching her jaw tightly and meditating a cutting reply, she answered instead, "No, thanks. Can I get one for you?"

"Later maybe."

She moved to the low doorway and watched him cutting carrots and onions for a stew. Slow and awkward with a knife, he still wouldn't accept her help. "Well, I'll take my things up," she said. "Will it be the same room?"

"Yeah, the one under the gable. Want me to carry that stuff?"

"No need to."

"Don't be shocked. It's bitterly cold in there. Hope you brought a sleeping-bag."

"Thanks, I did."

The room was halfway up the stairs to the attic room where he slept. She opened the door and smelled the familiar mustiness, but it was almost home. A release from the city; a place of peace. And at least this room was as she remembered it: bare walls, bare floors, bare windows.

Outside the wind was dying a little but still squeaked and whined through the cracks around the windows—the only sound until the telephone rang below. Through the old floorboards she faintly heard the murmur of his voice answering. She sat down on the bed, numb with cold, gnawed by uncertainty about the wisdom of coming alone to see this man she had loved so long. And she remembered, suddenly, the call from Ellie that had changed both their lives. That call had brought Don nearer after all, though in the intervening two years he had rarely seemed near at all.

In the dark the phone shrilled, went silent, then shrilled again. Her dream was splintered. She fumbled for the light, knocking over a glass of water. The phone pealed again. Dazed, she screwed up her eyes against the sudden glare to see the clock. Then she picked up the receiver.

"Maggie, Margaret—that you?" A girl's voice, talking urgently.

She sat forward, trying to concentrate. The end of the dream twisted in her mind, eluding her. "Yes, this is Margaret, but—"

"It's Ellie. It's me. I gotta talk to you."

"At three in the morning?"

"I know. But I'll go crazy if I don't talk to someone. Please don't hang up."

Margaret clicked her tongue. "Of course not. Calm down. Just tell me what's going on."

The voice on the other end of the line changed slightly, self-pity replacing frenzy. "You've just got to help me. The dean's thrown me out of school."

"Again." Margaret flopped back onto the pillow and coiled the phone cord round her fingers. "This has happened before, hasn't it? One little wiggle of McEnroe's finger and the college gets back in line for you."

"Oh, just great! What's the matter? You're never like this."

Margaret sighed. "Don't be stupid. But we've gone

through this before. Why don't you call me tomorrow when I can think?"

"It can't wait. This is it. Final. Period. Out for good."

"*Why*, Ellie?"

"Because McEnroe says he won't intervene for me this time. I'm through with everything here, and I'm not going home, either. Not on your sweet life."

Margaret digested this, anticipating what was coming. Ellie always had her way, but Margaret wouldn't give in, not yet. "What was the crime this time?" she asked with deliberate sarcasm.

"The dean called it 'chronic indiscretion'."

Ellie's mocking laughter brought a smile to Margaret's mouth. "Went to bed in the wrong dorm again?"

"You don't need the details."

"Oh, yes I do, if you're going to ask what I think you're going to ask."

"You don't need to give me such a hard time, either."

"Why not? Oh, the poor dean! I can see him now! Harried. Frustrated. 'How do I deal with this awful McEnroe woman *this* time? Will anyone please tell me what to tell her father? And what do I tell the trustees when funds stop coming for the McEnroe Theater Arts building?' Oh, poor little man."

Ellie was laughing and shouting at once. "Come on, Maggie. Can I come up and see you, or not?"

"I see. You want to visit for a couple of nights?" She kept her voice light.

"No. Maggie, you're being a perfect—"

"Stop. The phone's turning blue in my hand."

"Then cut out the big-sister routine. I'm only asking if you'll let me move in for a few weeks. I'll get a job in Boston. Just till I get on my feet. Okay?"

Margaret smiled. "I knew you'd ask," she said sweetly. "Sure you can come."

The relief was audible. "You're an angel! I know it'll work out. I couldn't face staying in Providence. Know what I mean? And I have a ride tomorrow. Will you be there?"

The dream turned toward her again, and then she remembered. Don—she had been with him again. That's always what she remembered: his arms still pressed around her. He loved her, after all. And Ellie watched from the shadows of a dark tree as the two of them rocked back and forth, dancing to soundless music. But the shadows swam and grew more distorted. Ellie melted. A phone rang. Water splattered onto the bedside table, and the hand that put on the light had shattered everything except the warm pressure of his arms.

Remembering, she wanted only to be near Ellie, to have her there just to have someone to talk to about him. "Yes, if you know when you're coming, I'm sure to be here."

"You're such a sweetheart! I can't wait to see you."

"*When*, Ellie?"

"He said we'd get to Boston around eleven. Of course this guy has no idea how much stuff I have stashed away in this room, so let's say twelve?"

A thought occurred to Margaret. "It's not . . . Don who's bringing you, is it?"

"Transparent Maggie! No, darling, it's not." She drew out the word "darling" as Vivienne Leigh might have said it. "You'll be there?"

"I'll be there," Margaret said wearily. She felt like swearing.

"Thanks for the graciousness. I'm sure I shan't be able to stand you for more than a few weeks anyway."

"Likewise, my dear." She didn't bother to mop up the water. Switching off the light, she tried again to see in the dark the face of the dream, but it had slid away.

———

The smell of the stew and the warmth of the stove

and the living-room fire had just begun to take the edge off the frosty room as she went downstairs again. Don was smiling to himself and setting out plates and forks. "You'll hardly believe this," he said.

"What?"

"Reality wins over romance, one to zero."

Her eyebrows flickered in puzzlement, and she felt her face grow a little warmer from the heat of the stove. "Too bad. Reality's so dull." She picked abstractedly at the paper on two wrapped packages she had carried downstairs with her and wondered what he was talking about.

He grunted. "Well, it's what I said before. This is no idyllic life. That was Ray Hammond on the phone complaining about the cows being out overnight too early in the season. He's right, I guess. Wants me to go back down and move them in." He scowled. "I should've done it before—thought about it." Then he shrugged. "So much for the candlelit dinner for two . . . and I forgot something else we'll need if you're going to be here a few days. Of all the jackass things to forget." He turned and stirred the stew for a moment, and the aroma of tomatoes and gravy wafted toward Margaret. "The milk!"

She laughed at him. "You work on a dairy farm and you're out of milk. Good, Don! Give me a pail. I'll run out and milk a cow."

"Sure! I usually get a small can before I come home. You put it out of my mind—and we can't drink water and beer all night or on our cornflakes. Or in tea—you still put milk in tea?" he pulled a face. "Looks like I'd better get myself down there."

She swallowed. "But you haven't even eaten. Couldn't Ray move them? Or what about the other hired man?"

"Didn't show. And Ray has lots of bookwork to do. This is what I get for being such a lazy cuss and trying to cut out early."

"You won't eat first?"

He put his head on one side. "Come on, Margaret. Don't put the mother-hen act on me. If you're hungry, you go ahead. I'd rather eat slowly and relish it. I won't be gone long." He took his jacket off the hook behind the door and started to pull on his boots.

"I could go with you."

He stopped, balancing against the wall with one foot on the floor and the other partly into his boot. "Heck, whatever for?"

She put her packages on the drain-board. "I brought these things for you . . . you can look at them later." Then she turned around again. "For company, of course. I'll fill up a can while you round up the cows." She forced a smile. *This was all a mistake. I should never have come without Ellie.*

He moved his shoulders indifferently. "Please yourself, Margaret. If you want to tag along, hurry and get a coat. I've gotta get moving."

"If you want to tag along." Was that how he still thought of her? Flustered, she rushed upstairs again, pulled on her coat, and bent for her oldest pair of shoes. *At least he can't say anything about my boots this time.*

In the jeep, he said, "So how's the world been treating you?"

She deliberately kept her eyes on the laser-like lines of snowflakes driving against the windshield and headlights. "So-so, I guess."

"You don't want to tell me?" He sounded amused, indulgent. It was the same tone he used with Ellie.

"There's not much to tell. I like the job, for now, and the principal likes what I'm doing. I just don't know if I want to spend the rest of my life as a second-grade teacher, that's all. But I've told you all that before. You read my letters, don't you?"

He didn't answer the question. "Couldn't stand it, myself."

"You're doing what you want to, though. It's different."

"It's not exactly what I want . . . but I do want to know about you." He leaned forward to light a cigarette from the dashboard lighter. "Smoke?"

"No thanks. You know I don't." She tried to gauge his tone. "What do you want to know about?"

"Oh—you know me. Always curious. You and Ellie both. You dating around?" The cigarette glowed, a red point in the dark.

"Ellie is."

"Naturally. My swinging sister. Anyone nice?"

She smiled. "Some of them—a few. But they're drifters. Some of them are a little strange."

He laughed. "She's good for a little fun, then off they go?"

"Something like that."

They fell quiet, and a parade of faces passed across her mind. She relived the early days in the apartment she and Ellie first rented.

———

They had moved early in the summer of '69 from Margaret's efficiency to a larger apartment. While Margaret wanted the extra rooms and space to prepare her lessons in peace, Ellie saw the new place as an opportunity to experiment with parties. Night after night under her art-nouveau wall hangings and cascading ferns and philodendra, the apartment rocked and reverberated to Dylan, Jagger and Joplin. Or it flickered in the candlelight of what Ellie euphemistically called soirees, which lasted long into the night and ended in a huddle of bodies and afghans on the living room floor.

On those evenings Margaret crossed the room ruefully as she went from bedroom to living room and back. It didn't matter that the new apartment was rented in her name, that she was only a year older than

Ellie. The friends made her feel, anyway, as if she was out of place and out of date; beside Ellie, she felt colorless and insignificant. She didn't know enough, she thought, about civil rights or the Kennedys or Vietnam or the proposed lottery system, to enter into the impassioned debates that generally continued for hours after she'd gone to bed. And because her brother David had gone to Vietnam as a medic and had returned alive, she felt as if what went on in the war had no power to touch her. She was not interested in all the discussion about it, either, and she hated the way it hung like a gray shadow over everything. She was tired of the nightly litany of village names, of "victories" and "defeats," of strategic maps, choppers clattering over the jungle, bursts of mortar fire—all on the twelve-inch screen of Ellie's portable television. Was there no escaping the meaningless peace talks in Paris, the flag-draped coffins, or the blank faces of the dead and dying in the pages of *Time*?

The nightly visitors in the apartment that summer were long-legged, large-eyed girls who worked with Ellie at the modelling agency and who darted quick, suggestive glances at all the men in turn. With them came a few of the disenchanted from Providence: men and women who, like Ellie, had crossed the dean of the college once too often. They thought of themselves as campus radicals who without degrees had nevertheless earned themselves tickets into the high circles of the New England political, intellectual and cultural aristocracy—unless the draft board intervened. Nothing was too bizarre or esoteric for their consideration. They argued, smoked and drank; drank, smoked and argued.

Then there were the withdrawn ones, most of them men. They lay back on the beanbag cushions, their adam's apples protruding, their eyes fixed on the ceiling or the plants. They said little, except perhaps to girls as quiet as themselves, or occasionally to another man when they passed around the ritual joint. They seemed unaware of whose apartment they occupied. Margaret often wondered, too, how Ellie had ever met them. Did they care if they came? Or would they rather have lain instead on Boston Common, staring through the neon glare at the faint stars and hearing in the distance the mournful insistence of the Hare Krishna chanters? For all their nonchalance, she could scarcely tell.

She would find out what they were thinking about, she had decided one evening when she was tired of being the middle-aged outsider whose only function was to clean up the following morning. She would find out.

Friday came and the rain was gusting onto the black night windows. Ellie lit candles and put cheese, wine and crackers on the kitchen counter. Margaret plumped the beanbags and fussed with her hair in front of the mirror in the entryway. *You've wit enough to keep ten men busy, Maggie,* her brother David used to say to her. But wit was no good by itself. How could she break into Ellie's circle with useless wit—when the men were discussing deferment, flights to Canada, draft-card burnings, and nuclear war?

No one had come. By nine o'clock Ellie, obviously deflated, lounged in the love seat filing her nails and occasionally leaning forward to switch channels on a television she wasn't even watching. Suffering from hay fever, she had to keep stopping to blow her nose. "We should have gone dancing in Cambridge," she grumbled.

"Didn't any of your friends tell you they'd come?"

"Sure. They always say they will. Some of them do; some of them don't. But who wants to come out in this kind of rain?"

Margaret looked at her watch. "We still could go over to Cambridge, I guess," she said doubtfully. "Rain doesn't bother me."

Then the downstairs doorbell buzzed. Ellie jumped up immediately. "Why don't you crack out some ice?"

Margaret hesitated. "No, you do it. I'll let them in."

Ellie gave her a look of exaggerated surprise. "You'll be staying around for a change?"

"Yes."

"Good. Go ahead, then. I was hoping you would." So Margaret asked over the intercom for identification.

"Chuck Ryan and Constantine the Great. But whose is the gorgeous voice?"

Her mouth went dry. "Margaret. Ellie's friend. Come on up." She pressed the door release and called back toward the kitchen, "Chuck Ryan—and Constantine? Okay?"

Ellie laughed gaily and clinked glasses. "Chuck and *who*? Very okay! Now I don't care if no one else comes at all."

"*Constantine*—is that the guy's real name?" She hesitated near the door. The air conditioner did not seem to be doing its job; the apartment was far too hot.

Ellie set drinks on the coffee table behind her. "Yeah. Family's Greek Orthodox, poor kid. He wanted to declare conscientious objection, but his draft board's ultraconservative—they're going to nab him anyhow. They told him he had an ancestor who was a Christian *and* a soldier, so tough luck to him. He's one of the first in line in '69—supposed to be inducted at the end of this month. And Chuck, you may have seen him before. I've been crazy about him for several days . . . oh, why don't you let them in?"

"Hello, baby." One of the men waltzed straight past Margaret to give a hug to Ellie. "I dragged Constantine along. And this." He held up a magnum of cheap red wine. Ellie's friend was tall and heavy with a reddish beard and small wire-rimmed glasses that rested ridiculously on a large nose. A sort of hippie Santa Claus.

"Lovely," Ellie was saying. "Great. We've got some

too. Come right on in. Your beard's so—mmm." She took his arm and led him toward the kitchen.

Behind came Chuck's friend, who nodded at Margaret and found his way to a beanbag. He sat down quietly with his hands on his knees and did not look up until Ellie brought them a drink. Then he gave Margaret a disarming smile and raised his glass to her. "So you're Maggie. We've been hearing of you. Never seen you, though."

She laughed, catching Ellie's eye. Ellie, already cuddled up to Chuck in the love seat, smiled back beatifically. "Cute, isn't he, Maggie?"

Chuck groaned. "Watch your language, McEnroe." He slid his eyes in Margaret's direction. "She ain't so bad herself. Look at that gorgeous thick hair."

Ellie punched him, but Margaret knew she didn't have to answer. She met Constantine's eyes over her glass, all the same. His were dark and alive in a mobile, expressive face with taut, clean-shaven skin and a cloud of black, curly hair. He was watching her, intent on her.

"Say, Ellie and Margaret—" Chuck began, "have you heard about this music and art fair they're having next weekend? Woodstock?"

"What? Where?" Ellie asked. She wiped her nose and eyes again. "Curse this hay fever!"

"Bethel—someplace in upstate New York. I don't know where it is. But it sounds good. Sounds like everyone's gonna be there. Janis Joplin—" He gestured wildly toward the stereo. "Jimi Hendrix, Joan Baez, Arlo Guthrie, Jefferson Airplane . . . they're billing it as a peace celebration, expecting fifty thousand people. Wanna go?"

Margaret avoided Chuck's eyes, but Ellie turned immediately with a smile. "Sure we'll go."

"We could use my camper. Plenty of room. The festival's on some freak's farm. I don't fancy camping, but the van'd be cozy." He leered at Ellie.

Margaret wanted to laugh. *Well, she's getting what she wants*, she thought. "Count me out," she said. "But thanks."

"I might go. It'll be the last weekend before—" Constantine stared with a wry face at the farthest wall. "—I get my hair cut."

Margaret swallowed and turned her head sharply toward him. *That's right. He's going away.*

Chuck knocked back the rest of his wine and held out his glass to Ellie for a refill. "Heck, Constantine, and I thought Ellie and I had you all fixed up."

Ellie laughed, throwing a mischievous glance at Margaret.

I bet she had all this planned, Margaret thought. "Should've gone dancing in Cambridge, Ellie? Oh yeah!"

Ellie shrugged. "Well, why not?"

The wine had relaxed her. She murmured, "Why not?" But she didn't look at Constantine, and she didn't want to spend the next weekend out in a muddy field listening to music, even if it was his last weekend stateside.

They drank the wine, laughed and talked: about Harvard, about the war. Chuck and Constantine, she discovered, were a year younger and had just finished their senior year at Harvard. Margaret could imagine Constantine in the library absorbed in a book, but she couldn't see him in jungle fatigues landing a helicopter or lobbing hand grenades at Viet Cong. Something inside her withered, shriveled as she watched and listened to him.

She left her glass on the table and stood up, suddenly afraid to think about it any more.

"How about some tea?" Chuck muttered to Constantine, leaning forward and uncurling Ellie's arm from around his shoulders.

"I can get some," Margaret answered, puzzled.

Ellie looked up, her face reddening as she burst into waves of laughter that shook her body. "No, no, silly. Not *tea*. Chuck means grass, honey. Marijuana, you know? We'll get stoned." And she turned to Chuck. "Maggie here's such a good little girl—I'll bet she never puffed a joint in her whole life. Right, Maggie?"

"No thanks, Ellie McEnroe." She felt stupid.

"Such a good girl." Ellie's voice was already slurred. Margaret's return smile was pasted on.

"Sickening," Ellie went on. "Imagine, she was the one held up as a good example in school all the time. Sickening! Can't imagine why I'm sharing an apartment with such a good girl." She gestured wildly, giggling and falling against Chuck. Then she had to blow her nose again.

Constantine was reaching into his pocket. He threw a small unlabeled packet to Chuck. "Here, you take it. I guess—I don't want any. Finish it if you want." His eyes came up to meet Margaret's. "Want to go out for a while?"

She hesitated. Was he trying to save her from the situation? She moved her shoulders slightly. "Sure, we can go out if you'd like." Then she remembered the rain. "That is, if you don't mind wading across the Common or wielding my hideous umbrella."

"The rain was stopping when we got here," he said. Ellie was crooning and swaying in her seat now.

"Have yourselves a grand time, kids." Ellie waved and giggled as they went out. "Ma and Pa'll keep the place warm for you."

Out on the street, Constantine immediately put his arm round her. "Your friend's crazy," he said.

"Always has been. But I love her a lot." *Yes, and I love her brother far more*, she added mentally. For a moment she felt like a betrayer. What was she doing wandering around Boston in the dark with a man she did not know, when the man she loved was miles away?

But he does not love me. She tried to shrug off that photograph in her mind of Don's arm around her shoulders.

"D'you mind if we walk a bit?"

She pulled herself back to the present, and to the man whose arm was warm around her shoulders now. "No, I'd like that. The apartment sometimes gives me claustrophobia."

"It was hot."

"Yes, and we weren't wanted, either. But I'd much rather be outside, anyway."

In open-toed sandals they splashed along between the puddles on the sidewalk and came down Spruce Street toward the Common.

"After the rain, even Boston air smells good," she said. "You can smell the ocean." She thought about the marijuana again, and was curious. "You smoke a lot, do you?"

"Grass? No—oh, once in a while. It's been less lately. And you, you don't do drugs?"

She shook her head. "No, but that must sound tame to you."

"Oh, you're one of those health freaks, I guess."

"Not yet."

"Wash with a loofah and eat yogurt and brewer's yeast, right?"

She laughed and dodged a puddle, losing his arm. "I just like to know what I'm doing, that's all."

He reclaimed her. "You can be stone-cold sober and still not know what you're doing, or why. Like in Nam."

The laughter had left his voice. *There is no escape from the war,* she thought. All she wanted was to live, not to think or talk about dying, not to die.

They found a bench that faced Beacon Street and watched the people walking by. Two patrolmen swinging their nightsticks stopped a few feet away from them, eyed them, then ambled away again still swinging their sticks. After they'd gone, Margaret dropped her head on Constantine's shoulder.

He said, "Hmm, that's nice. Chuck's right."

"What?"

"You do have gorgeous hair." He touched her head lightly. "It's thick and warm. All springy."

She smiled, feeling easy with him, and sleepy. They sat still for a long time, and he told her to call him "Con." "Most people do. Ryan was just having a laugh tonight calling me 'Constantine' all the time. And 'Con' makes me sound like one of you. Like all the Irish kids I hang out with." He waved his hands as he talked. "You're a Catholic Christian, I guess, like most of the Irish kids I know?"

She did not want to answer. Bishop O'Rourke's Academy was a memory of childhood she would rather escape, except that through it she had met Don. So she ignored the question. "*Con*. It suits you."

He gently pulled her nearer to him and began to kiss her. Then he walked her back to the apartment, where Ellie and Chuck had disappeared into Ellie's room. Without any invitation, for he hadn't needed one, Con took her to bed. But he did not touch her, and all night she stayed awake next to him, watching him. He would be in the jungle in a few weeks. She had forgotten most prayers from Bishop O'Rourke's, but now she wished she could remember how to pray for him. Someone had to, and she faltered through several prayers before giving up with a sigh. *Poor Con.*

————

Was all that only two summers ago? She shook herself, shifting in her seat, and watched Don as he steered slowly forward.

"And you with no vices, no smoking, no drinking— what about men, Maggie? When are you getting hitched?"

"Hmm? What?" His use of *Maggie* stopped her for a second. "Not for a long time."

"Not even going steady? You never mention a thing about men in your letters."

"Nope. None of your business." She was thankful he couldn't see her face. Her hands felt damp inside their gloves. "And you," she asked as lightly as she could, "have you got all the Vermont women's hearts clattering and tongues chattering?"

"Sure hope so! It's fun being the youngest eligible old man."

She laughed. "But what did you mean—this isn't exactly what you want? I thought you loved it up here."

He gestured. "Oh, it would take a while to explain. I was satisfied for the first few years. Ray's okay. I've learned a lot from him . . . about everything. But I've been here eight years, and tonight's typical. Even if I should've done it before, Ray could easily have taken a few minutes from his desk to get the cows. But no, he can sit on his backside and call me while his wife makes supper for him. I'm thirty-one, Margaret. I knew it would take time to set myself up without McEnroe, but I need to be working for myself—like you and Ellie. And that cottage—it's never really been home. Could've been, I guess. But I haven't wanted to bother. I've been saving everything. By next year, maybe. I promised myself by thirty-two I'd be out."

"You'll buy your own place?" Her voice was quiet, wondering.

"Sure, that's what I've wanted all along."

She found she couldn't answer right away. At last, she said, "Where?" and her voice sounded small even to herself.

"I'm thinking Western New York somewhere. I've been keeping my eyes open, and there's a couple places I'm interested in. Longer growing season there, and the land's not so expensive, either." He swung the jeep into the yard. Snow was falling fast, big flakes that plashed onto the windshield. "Well, you'll have to wait for details some other time. Go on in the parlor. It's not too cold, and we'll be back up in twenty minutes or so, if the cows are as eager to get in out of the snow as I'll be." And he disappeared into the dark with a flashlight and one of Hammonds' dogs.

She went in and sat on the hay. The only light came from one bulb by the door; she couldn't find the switch for the others. So she sat in a circle of feeble light staring around and listening to the slight scratching of mice along the walls and under the straw-littered feed troughs. If Ray came in, he'd be surprised to see her.

But no one came except a white cat, who, having crouched unseen and silent under a trough for at least as long as she'd been in there, shot out and nabbed a mouse in the nearest corner: a mere limp shadow in its jaws. She heard some scuffling, then the snapping of small bones. The sound made her shiver.

Restless, she got up and went to the bulk tanks. Remembering how to open only the oldest of them, she went up on a stepladder, unlatched and raised the hinged lid. . . . A round lake of bubbling white. Then she closed the lid and searched by the sink for a clean can. All those she found were too large, so she sat down in the hay again and began to wish she had stayed in the cottage after all. Or perhaps she should have stayed in Boston, in the apartment. What if he didn't have Saturday off, as he used to?

Just when the cold from the cement floor had penetrated her shoes, and her face and fingers had begun to feel pinched, she heard the familiar bellowing of cows in the pasture behind the adjoining barn and knew that Don would soon have them inside. Sure enough, the dog was scratching and snuffling at the door within a few minutes. She let him in, and with him a cloud of snowflakes blown off the roof. In only

half an hour snow had fallen ankle-deep in the yard . . .
drifting too.

The dog sniffed and wagged at her. Then she heard
Don stamping his feet and whistling outside. "All set,
Maggie."

She called back, "I couldn't find a can."

He came in, his cap, jacket, and hat crusted with
snow. "Here, I'll get one. Then let's get back. You're
shivering with cold." Shoving the dog out of his way,
he washed his hands at the sink. "The can's under the
tank. Get the scoop off the other tank. Okay?" Then he
leaned over the old tank and with a look of intense
absorption creamed off the fresh milk froth. He tasted
and offered some to her.

She reached up and sipped: bitingly cold, smooth,
creamy.

"The best drink on earth, isn't it?" he asked, and
caught her eye.

"Like this it is, before they pasteurize and homog-
enize and vitaminize it."

He grinned. "A purist. You'd make a good ad for the
Agricultural Department. That's how I like it, too.
Straight up." He poured the milk foaming into the can.

The jeep already lay under a thick hat of light snow,
and their tracks from half an hour before had vanished
as they turned out of the yard. More snow drove against
them all the way back to the cottage, and Don steered
cautiously, guided by telephone lines for the length of
the track. Margaret watched his tense face in the green-
ish glow from the dashboard. "If the wind comes up
hard again—and it will—this'll be a terrible mess," he
said.

"It's only a few inches."

"In a couple hours! And you know how this land
rolls. The wind can roar up over here. I've been completely stuck before—in only six inches—but with
three-foot drifts. These late storms are the pits."

She shivered and edged farther down in her seat, as though the movement would warm her. But she felt cold until they were inside again and eating the stew: tender braised carrots; onions and tomatoes; rich beef and gravy. Without candlelight.

"You cook well, I have to admit." She watched him mopping up gravy with a piece of baked potato. The kitchen and living room were warm now. She felt like basking in front of the fire with a book. Or with him. So what if the snow kept them in?

"Thanks. Ellie's never said so."

She leaned back to survey him across the table. It was a kind of game. He knew she was watching but made no acknowledgement, and she knew that he knew. But she went on staring anyway at the wide shoulders, rounded in relaxation; the large forehead, heavy jaw, and thick dark hair. She examined him slowly. After all, it was three years since she'd seen him. . . . *Not like anyone else I love. Then why?* She went on staring, trying to analyze the old attraction.

It defied analysis. Her internal voice moaned, *He's everything I want. Solid. Roots deep in the seasons* . . . The voice stopped, and her satirical mind laughed at the fancy. Conscious and unconscious metaphor failed at all attempts to fathom this strange, unknown soil people call "love." It was there. That was all. Real, fertile and waiting.

Words seemed weighted and irrelevant. She was not sure, yet, whether her outward voice would sound like her own. So she kept quiet, waiting. But then she laughed at herself. If Ellie were here, she would have kicked her under the table by now.

He looked up, finally. "What is it?"

"I was wondering—" She looked down and leapt the gulf from within to without before raising her eyes. "Oh, I was just wondering what you'll be doing this weekend." She had to look down again.

"Don't you remember? It never changes. Off every Saturday since I came. Morning milking's all I have until Sunday, and some weeks until Monday."

"You don't have to get up early tomorrow, surely?"

"Sure I do. I like to. I hate to waste the whole day."

"Then what?"

"Depends." Unconsciously he was rubbing his hand up and down the cracked grain of the table. "Sometimes I study. Not exactly starving for fresh air in my profession! Some days I take off to Rutland, or Middlebury, or Barre . . . just depends how I feel. Tomorrow looks like a reading day. I'll be lucky if I even make it down to Hammonds'. Probably have to use the snowmobile. The snowplow never gets up here early enough." He lifted the dishes into the sink.

She hesitated, thinking how he disliked Ellie's help. "Shall I do them?"

"Nah. Let's go in the other room." He led the way. "I want to see what you brought."

Proffering the small parcels, she said, "Both for you."

He took them in one hand and bent with the other to poke the fire in the stove. Then, subsiding with a groan into the broken sofa, he rustled the wrappings open. "From Ellie?"

"No. From me." She hesitated, then sat down beside him.

He held on his lap the jar of dark purple jam and the large slab of fruitcake. "You made this scrumptious cake?"

"No, Momma did. For Christmas. It improves with keeping, so I saved some for you. But I made the jam. See the label?"

" 'Blackberry, September 1970. Fuller'," he read.

He pulled off the seal and dipped a finger into the jar. Licking it, he made noises of smacking appreciation, grinning broadly. "Good little jam-maker you are," he said, and he reached over and gave her a pat on the shoulder. But then, with an impish grin she had not seen on his face since her arrival, he suddenly wrestled her arm backward until she was bent double and he was laughing down at her. It always happened this way—his old trick with her and Ellie: a sort of "in" joke between them. How to persecute Ellie and Maggie without really trying. Ellie had even suggested once that Don write a manual on the subject.

Twisting her neck round, Margaret winced, "Come on, Don, for goodness sake. That's kids' stuff."

He tightened his hold on her arm again, still grinning. "Ah, but this is what you sat next to me for, isn't it?"

She felt her face go red, but she laughed anyway and lunged out against him with the full weight of her body and swung with her free arm. He grabbed for her with his other hand.

A crash stopped them both. They weren't children any more. He freed her, and she jumped up, flushed. The jam lay in shards at their feet.

"Now look what you made me do," he laughed up at her, stretching to put the cake onto the coffee table and stooping to gather the fragments of glass.

"No, it was your fault," she answered tonelessly, and walked away to find a dustpan in the kitchen.

The moment passed, and with it any delight in his brief closeness. Dully she watched him turn on the television, stretch, drowse, and jerk awake again. The room became quiet except for the ticking of an alarm clock on the mantelpiece, the noise of the wind in the windows, and the murmuring of the television on low volume. Still she watched him.

At last he woke again, rubbed his eyes, and ambled off to find extra blankets for her. Even ten o'clock was late for him. And when he had gone upstairs with a gruff goodnight she spread the blankets in front of the fire. She sat there cross-legged, thinking about him.

We might as well be strangers; whatever understanding there was between us doesn't exist anymore . . .

She stared at the flames for a long time, watching the logs turn from glowing pink, to red, to gray, before she moved beyond the fire's radius to go up the wooden stairs . . . She was alone now in a cold room at the turn of the creaking stairs where Vermont March crept in at the windowpanes.

Opening the drawer she found them: the pictures she had brought with her, all the old photographs of those long summers with Don and Ellie—the ones she usually kept pinned to her bedroom wall. They were part of her identity, reminding her of where she thought she belonged. Among them were no pictures of her lost father or her mother. Instead, here was Don delivering a calf, Ellie's gangly teenage legs in short shorts standing behind him, her mouth distorted by the snapping lens, gawking, horrified. Here was Ellie at seventeen holding Don's beer glass at a party given by the Hammonds for his twenty-fourth birthday. Here they all were, Don in the middle, his muscled, tanned arms around the two of them: braces and untidy bangs, fresh party dresses and freckled party faces. When was that? 1964? And here was Don with his arm around her that Christmas she had spent at Ellie's home . . . How old had she been? Sixteen? It was the most crinkled and battered of all these old pictures. She stared at it blindly while the snow drifted against the side of the house in the darkness. The snow drifted . . . she drifted . . . and Ellie's voice, Don's voice, whispered in her mind. Sometimes, 1969 seemed more real than 1971.

———

"Let's go home next weekend and see if McEnroe'll

kill the fatted calf for his prodigal daughter," Ellie had said. "I need some cash, anyway. Woodstock . . . well, I blew too much there."

"But I thought you never wanted to speak to them again," Margaret reminded her.

"You'll be back to work any day; then we won't do much together any more." Ellie was slumped in a rattan chair, her legs dangling over the arm, carefully applying nail polish as she talked. "Come on. He ought to be glad to see me. I've got me a steady job, off marijuana already. Quite an exemplary little girl, don't you think?"

Margaret grinned. "No, but let's go anyway. I haven't seen your parents in a while. Labor Day weekend—you talked me right into it."

"Great!" Ellie laughed. "And," she added slyly, "you might see Don."

But Don could not leave Hammonds' for the holiday, so Ellie and Margaret basked without him in McEnroe luxury and early September sunshine.

"You girls sure surprised us," McEnroe said. He had just returned in the middle of the afternoon from the eighteenth hole to find Margaret relaxing by the pool.

She squinted up at him: the familiar, thick gray hair; the crow's feet at the corners of his eyes; the blue wreath of cigar smoke; the abdomen that had begun to sag slightly above his belt. "We surprised ourselves, I think."

He laughed. "Well, how about that. And, Maggie, how did you ever talk our Ellie into coming home for a visit?" He dropped into the chaise lounge beside hers, propped his feet, and tapped a small disc of ash off the end of his cigar.

"I didn't. It was her idea."

"Tell me another one! Hey, I thought I could always count on you for the truth."

"I'm giving you that right now."

He winked. "She feels it's safe to show her face now

that she's a responsible citizen?"

"I guess so," she muttered, looking away and thinking of Woodstock. *Responsible citizen.*

"Her mother was amazed when she called us."

"I'm sure she was."

"It's a treat to have her here again. You too. I hope this'll be the first of many weekends. Quite like old times."

She couldn't return his direct gaze. "I hope so too," she agreed lamely, feeling like a hypocrite. She knew that Ellie already felt constrained and could hardly wait for Monday evening.

"You know you're welcome alone, too, any time. If the city gets you down . . . just give Marianne a call. You don't have to wait for Eleanor's pleasure. We think of you as one of us, too. You know that, don't you?"

From anyone else, the comment would have been patronizing, but she knew his sincerity. She nodded, counting the swirls of color on her swimsuit, still not looking up. "You've always made me feel that way."

"It lifts Marianne's spirits no end when Ellie comes home. She's fun to have around."

Margaret leaned back, laughing. "I know it."

"Perhaps we didn't appreciate her enough when she was at home or back from college." He exhaled heavily; the smoke hovered above them, then vanished. "I may have nagged her too much. But I guess it's all turned out well so far. She's doing pretty well, from all accounts."

She knew he was probing. "Her boss thinks the world of her. I'm sure she won't stay at the agency for long. She's bound to get snapped up by a producer one of these days . . . You've probably seen how they're using her picture all over the place."

He was nodding. "We're pretty darn proud—now. It was a little hard to stomach at first. We didn't envision Eleanor as a college-drop-outer model. For the riffraff, that's what Marianne thought. But it's making her happy. I gotta learn how to keep my mouth shut, I guess." He swung his legs down and ambled off the patio to return with two glasses on a platter. "White wine with soda, right?"

"Thanks."

He stretched out again. "It was the same a few years back when Don took a notion to go up and work for Ray Hammond. When he went to the tech before, well, that was bad enough, but we didn't pay much attention. Figured being a country boy was something he had to get out of his system. But he wasn't going to, I guess. Oh, he made me so furious I was ready to cut him outta my will." He winked again. "I still might, if he doesn't choose the right girl . . . but I see now he has to find his own way. I did it myself, for heaven's sakes. Ellie has to, too."

She had heard his tale before; McEnroe was dearer to her than her own father, who had never returned home after his abrupt departure seven years before— though she knew where he was. He would not be coming home again.

"If I'd listened to my old father, God rest him, I'd still be running a second-rate marina in Gloucester and living on fifteen thousand a year."

She shut her eyes to the drenching late summer sunlight and listened as he went on as usual to recount how he had saved enough to put himself through Harvard Law School and later how he had set up legal practice in Bedford and married Ellie's mother. The phrasing, the rhythm, the epithets had hardly altered over the years that she had heard the story. Small wonder that Ellie—attorney's daughter, politician's daughter— had the gift of the gab.

Then the story was drowned by a sudden burst of music. From inside the house came the thump of drums and a wail of voices that made the hair rise slightly on Margaret's arms. Ellie would be playing some of her Woodstock recordings for Marianne. She couldn't imagine that Marianne would be interested, but could picture her listening with polite attention as Ellie shrieked and exclaimed above the noise.

"And then it rained—how it rained! They told us all to cover up, but it didn't make a hill of beans' difference whether we did or not. We were sitting in a sea of mud anyhow." She was shouting with laughter.

There was a pause. Marianne must be answering, but Margaret could hear nothing now except the thrum of the music, insistent and hypnotic. She almost wished she had gone to Woodstock herself.

Behind her, as she lay with her eyes still shut, the roar of the half-a-million-strong crowd rose to a crescendo. "We must be in heaven," she heard a man crying in a rapt voice. "There's a little of heaven in every disaster area."

The words made no sense to Margaret. They drifted, disconnected, in and out of her brain. *Disaster area?* Perhaps it was. Certainly Ellie had come back ill and confused. But now—?

"So here you are, honey." Marianne's bright voice preceded her out of the french windows, and within the house the music died down.

Margaret opened her eyes as Marianne came and stood beside them on the patio. Ellie followed more slowly behind her, wearing a sleek red swimsuit. The hot pink towel she had draped with apparent carelessness over her shoulders clashed, but Margaret had observed her long enough to know that she chose every fabric that touched her body with deliberate thought. No matter where she was, whether in patched jeans or a velour catsuit, eyes followed her.

McEnroe craned his neck back and whistled at Ellie under his breath. "Yeah, just got back. It's good to relax for a change, isn't it?" He reached over and pulled another lawn chair next to his. "There you go, Marianne. Been having girl-talk with Eleanor? How nice. Want a drink, honey?"

Marianne shook her head. "No, it'll just give me a headache, especially in this heat."

Ellie dropped her towel onto the flagstone and dived straight into the blue stillness of the pool. She surfaced immediately, shouting about the cold and splattering droplets from her hair, then began to swim up and down with easy, powerful strokes.

McEnroe watched her absently and then inclined toward his wife. "Headache? Nonsense!" He patted her evenly tanned leg. "You worry about yourself too much. Look at you! You're gorgeous! You're healthy. I'll get you a Bacardi."

Margaret watched her look up to answer: the thick mass of curling blonde hair, the savagely blue eyes, the pouting mouth, the clever cosmetics that concealed the pale mask of freckles over the nose and the treacherous lines around the eyes and mouth. *She's still as stylish and beautiful as Ellie*, she thought.

"All right. You win." Her eyes followed her husband into the house again and then smiled at Margaret. "He's good to me, you see."

She didn't need an answer, Margaret decided, taking a sip of her own drink and lying back again. She shut her eyes. Beside her she could hear the tinkle of ice in the cocktails, the slap of water in the pool, the ebb and flow of the McEnroes' conversation; and all around her, as if it were mysteriously part of the heat itself—soaking down from the sky and radiating back from the stones and the lawn—the whir and whine of crickets and cicadas—incessant and invisible, answered by the rhythmic, sometimes lyrical, singing from Woodstock. The sounds were palpable, far more real than the drowsy weight of her own body in the lawn chair.

Her mind drifted and floated free on the lap and splash of the water in the pool. She was at Woodstock, but it was not raining. Sun was pouring down from a golden sky, and around her were throngs of singers all with their arms raised in greeting to someone invisible and beyond her reach. She felt herself suddenly and completely warm and loved.

Cold water immediately prickled her hot skin. "Wake up, you lazybones! Come and swim!"

Ellie threw a long, slender shadow across the sun as Margaret opened her eyes. Dazed, she muttered, "Oh, I went back to sleep." She shook her head and pushed back some loose ends of hair glued by sweat to her face.

More water splashed down as Ellie laughed at her. "Hurry up. The sun won't keep, you know."

She stretched languidly. "I'd rather stay here, I guess." Ellie dropped down beside her. "Okay, then. I'll dry off here."

Marianne glanced up at Ellie. "Good swim?"

"Sure was. I'd forgotten how much I loved this pool."

"I don't suppose you gals get much sunning and swimming in town, do you?" McEnroe said.

"No," she conceded. "But I wouldn't have time even if Maggie and I had our own pool on the roof." Ellie chortled to herself. "What a thought, isn't it! Can you imagine the landlord. . . ?"

Margaret joined in the laughter.

"Then all this makes a nice change for you," McEnroe pursued.

"Yes, it does." But Ellie's voice was grudging, and her eyes had slid away from her parents, out to the smooth slope of the lawn beyond the pool.

Marianne cleared her throat. "You haven't said much to Daddy about your job, Eleanor."

The brown eyes came back, swerved briefly to Margaret's, then fixed on her mother's immaculately made-up face. "I like it. What more can I say?" She fingered a large silver ring on her right hand and moved her shoulders. "Gerard's all right. He treats me well. I don't take any funny-business from him—not like some of the girls. He likes directness, and that's what I like; so we understand each other just fine."

McEnroe winked at his wife. Margaret saw the wink and hoped it had escaped Ellie.

"It's a dog-eat-dog business. But I intend to make it to the top."

"That's the spirit! Wouldn't be a McEnroe if you didn't."

Ellie's mouth screwed up at the corners, but she went on. "I like the hours. We can come late and stay late. That suits me, as Maggie could tell you." She smiled slightly. "Gerard says I have the best legs on any model who's worked for him in ten years." She tilted her chin. "I can't prove it, because I don't always know what goes on in the back office or over the phone, but I'm sure he often gives me preference."

"Of course he does!" her father almost shouted. "He ought to know a beautiful woman when he sees one, and talented on top of that." He nodded in Margaret's direction. "That's why we see your face, Ellie, every time we ride the subway or your mother opens a fashion page."

Ellie's face lit up, but only for a moment.

"So when's the big movie signing?" Marianne sounded faintly acerbic.

Ellie swore. "I've only been in this a few months."

"But it'll happen soon, of course it will," Margaret interposed quickly.

"Sure it will."

"Nothing definite though, huh?" McEnroe's blue eyes searched his daughter's face keenly.

She looked away. "Why should there be—yet? I told you, I'm just starting." She pushed her hand through her hair with visible exasperation.

McEnroe drew slowly on the cigar and kept it between his teeth. "Well, I'll have to see if I can turn a few stones for you. Dan O'Grady owes me a couple, and he's got connections in your—"

Margaret held her breath. She saw the old shutters drop over Ellie's face. The guardedness, the smoldering resentment against power that came with a price tag, affluence that ultimately exacted a return. Torn between the friend and the parents, Margaret watched as Ellie looked straight through her father, picked up her towel, and coolly strolled back through the french windows, leaving only a trail of damp footmarks.

McEnroe sat forward and dropped his cigar. "Now why's she so darn touchy?"

"Don't get excited, honey."

He slumped back and wiped glistening sweat off the back of his neck. "She's forgotten how darn nice this pool is, and I've forgotten how frustrating she is." He swore, emptied his glass and lit another cigar. His face deadpan, he turned to Margaret again and said, "How's your mother, Margaret?"

She smiled back. It was easy to take refuge in this old joke. "Still voting Democrat."

He slapped his thigh and roared, "Ha! That's what I love to hear. You wait. We'll make idiots out of them all yet. Your mother's a smart lady, Margaret. I always said so. People like Gwen Fuller, Marianne McEnroe, Julius McEnroe—we'll see the Republicans out of Washington in style, you mark my words."

Margaret laughed. McEnroe had never met her mother, not even in Bishop O'Rourke days. And her mother's name was Laura, not Gwen.

———

Don had called a few weeks later. She didn't recognize his voice at once because of a low, static rustling.

"Eleanor?"

"No, this is Margaret, her roommate."

The voice changed. "Maggie, hi!"

Then she knew. She felt her stomach tighten. She hadn't heard that voice for a long time.

"I want to speak to my kid sister. Is she there?"

"No . . . what time is it?"

"I woke you?"

"I guess so. I must have fallen asleep . . . trying to grade school work sheets."

"Oh, you poor kid."

"Well, anyway, she's not here. Away for the weekend. She and Gerard went to a show in New York City."

"What sort of a show? That's good."

Margaret struggled to give the impression that she knew what she was talking about. Her throat was clogged and her brain was clouded with sleep, yet the tone of his voice was oddly comforting, and she felt somehow that it didn't matter to Don how she sounded. "She's going to be showing some of the latest things, I think. Some artists and designers from *The New York Times* are supposed to do sketches of her for the Sunday edition. Ads for Lord and Taylor or someplace like that."

He whistled. "Ellie sure lands on her feet."

"She's doing what she wants to."

"That's what I love about my sister."

The static over the wires intensified. Frustrated, she raised her voice. "Don—how're you doing?"

"Fair. Everything's pretty much the same. Nothing particular happening."

"You've had a good harvest?"

"We got a good crop of barley and oats this year. The hay wasn't so good—too much rain at the wrong times. And what about you, Margaret? How can you stand to live with my sister?"

She laughed. "We've been having fun. Life was dull until she moved in."

"You don't ever wish it were dull again, once in a while?" He was chuckling.

"Sure, sometimes." The conversation began to irritate her. It was going nowhere. If she'd had time to think—if she hadn't been so surprised to hear from him—she would have had questions. She felt the familiar prick of urgency, knowing that if he couldn't talk to Ellie, he wouldn't talk long. She had to make every second valuable.

Just as she was going to ask about his studies, he began, "Say, you mentioned in a letter not long ago that you were over at McEnroevia on Labor Day."

"So you do read those letters, after all."

"Sure! And my mother said something about it, too. Said it didn't go too well—sort of a fiasco between McEnroe and Ellie, huh?"

"You know how it is," she said. "They just never get along."

"They're cut out of the same bit of cloth. So like each other they hate each other's guts."

Laughter bubbled up inside her. "And don't you think you're a little the same way yourself?"

"Yeah, maybe! I don't see much in common, myself, between a hick farmer and a politician."

She didn't want to pursue that avenue; it was too personal. Instead, she asked, "When will we ever see you?"

"Oh, I don't know. The cows need me. You know I don't get away often."

"You don't want to, anyhow," she accused.

"No. How did you guess?"

"See, I told you—" and she was going to say, *You are like Ellie, pig-headed, like your father*, but thought better of it. "We would like to see you."

"I doubt if you're speaking for Eleanor McEnroe."

Margaret felt her face grow warm. "Sure she'd like to see you."

"As long as I didn't disrupt her agency schedule or social calendar. Right!" he teased. "Not that you'd be worried about such trivia. You'd want to see me."

Her voice sank down. "Yes, I would."

He hesitated. "Then you and Ellie will have to come out some weekend." He sounded vague, and she knew he was merely being polite; the idea was completely remote. "You haven't come in such a long time. Your senior year, wasn't it?"

"Right after I graduated, I think," she answered drily. She could have told him the precise dates if he had asked.

"How about Thanksgiving, or Memorial Day?"

"No, you should come to Boston for Thanksgiving, Don."

"No thanks. Not back to Bedford. I always find my mother's Thanksgivings stifling." Then he went on more seriously. "So why don't you come out? Memorial Day, Labor Day? I don't care. Any time you have a long weekend."

Equally vaguely, she said, "We'll try to plan it, if I can pin Ellie down."

"Okay, you do that, Maggie." He shifted into his big brother tone. "And you take care of yourself, d'you hear?"

"I will, Don. We'll hope to see you soon."

Hanging up, she slumped down by the telephone. As always, she was shattered. His calls—placed to Ellie but always by default to herself—left her shaken, sometimes tearful. She stared at the wall opposite her but saw nothing.

————

"You're sure you can't come for a *Fuller* Christmas?" Margaret asked.

Ellie wedged a cashmere shawl into one of the crevices of her bulging suitcases. Without looking up, she answered, "I wish I could." Then she winced. "Ouch. That wasn't much of a pun, Maggie."

"You really can't stand to go home, can you?"

"No, but what choice do I have?" Ellie frowned. "It'll just be Labor Day all over again, with a few diversions—relatives, gifts—and Don." She screwed up the corners of her mouth. "Anyway, McEnroe hardly needs Christmas! What can you give a millionaire? A trip to the Caribbean? He's such an old stick-in-the-mud he never sets foot outside the state. Holy Massachusetts! Pilgrims, fish, and Democrats!"

They both laughed.

"I'm sure he doesn't want anything, Ellie."

"Of course not. But I'll never hear the end of it if I don't take him something. Don? Well, he's easy. Sweaters, cigarettes, almanacs and the Whole Earth Catalog, and chocolates—simple tastes. Mom—I'll take her out for a woman-to-woman meal someplace. Or we'll go shopping with plastic money. But McEnroe—any ideas?"

"Liquor?"

"I can't afford what he drinks."

Margaret blinked in astonishment. "I thought you got paid yesterday."

"I did. But so did my creditors—well, some of them. Things look bleak for the big spender with the big suspenders." She made a funny face, but her smile died quickly. "And you—are you rolling in the dough this merry Christmas?"

"Hardly. Did you ever hear of a Boston teacher who was?"

"Nope."

"But I've finished my shopping, and I'd be glad to lend you a few bucks to buy your dad—"

"You would?"

"You know I would. Why didn't you ask?"

"Because you earn so much less money than I do anyhow, and I waste mine."

"But for something specific? Heavens, how much can a bottle or two cost these days?" She walked to her room and returned with her check book and a small box wrapped in bright red paper. Then she sat on the end of Ellie's bed next to the muddle of holiday packing and wrote out a check. "Will this be enough?" She passed it to Ellie, expecting her to exclaim that it was too much.

She didn't. "That ought to help" was all she said. She bent and ruffled Margaret's hair. "Thanks. You're so sweet . . . and that—what's that?"

"Your Christmas present, dummy."

Ellie bit her lip. "Oh, I didn't get you anything."

"It doesn't matter, really."

"Oh, but it does. I wasn't expecting—"

"Shall I take it back then? If you protest any more . . ."

The paper peeled to the floor. "Well, I guess I'll give it back if I don't like it." Ellie grinned.

"You'll like it."

"Maggie! Oh, they're perfect!" She held up the earrings Margaret had bought her, then bent again and hugged her. "You're a darling, a real doll."

Warmth spread through Margaret. "I told you you'd like them."

Ellie's face showed her mind was jumping ahead. "You wait. I'll get you something really special, too. Nothing you could get in Filene's or Jordan Marsh's either."

"I'll settle for your brother, no less."

"So it's all a bribe! I wish he were mine to give you, for pete's sake. John the Baptist on a plate."

"Ugh! No thanks!" Margaret shivered.

"And I'd simply love to do the dance of the seven

veils. But I don't even have one."

"Don't bother."

"But I could do something for you, I guess."

Margaret smiled. They'd talked about Don almost too much lately.

"Didn't you say a few weeks ago he wanted us to go up to Vermont some weekend?"

She nodded. "Yes, but—?"

"Well for heaven's sakes, let's do it."

"In the spring?"

"Why not? We haven't gone since the summer before last. That's far too long."

Margaret smiled uncertainly. "I'd like to go, of course, especially since he suggested it."

"You're not aggressive enough. Haven't you read any of Gloria Steinem's women's lib articles? Don't wait for him to wake up."

"You're pretty funny. I'm not made like you, Ellie."

"Meanwhile—" Ellie rubbed her hands together gleefully. "I'll snip off a lock of his hair for you. How's that for a Christmas gift?"

Margaret got up and went to Ellie's dresser, where she stood with her back turned, fingering absently a vase of dried flowers. "No, you don't understand."

"What?"

"Locks of hair. Weekends in Vermont. That's all froth. I want the real thing, Ellie. Something strong and durable and warm, like your folks have. Trust, commitment, support—all those big wonderful words that can be real . . . for some people." She thought briefly of her own parents' broken marriage—dissolved a few years before and still a source of sadness whenever she remembered it.

The room lay quiet for a moment as Ellie stopped pushing clothes into her bags. Margaret's shoulders tensed in the stillness and then relaxed again. "Your brother's everything I've ever wanted. He just hasn't realized I'm out here yet, that's all. He will one day, but meanwhile I doubt if an occasional weekend is going to help any."

Ellie tried to laugh it off. "But—but you gotta start—"

"Not with that, though, I don't think. I've gone over it in my mind hundreds of times. But Don has to realize—first—what we could have together. All that stuff about assertiveness is irrelevant. I've bared my soul to him already. Now I have to wait."

Ellie clicked her tongue irritably, and Margaret heard her cramming the last things into one of the bags. She grunted, straining to shut it. "Well, I gotta hand it to you; you're patient. I sure don't have your patience, or your brass certainty. Men grow on every tree. If they aren't interested in me, shucks! I can do without. You're right. I don't understand at all. I've never felt that way about anyone. Don't intend to, either." With a final jerk she snapped the sliding locks into place.

"Thank God for differences, huh?"

"Thank God!"

Margaret turned. She felt more composed now. "Anyway," she said, "I wish you could come visit with us."

"And I wish you could come with me, too."

"Don'll be there?"

"If he shows. Two days, I guess. Too bad you—hey, couldn't we all get together for a drink, or something?"

She shook her head. "Probably not. David and Martha are spending the week with my mother. And this'll be their first time off the island with the grandchild. We hardly ever get to see them."

"Oh, I guess not. What's the kid's name again?"

Margaret smiled. She must have told Ellie half a dozen times. "Rebecca."

"Sounds very Jewish. Reba? Or Becky?"

"Not Jewish. 'Biblical' is what Martha says. She's a Mennonite."

"A what? Oh—one of those born-again Baptist types, right?"

Margaret shrugged. "Don't ask me. But they're into some little old island church. Helping to finance it. I'm not quite sure what David thinks about all this, but the sun rises and sets on Martha, so I guess David can thumb his nose at the Vatican if he wants to. Whatever she does is right."

"All sounds very cozy and quaint."

"Actually it all sounds quite nice to me," Margaret said lightly, "but I'll keep you posted after Christmas."

"Won't it be rather dull at your place with five adults all fussing after a one-year-old?"

She lifted her hands and let them drop. "Not for me. I like that kind of a holiday, and we'll have plenty to talk about. Anyway, Martha's four months along with the second."

"I wouldn't fancy it, myself," Ellie muttered.

"What?"

"No night-life, a house full of brats, and only an island hospital to have them in." She gave a theatrical shudder. "Who'd live on Nantucket!"

"David's a doctor, remember. And it's a good hospital."

"They should build a better one, never mind the church building fund. How crazy can you get!"

"Like I said, we should be glad of the differences."

Ellie laughed. "I guess Don and David and Martha and you and I wouldn't have a whole lot to say to each other over a drink, anyhow."

"I doubt it. Martha doesn't even drink."

"Or David? Oh, Maggie, they do sound boring!"

Margaret looked around the room at Ellie's colorful clutter: on the walls—playbills, newspaper clippings and photographs from Woodstock, and a huge poster

that said "Make Love, Not War"; on the chairs—rain-
bow-striped socks, unmated shoes, and silk under-
wear; on the dresser and bureau—candles, stereo albums, and dried flowers. "No," she said thoughtfully.
"They aren't in the least boring. Just different."

———

She woke, suddenly, in the darkness, hearing the
sound of heavy steps. Except for her face, she was quite
warm. Don was already stirring, preparing to go and
see to the cows. His feet went back and forth across the
creaking attic floor, then softly down the stairs past her
door and out of the cottage. Still drifting in and out of
consciousness, she waited until she heard the sound
of the snowmobile dying away, then slowly slid out of
bed. She would fix breakfast and surprise him when he
returned.

The wind had dropped completely now, but the
snow had banked up against the side of the cottage, as
he had said it would. The world was silent, sound dead-
ened. Margaret stepped outside to all this, and to see
the first line of dawn show ashen in the east.

She warmed herself with a flurry of work. First she
heaped the stove with wood; then she scrubbed the
cracked wooden table in the kitchen and washed a pile
of dishes that had accumulated in the stone sink. She
mopped the kitchen floor, cleared the living room grate
and flung the ashes outside. She found an ancient vacuum cleaner and went over all the carpets; but then,
reminded of the bare windows everywhere, she stood
still in the middle of the room and decided to make
some curtains for him as soon as she got back to Boston. But how to measure the windows? She would have
to use her arms and record the measurements as
closely as she could, say, middle fingertip to top of
shoulder, top of head to knee . . . then she would send
them to him. And every time he drew them, she

thought, he would remember her.

She started breakfast: coffee steaming, bacon sizzling, and toast turning golden under the broiler. He would be so pleased . . .

Someone knocked at the kitchen door, once, then again. "Margaret?"

Why is he knocking at his own door? Has he locked himself out?

"Margaret? Are you awake?"

She rolled over in bed and sat up abruptly. No coffee, bacon, or toast. No clean kitchen. She had fallen asleep again. "Oh, Don, you're back already?" She pulled the covers around her—at the same time willing the door to open—but the old latch did not move. "I was going to fix breakfast for you."

"Don't sound so disgusted with yourself!" he called back. "It's done already. Come down when you're ready."

Rubbing the sleep from her eyes, she dressed quickly in the chilled room, disappointment nagging.

He was pouring the coffee and buttering toast—almost like the dream—when she came downstairs. The tail of her dream writhed, the invisible creature slinking away into some recess of her brain and hiding there, twitching, not revealing itself fully. Then in the harsh light of the kitchen it slid away completely, and she had to concentrate instead on what he was saying.

"There was a weather forecast just now. Today's going to be clear. Then we'll get slammed again tomorrow. The usual low coming down from Canada—it might storm for four more days."

She sat down opposite him and understood immediately what he expected her to say in return. But even though things might be better that way, she would not give up too quickly. Stirring sugar into her coffee, she murmured, "Oh, really?"

An edge of impatience sharpened his voice. "If it

does, Margaret, you'll have problems getting back. I was thinking—"

No, she would not give him the satisfaction of saying it, after all. "That I should leave?" She did not look up from her plate. "Yes, it might be better. I'll leave right after breakfast."

"I'm sorry. It's too bad."

"I guess it was stupid to plan a weekend up here in March. I should've known better."

"Maybe you and Ellie could get up here for Memorial Day or July Fourth."

"Maybe we could." Her voice was listless and non-committal; they had planned such weekends before. She decided the trip had been an utter failure; he did not even have the grace to sound sincere.

The silence in the room was broken by the town snowplow clanking and scraping its way up the road. Its orange strobe light bounced madly around the kitchen walls in the feeble light of the overcast morning. She ate mechanically now, hardly tasting the food. He wanted her gone, and she wanted to be gone, herself.

He drove her down to Hammonds' in the jeep and helped her clear the snow off Ellie's Buick. All he said was, "Isn't it about time she bought a new car? She can afford it, can't she?" Then he swung her bag into the trunk and held the door for her. "I'll call you sometime."

"And I'll write."

"You do that."

But she knew he wouldn't notice if the letters stopped. Sad again, she rolled down the window and put out her cold face to be kissed. He would kiss her, at least; surely they both knew that. Like New Year's Eve at Ellie's house that year . . . *Should auld acquaintance be forgot and never brought to mind* . . . Instead, he patted her gloved hand and stepped back, gesturing

to her that she should close the window. A few flakes
of snow were whirling out of the sky again, and she
thought for a moment of the old photographs she had
folded carefully in a sweater in her bag. At least nothing
could change those still, warm, still-warm images.

PART II

Negatives
March – May 1971

Snow falls in spring, banking
Over the city in great crests
*   of drifting white.*
Over-exposed, they said, the photographs
*   gleam empty, harshly white;*
But the negatives stare back, black,
As I dimly watch you walk away
In shadows dark with sorrow.

Having turned the key in the lock, she braced the front door with her back and shoved the bag through it as a wedge before it could slam itself shut again. Inside, the stuffy warmth of the heating seared her eyes and made them run after the wind and cold of the street outside. She tried to make herself adjust again to the world of the city, of this closed brownstone apartment house, of her own routine. Don's cottage lay an ocean of snow away: strange to her now as Boston would have looked had she seen it through the snow of the Vermont hills that morning.

Halfway through the hallway from the elevator, she noticed as usual the mess on the wall left by one of Ellie's friends after the first party Ellie had thrown in the place. The red wine stains had long ago turned brown.

She opened the apartment door and stopped in the doorway. The place was oddly quiet, but lights were on . . . and there was a sweetish smell, faint but quite discernible, that she couldn't identify right away. Then the toilet flushed, and a man came out of the bathroom.

He hardly surprised her. Ellie frequently had friends in when she was gone. But this man was different; he wasn't tall—a characteristic Ellie always seemed to require—but he wore neat, expensive clothes, close-cut black hair, and the expression of a man who knew his purpose. No vague and abstracted dreaminess like that of most of Ellie's other friends. Here was a man who belonged in the McEnroes' class: the sort of man Ellie's mother Marianne might have chosen for her. Margaret took in all these impressions quickly, as they stared at each other.

"Who are you?" The man's voice was a smooth, musical tenor, exactly as she would have guessed. But the eyes seemed out of character. The mouth smiled; but the eyes did not.

"Margaret Fuller," she offered. Then she laughed, catching a glimpse of her own drained face in the entryway mirror. "I live here, you know."

"Oh." He turned away with slight distaste. "Eleanor did not tell me." He moved ahead of her across the parquet floor of the sitting room and dropped onto the love seat, propping his legs on the glass top of the coffee table.

Margaret frowned. His easy assumption of his right to do that irritated her. Then she noticed the high polish on his black shoes, the roses he must have brought Ellie, and the monogrammed luggage that stood near his feet. *Class, all right. Just not Ellie's usual choice.* She set down her things on the other side of the room, against the wall of her bedroom, and stood with her hands on her hips. "I don't know who you are, but you can take your feet off that table."

He removed them instantly but without the slightest acknowledging change of expression. Then he lit a cigarette and blew smoke at the ceiling.

She stood her ground. "You're staying here tonight?"

"Yes."

"Fine. Just so I know. Where's Ellie?" She picked up her coat and bag again.

"Changing her dress." He pointed toward Ellie's room. "But she wanted to be alone for a while. Perhaps she would not want to talk tonight to you."

"Maybe not. Then I'll see you later."

"I think so."

She listened carefully, still measuring him. She realized he might not be American. The intonation wasn't quite right. Well, she'd find out soon enough. She went to open the door of her room, but then stepped back in surprise as with a few quick strides he had come to open it for her. Murmuring a half-hearted thanks, she passed him to go in.

"You would like company for a while?" he asked unexpectedly. "Eleanor said she wanted half an hour by herself. We could have a drink together?"

She relaxed, turning to look at him afresh. He was as nice as he looked, after all. She smiled, "Yes, let's do that. Did Ellie. . . ?" How long had they been there already? "Did she show you where we keep the drinks?"

"No. I found them myself. What would you like?"

"Whatever you're having. On the rocks."

"Sure."

She hung a few clothes in her closet, outlined her eyes with fresh make-up, and went out to join him again. His feet rested next to the roses on the coffee table again, but so did two martinis. She didn't complain this time about his feet but dropped into the rocker opposite him.

"You live with Eleanor?"

No, she lives with me. But so what. She sipped the martini, suddenly uneasy under his appraisal. "Obviously," she returned drily. "And you? Don't I get to know who you are?"

Over the rim of his glass his eyes were dark and steady. "Certainly. Steve—Garshowitz. I met Eleanor a few weeks ago—when I last came here on business."

"Oh? She didn't tell me."

"And you tell her everything?"

"Yes, quite honestly. We've known each other for years." She looked away from him at the zigzag design of the floor. "We've shared an apartment for two years. Before that we knew each other in school—Bishop O'-

Rourke's Academy—one of the big schools in town. We kept in touch while we were at college. I've always . . . gotten along well with her family." Spoken, the words made the feeling behind them seem fatuous. She looked up, challenging him with her eyes to dismiss what she had said.

"Really? How interesting." He continued to watch her without evident interest, but without blinking either.

She ventured, "So I gather you're not from Boston?"

"You are right. A good deduction." He was mocking her. "From Miami, in fact. At least, I live there sometimes. I travel often."

Margaret wished she had simply gone to bed. She felt tired and suddenly didn't care to make small talk with this man. All the same, she went on with mechanical New England politeness, "Your family is in Miami, too?"

His smile was patronizing, as if she'd asked a childish question, but he hesitated before answering. "No, alas. I never knew my father. My mother is Peruvian. She lives alone now in Lima. I do not see her often. It is sad."

"It must be hard for you." She played with her drink, rattling the ice around the glass. Then she thought, *I don't have to do this. He can quite well entertain himself.* So she drained the martini and stood up. "You must excuse me. Tell Ellie hello. And Don—her brother—sends his love . . . I've had a long day."

He looked up, more interested now. "Her brother?"

"Yes. I've been visiting with him. He's a farmer, in Vermont. As I said, I've known the McEnroes for a long time . . . The weather was awful coming back. It's usually three hours, but today it was nine or ten." She knew she was rambling. "So please excuse me."

He stood up, either genuinely concerned or feigning solicitude; she couldn't decide which. "Naturally. Sleep well. I shall tell her what you have said."

"I'll see you again?"

"Not in the morning. I must go early. But I expect
to be back." He grinned for the first time. "If Eleanor
likes me."

She went in and undressed slowly. Her head felt
light. Usually she would have showered, put on her
dressing gown and sat at the kitchen counter with Ellie, gossiping until midnight over toasted cheese sand-
wiches, coffee and apples, with Dylan and Sebastian
shouting in the background. Not tonight, though. The
man's presence was vaguely disquieting, and she didn't
have the ambition even to make a sandwich. She'd go
right to sleep and wait to see Ellie in the morning.

She stretched out on the bed and pulled up the covers. Then she heard the murmuring of voices from the
other side of the wall. Water ran in the bathroom, and
Ellie's door closed.

She got up again, very quietly, and opened her door
a crack. The living room lights were still on. One of
Steve's bags lay open on the floor, but he wasn't in the
room. She could still smell that half-remembered scent.
A herb of some kind? Aftershave?

In boots, faded jeans, and an old jacket, Margaret
walked out in the morning snow for the Sunday paper.
Later she sat on a bar stool in the kitchen and relished
the warmth of indoors. She scanned the headlines,
poured a second cup of coffee, and made herself some
toast. Her almost unvarying Sunday routine.

Ellie found her still hunched over the counter when
the stove clock read 11:45. "Up early, aren't you?" She
came and stood in her bra and silk panties in the middle of the room. Yawning and stretching, she rubbed
her head. "Oh, Maggie, I feel awful."

Margaret glanced at Ellie's tangled hair, red-rimmed

eyes, and white face. "You look awful, too."

Ellie retorted, "You don't look so gorgeous yourself, honey."

Margaret kept her eyes on *The Globe.* "Probably not. I was beat last night."

Ellie opened the fridge, muttering, "I'm thirsty."

"I made some fresh juice."

"Thanks. Just what I need."

"Want some toast?"

"No—but I'm sure dry."

Margaret pushed the paper aside and watched her. "Did your friend leave?"

"Oh, you met him?"

"Yes, when I got back. You were closeted at the time."

Ellie turned, frowning. "Oh, that's right. You were up to see Don. But wait a minute, I thought you were gonna stay there until Monday."

"So did I."

"You'll have to tell me all the details when I wake up. Heck, what time is it, anyway? I don't even know when Steve left. I was dead. Probably early. I mean, earlier than now."

Margaret laughed. "It's noon, Ellie."

"Really? So it is." She reached for the coffee pot.

"You'd better eat something."

"I told you, I don't want a thing. Anyway, I can't afford to gain another pound or they'll fire me because I can't model Twiggy clothes anymore."

"Baloney! Twiggy's been out of style for months, and you know very well you're the thinnest woman Gerard's got."

"Most *slender,* please." Ellie reached for the sugar bowl and put two heaped spoonfuls into her black coffee. The third poised above the cup, she stopped, cursing herself. Then she stood up to pour all her coffee into the sink. "Speaking of which, I just have to kick the sugar habit. Black coffee, unadulterated, here we come." She poured another cup.

Shoulder to shoulder with Ellie at the counter, Margaret stared at the smears of butter, toast crumbs, and small coffee rings in front of her and felt glad, suddenly, that she worked with second graders, not with competitive models or with agents she silently dubbed "dealers in thin skin." At least she didn't have to worry all the time about every angle and curve of cheekbone and thigh. *Don doesn't care about those things, either,* she thought . . .

Or did he? She knew too little about what he thought, and their parting still stung her. She wanted now to talk to Ellie about him, but Ellie was sitting quite still beside her, lost in her own thoughts.

"I'm madly in love, Maggie." Ellie neither moved as she said it, nor looked up; so Margaret was caught off guard.

"Oh, you are?" Usually she would have shot back automatically, "Oh, again?"

"Steve, the one you met last night."

Margaret knew Ellie needed to talk, too. "How'd you meet him?"

"How? I don't know . . . but about six weeks ago, so *he* says." She grinned. "I honestly don't remember."

"He made a big impression, I can tell."

"I should've known you'd say that. But we met again at a party on Friday. What a party! It was the wildest thing I've been to in years. You'd have loved it."

"Are you sure?"

"Honest, I think you would. Sure, all sorts there: Jews, blacks, WASPs . . . and one or two red-headed models who gate-crashed." She winked. "Teachers, economists, an absolutely enchanting artist who wanted me to pose, politicians—I steered clear of them in case anyone recognized me—lawyers. All sorts."

"And what was Steve's ticket into this party? He's Jewish, isn't he?"

Ellie's eyebrows rose dramatically. "Heavens, no. He's Peruvian—half, at least. Couldn't you tell? With a name like Garcia, no way he's Jewish."

"Oh, excuse me!" Margaret jibed. "But he told me his name was Garshberg, or Garshowitz—something like that. I'm sure he did."

Ellie shook her head. "No, you must be thinking of someone else."

Margaret shrugged. "Well, I guess I was pretty tired. I remember he did say something about South America—still . . . I thought—"

"Never mind. Oh, we had such fun together Friday. He was the perfect gentleman. Escorted me to the door, kissed me goodnight like he was my politest cousin, and asked if I'd be free again on Saturday. 'Am I?' I wanted to scream at him. 'You bet I am!' " She laughed. "I had plans, but nothing that mattered. So he came over last night with a handful of long-stemmed roses. I hardly even know how to act around anyone like that. No one ever treats me that way."

"And took you out again?"

"The works—in style. First dinner. Then another party. He's unbelievable. Everyone seems to know him." She looked down. "Another great party. Everyone was high as a kite."

"Drunk?"

"No—stoned. Marijuana. You name it . . . Don't look so horrified! Two years—I've been good all that time. And it was quite innocuous stuff. I told him no at first. But then I think I drank quite a bit, and he was coming on a bit stronger, you know, the hot Latin bit, so I took a couple puffs. Then a couple joints. Can't even remember why I stopped smoking anyhow."

Margaret watched her. "You can't?"

Ellie ignored her. "Then he brought me home . . . I asked him to stay. So he checked out of his hotel and, well, you know the rest. Oh, Margaret, he's such an amazing guy. I'm crazy about him. So clean-cut, but so much *fun!*"

"Clean-cut? Since when did *that* matter. You mean rich?"

Ellie's eyes widened. "Sure he's rich! Owns his own business in Miami. It's fabulous! He has money just oozing out of every pore."

"You've missed that, haven't you?"

Ellie looked up sharply and shuddered. "Not Mc-Enroe's money, I haven't. Too many strings attached. But—yeah—I am sick of money-grubbing for every little cent. And driving that old wreck—it got you there, did it? Amazing! And breaking my back for a job with no prospects except retirement at twenty-six and that's after two years of slave labor, and no real breaks." She fell into a meditative tone. "It looked so bright at first, but things just haven't moved fast enough."

"And I suppose Steve's looking for a promising young woman like yourself, smart, attractive . . ."

Ellie rocked back dangerously on her stool and pushed a hand through her curls, laughing. "Oh, I get dizzy just thinking about him!"

" . . . to work with him."

Ellie blinked and leaned forward again. "Maggie, I swear you're psychic! He did say something about it."

"No wonder you're sold."

"Oh, he was just joking."

"Of course. When's he coming back?"

Ellie's eyes clouded. "He didn't know, exactly. Said he had some important deals to tie up, and he had to go see his parents."

"Parents?"

"Yep. Ma and Pa. You know? I told you; they live in Peru. His father's a doctor, I guess. He doesn't see them often, but he'll be back." She hugged herself.

Puzzled, Margaret tried to recall what the man had said. Wasn't his mother dead? Or his father? Nothing seemed clear. Not that it mattered, though.

"He'll call me soon as he's back in town, he said."

Margaret returned Ellie's smile. "He will, I'm sure, Ellie." She got up and began to wipe the counter.

"No, I'll do that." Ellie jumped up suddenly and took the dishrag away from her. "Why don't you tell me about Don? You did make it up to Hammonds', didn't you?"

Margaret rested her chin on her palms and looked out of the kitchen window at the wall of the apartment house next door. She tried to see in its grayness the snowscape of Vermont, the red farm buildings, the thick-walled cottage, and Don himself . . . three hours away.

"Maggie?" Ellie had stopped beside her and was watching her face.

"Yes, I made it," she said slowly. "But things didn't work out well at all. That's why I came back early—that and the weather."

"He was rude? He can be such a boor sometimes."

"Oh, no. That wasn't it."

"My matchmaking never works."

"Matchmaking! You know very well—"

"Yes, poor Maggie! It's been so long, and I didn't have a thing to do with it, did I? Just took you home a few weekends . . ."

Margaret answered softly, "It never had anything to do with you, Ellie."

"No, it didn't. But I think my brother's such an imbecile at times, especially about you."

"It's not his fault."

"Oh, you excuse him all the time."

"But he's known me too long. You and I—we're just his kid sisters. He still talks that way. 'If you want to tag along . . .' "

"He said that to you?"

She shrugged. "Sure."

Ellie clenched her teeth. "He's stupid. Maybe he doesn't like women."

"Ellie, it's just that he doesn't want me."

"Well maybe he *doesn't* like women," Ellie insisted. "When did you ever see any sign of women around his place?"

"Never, but he's never there anyhow. If he's not over at the farm, he's out to Middlebury or someplace. That cottage—he doesn't care, and he still says so. Homemaking's just not his thing."

Ellie laughed. "Must run in the family! But he sure must be slow-witted about women."

"He's saving to get out of Hammonds'. I'm sure he doesn't want to spend all his money on women."

"There you go again, excusing him."

"But it's true."

"He told you he's going to leave there?"

"Says he's going to Western New York. Upstate."

"That'll be the day. Oh, won't McEnroe blow his stack over that one! This farm bit's all a little hard to swallow, but even worse away from New England. Poor old Daddy."

"Where's your respect, Eleanor?"

"Ain't got none." She touched Margaret's arm. "So, you're still in love with my creep of a brother?"

Margaret couldn't answer.

"Sure you are. Sorry. Oh, poor Maggie. What a pair of old maids we'll be, crying into our tea!" She moved away from the counter. "You for a blind man who doesn't even give you a second look, and me for a dreamboat who sails in and out of Boston now and then but sure isn't the type to drop anchor."

"And neither are you."

Ellie turned in the archway with a grin. "No, well, I'd better take a shower."

"Catch you later . . . oh, by the way, what was that

funny smell in here last night? I couldn't think what it was."

"Smell?" Ellie frowned. "I didn't smell anything."

"Herbs, or something. Does Steve use some weird aftershave?"

"I don't think so—oh." Ellie exploded into a giggle and bent over laughing. "I know what it was. Grass! We must have been smoking right before you got back. How could you forget? This place used to reek of grass every night."

She shuddered. "That was it."

"I swore off it after Woodstock, right? With—what was the guy's name? Ryan somebody?"

"Chuck Ryan." Margaret remembered him only because of Constantine. "Chuck Ryan. You got very sick on it that weekend, remember?

"Vaguely. That's right, Chuck Ryan."

"The one you were so *madly* in love with."

Ellie grinned back and slammed the bathroom door.

————

The bell in the corridor rang, and the children stirred. One more period, and they could all go home. By Fridays Margaret went through the motions in a zombie-like trance: grading gum-and-ink-smudged papers clumsily written in a #2 soft pencil, sending the sensible girls down to the office with messages of doubtful importance, listening to the slow boys stumble miserably through another page of the Houghton Mifflin Reader; the stories, the counting, the repeated questions. "Are you listening?" "Can you see the blackboard?" "Would you please come here?"

Half in a trance: that's how Margaret existed now, at 2:15 on this dull early April afternoon. The unconscious part of her continued the routine, asked and answered questions, wrote on the board. But her brain consciously registered other things far removed from the second-grade room. Only a few days ago, she'd been on her way back from Vermont. Snow had drifted over the highways and farms, and unmitigating whiteness sliced into her eyeballs. In that intolerable weather she had stopped at Howard Johnson's to give herself a break and warm herself. By then the early darkness had already settled over the hills, but the polka dots of snow in a black New England night eased her eyes no more than the glare of snow in daylight.

And then she'd come back to find Steve, not Ellie. Steve . . . he'd seemed to live with them all week. As Ellie discussed him, his presence sat at breakfast and late at night with them. He reappeared genie-like in the smoke of marijuana he'd left for Ellie, in the fading scent of the red roses that had drooped and dropped their petals on the coffee table. And he had talked in low murmurs to her over the telephone. But Margaret could associate none of this with Eleanor McEnroe. Ellie had never stayed in the apartment every night and turned down all dates, had never talked constantly about one man; nor—since Woodstock—had she used marijuana. And when Ellie didn't sidetrack Margaret's evening work with anecdotes about what Steve had said on the telephone, she stood in the middle of the room smoking, her face preoccupied. She was jumpy and irritable. It was as if Eleanor McEnroe had moved out and someone else, someone who looked like her, had moved in. Someone with an obsession.

"Bisses Fuller!"

She looked down sharply. One of the youngest and most despised boys in the class, Paul, was trying to get her attention. He stood with one grimy hand over his face and couldn't meet her eyes. He always called her "Mrs.," but she had given up correcting him months ago. "What is it?"

"Rickie threw his book at be. By dose is all bloody."

The unconscious part of her moved down the aisle

between the sticky desks, hauled the offender out of his seat, and put him in an empty desk near her own. The unconscious part of her mechanically took the smaller boy over to the sink and made a pad of cold, wet paper towels for his nose, while behind her the children fell unusually quiet and made a great show of scratching away with their pencils.

The conscious part of her watched the tearful brown eyes over the bridge of soggy paper, observed the dirt ground into the moon-shaped nails that pressed down on the towel with her help, and thought angrily, *One day this will be my child. Dirty, hurt, staring at me over a bloody nose with his father's eyes. Poor kid.* But then consciousness and unconsciousness met and detachment set in. She tried to focus on what she was doing, and for a while Don and Ellie receded from her mind.

Later, when she let herself into the apartment, she found a large piece of paper taped to the floor in the entryway. Ellie's writing sprawled boldly across it in red ink. "Steve arrived unexpectedly. Friends of his in Newport are putting their yacht to water this weekend, so he's invited me to go down and join them. Won't we have fun? I'll see you Monday night."

Folding the paper, she stuffed it into her coat pocket. She was glad for Ellie; yet in the corner of her mind, anxiety nibbled. She knew it was baseless, but it stayed there, nevertheless, goading her to doubt. She tried to tell herself it was just an old Puritan hang-up of hers to fear people who were rich—though that wasn't it, for she'd never feared the McEnroes—to fear people who moved and acted as quickly as Steve had done. Oh, Ellie was rich; Ellie was glamorous, Ellie made decisions impulsively. But that wasn't it, either. There was something else about Steve that was not spontaneous, not impulsive; there was something calculating about him. And that combination—the affluence; the seductive, fashionable glamour; the seemingly cool shrewdness—stirred up misgivings.

Over and over again during the weekend she thought about Steve and Ellie and tried to dismiss her bias against Steve, to dismiss the vague anxiety that went with it. She thought about them while she wrote to Don. She thought about them while she read the Sunday papers and baked cookies. She thought about them as she drove out of town to walk on the Gloucester waterfront. She wondered, too, why Ellie had said, "See you Monday night." Why wasn't she returning on Sunday to go to work as usual on Monday?

As it was, Ellie arrived neither on Sunday nor Monday night. Late on Monday, in fact, after Margaret had been in bed for a while, Gerard called from the agency, asking where Ellie was. Relieved to hear from him, she still could help him no more than he could help her. "When she gets in tonight, I'll tell her you called," she just said. Then she got up and pasted a note of her own to the mirror in Ellie's room. "Call Gerard."

Tuesday, when Margaret returned from school, Ellie had still not come back. But around nine, when she was soaking in the bath, she heard the apartment door open and Ellie's familiar heels click across the floor.

Doors banged, and there was a thud in the entryway. "Maggie! Where *are* you?"

She sprang out of the bath, wrapped herself in a towel, and went out dripping wet.

Ellie stood back as if afraid of her. Her eyes were enormous, her face pale. "*Don't.*"

"What's the matter? I'm glad to see you."

Ellie snapped, "Yes, of course you are."

"Well—" Margaret was stung. "You did shout for me."

"Oh, I'm sorry." She flung her jacket onto a chair. "Yeah, I'm glad to see you, too." But her voice sounded lifeless.

"Isn't Steve with you?"

"Steve? Oh, no. He left me at Newport. Got one of his friends to drive me back. He was flying out of Kennedy down to Miami again."

"You don't look as though you had a good weekend. Did something go wrong?"

Ellie did not answer immediately but subsided into the love seat. Looking at her hands and idly picking at one fingernail, she eventually murmured, "Frankly, I don't know if anything went wrong or not. I was out of it for most of the weekend."

"Smoking?"

"Yeah—no—not really."

Margaret wished she could understand. "Don't you want to see Steve again?"

She nodded. "Oh, yes, I'll see him again all right. He may be up on Friday or Saturday."

"He's coming just to see you, is he?"

She nodded again, half smiling. "Right, but for other reasons, too. He hopes to expand his business here. I think I'll be seeing a lot of him now."

May

"That smells pretty good." Ellie stood in the archway and watched Margaret taking a casserole out of the oven.

Margaret smiled to herself, pleased they had time for a meal together. There had been so little time to talk. "Hungry?" she asked.

"I guess." Ellie walked to the cabinet, took down two glasses, and uncorked a bottle of last year's Beaujolais. "I don't know if *red* wine's what I want now, but it's better than nothing."

"Let's eat, anyway." Margaret was already filling the plates: a colorful mixture of seafood, pimento, green peppers, and noodles.

Ellie stopped beside the counter and poured herself a full glass. "There. I'll drown my sorrows with some old Beaujolais. Heaven knows when he'll be up again." In spite of her complaint, she was half smiling.

"You've said that every week for six weeks, and he comes every time."

"Almost every time . . . oh, Maggie, I can't eat all that. Just because *you're* hungry doesn't mean *I* have to eat like I've not seen food for five years." Irritated, she spooned some of hers back into the dish and took a few small bites.

Margaret watched her. "I thought you were hungry. You love this recipe . . . and I doubt if you've eaten much of anything this week."

Ellie threw down her fork and shoved back the bar stool so violently that it fell to the floor. "For pete's sake, let me alone! You're forever strutting around here like you're my mother. Utterly neurotic! I've had it with you, Maggie! All you do is tell me, 'Eat, get some sleep, don't you think you need some vitamins?' You're like a mouse in a maze in someone's science lab—treading out your comfy little routines like there's no other way to live. You make me sick! No wonder you can't fantasize about any guy except my stupid brother—you haven't got the imagination. It would be far too risky and terrifying for you to push your boring little snout outside your maze and see what life's *really* like."

Margaret set her own fork down. She couldn't answer. Ellie's face had hardened in rage, anger entirely out of proportion with anything she'd said. She stared back, wanting to apologize and say that she would try to leave Ellie alone more, but before the words came, Ellie stopped her with a sharp question.

"And another thing. Why do you always hang around every time Steve comes?"

Familiar ground for argument, that one, and this time she wouldn't sit meekly under the stinging words. "Why not? This is my place, too. And does it really matter to you, if I'm shut up reading and grading papers? You two go out, anyway. I hardly even cross paths with you." She looked at Ellie with a mixture of frustration and defensiveness.

"Yes, it sure does matter. And if he shows up this weekend, I wish you'd just push off for a change."

Margaret turned from her food toward where Ellie stood behind her with her chin raised and her eyes fiery. She said calmly, "I don't see what your problem is, and I don't know why you're so uptight all of a sudden. Do you think I'm after Steve? Is that it? Believe me, I don't want to interfere at all."

Ellie's tone softened just slightly. "Then why don't you clear out for a few hours next time? You've lost your sense of humor, and I feel like you're criticizing him, and me."

"Sorry I give that impression," she answered stiffly. "I'd like to be alone with him once in a while."

Margaret laughed bitterly. "Haven't you been?"

"I mean—not at some party or bar. I want time to talk to him." And Ellie leaned forward as she said it, to make the point. "If you're around you act like you have a license to cross-examine me afterward. But it's my affair—it's got nothing to do with you."

No longer hungry herself, Margaret impatiently pushed away her plate. "Don't talk such drivel, Ellie. You've wanted to discuss him . . . ever since it started. Frankly, I'm sick of hearing about him. Believe me, I won't ask you another question unless I have to. Why d'you think I hardly talk about Don these days? Because I know it would bore you to death, even if—"

Ellie cut her off irritably. "Don't be so self-deprecating and martyrish. It doesn't suit you one bit. All I'm saying is—don't crowd me. Okay?" She spread her hands and raised her brows in entreaty, but the anger still lurked behind the eyes.

Margaret turned away, her own temper rising, pretending to pick at her food but still feeling Ellie's eyes boring into her back. "This is my place, as I said, Ellie. You can feel free to move out any time."

"Of all the—"

"But I wish you wouldn't. We've had some great times. You could have moved long ago, but you didn't. You wanted us to stay together for a while. But it's certainly not as if you need me any more."

Ellie stalked across the room. She leaned against the counter as if to make sure Margaret would hear her out. "I have no intention of moving out unless you kick me out. The lease was in your name, right?" She attempted a winning smile but failed. "I don't want to live alone." She took a quick breath. "You're right. We've had some good times." She shrugged, looking down. "But maybe it would all change—if Steve lived up here all the time."

Margaret was caught by surprise. Pushing back her hair, she said, "That'd be great for you, Ellie. I really don't want to fight with you . . . I thought Steve was opening a new branch in the city anyway. Oh, dear, I'm not supposed to ask any—"

"I raised it, Maggie." Ellie regarded her with a steady, almost pitying look. "Anyhow, Steve's line of business doesn't have storefronts or office space, exactly."

"Then—?"

Without another glance at Margaret, Ellie reached for more wine. "He has sales people working for him—privately, traveling. But—" she rushed on, "I don't know much about the market, so I might give you misinformation . . . Well, enough of that. You don't want to talk about Steve. I guess I don't, either. Let's talk about Don, after all."

Margaret watched a mask shadow Ellie's face and felt the tug of grief and love. Don had pushed her away. Now Ellie was doing the same. She had so many masks: one for Steve, one for her family, one for Gerard. She'd always flattered herself that she'd seen Ellie without the mask: Ellie who loved to be with friends; who enjoyed as much as she herself did the mere pleasure of being alive; who maintained a mischievous skepticism about politics and fashion; and who made fun of them—using the same cutting humor McEnroe used in the State House, and to the same effect. But perhaps she had never understood Ellie after all. Perhaps she had only seen another of the masks.

Ellie was still talking. She raised her glass. "Anyway, Maggie, here's to this apartment, and us." She took a generous swallow and waved the glass. "Here's to your best beloved, whoever he may be, and here's to—"

The phone rang beside Margaret. It was almost a relief, and she reached for it immediately. "Hi." She always used the non-committal, deadpan voice, never identified herself: fingers ready to cut the call directly, if necessary.

"Hello, Steve here. May I please talk with Eleanor?"

Without comment, she handed the receiver to Ellie and went to her room. Only a few moments later, Ellie was pounding on the door, her voice high with excitement. "Maggie!"

"What?"

Ellie opened the door halfway. "Could a contrite sinner borrow your car keys?"

"Keys, or car?" Margaret answered mildly. She reached for her handbag.

Ellie grinned. "Both, you loon. The Buick's not going to be ready until next week. Guess what? He's come!"

Margaret raised her eyes toward the ceiling. "What did I tell you? Shall I leave?"

Ellie hesitated, twisting the keys in her fingers. She frowned. "We do need some time alone. I meant that. But I guess there's nowhere for you either, unless you have a date?"

"Not this weekend." *And not any weekend,* she thought; but she made herself smile brightly.

"Then would you feel bad staying in here pretty much? Look, I know it's a lot to ask. I won't ask again, and Steve and I'll go out for a while, in spite of what I said. He always needs to touch base with a few guys as soon as he gets in town."

Margaret gave her a steady look. "Okay, Ellie, this one time. But, listen . . . it's no good. You and Steve should get a place of your own. He can afford it."

"We'll talk about it, I promise." Her face, dull only fifteen minutes before, was glowing. "Oh, I get so excited when he arrives, I think I'll burst sometime."

Ellie's fragile effervescence unnerved her, but Margaret joked, "Please arrange for someone to scrape the bits off my car, if you do."

"Get lost, Maggie."

"Break a leg, Ellie."

Ellie whirled out into the entryway. "I might, at that. We're bound to go dancing."

"In some crowded room, no doubt, where you can shout in each other's ears."

" 'Some enchanted evening—' " Ellie bawled. "Ah, well, never mind. We'll talk later—in bed. Ha!"

The apartment door slammed, the sound hollow in the dead air of the hallway outside, and Margaret found herself alone. *Oh, I'll be so stale by the time I turn thirty*, she thought wearily. Ellie's cruel words rang in her ears like a mockery. "You're like a mouse in a maze in someone's science lab. . . ." Perhaps she was right. She was by herself in the sterile vacuum and Friday-evening letdown of an untidy apartment and another lethargic weekend. By herself to brood over the paucity of social life, the repetitive routines of her existence. Although—hadn't she chosen them? It was no use seeing things through the distortions of Ellie's life. She wouldn't, she told herself, enjoy Ellie's way of life anyway.

If she were honest, she comforted herself as she cleaned up the kitchen, she did relish the rhythm of five days on and two off, the regular order of it. She held to it as happily as she did to the changing seasons outside—something Ellie disregarded altogether. She felt relieved of a certain tension when the heady days of summer gave way to the discipline of fall. And she felt equally unburdened when the Charles River thawed, the ice disappeared from the cobbles, and the geese flew north in freedom, clanking their wings and voices over the Boston skyline. In the same way she relished even the quiet boredom of most Friday nights: the silence when Ellie had gone out and she could read, bake, or sleep. It was not something she needed to despair about, after all. It was just the natural order of her life.

She turned on a recording of Jefferson Airplane. Then, because the music only made her think of Ellie and start brooding again, she lifted the needle and replaced the record with a Simon and Garfunkel album. Settled under the lamp, she began to write to Don—something else she did almost every weekend.

The letter was really a journal. She knew she wrote it more for herself than for him, driven by some unexplained need to share details of her life with someone she loved, even if he hardly read them and even more rarely answered them. Once, he had said he liked hearing from her, that she wrote good letters; but lately if they'd talked on the telephone he had made no reference to them. Though it didn't matter—they were one way she had of talking to him—a way which, unlike the telephone, held no threat for her.

The phone rang again, interrupting half-formed thoughts about Don, interrupting a sentence she was writing. She got up to answer it, trying to think how she would complete the line. "Hi," she said mechanically.

"Is Eleanor McHenry there?" A man whose voice she didn't know.

"Who's calling?"

"The name doesn't matter. I want Miss McHenry."

"I can't help you. Sorry." *McHenry? Why the confusion? Or was it deliberate?*

"She's out?"

"Right."

"Did she by any chance go to meet a guy called Garshowitz?"

"No." *That was the name!* She *had* heard another name that first night, after all. But he had told Ellie "Garcia." "I can't help you, I guess." And she was about to cut off the call when she heard a gasp of frustration at the other end.

"Listen, it's okay. I'm a friend of Steve's . . . Okay?

You don't need to cover for him. I need to see him, and this was the name and number they gave me . . . You're Eleanor?"

She felt the receiver go sticky in her hand. *"No!"*

"For crying out loud! I need help! I have to see Steve tonight if he's in town. Please, I—"

Her heart quickened. A kind of dread seeped into her. "I'm not Eleanor," she said reluctantly, "but I think you have the right number. You'll get the person you want if you call later."

"One?"

"Probably."

"Why all the short answers?"

"Because I don't know you, and I don't trust your friend, either."

A cynical laugh. "Most people don't." Then the line went dead.

She went around the apartment and pulled all the shades, turned on all the lights, and turned up the volume of the music. *Fear.* But then she collapsed into the love seat and laughed at herself. Maybe the guy owed Steve money and was nervously waiting to make a late payment. Or maybe he was a new salesman working for Steve and had blown an important deal. Whoever he was, he didn't like Steve any more than she did.

She went back to the letter. By the time she sealed it she had almost forgotten the call. The fright subsided, and she slipped again into the somnolent afterease of a "talk" with Don and a pot of tea in her room. Finally she closed the door and slept.

———

The phone by her bed woke her, but she didn't reach for it immediately and so heard it stop in mid-ring. She could faintly hear that Steve must have answered it in the kitchen. *The same caller again?*

She rolled over, her heart still thudding from the sudden awakening, stretched to turn on the light, but then decided to sit up in the dark and wait. The dread returned.

"No . . . cannot talk now . . . in touch with you to-morrow. It can wait. You—" The voice dropped too low for her to hear more. But then he shouted, "Do not call again. This was for an emergency . . . always a risk. You hear? No, it is not . . . tomorrow."

The telephone beside her gave a small click, and she knew the call had ended. She remained still, hugging her knees. Everything went quiet for a while; then she became dimly aware of a human noise that went on and on: laughter, but not the usual rolling giggle of Ellie. More a frenzied laughter, something uncontrolled and not enjoyed. It stopped abruptly, and someone crashed clumsily into the bathroom.

"I'm going . . . oh, I'm going . . ." Ellie's voice moaned.

"Get yourself together." That was Steve. No tenderness at all—but a barked command.

Margaret pushed back the covers and jumped out of bed. The floor, cool on the soles of her bare feet, arrested her. Whatever was happening, Ellie wouldn't want her, and nor would Steve. They thought she was asleep, and she did not dare turn on the light, even now. Helplessness and doubt seized her. She sank down on the edge of the bed with her fists clenched, only to hear the moaning begin again.

"I'm going to throw up . . . terrible. *Please*, Steve." Ellie sounded choked, desperate, barely recognizable. "Give me something. You gotta—"

But the reply came back direct and harsh, "Shut your mouth. You vomit; that is all."

"I'll never touch . . . that stuff again."

"It was the booze you drank."

Ellie coughed and retched. In anguish for her, Margaret shivered and broke into a cold sweat. Water ran, and someone moved across to Ellie's room and back to the bathroom.

"You will be fine, I said."

"You don't give a damn, do you?" Ellie's words were clearer now, spat out bitterly from between clenched jaws.

"Not when you do like this."

"Fine, then get out. Find a hotel someplace."

"Ellie—for heaven's sake—we had a great time, re- member?"

"Are you sure we were at the same party? Don't you wheedle. *Get out!* You don't care about me. You men are a dime a dozen."

"You lose touch with what is real."

Ellie laughed again: the same mirthless, wild laugh. "What is reality, Steve? You of all people presume to know?"

Margaret could visualize her face twisted in mock- ery and despair, as it often was when Ellie felt least sure of herself; equally she could see Steve's frustrated shrug, the characteristic Latin lift of palms and eye- brows.

"Is it Monday through Friday when I can't cop be- cause you're gone? Or is it Friday through Sunday when—

Steve must have shaken or slapped her. "Shut up before you wake *her*."

Ellie cried for a few moments, then a partial silence ensued. Soft footsteps came to Margaret's door and stopped. She held her breath in anticipation but then let it out heavily; Steve would expect to hear her breath- ing. A few more breaths like that—as even as she could make them in defiance of her ragged heartbeat—appar- ently satisfied him.

"Please come out here, Ellie." The tenderness had returned to Steve's voice.

She heard dragging footsteps and the small squeak of the castors against the parquet floor as they sat down together. Ellie would be leaning on his shoulder, subdued.

"We had a good time, sweetheart?"

Ellie paused, and her answer came as a loud sigh. "We always . . . do. But I don't know how long we can—or I can—go on this way."

"You mean?"

An edge of bitterness crept into Ellie's voice, which sounded otherwise more normal. "You have money, and I don't. Oh, I get along, but I can't go on dipping into my trust fund for ever to keep up with you."

"Ah, I have an easy solution. I told you."

She ignored him. "My father's bank is bound to rat on me sooner or later. And I never told you, but Maggie's doing me a favor keeping me here. It's really her place; she pays more than I do. Even if she sometimes gets on my back, she's a good kid." There was a long silence. "She lends me her car, and I lend her mine. We've looked out for each other since ninth grade. She lends me money when I need it. But she's made it pretty darn clear she won't share a place with me forever, not as long as you're in the picture."

Margaret's eyes rose in surprise at the construction Ellie put on their domestic arrangements. She smiled a little, but then began to ache. *"She's a good kid."* Was that all Ellie thought? The words were eerily reminiscent of Don's. *"You can tag along if you like."*

"And she's naive. Has no idea half the time what's going on right under her nose."

"Convenient."

"But I need to accommodate her more. I can't keep borrowing cash. See what I mean?"

"You always complain about cash. I *told* you—we can do something about it."

Again, she seemed not to hear him. Her voice

droned on in a monotone; she was trying to sift her thoughts aloud. "I can't go on like this for ever. I'd have to sell myself to Gerard altogether, or to some of his weird friends. Or I'd have to rob McEnroe."

"You never have a good word for any of them. Maybe you *will* have to." Steve sounded cool and steady.

Ellie, on the other hand, began to slur her words again. "Oh sometimes you're a cruel b—"

"Enough." His voice stopped her like a slap. "You make me weary. We shall go to bed."

"Not so fast." She matched his coolness by her own. "You told me tonight you loved me. I was a fool to believe you—just because I've wanted to hear you say that for six weeks. An hour later you tell me to sell out—to Gerard! If I need money, you say, I can get it from him, or my father. *You're* out of touch with reality, not me."

His response was subdued laughter. "You little monster! Come here."

"You do love me?"

"Of course."

She flashed back at him, "Then let me have it for nothing."

"I cannot do it. You said just now you do not want more."

"Yes, you can—and I do."

"Not unless you come in with me. We spoke of all this before. You need me. . . ." He dropped his voice to a caress, "and I need you . . . to sell for me." He went on, fast. "Listen. You shall have all the money you want, and a new car. Your old one is too conspicuous. You have a clean storefront here. And Boston—a rich town. You know just the people who will want to buy. Friends of the family—"

She jeered at him.

"You laugh? I could give you a list that would make your revered father resign overnight in sheer embarrassment, to—how is it?—save his skin. Gerard's men.

Those film people you are connected with . . . Just think, Ellie. All the parties, all the important people who will look to you, need you."

"Right! Uptight suburban housewives and their executive hubbies! Sure, they'll get in line for it. Sure!"

"They will. I told you. They get bored. They want some fun. It does not hurt their jobs, just adds a little . . . glamor. Your work does not suffer, does it? It is all clean, all fun."

Can't she see what he's doing? Margaret thought desperately.

Ellie seemed to waver. She had stopped arguing back. "You really believe it yourself, don't you?" she said levelly. "Fun, as long as I don't get hooked myself, right?"

"Right. And you do not. You are a strong woman." He was coaxing, wooing her to him. "These Boston people are intelligent, Ellie. And they will see you are intelligent, too. That makes them feel safe. You make the contacts. They just telephone you; then before you know it they start buying regularly."

She hesitated. "It's really that simple?"

"Look at me. You can see it is."

"All clean, all fun, huh?"

"And free cuts for you."

"Let's go to bed, Steve."

Margaret didn't hear his answer, but they obviously moved out of the room. She heard them coming and going, the closet door opening, the shower running, quiet sounds in the bathroom . . . and then nothing.

In the blank dark, now feeling numbed even in the mildness of early May, Margaret remained still and tried to sort out her feelings about what she had so unwillingly heard. Ellie—the free spirit that she herself couldn't and wouldn't be—that personality was a mask, too, after all. Yet Ellie had apparently needed her, and she had needed Ellie almost as much. It *wasn't* just because of Don, she told herself. It *wasn't*. It was because Ellie's being—her otherness, her difference—somehow complemented and completed her own. So that was why she herself hated Steve, she realized: because he was chaining her up; because he did not love Ellie; because he would destroy her. Yes, and in the end he would destroy her own links with Don, too.

At last she was certain that they must be asleep. Driven by all the tea she had drunk, she tiptoed softly out to the bathroom. The light on, she saw that they had been careless for the first time. On the hightopped table where Ellie kept her make-up rested a small sheet of aluminum foil that had been torn from a roll. The foil was lightly scored by a razor blade that lay on top of it. A plastic drinking straw, bent and discarded, lay beside the foil. Minute traces of a fine white powder remained on the foil.

She stared at it, then caught in the mirror a picture of her own pain and horror. "Oh, God," she whispered. "Oh, my God, my God."

But no one answered.

PART III

Flash Photography
May – December 1971

Numb with unbelief you stand on a stony shore
Emptying your voice into the tide.
Left by the same long outgoing water of lament
I watch from my island
The sea ebbing away
While both of us look for another headland
    for the turning tide.

For the second Memorial Day weekend in a row, Margaret was staying on Nantucket Island with David and Martha. A stiff sea-breeze drove the breakers into white caps and sent her scarf whirling around her head. Beginning to feel chilled, she and Martha with the two children turned away from the waterfront and took refuge for a while in the steamy warmth of an inn close to the public beach. When they were warm again, they walked down to Old South Wharf.

"Here's a gallery you might like," Martha said. She led the way to a gabled building more reminiscent of a fishing-hut than an art gallery.

"I saw a much larger place on Main Street," Margaret commented.

"Yes, it's bigger. More polished, too, but not nearly as interesting. Come on. You'll see." Martha lifted Rebecca into her arms, murmuring, "I'll have to carry you for a bit." Margaret had Jonathan in a carrier on her back.

Martha's enthusiasm was hardly infectious; doubtfully, Margaret followed her sister-in-law over the damp boards and through a low doorway. Shifting Jonathan's weight, she stepped down into what she almost expected would be a dank, poorly lit cellar smelling of fish. Instead, fresh ivory paint and clean gray burlap covered the walls and ceilings between beams. Far from dingy, the gallery radiated with unobtrusive track lighting that lent an amber clarity, a sort of luminosity like that of the light on sea and sky outside. A clean smell of linseed oil pervaded the place.

Martha smiled at Margaret's surprised face. "Isn't this—?" She spread her hands.

"Yes, I love it."

"I'll take Jonathan, if you like. You ought to look around."

She peered over her shoulder. "No—he's sleeping. You can have him back later."

Martha grinned. "All right, then. I'll take Rebecca out on the wharf again for a few minutes. I'm afraid she won't last long in here—will you, honey?"

Rebecca squirmed in her arms. "Let me down!"

"In a minute. We'll leave Maggie here and come back."

"Just give me ten minutes, okay?" Margaret asked. "I could look round some other time."

"It'll be closed on Monday. Take your time."

Margaret moved around slowly to one seascape after another: clear, blue-drenched oil paintings of the Atlantic, of sea gulls banking over gull-gray houses, of dilapidated wharves, and white, bell-topped church towers throwing their reflections into dappling harbor waters. Neat white tags beside the paintings identified in bold calligraphy varying interpretations of Madaket sunsets, Brant Point rain squalls, Nantucket yachts and schooners. But never was the light the same.

In the back room she came upon an anomaly in all this wash of cobalt and ultramarine. Hanging in one corner was an oil that on first viewing looked artificial and ill-conceived: a windy ocean of viridian and emerald green surging around a red lighthouse. But stepping closer and adjusting her eyes, Margaret saw not a red lighthouse but a silo painted in cadmium. A spray of white oaks and red maples masked the adjoining barn, and beyond it the soft fields melted from earth greens to the grays of the horizon. She stepped back, laughing with pleasure. From this new vantage point she saw what she had at first missed: two tiny figures running, shadowed and almost hidden by the trees; a little mongrel by the barn, barking at the wind that took the trees and beat them against the red siding. The painting lived and moved. "Vermont Seascape," the tag drily announced, then in smaller letters below, "John Coffin, 1965." No price was listed.

" 'Vermont Seascape,' " she muttered in amusement. But then, inevitably, she thought of Hammonds' rust-red barns and became wistful. If only she could take the painting . . . She would hang it in her room: a window on Vermont from seascaped Massachusetts. Then the seething trees would dance for her, day and night; and the two diminutive figures would run under the cresting tree-waves, never inundated.

She was still standing before the painting, unconsciously rocking from side to side to lull Jonathan, when Martha returned.

"What've you found? Oh—isn't that a clever picture?"

Rather at a loss for words herself, Margaret gesticulated. "Oh—I—"

"You like it?"

"Very much. I didn't figure it out right away."

"I met Mr. Coffin once," Martha began. "I wanted to ask him to explain this one to me, but I didn't quite have the nerve. Most of the artists around here just shrug and say, 'It means what you want it to mean. You're part of the art, yourself.' Or something like that." She smiled. "Well, are you ready to go back?"

Reluctantly, Margaret threw a last look at the painting and went up the stairs again. The two women carefully transferred Jonathan onto Martha's back and made the trek through the most crowded part of Nantucket back up to the Cliff Road.

As they reached the house again, both were rosy-faced from the walk. Jonathan lay asleep against Martha's back, his head lolling. A thin necklace of drool strung out of his open mouth to the shoulder-seam of her jacket. In a fluffy white parka, Rebecca ran in circles around them like a small overjoyed rabbit.

Humming to herself, Martha pushed open the white gate and held it for the others. Margaret glanced up as she passed and saw her, suddenly, as if for the first time. Her sister-in-law's plainness had always struck her before; but now she saw—instead of the straight brown hair in its untidy ponytail—the opalescent, clear eyes with fine lines at the corners; the curved, full mouth that could laugh or draw softly together but which never curled in bitterness like her own. The open serenity of Martha's face was what drew her—the unaccustomed freshness that contrasted with the void expressions she saw daily on the train. That indefinable sweetness—no wonder David loved her.

Oblivious of the scrutiny, Martha trailed up the path after Margaret, while Rebecca tugged impatiently at the unlocked doorknob. "I can't! It won't open!" she wailed.

"Try again," Martha advised. She turned to Margaret. "Look, David's back already!" His bike stood against the side of the house. "That's good. Must've had a lighter day."

Rebecca at last wrenched open the front door and stood on the doorstep, reaching up to the bell and shouting "Ding!" every time she pressed it.

"You old dingbat," Martha said, scooping her up and balancing the weight of the two children front and back.

David came out of the kitchen with a fistful of letters and a folded newspaper. "Hi, everyone, been for a walk?"

"We got berry flowers and violets . . . and then Maggie had to look at some old pictures—"

Jonathan's voice drowned his sister's. He bent

backwards in the carrier, stiffened his legs and began to cry furiously.

"Poor little guy," Martha muttered. She turned so that David could lift him off her shoulders and then leaned over to kiss both of them. "How's the hospital?"

He grinned. "Oh, quiet for a change. I just got back. One of the tourists got a hook in his leg—surf-casting. That was the worst." He smiled. "I see you made a cake." He pulled a face and pointed at Jonathan. "See, Maggie, the filial gratitude we get for giving him a birthday cake."

Rebecca grabbed Margaret's hand and began to hop up and down. "I want cake!" she shrieked. "See how good I can jump?"

"*Well*," David insisted.

"Well what?" Martha asked.

"How *well* she can jump. Where's her English these days?"

"She's been charming the fishermen a good bit of the day, I guess."

"That explains it. Washingtonians . . . New Jersey-ites . . . what d'you expect?" He winked over Martha's head at his sister. "And Vermonters . . . any of them handsome enough for our Margaret? What are they catching these days, anyhow? Whale?"

"Bass, bluefish, and swarms of children," Martha said.

"But no women," Margaret assured him.

"More fool they." David wiped Jonathan's face. "Hey, let's have your cake, huh?"

"He won't appreciate it, I don't think." Martha lifted the child out of David's arms again. "Let's eat it later. He can go down for a bit longer."

Rebecca began to fuss about the cake.

"And you, madam," David said, "can have a little nap, too." He hugged her, lifting her nose-to-nose.

"But I want cake! I want cake. Oh—"

"No, you burned out on the Wharf, I think. You can stay up late tonight with the grownups, okay?"

Margaret was left standing in the low-ceilinged kitchen as the children were put to bed. Upstairs the nursery floor creaked and the wails grew fainter. Downstairs the house lay peaceful. The kettle began to hiss softly, and wind lifted the curtains a few inches off the sills. She crossed to the sink and stared out of the screened windows toward the water. Above the beach a red and blue kite bobbed on the air currents and was echoed below by a red and blue sail scudding across the Sound.

I can't bear to go back to Boston, she thought with a sudden heavy dread. *It isn't the school . . . not even the chaotic apartment . . . but to be with Ellie again— that's what I can't bear.* She visualized the apartment as it looked when she left the piles of clothing, dirty and clean, dropped all over the floor; the dead plants in Ellie's room she had tried to save from dehydration; the empty bottles and wine-sticky glasses left in the kitchen; the unmarked packages that appeared and disappeared, supposedly without her knowledge, from corners of a high shelf in the living room. The apartment would smell stale and strange. The phone would ring again and again, and voices she didn't know would ask for Eleanor McHenry—too many times for the last name to be a mistake. . . . Just how long could she endure all this?

Her own life had gone underground for the weeks since she'd heard Steve and Ellie talking in the middle of the night. Everything had become alien and joyless to her. She'd gone on, running on habits and routines—a clockwork doll. Not that she herself in the midst of it all could have recognized what was happening—for the plumb of unhappiness had descended slowly. But now, distant from Ellie in the retreat of an island peace, the soundness of her brother's life here

struck her as far more real than the existence she and
Ellie had in the apartment.

Once before she had accused David of isolationism.
"It's all right for you on sleepy little old Nantucket,"
she'd said. "You've got island, sky, and ocean. No wonder you have peace. No ghettos, no crime to speak of
. . . no wonder you and Martha can go on a Jesus trip.
You don't even live in the real world."

But now she began to question herself. Ellie had
lectured her with persistent incoherence about what
she called a "deep reality": a new communion with the
world, a fresh perception of herself and her circum-
stances. *I feel so strong now, with Steve. More competent, and much sexier. Perfect!* But were Ellie's deep
reality and perfection real at all? Even as Margaret
watched, drugs had dwarfed the mundane things
around Ellie, rendered them suspect or at best objects
of complete disregard. Only Steve and the rush of cocaine or the mellow after-ease of wine and marijuana
were real to Ellie. And in the crumbling and dissolution
of Ellie's external world, Margaret could already foresee
shadows of Ellie's internal dissolution. Perhaps her
own, too, if the shadows fell far enough.

Was all this more real, then, than surf in the Sound,
the play of light on the ocean, sand dollars on the
beach, the Vermont seascape, men in the emergency
room with fishhooks in their legs, kites and kettles, the
push and swell of Martha's growing baby, birthday cake
for a crying child? Which the light? Which the shadows?

The kite dipped suddenly and dropped out of sight,
reeled in by an unseen hand. At the same time the
kettle began a baleful whistling. She turned it off and
made tea.

"Ugh! Maggie!" Martha had come in soundlessly.
"Milk in your tea? You and David . . . disgusting."

"No, it's good." She looked an appeal to her brother.

David stood with amusement in the doorway, then settled himself in a rocker. "It's a futile argument, Maggie. Martha's just an ignorant New Yorker."

"Any more states you care to bash?" Martha returned lightly. "You've got it in for them all today."

Margaret thought of McEnroes. They did the same. Massachusetts might as well have been the only state in the Union.

"Oh, I'll allow Vermont, I suppose," David teased. "But no others. Not a one."

Margaret grinned. "Very magnanimous of you. But I think Vermont may be moving to New York one of these days."

Martha sat forward and rested her mug on one knee. "Don—in New York?"

"He said so in March . . . when I visited him." She felt warm, suddenly. Why had she done this? Could talking about him somehow summon him for the claiming? It was so tempting to imply more of a relationship than had ever existed. Tempting—but pointless.

"Not the city," David pursued, watching her.

"Oh—no way—the western end of the state." She frowned. "I don't know exactly where."

"Then what, Maggie?" he asked gently. "Aren't you ever giving up on this guy?"

She looked away, wishing again she hadn't steered the conversation toward Don. David always ferreted out truths she didn't dare confront herself. "No, I don't think so. If you met him, you might understand." The talk had suddenly become far too serious.

"We don't, honey. But if he's like his sister—"

She jerked up in her seat as if he had heard her thoughts by the window. But all her protective feelings for Ellie flooded back. "Dave! This isn't like you . . . would you want people to make conjectures about *you* from watching me plod around the way I do?" She smiled briefly, but it was a tight smile. "And you don't know Ellie, either, not really. You met her *once*, that's all."

David rocked harder. "I guess. Sorry. I don't want to judge."

His keen eyes blazed toward her, and she thought for a moment that this must be how he looked at his patients in the emergency room: with absolute concentration, not missing a single detail of facial or bodily movement. "But I want—*pray* for—the best for you. And I'm not sure that McEnroe can give it. Are *you*?"

She met his eyes. "Positively. It's been the most certain thing in my life, for nine years."

David shot a meaningful look at Martha and then turned back to his sister. "Well, I like your conviction."

"And Ellie—?" Martha interposed. "You said something on the phone one day about some problems. You and Ellie still getting along?"

Holding the tea close to her mouth, Margaret was careful to look no further than the rim of the mug. "Oh, basically." She made her voice vague but immediately caught another look between the two. She must be cautious, she decided, to reveal nothing. Perhaps she could skirt the issue. "It's just . . ." She fumbled for an idea. "Well, she doesn't like to get going in the morning or go to bed nights. We have different lifestyles . . . that sort of thing."

Martha smiled. "Can't get up in the morning? Can't sleep nights?" She set her tea on the table and stretched her arms out over her head so that the outline of her belly was clearly defined against her smock. "What she needs is some ADT. Right, Dave?" She began to giggle.

David joined in, almost choking on his tea. Their laughter bounced against the walls of the old room and caught hold of Margaret, too, even though she didn't understand it.

"ADT?" She was relieved at the change in their mood.

"You tell her, Dave."

"Before we came . . . there was an ornery old family doctor here. Years ago, I mean. And a druggist who was in cahoots with him, so we're told." He started to laugh again. "They'd both have their licenses revoked nowadays. The old doctor had a standard remedy for whatever ailed anybody—especially those nice old ladies who just wanted a chat, you know: ADT."

Martha covered her mouth with her handkerchief, laughing helplessly, but Margaret felt left out of the joke.

"The druggist made it up, and all the old dears flocked in and got their bottles. 'Oh, doctor, that medicine sure works wonders,' " David raised his voice to a querulous treble.

"What *was* it," Margaret prompted.

David shouted with laughter. "Any darn thing."

"What?"

"Any old thing the druggist had left over! He kept a barrel in the back of the store. Used to pour a little of this and that in it and fill the bottles out of the barrel. Never tasted the same, of course."

Margaret subsided against the back of her chair. "Oh, you two! I don't believe a word of it."

"He did, truly," Martha laughed. "Whatever he had."

"He could have poisoned someone."

"So he could. Probably did. But everyone swore by the stuff."

"And so you prescribe ADT, I suppose?"

"Wish I could sometimes."

"David Fuller!"

"Margaret Fuller!" he mimicked her. "Just think what modern medical science is missing. A cure for measles or cancer or insomnia or the common cold. You name it. ADT does it all."

The room became quiet for a minute and lulled Margaret into a false sense of security.

"So what's Ellie's real problem?"

She should have known that his dogged nature wouldn't leave the topic unfinished. Still, she wasn't quite ready to answer, but her unconscious and desperate desire to unburden on someone took hold before she could think of how to avoid it.

"She thinks I don't know what's going on." The words broke out, sharp as the tip of an iceberg about to ram a hole in all her old hopes and dreams.

David's rocker stopped. His face sobered. "Can you tell us?"

"It's difficult."

"Martha knew something was eating you up."

Margaret looked sharply at her sister-in-law. She wanted to let go, but she wanted to hold back, too. She sat still for a long time with the others looking at her, waiting. Finally she said, "I can't see what good it'd do to tell you anything. You couldn't do anything for her, anyway. And it'd just confirm any prejudices you have about McEnroes."

"Let that one go, Margaret. We've never met Don, as you reminded us," David said. "But if we could ease your mind . . . that would make it worth your while to talk, wouldn't it?"

She could still walk around the subject, she realized. They could draw their own conclusions. She took a deep breath, but her voice came shakily. "Gerard— her boss—I've never seen the guy except at a couple of her zany parties, a couple years ago. He keeps calling and complaining about her." Her voice fell lower, in exasperation. "And I don't know what to do! She's not getting to the agency half the time, and he's prepping someone else as his prima donna. He complains to me on the phone and asks me all the time, 'Where is that girl? What the heck's going on?' " She shrugged a gesture of dismissal. "And what can I tell the guy?"

"The truth, I guess," Martha said simply.

She shook her head. "No, it's not that easy. She's working for someone else now, as well. Someone I can't stand." She gritted her teeth. "And it's all strictly . . ." She let out a long breath. "Steve—you've never met anyone like him."

"Her other boss?"

Margaret's mouth curled. "No, not exactly. Her lover. Looks like a graduate of Princeton or West Point. But he's crooked as your elbow."

"Mafia?"

She laughed bitterly. She was dropping the story out, pebble by pebble of it until the trail of pebbles led to a place they recognized. She didn't know how else to tell them. The truth was too brutal, and she couldn't accept it herself, even after all she'd heard and seen. "No, not Mafia. He's Peruvian—half—or so he says. I can't tell. Says he's from Miami, but he jets up to Boston and down to Peru—so I don't know—" She broke off, stopping short of throwing out the last pebble. She would take another path.

"The phone rings constantly. People I've never seen in my life drop by and get things or leave things for Ellie or Steve—except they call them by other names. I answer the phone; I sometimes have to take in those awful deliveries . . . and they think I don't know what's happening!"

David and Martha remained silent. The curtains flapped in the window as a breeze came up again.

"McEnroe—I mean her father—that's what they all call him, even Ellie—and Don . . . McEnroe calls and gets mad when she's never there. He's no fool, either. Sooner or later . . . and Ellie's suddenly got money. Her old Buick's gone. She drives a Lincoln Continental—custom built. She spends wildly and still wants to borrow—"

"Wait a minute, Maggie." David's long fingers had turned white; he pressed them hard against each other. "You do know what's going on, you say?"

She didn't answer.

"I don't," Martha said, full of concern.

David looked across at her, then back at Margaret.

"Mind if I ask you a couple of things?"

Margaret sat back. Her breathing wasn't right, and her heart raced. "Go ahead."

"Ellie used to smoke marijuana, didn't she?"

"Yes."

"Has she gone on smoking?"

"No. She stopped after she went to Woodstock. Had some kind of reaction to it—made her very sick."

"That doesn't usually happen, unless she was using something else as well."

"She stopped," Margaret said slowly, "but Steve got her started again a few weeks ago."

"And this Steve—what's his line of business?"

She stared back dumbly.

"He smokes too?" David pursued.

"Yes."

"Oh, Maggie, can't you come right out with it? This needn't be a game."

"I wasn't trying to play a game," she snapped. "I told you. This is *hard*." The tears welled up suddenly, surprising her.

David moved from the rocking chair to put his arms around her.

"I think you just told me everything," he murmured.

Her voice slid up to a squeaky sob. "I've been afraid for her. There was no one—"

"Steve's peddling dope, right?"

"Right. Oh, but David . . ."

"Not just pot, huh?"

"Cocaine. She knows I know about the grass—never tried to hide it. But the cocaine . . . I discovered it by accident. I wasn't sure at first." She wiped her eyes with her wrist.

"It figures. Easy victim."

"Not just a victim. He's got her working with him in the city. Selling to others, as well. A whole ring of people, far as I can tell. She's out in the worst parts of town. And it's all dirty, filthy. I know just what's going to happen . . . people are shot and knifed all the time. She's fooling herself." She took a breath, her face pained. "I'm sure all the excitement of running against the law makes her feel better, more important. Steve had her figured out to a nicety." She shuddered. "All the style, the glamor, her job, the people she hangs around with . . . everything. It's fake. And now she's getting so out of control she can't even see it herself."

"Poor, poor Ellie," Martha breathed.

David sounded somber. "Oh, if only she could see some of the cokeheads—"

Martha quickly reproached him, "Don't say that."

"No, you're right," he nodded. "But, Maggie . . . I've treated addicts here sometimes. And before, when I was interning at Mass. General. And in—"

"But I thought you couldn't get addicted to cocaine," Margaret said painfully.

"There's a lot of argument over it. Coming off doesn't leave you physically broken, it's true. But you're wrecked psychologically. Not to mention financially. And there *are* physical risks for users. Nasal infection, emaciation, respiratory depression . . . sometimes even cardiac arrest."

"But I thought it was the kind of drug people could take or leave? It's so expensive, isn't it? And I remember reading that people often don't use it a second time."

"I wouldn't know about that, but I doubt if it's the kind of thing you get into in moderation. You crave it, cry for it, steal for it . . . kill for it."

Margaret thought with a chill of Ellie's desperation, her sell-out to Steve, her willingness to risk her job, her life—everything—to assure her supply of cocaine. The memory left her with even more anguish. "That's what I'd begun to think I was seeing. She doesn't think of much else now, I'm sure."

"The people I saw were all in pieces. They were sniffing all the time. One patient—he was shooting up as well—probably selling, too, but I don't know—when I saw him he was covered with needle marks and welts and sores. He hallucinated so badly he thought spiders were running all over him. He'd torn himself to pieces."

Martha's handkerchief was over her mouth again, but this time in horror.

"Nothing glamorous about that stuff. You think you're in touch with God. That's what the Incas thought. But you've betrayed yourself to a demon."

Margaret brooded over her tea. "Steve doesn't use it much," she said, half to herself, still thinking hard. "It's Ellie who can't live without it."

"If he's a full-time pusher, he's far too smart for that. And he probably doesn't need a bolster for his ego, either, the way she must. Do you think she's sniffing, or shooting?"

Margaret found herself grinning suddenly. "How come you know all the lingo, Dave?"

"Vietnam, honey, remember?"

"Sure." She winced. "I don't know what she's doing, not for sure. Sniffing, I guess."

"Seen any syringes? Water pipes? No? How did you discover it, anyway?"

"In the bathroom. A straw. A spoon. A *tiny*, tiny bit of white stuff. I knew enough to figure it out after a while."

"Well, there's a little hope, then."

"How?"

"Free-basing and hypodermics—they're not so common, but much more dangerous—for lots of reasons. When the flash comes, it's a terrific jolt for the old body. And the paraphernalia itself can kill you. It can explode—the water pipe, I mean. Or the needles may be contaminated."

Margaret shut her eyes and sagged back in the chair. Through a haze of dismay, she murmured, "Then what can we do? I love Ellie, Dave. She's destroying herself."

"Not yet, but she might." He matched her low, grieved tone. "Do? Nothing—as you thought. She has to want to be helped. Turning her in won't help anyone."

"She doesn't want help."

Martha had listened for a while in silence. Now she spoke up. "It seems to me, Maggie, that you're in as much danger as Ellie is, in some ways."

"Oh—*I* won't touch it."

"No—but you're involved. You're living there. What if you took one of those deliveries from the wrong person—the FBI, for example?"

"Don't be ridiculous, Martha," David scoffed. "She'd be pretty glad if the FBI or the drug enforcement guys arrived."

"If she went to jail for possession?"

"You're missing your own point, honey. What's far worse is the problem of this . . . Steve, himself. She knows rather too much."

"But I told you—they think I don't know anything," Margaret objected.

"But for how long?" He raised his eyebrows. "How credible is naivete in a woman of twenty-four or -five?"

She was silenced.

"I think we'd better go back to Boston with you. Or I will, at least. We'll move you out of the apartment."

She regarded him steadily. "No, I won't move."

Her brother's forehead drew together over his dark

eyes. "Then I'll move your things myself, without your help, if necessary."

She burst out, "But I can't leave Ellie!"

"You won't help her by staying there. You need to move, Margaret."

She hunched forward. "I won't move," she insisted, catching the look of appeal Martha sent to David.

He did not answer her for a moment, then he said grimly, "Listen, who needs whom, I'd like to know?"

The question hit home. Margaret's determination disappeared into an aching abyss. She bit her lip and moved her hands helplessly. Her feelings swung back and forth between blank despair as she contemplated never again seeing Don, and wild relief at the thought that she'd no longer have to return to their apartment with dread; she'd be free of Ellie's vagaries, Ellie's friends, Ellie's dope, Ellie's own swinging emotions.

David held off, seeing the pain on her face. Finally it was Martha who said, "You don't need to answer that one, Maggie." Her voice was very gentle.

Margaret's throat began to clog. "It's true," she managed. "I don't understand it, but she's important to me." Her eyes had filled again. "She's unpredictable, capricious, selfish, vain—but I care about her."

"That's good," David said softly. "That's very good. She's got a better friend than she knows. But you can't destroy yourself. You might be able to do more by living somewhere else and keeping in touch."

"*How*?" she laughed bitterly. The thought of Don kept coming back. What would he say? Would he be able to forgive? He loved his sister the way he loved free wild birds and animals. Would he forgive Margaret for standing aside while Ellie chained herself in drink, dope, and dead-end dreams of a drug-peddler? But what could she do? What could she *do*?

"It's her brother, isn't it? That's what's—"

She began to weep again. "What on earth can I do?"

David's arm was still around her, and Martha's eyes, though troubled, remained steady. "Let's not push her, Dave," Martha said. "Maggie, we'll think about it some more—together. Okay?" She stood up. "Excuse me, would you?" She went out, leaving them alone together.

David pulled out a tissue and gave it to her. "You're my emergency today, I think."

Margaret nodded weakly, but the tears still gathered. She wiped them away again and turned to her brother. "Basket case."

He moved back to the rocker. "Martha's gone to pray about things, I imagine." He hesitated. "Would you let me pray with you—for Ellie—and Don—and you?"

That stopped the tears instantly. "No! This isn't kindergarten, Dave." She found his intense eyes suddenly unbearable. "What good did prayers ever do? Empty words to an empty sky."

Instead of looking outraged, as she expected, he actually nodded. "That's what I *used* to think, too."

———

Somewhere between Hyannis and Boston on the long, dull stretches of Routes 6 and 3, David convinced her she should leave the apartment. Whether it was his insistent logic or his reassuring presence that finally swayed her, she couldn't decide afterward. In any event, by the time they pulled up in front of the familiar apartment house, she had surrendered her gut feeling that she should stay to a vague notion that it was pointless to go on living in the world of chaos and artificiality that Ellie chose to inhabit. Not that the decision left her with any sense of relief; instead, she felt numb, weary, curiously indifferent.

"I'll run up and check to see if Ellie's there," he said.

She looked down the block for the place where Ellie generally parked. The glossy black paint of the Lincoln Continental was nowhere in evidence. All the same, she cringed at the thought of seeing Ellie return now when everything was still so painful and unaccustomed; it would be better if she and David could get everything out fast and avoid her altogether. The question of where she'd live now wasn't nearly as pressing as the uneasiness she felt at the prospect of a fight with Ellie. The apartment would have to be signed over to Ellie, and Steve's "clean storefront" would be gone . . . things could get unpleasant.

"You'll need both keys. Here." She took them out.

"I'll be right back for you," he said.

Watching David enter the front vestibule and disappear, she was soon seized with doubt. What if Ellie came right now? What if she was there already and her car parked somewhere out of sight? Her hands began to sweat.

Without really seeing them she watched a few people passing David's car: a heavy woman with a child whose jaw was oddly misshapen; a tall black man who whistled and leaned forward as he walked, his hands shoved deep in his pockets, his eyes straight ahead. Then another man by himself, square-shouldered, thick blonde hair to his shoulders, feet not hurrying. He paused by the front of the apartment building, stared up at it, then began looking into all the cars beside the curb. Margaret was not fully aware of him until he stopped near the car and bent to get a full look at her. Automatically, she turned her head when he caught her eye; she remembered that the doors were locked and felt secure in ignoring him. She expected him to move off, but he didn't. Close to the glass, he made motions with his hands that she should open the door; he nodded and grinned suggestively.

Used to this, she turned an angry face toward him. "Go try someplace else," she shouted. "My husband's coming out in a minute."

Giving her a peace sign and another parting leer,

the man shuffled on up the street but then loitered on
the corner, still watching her. What was keeping David?
She wished she'd gone in with him. She watched the
seconds tick off on the dashboard clock. The wait
seemed interminable.

At last he came out of the building. He'd shed his
jacket, and his shirt sleeves were rolled up to the el-
bows. He was lugging an armful of Margaret's books.
"She's out. Might as well start right off," he said. "Help
me with these, can you? . . . You could open the trunk."

She stepped onto the curb and threw a quick glance
down to the corner, but the man had vanished.

"It wasn't hard to figure out which room was yours
. . . what did the place look like when you left?"

"Same as usual."

"How, then?"

She slammed the trunk shut. "We're being
watched," she laughed.

He didn't laugh. "By whom?"

"Some guy was trying to make a pass at me while
you were inside . . . don't worry about it . . . didn't look
like the FBI, believe me."

"You're not taking this very seriously, are you?"

They stood on the step briefly with the humid afternoon sunshine filtering down onto their heads.

"The move? Yes—very. But the idea of my being in
danger . . . not really."

"Maybe you should."

She shrugged. "Maybe. But it doesn't matter if I'm
getting out now. Come on, let's get going."

In the elevator, he asked again about the apartment.
"Was it bad in your place when you left?"

She had to measure her tone before she replied. She
felt cold inside when she thought about the difference
between the bright, artfully conceived decorating Ellie
had done two years before and the squalid mess she
had left on Friday, but she wasn't giving up com-

pletely—yet—on her habit of covering for Ellie. In the hallway they passed the old stain on the wall where Ellie's friend had shattered a wine-glass. *I should have known then*, she thought.

She said, "Housekeeping's never been Ellie's forte. She was always the scintillating hostess, and I was the housekeeper. It worked for a while."

"Your understatement just underscores it. The place is a junkyard—it stinks, Maggie." He pushed open the door and held it for her. "For pete's sake why didn't you tell anyone about this before? It must have driven you crazy."

Inside she took in the slovenly litter of discarded clothes, half-eaten food, unopened mail, open closets, broken light fixtures, and dust-streaked floors. "It hasn't been like this for long." Her voice softened. "I wish you could have seen it—even a couple of months ago." She shook her head wearily. "I'm sorry now that I always see you at your house. You and Martha should have come over—you would have liked it. But lately . . . I just couldn't keep up with it all. I gave up . . . a few weeks ago. I didn't know what to do."

David reached out and put his hand on her shoulder. "I know you're hurting. But this is best."

She darted a sardonic smile at him. "The patient has to feel the stitches before she's all sewn up again, right?"

He looked at her steadily. "That sarcasm doesn't suit you. Why don't you go ahead and admit it."

"The sarcasm?"

"No, the hurt."

"I'm sure it's been obvious all weekend."

"I can read you like a book, m'dear."

"Read on, MacDuff."

"The book says 'I'm scared to death of losing that man I never even had.' "

"Ouch, David—"

"Feel those stitches going in?"

"Yes, you brute."

"Then don't cover it all up, sweetheart. It's part of you. If you're meant for him, and he for you, you'll be together some day."

"You're preaching."

"Ellie's the only person you could talk to about him, huh?"

She closed her eyes for a moment and then stepped aside to avoid the pressure of his hand on her shoulder. "Oh, Dave . . . You don't need to stick me any more to see if I bleed. I'm hemorrhaging. Yes—if you want to hear me say it—yes, I needed Ellie." The hot tears made him swim across her vision. "See—I cry, too, as well as bleed."

He held her against him for a moment. "I'm not trying to make it worse, honey. I want you to believe this is best. I didn't want to make glib talk just now. I really meant it. If you're for Don, moving out and away from Ellie won't change a thing."

"And if not—?"

He didn't answer her. "Let me make you a glass of ADT—if I can find anything in this pigpen. Then we'd better pull out."

She submitted to his talent for managing others in a crisis. It was comforting for a time to make no decisions. She drank the concoction he made her—"Fruit juice with a pinch of salt," he called it.

"To be taken with a large grain of salt, I presume," she laughed, smelling the slight aroma of brandy. "You wouldn't even drink this yourself, would you?"

"Almost every medication has alcohol in it—even ADT."

"Hypocrite! You think I need a sedative?"

"It won't hurt—though I wouldn't give it to Ellie."

"Enough, Dave."

While he went to see the landlord for her, she

stripped her bed, piled the clothes by the door, and began emptying her closet. Then together they moved her bits of furniture out into the hallway. They were half way down the stairwell with her dresser when he announced, "Oh, by the way, if you were wondering what took me so long in here by myself . . . I made a couple of calls for you. I found someone who might—"

"Oh? What—"

"He may have a place where you could live, at least for a while."

She looked at him over the scratched wood surface as they carefully turned the dresser around a corner. Between her teeth, she grumbled, "I *hate* moving."

"But at least you may have a place to move *to*."

"Why didn't you tell me before?"

"You were pretty upset."

"*Were. . . ?* Well, where is it? Oh, let's try to get the next piece in the elevator. This is ridiculous. We need a U-Haul, and a trucker to go with it."

"Come on—you're a strong woman . . . it's a couple of miles—on the other side of the river. In between Harvard and MIT."

"In Cambridge, you mean."

"Right."

They set the dresser out on the pavement. She was sweating under a thin cotton blouse. She knew he saw her defeatist look, the eloquent *How-can-we-possibly-move-all-this-stuff-now?* question in her eyes.

"We'll make it, Maggie."

She pushed up on her hands and jumped to sit on the top of the dresser. "Tell me more."

"Walt's doing his residency at Mass. General. I knew him when I interned there. Just married . . . bought a house . . . Cindy got pregnant right away, and he said something a while back about converting their downstairs into an apartment to help pay the mortgage."

"And did he?"

"Apparently. He told me he'd rented it once, then someone broke a contract and left him in the lurch. He's got several people interested again, but no one's made a down payment."

"So it might work out?"

"Might. He said he'd double check with one other possibility and call me back—here. But I think it's yours. He sounded very pleased I called."

Her hopes lifted slightly. "It sounds okay."

"There's a catch."

She examined her fingernails, not looking at him. "Always is."

"He'd need the down payment today—no—Monday."

"Tomorrow? The banks aren't even open."

"Then Tuesday. Right away, anyhow. Could you do it?"

"How much?"

"Two-fifty."

"I don't know."

"Would you let me bail you out? A loan, I mean."

Her lips curled. She knew he wanted to help her keep her pride. "Sure. I'd take it . . . so what's the other catch?" She swung down off the dresser and helped him lift the drawers into the trunk.

"No—nothing."

"I thought you were going to tell me the wife had left him and Walt's a lean and hungry bachelor again, with a sad kid who needs a mother."

"Not in the least! They're toughing it out, but they're wild about each other."

"Sounds better every minute."

With careful maneuvering they squeezed the dresser itself into the back of the car and locked it in.

"If he clears it for you, you'll take it, then?"

"I can't be too picky, can I? What's it like?"

"I've never been there. Haven't seen him since their wedding. He said it was comfortable—new carpets, new drapes, modern kitchen, but kind of small."

"That's all right. When he calls again, you tell him
. . . I'll take it."

"Good. You'd like them."

They took the elevator upstairs again and began
making more piles by the door. She caught herself saying, "Anything would be better than this."

They had filled her car. They couldn't move any
more until Walt telephoned.

"Aren't you warm?" she asked him.

"Plenty."

"I'll find you a drink."

"No hidden extras, okay?" he laughed.

"No ADTs?"

"No—they give me the DTs."

"Oh—you're awful. How did I ever rate a corny
brother like you?"

"You love it."

She washed two big sour-cream containers and
made a jug of fresh orange juice. Though the entire
kitchen was sticky and greasy, she wiped up what little
she'd spilled, without even thinking. Then, opening the
refrigerator to put the pitcher away, she heard loud
voices just outside the apartment. She froze by the
counter, her eyes focusing unseeingly on the gray mortar of the building next door. All her senses were tuned
to the other end of the apartment.

Laughter first. Snatches of sentences . . . Some
kind of a joke, I guess . . . Maybe the landlord . . . "Margaret's stuff!" Then the laughter turned spiteful. "What
the—? Margaret!"

She remained still, her heart racing against her
ribs.

David stepped out of her room toward the front of
the apartment. "Hi—I'm—"

Ellie stopped short. "Who are *you*, for pity's sake?"

Quickly, Margaret jumped to answer. She saw a loophole that might make things easier—unless Ellie remembered. At the top of her lungs, she screamed out, "Dave!" Then she ran headlong to the hallway and grabbed hold of him before he could say another word.

Steve and Ellie faced them by the door, a clutter of bags, boxes and furniture around and behind them. Irrelevantly, Margaret noticed that Ellie was at least two inches taller than Steve. As usual he was immaculately groomed, but his small build suddenly caught her attention, and she was grateful for David's lanky height. Breathless with fright, she stumbled over the words.

"Ellie—Steve—" she burst out. Would they mistake her terror for excitement? "This—is David. He's moving me out. We're—we're—" She looked up at David with coy devotion on her face and dared him to contradict her. For an instant she remembered him saying "I can read you like a book." He'd better! "Ellie, Ellie—we're going to set up an apartment in Cambridge today—" She pinched David's arm hard, coveting Ellie's flair for dramatics. "Isn't it *wonderful!*" She accentuated every word for David's sake, beseeching him with her eyes not to undo the pantomime. She hadn't lied yet, so he might play along with her. If only they hadn't been taken by surprise . . .

His arm went around her, and he pulled her close against him. Relieved, she looked up to see a Cheshire cat's grin. "Well—what d'you think?"

Ellie's eyes dilated and her mouth opened slightly. "Well, if you aren't the slyest woman. . . !"

Margaret wanted to look at Ellie but found her eyes pulled against her will to Steve's. She saw again that shrewd hardness that she'd noticed the first night. He was looking from her to David and back again with a steadiness that completely unnerved her. But glancing back at Ellie she saw no recognition there of David, only laughter and amazement.

"So all this time you've been setting a high moral

tone, Maggie Fuller, you've been plotting to move out on me and shack up with someone yourself! What a nerve!"

"Oh—well, I—" Her wits forsook her completely.

"Come on! This calls for a bottle of champagne. It's a bit of a shock, you know—pouf! And out she goes, just like that! But let's drink to it anyway."

Leaving Steve standing with David, Ellie went ahead of Margaret to the kitchen. Following her, Margaret half-heard David saying something to Steve.

"*Orange* juice?" Ellie asked disdainfully, looking at the glasses on the counter.

"Well—we got hot—all that stuff—" She knew she would become incoherent in a moment. The charade would fall apart. They should leave—and quickly.

But Ellie was bending toward her confidentially, with a friendly look so like her old self that Margaret felt a pang of sorrow. "So, tell me, how'd you connect up with that gorgeous man?"

Not thinking quickly enough, she took a risk. "Remember—I've gone to Nantucket several times lately . . . We met there . . ."

"Aha! You sly old thing! And he's married, too!"

She swallowed hard. "*M-married?*" she stuttered.

Ellie's forehead crinkled. "Yes—the ring. I saw his ring—is it just—?"

She tried to think. If she confirmed that he was married, Ellie would dramatize this shock and scandal even more; if she said he wasn't, there might be other questions. "Look, let's not talk now, okay?" She said with a helpless gesture. "I'll call you . . . in a couple of days." But she was immediately furious with herself for the whole pretense. She had enmeshed herself in a net of lies that would be hard to escape. Would the truth have been simpler, even if it meant a torrent of bitter words or even threats—or violence?

Ellie pulled a cold bottle from the bottom of the refrigerator and held it up to the light. "No champagne. Too bad. But this'll do just as well. Grab some glasses. Oh, Maggie! Now you're rid of my slow-poke brother! What a coup!"

Margaret felt the color drain out of her face. "Don't—" But Ellie misinterpreted her pallor. "Oh my gosh! Sorry. I guess it's not quite *au fait* to say another word about Don in present company." She blithely took the bottle back to the living room with a corkscrew.

Her hands shaking, Margaret took four wine glasses out of the cabinet and put them on a platter. She picked it up, then caught her elbow against the refrigerator. Veering to one side, she saw in horror one of the glasses begin to slide. She lunged toward the counter, but the entire platter crashed to the floor. Crystal splintered everywhere.

David was beside her instantly. His arm went around her again. Behind them, Ellie was laughing heartily, "Oh, see what love's done to moral Margaret! Just look at them, Steve!"

"It's okay, you hear me?" David whispered.

She wanted to cry. The tension was unbearable.

"I'll clean this up. Walt'll call any minute, I'm sure. Then we can clear out."

"You won't—?"

"I'm not going to mess it up, Maggie. Not with what's at stake. Keep cool."

Margaret was not sure afterward what happened during the next half hour. She saw a side of David she'd never seen before, an intelligent, smooth self-possession she wouldn't usually have attributed to him. While she huddled against him in the love seat and studied her drink, he sat with one leg thrown casually over the other and balanced his glass on his knee as if the conversation were quite the most natural thing in the world. Steve didn't say anything, she noticed, but David kept up a light, flirtatious patter with Ellie that awed Margaret completely. He held the glass to his mouth periodically but hardly touched the wine. She took a cue from him and left hers alone, too. Terrified and confused as she was, she didn't need anything else to befuddle her now.

At last, Ellie said, "Well, guys, we'd love to help you more, but—oh—Steve, it's getting late. Aren't we supposed to. . . ?"

Steve looked at Margaret coldly and then back at Ellie. "Yes. We should go. We came to get something." He looked at Margaret again, a fierce stare she had no difficulty interpreting.

"You're—er—going to a party?" she mumbled.

"Exactly."

"Go ahead. We should be all set before tonight," David said, grinning at Ellie. "The place is all yours now."

A momentary frown crossed Ellie's face. "Oh—I guess so . . ."

"I put the rent book on your bureau," Margaret said, recovering a little. "Call me if you have any problems."

Ellie's eyebrows quirked. "We're paid through May, are we? Hey—I don't know your number."

Margaret looked quickly at David. "Do you, darling?" she asked.

"No—phone's not in yet. We only rented the place today."

"I'll make sure you have it," Margaret said. In the back of her mind, she thought, *When Steve's gone back to Miami . . . I'll tell her the truth then.* "And we're paid through June as well . . . We took care of it today. The landlord told Dave he'd expect you to come down and sign for yourself. Okay?"

Ellie smiled. "Thanks—that was sweet of you." She nudged Steve. "Ready?"

He stood up directly and made a mock bow toward David. "Que le vaya bien." Then he turned to Ellie. "You have something to get. . . ?" His voice was low.

"Oh—in a minute!" Seemingly on impulse Ellie reached out to Margaret and hugged her. "The end of a long era, Maggie," she said.

Again Margaret felt guilty. Ellie hadn't been this warm for weeks. Her throat was blocked, and she shut eyes against the sting of tears and against the wrenching pain of cutting her closest tie with Don.

"You're shaking," Ellie said gently.

"Am I?" She tensed. Steve was eyeing her strangely, and she couldn't rid herself of the idea that he'd seen through their play from the very beginning.

Ellie pushed her toward David. "You'd better look after this woman pretty darn well," she said. "She's a good, good person."

David took her hand. "I *know* it."

"Won't you give Steve a kiss, too?"

She tried to feign complacency, released David's hand, and moved stiffly toward Steve.

His arms went round her ribs crushingly hard, and he bent his mouth to her ear. "Keep quiet. Understand?"

Had she heard it right? She flushed hotly. "I will." Then as a last desperate attempt at naturalness, she added, "Take care, Steve."

"Oh—Maggie—you're red as beets! Steve—let her alone, for heaven's sakes!"

David claimed her again, and Steve returned to the entryway without another look at Margaret. Ellie went into her room and came straight out with a different bag slung over her shoulder, waved gaily, and shouted back, "Call me soon, okay?" Then they were gone.

David turned to her. "I *like* Ellie," he said.

Flabbergasted, Margaret stared at him. "Oh, you're a cool luke. Whatever makes you say *that*?"

"Because I do. She's attractive. She's got a lot going for her—if she doesn't waste it. I see why you like her, too. And Steve, I can see why—"

"Why I don't like him?" she parroted, finishing his sentence. "Please—cut this out! Could you *see* that he knew exactly what we were doing? Did you *see that* in all you *saw*?" Her voice was strident. "Either you're far cooler than I thought, or you're even more naive than I am."

He dismissed it. "I don't think he knew."

"I do. He told me to keep my mouth shut."

David snapped, "When?"

"In that phoney embrace of his." She recoiled from the memory of it.

"But he would have blown your cover if he'd known. He'd have no reason to keep it from Ellie."

She hesitated. "I wish . . . I could believe you. Oh, why did we ever get into this story anyway? I'll have to burn every last bridge to Ellie when I tell her the real reason I'm leaving—if I do—and that's—"

"—the last thing you want to do, I know. Oh, *dear* Margaret! Things didn't go so well. . . ."

She shrugged. She didn't want any more sympathy now. She didn't want to think of Don anymore. "I'll manage. I'd feel better if Steve weren't around to haunt me—he gives me the heeby-jeebies." She shrugged again. "But—you're right. It's best."

The phone rang. David's face lit up. "Walt!"

"Well, thank God for that."

David lifted the receiver in the kitchen.

"Who? Oh—you want Ellie? . . . No, she's out right now . . . No, this is David, Margaret's brother . . ." He stood still, put one hand on his forehead and pushed it back into his hair in a gesture of bewilderment she remembered from his high school years. "You too. Yes, you want to speak to her?" His face had changed color, and he motioned for Margaret to come to the phone. "She's right here."

She took it from him.

"For you," he said lamely. "Listen, I'll go down and

call Walt from the landlord's apartment. We shouldn't hang around too long." His grave look added weight to the words. "Keep it short, Maggie."

"Margaret?" The call was long-distance. She could tell by the hollow sound of the voice at the other end: like talking to someone at the end of a long pipe. "It's Don."

She was utterly unready to hear from him now. A rush of adrenalin flooded her and seemed to heighten every inflection in his voice. "Oh, what a surprise!" She shut her eyes briefly.

"I thought you went to Nantucket," he said. "You mentioned you were going—last week's letter."

"I did go. Just got back—a little early."

"I gather—your brother said Ellie went out."

"Yes, she came back a while ago but then—" Her voice trailed away. It was hard to finish a thought of her own. She'd rather listen, first.

"I was planning to call tonight, then I decided I couldn't wait any longer. And I figured she'd be out tonight anyway. What's the boyfriend's name now? I never can keep them straight."

Her voice dropped low with suppressed anger. "Steve."

"I want to tell her what's happened here. Fantastic news!"

Her heart constricted. He was getting married, perhaps. The end of an era, indeed, if so.

But he didn't wait for an answer. "I might as well tell you, since you're there. And you've always shown an interest."

She made a small, noncommittal sound, resenting the patronizing tone and wanting to run away from the raw animal pain of it all.

She heard the quick intake of his breath, the unmistakable quiver of joy. "I've closed on a farm over in New York. It's all set."

It was the last thing she had expected now. The possibility of his leaving Vermont as he'd predicted hadn't seemed real to her—even though she'd talked about it herself; it wasn't something she'd wanted to fantasize about. She'd decided to accept the news when it came . . . but not now. Not now when the opposing pull of guilt and relief racked her, when the barbs of her own deception of Ellie still stung her, and the hissed threat of Steve pricked at the back of her brain. Her mind jolted, couldn't readjust.

"You still there? I said I bought that farm!"

"You did!" Her delight almost matched his now; she was pleased by the spontaneous sincerity of it. He was still free, at least, even if lost to her. And this was what he'd wanted all his life: to be an independent farmer. "Oh, Don . . . you got it . . . really? When?"

"Friday. I came back yesterday . . . it happened faster than I thought. Remember I told you in March I was working on it?"

"Sure."

"It's an old farm—family-run for years. But they haven't been making the money he thought they should, and he was ready to retire. The boys didn't want the farm, and the old guy decided he wasn't going to wait for one of them to change his mind. I'd been hounding him for a while—saw some ads in *American Agriculturalist*; he liked me, I think. So he finally upped and went to his attorney and the county extension service, and I started getting calls . . . Ray Hammond's a bit frustrated. I've been driving back and forth for several weeks. The land contract's all arranged now; I got some good loans from the FHA to help with the cattle. The land—that was a deal with the owner—he'll hold the mortgage for a while and I'll be leaving Hammonds' at the end of June. I didn't say anything much to anyone until I could get things pinned down—"

"You must be excited out of your mind."

"High! Unbelievable! Tell Ellie to crack out a little champagne and drink a toast or something."

"She will, I know. Don't you want to tell her yourself?" Their conversation began to seem unreal, and she hardly knew how she would sustain it.

"Oh, I could, if you know when she'll—"

"Well, I don't."

"Want to hear more?"

"Go ahead. Where is it, anyhow?" She could listen, at least.

"Arcade—near Arcade."

"Never heard of it."

"Nor did I until last winter. It's in the snow belt, south of Buffalo. Not exactly what I thought I'd find . . . Ray's been pulling my leg about it for a while."

"Oh, why?"

"He's all for a free-stall system—so am I, too—and this place is about as traditional as you can get. Stanchion barns."

"That sounds okay," she ventured cautiously, hearing dissatisfaction in his voice.

"Oh, it is, if you like to milk one cow at a time and keep them tied up most of the time."

"I see." She wished she knew more.

"That'll change, though. I couldn't stand it for too long. The place has what McEnroe'd call potential. But it'll take a lot of time and capital."

"You're dreaming already."

"Sure! I've waited so long I'd begun to wonder—but I did it, finally. No help from McEnroe, either."

She thought how like Ellie he sounded, suddenly. "You've told them?"

"I called them around noon."

"What'd they say?"

"Oh, they grumbled. Mother especially. She thinks Vermont's uncivilized enough anyway—the only time she deigned to set her dainty foot up here she made

McEnroe get a motel room. But the wilderness of New York! 'Don, you're getting more eccentric every year.' But McEnroe's more philosophical. Said he figured I'd do it sooner or later, and wasn't it about time I settled down anyhow, and when was I going to get married, and didn't I need any cash to sink into a prime herd. . . ? All the stuff I knew he'd say."

"Base ingratitude, Donald." She laughed suddenly, a deep gurgling, healing laugh that lifted a little heaviness from her. She wished he were beside her now, where she could share directly in his joy, and where he could share her fears about Ellie. But their relationship just wasn't built on that kind of understanding.

The curtain of uncertainty and misery fell again almost immediately, as David returned and sat where she could plainly see him growing impatient with the length of the call. He gestured that he needed her attention; so eventually she gathered enough conviction to stem the flow of Don's talk. "Don—things are hectic here, too."

"Oh—in what way?" he sounded indifferent.

"I'm moving, too," she blurted. "Right now, in fact."

He shouted back, "Out of your own place?" The sharpness of his voice made her blink.

"Yes."

"But why?"

"I need a change," she answered, deliberately evasive. "We both do. You can ask Ellie. She'd say the same."

He didn't reply immediately. Then he said, "Well, I'm sorry to hear that."

"I'm sorry, too."

"You and Ellie been fighting?"

"I'd rather not answer, Don. Please . . . you can talk to Ellie. She'll tell you I'm going to live with someone . . . a guy. That's what she thinks."

He burst out laughing. "You're joking!"

There were too many ways to interpret his laughter: bitter, scornful ways. She couldn't think about it now. "You can believe what you like."

"I wouldn't believe that, especially from my own sister."

"You can believe what you like," she insisted.

"Hey—wait a minute. You sound sour as last month's milk. What's going on?"

"Dave—er—Don, I need to get going now. I'm sorry.

"You're so strange, Maggie. I called you up to tell you—"

"You called *Ellie* up," she corrected.

"Don't nit-pick. I gave you the best news of my life, and you spring this on me, cool as cucumber. What the devil is the story, anyway?"

She wanted to say in anger, "Does it matter? You don't need to know." But he did need to know about Ellie, and, paralyzed, she couldn't tell him.

And he ought to know, finally, how much she loved and wanted him, not how much she also resented him. This might be the last time she'd hear his voice; she didn't want to end her dreams that way. She couldn't keep the desperation out of her voice, however, whatever she said. "I'll be living in Cambridge, Don. Alone." How flat. How deadly.

"Where?"

"I don't know yet." She threw a look at David.

"Will you still write?"

"Do you want me to?"

"Why ever not?"

"Well—I don't know."

"God, I'll wring the truth out of Ellie if I have to. You're both really insane these days. Crazy as junkies . . . You're moving out this very minute?"

"Yes . . . that's why David's here."

"Would you do something for me, if you've got one minute?"

She hung over the precipice of tears again. David was watching her clouded face, and his jaw clenched as she said bitterly, "Sure, if I can muster enough sanity for it."

He didn't rise to the bait. "You can write Ellie a note. Tell her to call me at once, not home . . . well, I guess she wouldn't call McEnroe, anyhow. She's to call me whatever. Got that?"

"Yes."

"*Would* you write? You want to keep in touch, don't you?"

He didn't say, "I want you to keep in touch," she noticed. Any real answer to that would send her grovelling in grief and abject sentimentality. She caught her breath. "Goodbye, Don." And with her hand she clicked down the cradle even before he could answer.

Summer

She had expected to lose sleep for the first week in the new apartment. Walt, the landlord, went in and out, early and late, never bothering to muffle the slam of the front door. Cindy trod back and forth above her for most of the day; sometimes she'd hear her, too, in the night when the child cried. Strangely, though, none of this disturbed Margaret. She slept deeply and woke with a feeling that sometimes approached exhilaration; she was independent again, could live by her own patterns. She felt liberated.

She had expected, too, to feel lonely without someone to talk to in free moments, but she didn't. Once school was out she frequented the Harvard library by day—got herself a reader's card—and went to concerts and plays at the University. At night she had more time than usual to read the papers and keep abreast of the Apollo 11 mission, the ugly unravelling of the Chappaquiddick story, and above all the draft protests that were heating up again in the aftermath of the latest battles in Vietnam and in anticipation of the third drawing of the draft lottery, due in August. Occasionally she drove to Dedham to see her mother, or north to Gloucester to walk on the beach or browse in the boutiques, glass houses and galleries she'd somehow never had time for before. She might have been solitary some days, but she rarely felt lonely.

She grew attached to the new apartment immediately. She might have sacrificed Ellie's flamboyant artistry and design for Walt's aluminum and polyester expediency, but at least the apartment was relatively quiet, uncluttered, easy to clean. If she stood in what she thought of as her den, she could look out of the front onto a street lined by similar houses, most of which were rented or owned by married law students or other interns, friends of Walt's. The front of the house generally fell under shadow, but light poured in at the back, where her bedroom was, and she shared a ten-by-ten patio with Cindy and Walt there. The cramped kitchen and bathroom, once Cindy's kitchen, were divided now and occupied the middle of the apartment on either side of a short, narrow hallway to the bedroom. The eye-level oven set in a brick-faced wall gave the only clue to the ambitiousness of the landlord's former plans for an up-to-date, more spacious kitchen. The kitchen was hot, though, and poorly ventilated; she wouldn't enjoy using it until the weather cooled.

She ate out as often as she could in June and the first part of July, sometimes with other friends, occasionally with Walt and Cindy. Cindy talked fast and joked about her Italian parents who refused to cook pasta "because it was for American peasants who thought they were eating Italian food!"

Their child, Peter, became another nephew for her, a substitute for Jonathan. Margaret melted at the upward gaze of his soft, chocolate eyes, at the long lashes and damp kisses; but Cindy laughed and called her a sucker for Peter's flirtatiousness. "You'll spoil your own kids rotten," she said, and Margaret wondered with longing if she would ever do more than share other people's children.

Walt had drawn a high lottery number and had thus, unlike David, avoided the war. If they watched the news together when he returned home from the hospital, he always had plenty to say about the evils of the war and the Republican party. Margaret teased him, lobbying for Nixon and Agnew, until she almost convinced them she was a Republican herself. Some nights she read up on the conservative columnists, then often went upstairs and ragged them mercilessly for "liberal" politics.

Waking one morning in mid-July when she felt no particular hurry to get out of bed because of the gray Atlantic rain drumming on the window, she thought over her new existence. This summer seemed a time of healing. Bruised and even a little confused by the months of hostility with Ellie, of chaos—palpable and impalpable—that had dogged her through May, she was just beginning to feel better again. And, returning to herself, she began to realize just how drained she had been before; how wise David and Martha had been to urge the move on her. Guilt had plagued her all through the month of June—a leaden feeling that she had betrayed Ellie by leaving her. But now a more balanced view asserted itself—the view that she couldn't have done anything for Ellie, anyway, though she still rebuked herself for never having called her again. She kept her own number unlisted now; so, unless they met downtown by chance one day, the ugly confrontation she anticipated would never take place. The guilt was melting rapidly into relief.

Earlier in the summer, too, she had lived in nagging fear about Steve. She made sure that she rarely went any distance alone, except to catch the trolley to school or to walk onto the Harvard campus. But even by the closing of school in June she was laughing at her own paranoia, and soon the fear lessened to an occasional jump of alarm if she passed someone in the street who reminded her of Steve or Ellie. Obviously, if he had wanted to hurt her or ensure her silence, he would have done so by now; he must have disregarded her knowledge of his drug dealing, dismissed it as little threat. Perhaps he had told Ellie by now of the deception with

David; Ellie would have laughed it off, no doubt.

"Well, let her go. Good riddance. I was tired of having her breathing down my neck. She won't talk to anyone about us, don't worry. The poor woman's so besotted about my brother . . . she's incapable of doing anything calculated to hurt any of us . . ."

Margaret went around town less cautiously now, glad of her anonymity, but she still thought of Ellie, still held imaginary dialogues with her in quiet moments.

"You nut! What'd you move out for? You loved that place!"

"Yes, I did."

"Then why?"

"Surely you knew, Ellie."

Ellie would look off toward the end of the street where they would have unexpectedly met. *"Steve said you lied. That was your brother, not your lover."*

"Steve's right. I couldn't take it anymore—the mess, the parcels, Steve . . . even you."

"How you've changed," Ellie would say. *"Gotten so snotty and critical. I couldn't stand you, either. I guess there's no love lost between us."* And she'd saunter away as casually as if Margaret were nothing to her. *"But what about Don, huh?"* she'd fling back over her shoulder.

Yes, that was the rub. *What about Don?*

Or, feeling more optimistic sometimes, she'd imagine something altogether different.

"Margaret? I've been trying to find your number for weeks. What the heck's going on? You were supposed to call me . . . hey, how's your gorgeous friend?"

"He's fine . . . but I need to talk to you, and explain . . ."

"Oh, you don't need to explain a thing! But I envy you. I decided to get out of Steve's . . . business." She would sound more lucid than usual as she said it; bit-

ter, but certain. *"He dropped me. I've been lonely, but . . . I think I learned some stuff."*

She'd blunder in, trying to express her delight, but Ellie would go on regardless, cutting her off.

"Say, could we get together sometime? We weren't talking much when you moved out. I could use a long heart-to-heart, myself . . ."

Wishful thinking, she realized, lying on her back with her hands pushed into the damp warmth of her hair and her eyes focused on the dismal rain outside. *Wishful thinking.*

But what about Don? Lately she'd even thought less about him. Ellie's absence cut down on the steady flow of reminders she'd had before; and she no longer settled in on a Sunday night to write him a letter; she no longer kept the old photographs pinned up in her bedroom. Distance and time had fallen between them— Newton's unalterable "universal law of gravitation"— any two bodies attract each other with a force inversely proportional to the square of the distance between them. Simple physics, that was all, and the icy immobility that had frozen her before Memorial Day had now thawed. The numbing coldness had gone, and she felt freer with the long distance between them to start a new life without the ice-jam of so many memories.

She still dreamed of him sometimes. After those dreams she'd wake to the sound of her own moaning and to a struggle with the hot tangle of bedclothes, angry with her subconscious for percolating the old fantasies through her mind when she had no control over it.

The dream would always be the same: Ellie under a shadowed tree, disappearing as she and Don danced together to silent music. She wondered what it meant, always, when she woke. But just as quickly she'd refuse to give in to any further consideration of it. She had a new life now without the McEnroes; and, as July rolled

on, the dream came less and less. She had not dreamed
of him for a week now . . . Oh, was she keeping track
of it. . . ? *Well, not anymore!*

Through Walt and Cindy and through colleagues at
the school, she gradually made new friends. She'd
spent less time by herself and more time at parties—
not parties like Ellie's, but quiet, relaxed affairs at
which the music came from Tanglewood via WGBH,
where there were no drugs, and where she could discuss the arts, education, and politics without falling
into an unpleasant argument with the kind of Harvard
students Ellie had once cultivated. Men whom she had
kept at a distance during the McEnroe era had suddenly found her more approachable; she danced, went
to the Pops, and sat at the table for hours of seafood,
wine and conversation with them. In their smiling appreciation of her ideas, she refound herself; Don had
never once told her that she was intelligent or beautiful; he had probably never even looked very closely at
her, for that matter. And she needed this new affirmation.

She rolled over in bed so that her back was toward
the rain, then slid again into the reveries of semi-con-
sciousness. Not long ago she'd taken the steamship
again for four days in Nantucket. This second visit had
provided an ending for her previous truncated visit, as
well as a turning point in itself. It marked for her the
quiet cessation of some of the emotional struggle and
the beginning of a measure of tranquillity. She knew
now that she belonged among a class of strugglers—
who were also the survivors. She began to have more
confidence in herself as a woman with enduring inner
resources, and she marvelled at them.

On Nantucket she'd found David preoccupied with
his work at the hospital. More tourists on the island,
as well as his colleagues' vacations, made for longer
hours. Martha, glad of her company, took her to res-

taurants, cafes, galleries, and to the beach. Margaret had fleetingly wished that she lived nearer to them, right on the island, and had even toyed with the idea of making applications to the Nantucket school and searching for an apartment for herself. But she belonged in Boston for the moment, she knew. At least for now, Nantucket could be only a temporary refuge.

———————

The evening milking behind him, Don stood out on the upper edge of one of the sloping twenty-five-acre cornfields and surveyed his new kingdom. Above him, the summer sky washed clean by yesterday's rain burned from delft blue to the chalky white of early evening. There was no haze left, though, and none yet rising out of the Cattaraugus Valley, where he had even by now come to expect it. In just a few weeks he had already grown to love his place; it gave him a deep satisfaction to stand on the hill as he did now, and to turn slowly around, looking.

In front of him stood the young corn, rank on rank marching down to the creek, acres below. The corn reached his thighs now, and some of it was beginning to tassel. The leaves grew up long and knife-edged, then bent sharply into dark green, criss-crossed shadows. He swung round. Now before him on the other side of a wide, rutted track, one of the sea-green oat fields spread over a flat twelve-acre expanse, an asymmetrical field truncated on one side by alfalfa; he could clearly see the short, knee-high growth of oval leaves. It was ready for the second cut; a few blossoms bobbed already, and if he waited any longer, it would be almost worthless as feed.

Diagonally opposite the first alfalfa, a smaller field of alfalfa marked the boundary of the oats on the other side of a field that swelled to another low hill, green with the same dense growth. One of his men—Larry or

Tony, he couldn't tell which—was cutting wide swathes of it now; he could hear the clatter of the tractor's engine and the whir of the haybine. The weather was supposed to stay clear for several days now: a good time for drying; he wanted to bale the alfalfa hay.

On the third edge of the oats, opposite and a little below him, lay the east pasture, land that had been badly overgrazed. He would wait to plow it until the fall, then reseed it in the spring with clover, timothy and trefoil. Beyond the pasture, flanked by two other cow pastures, clustered the farm buildings; and beyond them—invisible from this vantage point—the highway.

This, then, was the land he'd aimed toward for almost ten years. What happened here would be the result of a constellation of bonds between himself and the land, the land and the weather, the weather and himself, himself and the stock, the stock and the land. All his agricultural training would mean nothing if he did not enter into a pact with the inanimate. He was now scientist and steward, mathematician and romantic, calculator and idealist. At such a thought he trembled, was awed, yet exhilarated.

Taking his eyes off the fields he deliberately pushed his boot into the earth until a low dent was flattened by the rubber sole. Moving his foot again, he stooped to look more closely at the soil. Up here it was fine stuff, brown loam peppered with gravel. Down in the pasture, though, it had a compactness that warned of clay: the same stuff that made the creeks look slate-blue on cloudy days and tree-green under sunlight. All utterly different from Vermont with its granite outcrops, loose soil, rocks flecked with mica chips, and mountainous stands of hardwoods. Oh, there were trees here—he had a ten-acre woodlot—but no impenetrable forest of gray beech and white birch trunks rising for miles to pierce the horizon; no massed crowns of leafy greens growing thick as thunderclouds. The woods here, even when they covered hills at a time, instead grew with light between them, space for tracks and roads—a landscape with which he could feel at home, not at odds.

Thinking this, he smiled. Hadn't he just realized his own timidity and awe? Yes, but not terror. He could never have done what Ray Hammond had done and farmed for his whole life in Vermont—not if he'd held total responsibility. Marvelously, he already belonged here, felt a gravitational pull to remain here. The growing season would be longer, less harsh; the market for milk would be better than the Hammonds had in Vermont, and there was room to expand into a wider valley. He could ask for nothing better.

Still facing the oats and the pastured incline down to the sheds and barns, he tried to absorb the wealth of it all. As he returned slowly along the track, summer's smells invaded his brain: the earth hot and alkaline, lacking the peaty tang that had characterized parts of Vermont; the growing things intoxicatingly fresh, yet almost too ripe, too rank and full in their crushed-out fumes. He tasted the odors in his mouth as he brushed past them: dust, diesel, cut alfalfa, the bruised rough velvet of corn leaves—they tasted brown; they tasted green. Under his boots the ground yielded and then sprang back a little; it was soft from the rain, uneven from the transit of tractors, wagons and pickups; and a few dark pools still lay in the deepest ruts. Above his head a small cloud of gnats sang monotonously, a drone line for the somersaulting melodies of meadowlarks farther up. A blue jay squawked from the woods on the farthest hill, and pigeons called from the barns.

He turned left before a gate and cut between the alfalfa and oats to reach the east pasture. Now he began to think less of the beauty of the farm and more about hard numbers. Davies, the previous owner, had often

failed to raise enough to feed his stock of thirty cows.
David couldn't raise soybeans, he knew, but with careful management and a few experiments he ought to be
able to make the farm self-sufficient in other ways. After this summer he'd scrap the small sunflower and
clover crops; the nearest market for sunflower seeds
was Toronto, and clover wasn't as good a feed as alfalfa;
he'd rather save the space for alfalfa or corn to feed his
expanded herd of forty or fifty. He'd redivide the growing space, too. He'd fill not one but both silos with corn
and alfalfa hay, repair the barns and fences, and later
. . . he'd modernize. Put in an automated water system
for the cows; use all the stanchions. And if in five years
he could expand to a seventy-cow operation and borrow
from the FHA, he'd add a free-stall barn.

At the end of the east pasture he took the smaller
track that ran toward the house. The silos stood on one
side of the barns: twin blue towers in a landscape of
greens, grays, and browns: the newest of the farm ac-
quisitions, though he was only feeding out of one so
far. On the other side was the machine shed, a ram-
shackle affair that should be replaced soon. The dete-
riorating barns, once steel gray but now weathered to
a mossy verdigris, looked as if they had been built by
accident, not design. They shared a wall, but to get to
one from the other Don had to walk outside and back
in through another door. Both roofs sagged, and one
was pitched several feet higher than the other, its walls
leaning in to the concave. A jerry-rigged job, for sure.
For now, though, stanchions and all, these barns must
suffice. *His* barns, after all.

The track narrowed by the tool shed to a dusty foot-
path that crossed diagonally to the house through a
scrubby area that might once have been a garden but
had long since been ruined by chickens. A garden . . .
if only he had time! But the local farmers would laugh
at his absurdity. *Why would a farmer mess with a gar-*

den? No, a garden needed another to till, hoe, pick and can it. A garden was a luxury no one around here could afford in the daily round of milking, calving, feeding, breeding, record-keeping. If he thought of the work all at once, it overwhelmed him.

As he stepped inside the back porch, the telephone rang. Without pulling off his boots, he went straight to his desk to answer it. The four hundred pounds of 0–10–30 he had ordered for use in the fall on the alfalfa ground was in, the man at Agway told him. His voice was indulgent, tinged with mockery, as if Don had somehow made a foolish order.

He turned his back on the desk but remained on the swivel chair. It was an oak chair, the stuffed leather padding torn and uneven now, but he felt perversely sentimental about it. McEnroe's first law office in Bedford had been run from that chair; this farm would be, too. He swung around on the chair, resting his chin on his hands, thinking again. The muscles across his shoulders and back were knotted and sore.

The farmhouse had stood over eighty years. Passed through several generations, it had been neglected in favor of the land. Where were all his resolutions, now, to make a home of it? He'd been a stranger to his own bare cottage in Vermont, and he couldn't see how things would be different here. He felt as lost in this monument to the big American farm family as a Republican in a state assembly controlled by Democrats— one of his father's most hackneyed similes, he realized with a slight grimace. The place was so bare that it echoed. The screens, riddled with holes, hung or coiled away from the windows, and flies swarmed everywhere despite the sticky brown fly papers that drooped from the light fixtures. And the lights—even the best were cracked; the worst were tangles of bare electric wires that protruded from the sockets. Where should he start?

Except in the living room, no carpets graced the floors. Here at the back of the house in the room he'd chosen for an office, next to the back porch, the floors were stained, pitted and bare. What kind of wood lay under the splintered brown paint he couldn't tell. *Well, who needs fancy carpet in a farm office, for goodness sake?* But he couldn't see it quite that way, himself. Somewhere between the deep maroon largesse of his parents' Oriental rugs in Bedford and the ugly nudity of this floor—somewhere was a compromise.

The kitchen certainly looked no better and would soon present a more urgent challenge. Apart from the new refrigerator, everything was covered with filth; he had eaten at a diner in town almost every night so far. Dirt ingrained by decades of tramping boots lay thick enough on the kitchen floor to be chipped off with a chisel—if he had time. Some of the cupboard doors lay in a corner; the ceiling and sink leaked; the outside storm door was missing, and he knew he couldn't go through winter here without one. He hated so much dirt and chaos, but how could he do anything about it yet?

Leaving his boots under his desk, he trod cautiously out of the office, avoiding jutting nailheads and rough joints in the boards. He crossed the hall in front of the stairs and stood at the threshold of the living room. The taut muscles of his back suddenly relaxed a little. *At least one room in the house looks serviceable,* he thought. Obviously a room kept for company by the last owner, it conveyed a feeling of spaciousness and warmth with its wide stone hearth, sweeping bay window, and dark wool carpet. Otherwise, this room, too, was empty; he'd have to find furniture, and soon . . . perhaps at an auction . . . though most of what he'd seen at household auctions either cost too much or looked as dilapidated as the farmhouse.

Again, what should he do first? He was in a battle

against time and money. And somehow he lost both: crippled, made inert by the enormity of the responsibility. Should he call a plumber to fix the upstairs shower and replace the toilet bowl, or should he do the jobs himself? Should he extend his credit to the limit and buy furnishings for every room, or should he close part of the house immediately and comb the auctions? Should he, in fact, pour any capital at all into the house when the farm still needed so much?

He rubbed his head wearily. His stomach gnawed at him, but he couldn't face the diner again; so he went back and made himself a giant sandwich with thick wedges of tomato, cheese, and ham poking out between the lettuce and bread. Then he poured a long beer and went to his desk. Perhaps, he decided, he could make a list of all he had to do and assign some priorities. Sandwich in one hand and pen in the other, he jotted preliminary notes on an embossed Massachusetts legal pad. *McEnroe, I thank you,* he thought sardonically. *At least stationery's one thing I don't have to buy.*

The list grew. Fences, overhauls, plumbing, carpets, increase stock, meet with DHIA, water system, barns, tool shed—He flung the words down as randomly as the images came to him, then looked at them. *Depressing. Hopeless. What have I gotten myself into?* He compressed his lips wearily and tore the list into unnecessarily tiny pieces.

His eyes strayed to the pasture outside. The yellow bars of westerly light elongated it at this time of evening. He bit into his sandwich again and thought suddenly of his sister. She'd like the place, he decided. She'd exclaim over the plaster molding around the downstairs ceilings, the antique carved banisters, the obsolete copper pipes under the bath . . . *"I love it! Oh, Don, why don't you sell off the blasted land and use the money to turn this into a restaurant? Imagine . . . Ye Olde Farmhouse. I'd come and do floor shows for*

*you, and Margaret—"Darn! What does Margaret have
to do with any of this?*

Irritably, he remembered his last conversation with
Margaret. Sometime in May, or was it June? She had
sounded defensive, so strangely silent about his sister,
almost hostile. Her letters to him had stopped, and now
when he phoned Ellie the line rang and rang, but neither of them answered. Had Margaret really moved to
Cambridge, then? But why? And why could he never
find Ellie at the apartment? What sort of foolishness
was going on?

It irked him to dial a number more than a few times
when he needed someone, and if Ellie weren't his own
sister he'd have given up weeks before. What was the
matter with her, anyway? Hadn't Margaret left his mes-
sage? All he wanted was to tell Ellie himself about the
farm. He had talked to his mother and McEnroe several
times and asked them to leave the news to him; he
asked them, too, to tell her to call him if she telephoned
them—rather unlikely, he supposed.

Puzzles. What had happened to cause a rift between
Ellie and Margaret? Or was there some other reason
why Maggie had moved out in such a hurry? Didn't
Ellie care to know where he was and what change had
come to his life?

He stared at the telephone, muttering to himself,
"Might as well try again." And he dialed it without having to look up the number.

The ringing stopped abruptly after one peal. A woman's voice came on the line. He started to answer her
before he realized the voice was recorded. "Ellie, I
don't—"

"—you have reached has been changed. You may
reach your party by dialing—"

The first time he'd heard one of those maddening
recordings, just about a week ago, he'd hung up before
it was finished. Quickly he dialed the new number, not-

ing it down on his pad as it rang. No answer. What was going on?

He pulled a pack of cigarettes from his shirt pocket and lit one. He should go back out to the hayfield and take a more careful look at the alfalfa, but all this business with Ellie bothered him. He had to find out where she was. He had to talk to her.

Margaret would know. Ah, but he didn't know where Margaret was, either. He rested his cigarette on the ashtray and dialed Massachusetts directory enquiries.

"What city, sir?"

"Cambridge. Margaret Fuller." He chewed the pen and idly watched the flies buzzing and spinning in the broken screens.

"I'm sorry, sir, there's no number listed for that name."

He made a small, impatient sound with his tongue. "Look in the new listings. She just moved."

"No—no Margaret Fuller listed."

"What about *un*listed?" He knew he sounded angry, but he didn't know why.

"Yes . . . we do have a Margaret Fuller unlisted."

"Could I please have her number? It's important."

"I'm sorry, we're not permitted—"

He slammed down the phone in a rage. *Silly woman.* She'd kept her number in the directory before. Why not now? Perhaps she'd infuriated her family by moving out to live with the man she'd mentioned to him on the phone. Or had she? He searched his mind, trying to remember what she'd said. *'I'm going to live with someone . . . a guy. That's what Ellie thinks.'* But hadn't she then denied it? He couldn't be sure. What a thought . . . Maggie with some man he'd never met. Seeing her off from some Cambridge town house as she went to work . . . no, not till fall, she was on vacation . . . just another nameless suburban public school teacher lost somewhere in the sprawl of metropolitan Boston. He'd be taking her out to restaurants, up to the beach. She always loved the beach, or to see her mother. Walking with her. Sleeping with her.

Little Maggie—Margaret with another man. Those serious loam brown eyes that belied the repartee that came unexpectedly from her soft mouth. The quick way she laughed, the sly way she'd always watched him— perhaps she was giving all that to someone else, now. And the round curves hidden under those shapeless old clothes she wore in reaction to Ellie's fanatical fashion-consciousness. The level calm of her voice when she talked, the unwavering eyes . . . *Oh, well,* he thought wearily, *so what! She's got every right to shack up with anyone she wants to. Always was so mysterious and ornery. So what!*

He drained the beer in a few gulps, stubbed out his cigarette, pulled on his boots, and slammed the porch door hard behind him. He needn't think of her any-more.

But he did. Half an hour ago he'd seen everything through Ellie's eyes, and now he looked at it through Margaret's. Always the romantic, she would have seen the farm meshed in a golden web of wonder. The slimy pond in the west pasture would have looked blue to her. "Where are the ducks?" she would have asked, showing in her eyes reflections of white wings and curled tail-feathers. The cats in the barn would have drawn her next. Worm-ridden, scrawny, and worn down by litters of miscellaneous kittens: Maggie would have seen that they were all fed and doctored. Then she would have complained, "Oh, those poor cows!" seeing them stand-ing in stanchions in the twilight of the barn. "Why can't you let them out in the pasture all day?"

And he would have said indefinitely, "Sometime I will. I don't like this either. But the pastures are in terrible shape, still." And she would have smiled at him, pushed her fingers through that thick hair of hers, and shot back with some droll remarks about the cows that would have left him, as usual, bewildered by her contradictory impulses.

He retraced his way down to the track that adjoined the hayfield. The tractor had gone now, and rows of mown alfalfa lay like soft green pick-up-sticks all around the perimeter of the field. In the lowering sun the vegetation melted from rich green to a soft dun color. The edge was cut straight and neat, and the alfalfa gave off a warm, heady scent that reminded him always of his first experience with a farm: high school and a summer with McEnroe cousins in the Scottish Lowlands. Even in the long, cool evenings there, that hot, heart-breaking smell oozed up from road-side grasses, weeds, hedge rows. It was the same in Vermont, at Hammonds', and here. A universal, perhaps.

Darkness seemed to come fast once the sun had dropped behind the trees on the far side of the pasture. Except the tops of the trees and the silos, everything lay in shadow now, and even they were only faintly pink. That invisible green smell, then, surrounded and pressed down on him as heavily as something visible. And with it, hounding him so that he actually gave in to the urge to run back to the buildings, came tormenting little memories from those past summers . . . Ellie with hay fever, her face swollen, her eyes running. "You gotta get be to sobe doctor, Dod, or else drive be back to Bostod. Got that?" Margaret listening, her eyes full of tears, laughing, then saying, "But you don't want to go back yet, do you? Boston stinks in August. Please, please let's stay, Ellie." So Don had taken Ellie to the doctor, who'd given her some kind of antihistamine so strong that it had dried up her eyes and nose immediately but made her sleepy and half-drunk for the rest of their visit.

The first summer he had liked the big-brother-man-of-the-world stance, but it had quickly palled. During the day Ellie got in his way; Margaret had flirted and cracked jokes he couldn't always catch; both girls had been a nuisance, demanding more attention than he wanted to give. When he'd finished at night and changed his clothes, he'd take them out to a drive-in or walk them down to the village for a milk shake. Then Margaret had become quiet, withdrawn, her eyes lambent and watchful, her face dreaming. They had both driven him crazy.

That overpowering smell of cut hay faded behind him once he reached the barns again. Unutterably sweet, yet it drove him into an incomprehensible frenzy.

He crossed the farmyard with misgivings. That was another thing he had to do: install some lights on the porch and on the side of the barn.

In the kitchen he poured a glass of iced tea and picked up the paper. Third drawing of the draft lottery next month. Kennedy on trial for leaving the scene of an accident. Apollo 11 in space . . . Nothing he wanted to read about just now. His shoulders had begun to ache slightly again, but he wasn't sleepy. He decided to work on the kitchen floor a little—scraping and scrubbing.

Ellie drifted into his mind again. He dropped the brush into the bucket and went back to his desk. *One more time,* he thought, and dialed the new number again. Nothing. He let it ring ten times. Still nothing. He would call his parents instead; perhaps they would know what was going on. He hoped his father would answer, but usually it was his mother or the housekeeper.

"That you, Don? How ya been?" McEnroe's voice. His third martini voice: overly cheerful and very slightly slurred.

"Good to hear your voice, McEnroe. I'm fine."

"What can I do? Got some news?"

"Nope—nothing. But I've been thinking about Ellie. Where is she? I've called the number till I can dial it in my sleep."

Silence in Bedford for a moment. Don could picture his father standing at the phone table in the upstairs mezzanine. His shirt would be unbuttoned, his tie dangling, and he'd be standing with his free hand on his hip and his head tilted intently toward the phone. "Good question, son," he said after a while.

"You haven't seen her?"

"I'm trying to think—" He stopped to call out. "Marianne—when'd we see Eleanor last, hun?" Don couldn't hear his mother's answer, but his father went on again, "Your mother says the beginning of the month . . . what's that? Oh, no, she says June. I don't remember."

"She came up for a weekend, or something?"

"No, just for a couple hours. Said she was going down to Newport with a friend, and could she borrow some money."

He gritted his teeth. "Same old Ellie."

"Yeah, but we hadn't seen her for weeks, so I fell for it. Now we haven't seen her or the money since!"

Don's mind began to jump ahead of his father's slow account. "You think she's okay?"

"Damned if I know. I suppose so. Why wouldn't she be?"

"I'm not sure. I've been calling her, like I said . . . and now she's changed her number without telling anyone." He thought about Margaret's sudden departure and was just going to mention it: something held him back, though. If nothing else, he preferred to avoid reference to Maggie because he'd years ago grown weary of his father's predilection for matchmaking. "Well . . . I don't know. I have an uneasy feeling, somehow. Did you notice anything funny about her?"

Silence again. Then, "Maybe. Maybe not. Your

mother said she looked too thin, come to think of it."
He guffawed. "I just put that down to female jealousy—"

Don's mother protested loudly from somewhere
near the phone. "Well, *did* she look thin?" he rapped
out, growing impatient.

"I didn't notice it particularly, but she was awfully
pale—kinda white. And it wasn't just all that junk she
puts on her face. Her eyes—big as dinner plates. She
laughed a lot and talked loud. Matter of fact, she was
nervous as a cat."

"Drinking?"

"Not that I noticed."

"And Mother?"

"You mean drinking?"

He shut his eyes and said between clamped jaws,
"No—of course not! But, *you've* sure been at it, haven't
you! No—I mean, did Mother notice that she'd been
drinking?"

"Didn't say so . . . says she doesn't remember it,
anyhow."

"Listen, I'm worried about her. If she calls, you can
go ahead and tell her I moved, after all. It's not news
anymore, and probably no surprise anyway. But I'd do
almost anything to get her here for a weekend just to
see she's all right." He hesitated, knowing how angry
she'd be if she heard him say it. "Could *you* try to get
hold of her? Go down and see if she's still at the apartment in town?" He hesitated, suddenly irritated with
himself for dragging his father into a pointless search
for Ellie. Nothing to go on, after all; no substantial reason to get anxious, and he didn't want Ellie's flamboy-
ance cramped. His father would crash in as if he were
bludgeoning down a line of Republican opponents at a
committee meeting.

His father cleared his throat. "Well, I guess I
could—"

"But listen, I don't mean for you to hunt her down

or anything. Just a tactful fatherly check-up." Don winced inwardly. "You have an excuse, anyway."

"Right, the money. I'll try not to get her mad."

"She'll get mad anyway."

"Too bad. Won't be the first time—or the last," McEnroe said. "So, enough of Ellie. When are *we* invited over?"

"Soon. Not yet, though. The place needs a lot of work first." He couldn't imagine either of them here, especially his mother.

"Your mother won't come till it looks as good as the Bullfinch Chamber. I'd like to see it roughcast, myself."

"Then you should come out this fall. How about deer season? Weren't you a crack shot as a hunter once upon a time?" The laughter had returned to his voice.

"Batch it for a weekend? Oh, that sounds like fun."

"Fun—if you don't mind the antique plumbing and mouse-droppings and bare floorboards."

"*I'm* not afraid of getting my hands dirty," McEnroe roared.

Don chortled, "Good thing, in your job, I'd say! Then let's plan on it, okay? Meanwhile . . . go easy on her . . . but let me know about Ellie."

October

The habit of years was broken. Margaret didn't miss Don, scarcely thought of him or dreamed of him now. An empty kind of dissatisfaction and restlessness plagued her, instead. It was something she couldn't identify or assuage, though she tried.

The school year began well enough: a textbook class of average children almost all up to grade level—for a change. No whiz-kids, no dyslexic children, no children with obvious emotional disturbance. Average, but dull, unsatisfying.

Not that her colleagues made the job any more fulfilling. Even given the high staff turnover every summer, the faculty lounge discussions and disputes sounded all too familiar. The same male teachers still chased the same desirable female teachers, married and unmarried, with the same success. She noticed the same eloquent looks, the same whispers of tenderness or laughter when they thought no student or other staff heard. The same female teachers boasted about their grown sons and daughters in New York, L.A. and Chicago; gossiped about their menfolk; played bridge at lunchtime with the same liturgy of laments. "Aren't the cards *weird* today? . . . Terrible distribution . . . Won't you let my finesse work just this once, Helen? . . . Why does Mary always have all the aces?" Everything seemed so predictable, so colorless. It made her feel tired, as if she were only an observer of life, no longer a participant.

In the evenings, as she rode home to Cambridge in

the stifling heat of the train, she looked forward to the pleasantness and peace of her apartment. But that too had dulled—along with the new contract, promotion, bigger bank balance, and a wider circle of acquaintances. Her joy seemed to evaporate far too quickly now. She was achieving, possessing, living independently. But she was close to no one, and consequently preoccupied with herself, growing stale. But how to break out of the old patterns. How?

In October a possible solution occurred to her. She joined a racquet club in the suburbs and played tennis there regularly. She also signed up for ski lessons so that she could spend some of the winter weekends northward in Maine or Vermont. But every time she swung her tote bag out of the car after an evening at the racquet club, a letdown feeling stunted her sense of accomplishment, her pleasure at being physically fit. Weighing it all, she wondered if she were letting herself be consumed by the superficial, depriving herself of the heart of life.

But what *was* the heart of life? Was it the soul? *Did* she have a soul, which, like her body, had to be nurtured, made fit? Everything seemed smooth and easy on the surface: she coped well in the apartment, was respected by colleagues, sought after by several men. Despite a few unspoken doubts, then, she allowed herself to cruise along without making changes that reached deeply. She didn't know, anyway, what changes to make.

She still missed Ellie. Not just the relaxed times they'd spent together, but also—perversely—the clashes. They had been confidantes, friends, sisters, soul-mates. They had fought with each other but also for each other. Again and again she debated telephoning her, but fear of having to speak to Steve, misgivings about the emotional risks of having to face Ellie again, tugged against the impulse. And the longer she let it go, the harder she found it to make the call.

Once she actually gathered up the courage to drive over to Spruce Street and see her. She'd made a quick decision one Saturday morning as she dressed; she didn't let herself think further. Having parked the car and locked it with a shaking hand, she walked the last block. Then Ellie herself passed her, driving furiously in the black Lincoln Continental. That unmistakable head of red hair now strangely dyed black, the pale, taut skin and big eyes. Margaret had looked up in surprise, jerked her hand in an awkward wave, but then saw that Ellie hadn't even noticed her.

Five months . . . The shock of seeing her unexpectedly like that struck at her. She staggered to the nearest doorway and had to lean into it for support against the weight of anguish and sorrow that washed over her. She'd seen a stranger, and she ached. Later she couldn't even remember the drive back to her apartment.

Then McEnroe called: late one afternoon at school, during her free period. Could she take the day off, or half the day tomorrow? he wanted to know. Her mind cantered forward. What did he want? What was she to say to him? Flustered, she quickly agreed to meet him for lunch the next day and arranged to take the day off. But she spent the entire evening seething with anxiety and impatience. She turned over in her head all the things he could possibly have to say to her, considering what she might say in return, how she should react. She was hungry for news of Ellie and . . . perhaps . . . a little curious about Don, too, though she wouldn't think of him now.

All the next morning she wished she had gone to school for part of the day. The children would have distracted her until lunchtime. As it was, she expected to sleep late but instead woke at five and found she couldn't even doze anymore. She made a pot of coffee and went back and forth in the apartment, cleaning things she didn't need to clean and trying to divert herself with the paper and the inane sounds of television game shows and soap operas.

By the time she got off the train in the center of town, she was thoroughly disgruntled and a little disoriented. Despite the raw, salty chill of autumn she was drenched with sweat. A glance in the window of Filene's answered her with her own round, apprehensive face, hair untidy from the wind and cheeks flushed. And looking at the manicured, mascara-encrusted women who passed her on Washington Street with hair impeccable, silk blouses knotted gorgeously at the throat under furs and velvets, she thought, *Lord, I'll never belong here*, and added, *nor do I want to.*

To her surprise, McEnroe was already waiting for her in the lobby of the restaurant. He looked as keyed up as she felt, and dread momentarily closed itself around her heart like the jaws of a mousetrap. But because he made the effort to be cheerful and at ease, the way he always was with her, she in turn began to relax.

"Let's eat Italian," he said.

Thinking of Cindy's wonderful antipasto and Scaloppine al Marsala, she happily assented. But in fact all he wanted was pizza, so they ordered a big one together.

"Anchovies, peppers, pepperoni, mushrooms—the works," he told the waitress with a wink.

The girl knew him. "And two martinis, right?" The waitress was bright and pert, anticipating, Margaret supposed, the usual McEnroe largesse.

"No—not this time. Martini for me, yes, but the lady'll have white wine with soda." He looked across at her, and for a moment she saw Don's eyes. "That's still your drink, I presume?"

"Sure." She smiled, remembering Don's ungracious comment once: *"Pour yourself a drink; I guess you're old enough."*

She leaned forward. "Thank you . . . now, tell me, what's . . . what's. . . ?" She wanted to say, "What's going on?" or "What's on your mind?" or "Why did you call me at school?" But the questions died in her head, and she stared across at him with worried eyes.

Perhaps he heard the hesitation. He asked, "You want to know what on earth an old man like me's doing calling up a beautiful woman at work and asking her to take off a day she probably can't afford . . . right?"

She nodded, glad of his directness and even of his flattery.

"It's all on me, anyway. Even the day off."

"*What?*"

"You forgotten I'm on the school board? I talked with your—"

"Oh, but you shouldn't—" She resented somewhat the backstairs arrangements. She wasn't that poor, after all.

"But I did. No if's or but's, Margaret. We need to talk. Okay?" He looked serious.

She sat back, bemused, intrigued, but still in the grip of anxiety. The waitress came with salads and drinks, but she didn't notice them at first.

He was smiling slightly again. "Anyway, I want to treat you. My kids probably never do, and should."

She flushed. "You don't need to say that. And I can take a day off anytime I care to . . ."

He held up his hand. "Maybe . . . there, your health, Margaret."

Over the rims of both glasses she met his eyes. Blue. The old blue of New England, Ireland and Scotland. The shaggy eyebrows, broad features and generous mouth of a frank, intelligent face. A face she loved. "So—" she began, "you've been wielding your power with the school administration? Got them all scared, have you?" Her voice was light.

He grinned. "I like to keep 'em guessing. But listen,

girl, you've had *me* guessing, I'll tell you. You and Ellie. What the *devil's* going on?" His face darkened. "You're *never* home. You've changed your number. But I knew I could get you at school; that's why I called you there."

She toyed with her unopened red napkin, it was folded stiffly like a fan. "I've moved out," she said flatly.

"Oh. Just like that."

She felt like a child. His voice suddenly became bullying, the tone Ellie was perhaps accustomed to hearing. Her impulse was to complement his aggression with a quiet indifference or pretended coldness, but she knew he'd see through it in a moment. Fleetingly she visualized him as a political opponent might: she trembled at his tough, forthright expectation of honesty. "No. It was painful." She looked up with difficulty. "I moved in May," she added softly.

He set down his martini with astonishment barely controlled. "Well, that's a bit of a shock. Even Don . . . does he know—?"

"That I moved. Yes. I told him right then."

He swore and his brows came low over his eyes as he bit hard on the end of a cigar. A stranger might have thought that he'd finished talking, but Margaret knew better.

"He never said a word. But he's fussed and fumed at me for months now about his sister. He can't get away, so I'm running after her like a foolish doting old papa . . . but I haven't seen her since June or July." He laid his fist heavily on the white cloth. "*July*, Margaret. Now tell me everything's fine; she's just a flighty, silly female who doesn't care about her parents except when she's broke. Is that all. . . ? I hope to God . . ."

She put down her salad fork. Added to her consternation was the terrible and new weight of realization that she had done worse than merely walk out on Ellie—she had betrayed the whole family. No matter how much Ellie felt manipulated and pushed by her father, he loved her. *She should have called McEnroe!* All that time she had been scrupling about calling Ellie, she should have called McEnroe instead.

He was watching her as a cat watches a cornered mouse; there was no gleam of delighted triumph, though, only tension and doubt. But the look faded, and suddenly he seemed to change tack. He lit the cigar with slow deliberation, then turned his eyes on her again, more gently this time.

"You haven't asked me about Don," he said.

Her breathing quickened. "I don't think about him much anymore." There was no hurt or bitterness in her voice. It was an even, factual statement.

"More's the pity for him," McEnroe drawled. His eyes held steady, and his lips parted slightly so that she could see his teeth, clamped on the cigar.

She started. *Where are the jokes now?* she thought quickly. She could think of no quick banter this time. "We live in different worlds, you know," she said eventually. "I'm dating several different men at the moment . . ." Her voice trailed off; she tried vainly to make sense of the internal conflict as she heard her own voice mouth the words.

His lips turned up slightly at the corners, and he sighed. "You're a great little woman, Maggie. I have all the time in the world for you. Don and Ellie—you're worth twenty of them."

She shot back, "No. Not true. We're just different. Not compatible. Not Don and I. Not Ellie and I."

Equally quickly, he fired back, "That's why you moved out?"

She had expected the attorney's tactics, and here they came. "Yes. That's a big reason. Our lifestyles got further and further apart. The friends we had, the way we wanted to spend our time . . ."

"So when did you last see her?"

"End of May, I told you."

"Not since you moved?"

"No."

"Then I don't believe your story. *Incompatibility . . .* I think things ran deeper than that."

She ducked the hint that she'd tell him more. "I did see her briefly last month . . . she was driving by . . ."

It sounded lame, and he puffed out a cloud of smoke and laughed. "That doesn't count, though, does it?"

She stabbed at the salad with her fork and then sipped the wine and soda. She didn't know what to say.

"I think she's moved. Has she?" McEnroe asked evenly, his tone demanding an answer.

"I really don't know. I didn't think so . . . but she might have—"

"I went to the apartment, oh, twenty times . . . different times. I went to see the man at the agency where I thought she was working. He said she'd gone—in July."

Margaret frowned. She began to tremble far more for Ellie than for herself. "Didn't you say you saw her in July?"

He nodded. "Thereabouts."

"Where?"

"She came home. Said she was going down to Newport."

"You think she might be living down there?"

"I doubt it. Other people . . . and you've seen her yourself, you said."

"It makes me worried," she admitted, "that she left her job."

"Do you still have a key to the apartment?"

She was glad she didn't, and said so.

"Then I'm going to send the landlord in there."

"Can you do that?"

He scoffed. "Not legally, but I might anyway, m'dear. I'll have a warrant made out if the landlord says she's still living there. *He* must have seen her. Get the District Attorney to go in with me if I have to." He drew hard on the cigar, still scowling. Then he looked up, his blue eyes glinting with ice.

"So what's happening with Ellie? Why'd you move, Margaret?"

She abandoned all attempts to eat and drink. Her stomach knotted. "You asked me alread—"

"But you didn't really answer." He put his hand toward her. "Listen, honey, I'm sorry to grill you like this. But I know something's wrong, and I'll find out what. I'd rather find out from you, I guess. I don't want to coerce you. That's not my way. But I hired a private investigator yesterday, and one way or another I'll find out." He took a slow breath. "If you know more than you're telling, for pity's sake say it. Or you may have someone trailing you, too."

She was a little surprised, though not shocked, by the revelation. "It sounds like a threat," she said coolly. "You are coercing me, whatever you say."

He looked chagrined. "I don't *want* to, Maggie."

Her mind churned like a treadmill in a mouse's cage while her pulse and breathing seemed to slow to almost nothing, as if her body were gathering itself for the terrible mental leap she must make off the treadmill and into the trap. "All right," she said eventually. "But I feel torn in two."

"No," he said gently. "No, you won't betray either of us. I know where your heart lies, and it's in the right place."

She bit her lip and kept her eyes down on the cloth. "I moved out because—" she began slowly.

The waitress delivered her briefly from saying more. The girl came up smiling effusively. "Everything all right, sir?"

No it's not, Margaret wanted to scream back. *Can't you see our faces?*

"Fine, thanks," McEnroe used his cool public voice. He startled Margaret. "Go on, Maggie."

"I found out . . . almost for sure . . . that she's involved in a drug ring." She was glad, immediately, that she had told Martha and David everything in May. The telling now would be easier for that.

He sat forward quickly. His eyes were wide; she could see into the deep pupils. "Go on," he said again.

"She was smoking two years ago—no, more . . . d'you remember?"

"Yes. But she stopped—I thought."

"She did. You're right. Then back in the spring— no, it would have been February—the winter—she met a guy she liked a lot."

"There was a difference, you mean, between him and the others?"

She saw how patient he was being, allowing her to unravel the skeins of the story slowly and somewhat clumsily. "A big difference. She always said she'd never give up everything for anyone, never care that much. But Steve charmed her completely—if that's even the way to describe it. He's a smooth operator, subtle, good-looking. I couldn't figure him out at first. She was dazzled—said so, too." She moved her hands helplessly. "I saw she was crazy about him—but I didn't realize what else was involved . . . He took her to parties. She started smoking, then snorting cocaine. I heard them arguing one night. She couldn't afford any more cocaine and was begging him—"

His mouth clamped shut, his lips pressed so tightly together they barely made a white line in his face.

Margaret waited for him, expecting an outburst, but he said nothing. "D'you want me to tell you. . . ?"

"Eh? Oh—for pity's sake, yes." He seemed to shake himself awake.

"You look so—so—"

"I was thinking ahead, that's all." He gritted his teeth. "I'll break every bone in his body, so help me—"

Margaret thought dumbly. *That's what I'd expect.*

But Ellie made the choice. If only . . . oh, Ellie . . .

She tried to weave it all together for him. "She wanted him to let her have the stuff free. He's a professional, big-time peddler . . . wanted her to go in with him so she could take care of herself—"

"And that's when you moved?"

She looked down. "No, not right away. I—" Her voice came out with a strangled sound. "—I love her, McEnroe." His wide hand, dry and rough, covered hers. Her shoulders shook, but she steadied herself almost immediately. "But I don't know what use I am as a friend. That's when I should have gotten help."

"Maybe. Hindsight's easy. Always easy. So you waited?"

"A month . . . six weeks."

"And she got involved in the selling, too?" His voice grated harshly.

"I don't have absolute proof—just circumstantial things to go on."

"Like what?"

"Loss of interest in her job. Brand new car—luxury car. Suddenly had more money than she'd ever had. People called her—people I didn't know—lots—even though she always introduced her friends to me before. They called her 'McHenry.' And the apartment became the storefront—"

"And you got scared?"

"A little. Not much." She didn't want to think about that part of it. "But my brother—"

"He knows?"

"I had to tell someone . . . but he's silent as a tomb . . . don't worry . . ."

"Oh, I worry all right. Can you imagine what the press would do with this?"

"They won't get anything from me or David."

"Anybody else said that—I wouldn't believe them. You I believe." He sipped his drink thoughtfully. "Well,

I should have known. Heaven help me, I should've known. I'll take that investigator off Ellie unless she's moved, and I'll get him on to this creep, Stan—whatever the name is."

"Steve."

"You'll have to tell me all you know." His eyes darted back and forth around the room; he must have been thinking hard. Then they rested on her face again. "I'm sorry, Maggie, to put you through the wringer."

I owe Steve nothing, she thought. But she still felt uneasy.

"How much do you know?"

She gripped the napkin and twisted it harshly. "Not much. Now I wish I did."

"Tell me."

"The guy's a liar. I know that. Uses two names, at least—Garcia and Garshowitz. Has several different stories about himself. His father's dead, according to one. Or his mother. One parent is American, the other's Peruvian, but who knows which, if either. He claims he owns his own business in Miami, but he flies up and down to Boston and Newport as well, and goes down to South America sometimes."

"What does he look like?"

"Short, well-built, dark. He's good-looking. Wears tailored suits." She remembered his shoes resting on the glass coffee table. "Expensive shoes. But . . . I'm useless at describing. There'd be a thousand men in Boston who could answer to that."

"I'll have the detective outside that apartment twenty four hours a day . . . You think he's armed?"

"I don't know."

He took a deep breath. She watched him, thinking that he was reacting the way any angry father might react, but then she saw a hardening, a sudden resolve. He swore again. "I'm tired of worrying about clout," he said. "I'm not going to mess with any rinky-dink investigator after all."

She bit her lip. "What, then?"

"The DEA."

"What?"

"Drug Enforcement Administration.

"But Ellie—"

"Yes, she'll wind up in jail, too."

Margaret frowned. "That won't do any good."

"Nothing will," he said bitterly. "What's the difference? We don't want drugs and all the crime that goes with it in this city. I don't care if it's Ellie or some other dopehead—we just don't need it. I've gone out on a limb for Ellie often enough, as it is." He looked up sharply. "So have you. She's a child in arrested adolescence. I'm through with her."

Margaret began to feel hot, suddenly. Her voice grew indignant. "Then I *have* betrayed her."

"No. Maybe you've saved her."

Saved her. Saved her. The words bounced back and forth in her mind. Words Martha might have used in another context. "How?" she said angrily. "When her own father's going to see her prosecuted? Listen, I know nothing about the law, but I'd rather be jailed myself than stand up in a court and testify—" Her voice began to thicken; she almost choked. "It's unthinkable."

"You wouldn't have a choice. You think a crazy cokehead should be out on the streets trapping other people into the same destruction she's chosen for herself?"

Margaret shook her head miserably. "No. But I can't be that objective. Ellie's not just any crazy 'cokehead'—" she shivered, "as you put it."

He paused. "There are half-way houses, clinics, rehab centers . . . all those places that deal with down and outs. I'll see her into one of those."

She was puzzled. He was responding to her in fits and starts. First a detective, then the DEA, then jail, then a rehabilitation center. . . . First what seemed a true concern about Ellie, then a fury directed against Steve and Ellie, then anxiety about the press and about family position and influence . . . The impulses were baffling, contrary.

"That's what Don would want," he was saying.

She started, unnerved by the barrage of emotions that pushed her from despair to anger to frustration. And now he had to bring Don into it. She looked at him almost vacantly. "What?"

"I told you. Don's been fretting about her for weeks." He balanced the cigar on the edge of the ashtray and turned it slowly around until the dense ash dropped down. "Don's got his faults, but he's always supported Ellie, I'll give him that."

She decided to capitalize on his renewed caution and burst out with rather more warmth than she intended, "And he'd *never* forgive you if Ellie was treated like some skid-row trash to satisfy your desire to clean up Boston, a scapegoat for everything, as if Steve weren't far more to blame."

He seemed surprised, half amused by her sudden passion. He was nodding sagely. "You love Ellie far more than you ought to, and you defend Don well, too." His voice rang with irony. Was he questioning her comment that she no longer thought much of Don?

"Well roared, my gentle Margaret. You sound as righteously indignant as all the Pilgrim Fathers put together."

She looked down, but then suddenly laughed.

He grinned back. "Maggie! We need you at the State House. Ever thought of politics?"

She laughed up at him again.

"No," he mused. "I think you belong in a different arena. By the way, I'm heading out to Western New York in a few weeks . . ." A frown passed over his face. "If I can find Ellie first—listen—I lied about the detective, and I'm not bringing the DEA . . . not on her, at least.

Sorry, I know you trust me . . . but I wanted to get to the bottom of this myself. I can, now, and it can still be a family issue." His look of appeal came directly to her. "Understand?"

She nodded. "Yes. Of course. It's better—"

"I've got the Thanksgiving recess coming. Don wants me to go out deer hunting. Good hunting there, he says. I won't go if I can't take care of Ellie first." His mouth twisted. "And this Garcia or whatever. You'd not fight me if I went after *his* blood, would you? No? I'm glad of your good opinion." He made a wry face. "Remind me to hire you as political adviser next time I need one." He paused a moment, then looked directly at her. "And Marianne doesn't need to know. Not yet, anyway. But Don will know—everything. Can I tell him we talked? You're not in touch anymore?"

"No. It doesn't make any difference. Tell him what you need to." She suddenly felt very tired.

"What if he wants to talk to you himself?"

She rallied a little. "Oh, give me a break—He's sowing his oats in other places."

McEnroe's head went back in a big laugh, but when she looked at him again, she saw a gathering of water in his eyes. *Martini,* she thought, but wondered, all the same.

"You always had such a good sense of humor," he said. "But that's not what I meant . . . He may want to ask you more about what went on in the spring."

She shook her head slowly. "Then I think I'd rather he didn't get in touch with me."

"I hit a nerve."

She twisted her glass in the wet circle it had made on the cloth. "Maybe. It's an old one, if you did."

"I know. And you don't want him to know where you are."

"No. But that seems childish. Like a game, or something. Like 'I can't have what I want, so I'll pout and hide.' "

He shut his eyes briefly. "No. We all have to deal with pain one way or another. I respect your—" He parted his hands and breathed out heavily, "scruples, need to stay out of it, whatever." His blue eyes were warm, a father's eyes. "But you give yourself away, you know, my dear."

She blinked as he went on to quote her: " 'I can't have what I want.' "

She shrugged. "I don't even know myself, I guess . . . But, but—" She began to stammer. *Ellie's at issue here, not Don.*

"I know, I know. You want to know what I'll really do."

"Right."

"The rehab route. There's a place in Connecticut I remember I contacted before. Confidential. Discreet. Quite successful. A client of mine a few years ago got help there. Expensive, of course." He reached down and rattled the change in his pocket. "I guess I'll always be a foolish, forgiving papa. Ellie's life's too good to waste."

"I think so, too," she agreed warmly.

November

"It's been too long since I did this," McEnroe said. He struggled with the zipper on his trousers. Made of heavy gray wool, the malones were marked in the traditional indistinct plaid of red and green thread.

"Nervous?" Don asked.

"Heck, no."

"I always am. I get a sort of sick feeling in the pit of my stomach. Excitement, I guess."

McEnroe looked at his watch. "Or hunger. Oh, but this is an ungodly hour! Three-thirty in the morning! We're insane. Let's go back to bed." At last he buttoned the waist on his trousers; they were too tight now. "Just because *you're* used to the middle of the night . . ."

"No, come on. This is what you came for." Don shrugged into his new jacket.

His father grimaced. "You're a Halloween nightmare if ever I saw one. Who ever invented those ludicrous things? The deer'll see you coming a mile off."

"So will the other hunters, though. I feel a lot safer than I did in those brown things I used to wear."

They went downstairs and stood in the kitchen near the wood stove that Don himself had installed a few weeks ago. It gave off a dry, almost visible heat—as well as a thin powdering of dust that coated all surfaces in the room. But the whole house was warmer for it, and Don had felt a sense of fresh accomplishment from the splitting and stacking of wood.

"Get yours warm now, before we freeze," McEnroe

175

said, holding his wide hands over the wood stove.

"Nah—we won't freeze. You won't, anyway. Plenty of insulation you've got under that red coat of yours."

"Show some respect."

"It is red, too. And you think this orange is stupid?"

"*Orange*? It's a fluorescent light."

"Shoot, are we gonna argue all morning?"

McEnroe grinned, "Shoot, no, we're gonna shoot."

"Bad. Bad! Let's go. Got everything?"

"Flashlight, first-aid kit, rope, string, compass."

"Compass?" Don repeated with ridiculous emphasis.

"I don't want to get lost."

Don laughed. "Listen, I staked out these woods several times. We won't get lost, I promise you."

McEnroe rummaged around in the voluminous L.L. Bean bag he had used for thirty years. "I'll take the compass, anyway. And I've got slugs, my license, string, knife . . . er, let's see . . . cigars, bourbon . . ."

"McEnroe! For heaven's sakes! We're not going to the country club."

His father glared back. "I'll take what I want. Question is . . . what'll we take to eat, huh?"

"I wasn't planning to take a whole lot. I thought we'd cut out around ten and find ourselves a hearty breakfast down in Arcade. But I do have coffee, some chocolate . . ."

"*Chocolate*?" McEnroe jeered, echoing Don's mockery of the compass. "Garbage. No wonder you get sick to your stomach." He jerked open the fridge. "How about some good big chunks of cheese? Someone around here has to support the impoverished dairy farmers of America."

"Be my guest."

"I'll carry it. Anything I can carry for you?"

Don handed him the flask of coffee and a couple of

bars of chocolate. "Let's make do with one knife. Yours good and sharp?"

His father scrutinized the blade under the poor light. "Not the greatest," he admitted.

"Mine's sharp enough to cut off a Vermont mountain top. Here, take it."

McEnroe scoffed. "Exaggeration, Donald . . . but it looks fair enough." He sheathed it cautiously, then swore as he still managed to nick his left thumb with the widest part of the blade.

"See what I mean?" Don turned on a tap at the sink and reached for a Band-aid. "Fine start to the morning. Am I going to have a suicide on my hands before ten?"

Ignoring him, McEnroe ran his thumb under the water, cursing and grumbling. Then they muffled themselves in scarves, hats, and wool gloves, took up their guns and went into the wintry darkness. Outside, silence encased everything; the crack and crunch of their boots sounded like a blasphemy. An inch or more of snow covered the frozen ground, and a few more flakes drifted down as they crossed the yard. The sky hung heavily above them: thin clouds, a fitful moon, and every now and then the blink of a faint star between the clouds.

Don stood still a moment to savor the peace, but his father stomped across the yard in front of him, heading for the shed where the jeep was parked. *Quiet*, he thought. *So little sound, and this cold kills even the smell of cattle.*

The jeep rattled, coughed, and sputtered. Don turned the key again, pumping the accelerator hard. "She's cold."

"Should be used to it."

"I know. And it's not even bad tonight. Twenty, maybe . . . Got a thermometer, too, in all that baggage of yours?"

McEnroe gave him what was meant to be a withering look.

Don only laughed, and the jeep roared to life. They swung out around the house and onto the highway, the headlights picking out in white the uneven outlines of the two stone gateposts that marked the entrance to the farm. Wind and rain had battered the posts so that they leaned tipsily toward each other. As he had done so many times before, Don made a mental note to right them before they toppled forever.

"It's not far," he said.

"Too bad. I'm in no hurry to get frozen in this cold."

"I found us a good stand, if someone else isn't there first."

"No one will be, at *this* hour," McEnroe snorted.

"Don't be so sure. A lot of gung-ho Buffalonians are out early as you please."

"The first few days, maybe."

"No, I've been hearing them at the crack of dawn every day this week."

"Shows you who the real fools are, then, for starting out so early ourselves. Those idiot urban nincompoops who don't know their butts from their barrels. I don't want to be shot, either."

"Do you count yourself among the urban nincompoops—idiots, wasn't it?—or are you just a common hayseed like your son?"

"You're full of it, aren't you?"

Don laughed again, and the road hissed away underneath them. "Say, what do you think of using slugs instead of buckshot?"

McEnroe moved his shoulder slightly. Don could see him hunch forward: bulky frame, thick clothes tinged by the scent of cigar tobacco. "Better, I guess. I always did think buckshot was messy. Slugs—nice and clean, I imagine—just one wound if you do it right. But I'll tell you afterward what I think."

"You always used buckshot?"

"Far as I can remember."

They looked ahead at the darkened road. A miniature ground blizzard sent snow rippling under their tires, but little had accumulated. "Oh, this is cold country," McEnroe said.

"It'll do. Not as crisp as you're used to. But I like it. Everything's so open, see?" Don swept his hand to the left—to the wide hills that rose from the valley and to the yellowish glow that marked the location of Arcade on the side of the hills—but in the dark they could see very little.

"I can't tell now," his father mused. "But I did notice it—soon as I got over around Albany. The land's different altogether." He reached into his top pocket for a half-smoked cigar. "Do I have time for a smoke?"

"I doubt it. And the deer'll smell it. Can't you chew on it?"

"You telling me how to hunt?"

"No, McEnroe." Don sighed. He half wished he were alone. His father seemed like a liability; they hadn't hunted together for about fifteen years. "No, but our stand's half a mile away. We'll be parked in just a minute."

"Okay, okay." He crammed the cigar, unlit, into the side of his mouth. "Tell me about this great stand of yours."

"There's a trail off the road. You can see it from here in daylight . . . fifty yards after this sign." He changed gear and began to turn the jeep to the right. "We have to walk about a quarter mile—maybe less. Open fields on a hill there, and a big patch of brush and thornapple at the bottom. You'll see."

McEnroe rubbed his gloves together. "Now you've got me excited."

"Good!" Don parked the jeep and turned toward his father. "But we'd better shut up now."

"You *are* telling me how to hunt," his father said irritably. "I got a twelve pointer the year your mother and I got married, I'll have you know, and you were in wet diapers at the time."

"I hope I was—or nothing. The year you got *married*?" Don teased.

"Well, maybe the next. Anyway, you were just a bawling runt. So don't be telling your old daddy how to hunt."

Don reached out and pushed against the padded arm of his father's jacket. "I don't mean to. But I've been out in this brush and dreamed this hunt so many times I think I own those deer already."

McEnroe grunted. "Well, we'll soon see who owns what, I guess." And with the stealth of an old hunter he pushed open his door, dropped almost soundlessly to the track and closed it softly again.

Don sat still for just a moment before following him. For several weeks in the early fall he'd sat in the jeep with field glasses and watched the deer early in the morning and in the evening. They were fleet, savvy and shy of noise and movement. In the day they returned early from browsing in the fields and orchards to bed down by the thorn trees and evergreens at the base of the hill, where the brush was thickest. Then in the evenings they migrated under the twilight to higher, more open ground again. Later in the fall, when he'd searched out the stand on foot, he had seen them stepping out of the shadows of the trees, leaping along the furrows, and sometimes crossing the highway in enormous bounds. He had seen them, too, dead by the roadside: a trail of rusty blood on the road; gleaming hides stretched taut over the thinning carcasses . . . and the crows picking and fighting over them.

In front of the jeep the dim, circular pool of his father's flashlight had grown smaller but then stopped. He took a deep breath, forcing himself to leave the warmth of the jeep for the raw air and the rather uncertain pleasure of his father's company. *I hope he doesn't make a fool of himself*, he thought.

————

Streaks of muted yellows and whites appeared along the eastern fringe of the horizon. The two men stirred but made no sound. They stood shoulder-deep in the brush and watched; every movement, every sound in the stillness was a caricature of itself, an exaggeration. Don focused his eyes on the fields, turning his head again and again, slowly, so as to miss nothing. He drank some coffee. The scalding cup felt good in his numb gloved fingers.

McEnroe fumbled for the flask of bourbon. He undid it and took a sip. Don glanced at him for a moment and saw the flash of silver and glass in the eastern light. His father offered it to him.

"No." Don mouthed the word, shaking his head. "No. Anytime now, McEnroe." He turned his eyes back to the fields. In the growing light blacks turned to grays, grays to whites or duns, and duns to browns. The wind in their faces picked up; it drove the clouds faster overhead. He released the safety and squinted through the sights to the top of the nearest field.

Still no deer.

Then a shattering report split the air, and five does sprang over the top of the open hill, leaping toward them, bounding frantically for cover, veering apart and then together again. In the pale light he could see the lather on their haunches and around their mouths. He could almost smell their fear, almost hear the plunging heartbeats. *Guys on the other side of the hill*, he thought grimly. Then with quick relief, *They're out of range now*. He wanted no amateurs breaking their cover or shooting into this bunch. Beside him his father was poised to shoot. The deer closed on the stand. The wind behind them, the animals feared no enemy ahead—only the unseen agents of death behind. Then

Don remembered. *Regular license . . . antlered male
. . .* "Don't!" he shouted.

His father jumped in surprise and pulled the trigger; the slug went far over the does' heads. Abruptly the animals turned at right angles and disappeared along the edge of the brush.

McEnroe turned angrily. "What in *blazes*?"

"*Females*. Remember?"

In a rage his father swore and dropped the gun. "I *blew* it. Now none of the animals will come this way . . . *Does*. Oh!"

Don hadn't even shifted position; he expected at least one buck to follow the does downhill. But perhaps the hunters on the other side had felled him; none came. And by now the wind was carrying their scent to the does already behind them in the brush. Irritated, he nevertheless decided to make his father's escape dignified. Glancing at his watch, he said, "I'm cold. Are you?"

McEnroe stared at him, assessing the blandness of the remark, as if expecting a volley of invective for the rash shot. Then he answered, quite as if he'd been hunting all morning without a slip, "Yes, I believe I am."

Don consulted his watch for the second time, this time making sure his father saw the action. "We've been out here long enough for now. How about breakfast?"

"And then back here?"

"No. My afternoon stand is on the other side of this hill. I hope not where those other guys are . . . How about it?"

"Fine." He stretched and moved stiffly ahead of his son out of their brush hiding-place.

Don knew what his father was thinking. "Don't feel bad," he said. "I got excited, too. I could have done what you did, myself."

"I feel like a prize idiot."

"You'll make up for it," Don conciliated. "Anyway, I'm hungry."

While they waited for griddle cakes, McEnroe asked Don a few perfunctory questions about the farm but then lapsed into a prolonged silence. The waitress brought coffee, and both men endured the slow, painful thaw of their swollen fingers. Around them other men dressed for hunting held intentionally loud discussions about drinking parties the night before, last season's triumphs, the merits of one gun against another, and the prospects for the day's hunting. The only women in the restaurant were the waitresses; under the dome-like cloud of tobacco smoke and steam there was a noisy air of masculine conviviality; an atmosphere which smacked of the neolithic cave, which blurred the edges of the modern setting and seemed to carry them all back to a primitive age. Boasting rituals. Drink. Skins. Antlers. Horns for the womenfolk.

Womenfolk. Don glanced over at his father as the waitress brought two platters of pancakes and eggs. McEnroe had arrived only the previous afternoon, and Don had immediately asked him about Ellie. He had expected a sour, complaining response—not the silence he got. Not the brittleness in all McEnroe's jokes. "We'll talk about it later," his father had repeated adamantly. *This is later,* he thought, *and we won't be going back out for several hours.* Still, he waited for a few more moments until he could see that his father had begun to feel warmer. He lit a cigarette, then he said, "Mc-Enroe, I know you haven't wanted to talk about Ellie. But I know, just *know* something's not right with her, or you'd have been cursing her out."

His father took a couple of bites and leaned forward. He kept silence, not even looking up.

Don watched him with incipient concern and was suddenly shocked. *Why, he's getting older.* He'd always thought of his father as indefatigable: a Bostonian without some of the effeteness he associated with the city, a man with the Yankee energy and political know-how that might bring him the state governorship one day. Yet a man who was straight as well as shrewd, humorous as well as clever. Now, though, the unpretentiousness of his father seemed to have worn into shabbiness. He'd gained weight. His silver-grey hair was too long and unkempt now, and in his hunting clothes he looked like most of the frayed farmers in the diner: fleshy, sagging, the face reddened by years of drinking. *Old. And grieving*, Don thought to himself.

At last McEnroe said, "She's ill, Don. Very sick."

He wanted to thrash back against the tide of anxiety that washed over him. He saw Ellie suddenly as she had once been at Hammonds': her eyes swollen with hay fever and her face split wide with laughter. He wanted to defend her. But he wanted to shake her, too. Always so vulnerable. Always so comical. So he tried to dam up this wave of fear. "What now?" He sounded weary, but not indifferent. Never indifferent.

McEnroe sighed heavily. "She's been on cocaine. She's an addict. A *cokehead*. Your sister's nothing but a blasted *cokehead*." No anger, only corrosive sadness.

Don's mind leapt forward painfully, like the deer he had watched an hour ago. "So *that's* it. Oh, God help us." He stubbed out his cigarette. "I don't believe it. I can't believe it."

"It's true. Don't act so surprised. It's typical of her. Silly, flighty girl she always was."

"Don't you attack her, now. Maybe you've had time to get used to the idea. I haven't. And I won't. An addict!" His "Oh, no!" was a groan into his hands.

McEnroe sank back. "No, I didn't mean to talk that way. You think I mean she's just a common hooker, a bum, a drop-out? That's not what I mean at all."

"Then say what you do mean." His mind reeled from

the shock. He wanted to put his fist through something—anything.

"I mean she was always so insecure that she was prey to every fad and nonsense that came along. Preferably before anyone else got interested," replied McEnroe drily.

"Cocaine!" Don moaned.

"Well, what do *you* know about cocaine?"

"Not much . . . less than you, I'm sure . . . but, wait a minute, it's not addictive, is it?"

"Apparently it is. *Physiologically* non-addictive, I was told; but *psychologically* addictive."

Cold words! We're talking about Ellie. "So, what's she like *now*? What's happening to her *now*?" His mind had blinkered itself. He could see McEnroe clearly but could not summon Ellie's face from the shadows.

"She's in a private institution in Connecticut. I got her in there myself. They found she'd been injecting the drug as well as sniffing it." He frowned and seemed to shiver. "She's bordering on psychosis. You wouldn't know her. *Thin*, Don, oh, like something out of a third-world hunger appeal. Pitiful. Utterly pitiful."

Don groaned again and covered his eyes with his hands; he couldn't block out the mental pictures that formed themselves now.

"It's all I can do to tell you this," McEnroe said hoarsely.

Don looked up. Around them the hunters still bantered, smoked and boasted. The waitresses poured coffee and swung their hips between the packed tables as they carried trays of orange juice, pancakes, syrup, eggs, bacon. All indifferent to Ellie. All ignorant of Ellie. And life would go on the same for them. For him, though, the sameness was shattered and different, painfully different. He swallowed hard. The smell of smoke and food suddenly sickened him. "What else. Tell me, please."

"She was agitated, frantic, when I found her. I doubt she'd eaten much at all for weeks. She was shaking, terrified of me. She shouted and tried to fight me off. Her eyes were big—like black circles in her face."

"*Where*?" Don asked urgently. "Where *was* all this—and *when*?"

McEnroe began to talk fast. "Last month—I thought about getting a detective. Nothing added up about her. I found out she had a brand-new car, but she came to me for money—like I said. She didn't move, but she'd changed her phone number; Margaret moved out—you should have told me that—"

Don swore and ground his teeth savagely. "I had no idea that fact made any difference."

"No one's blaming you. But *why*? I asked myself. Why would she do that and tell no one? It didn't seem like Maggie either. So I went and saw her."

"Ellie?"

"*No*. Maggie. Through the school—remember? That's how I got in touch with her. By then I was desperate. Ready to do anything. I even said to Margaret that I'd get the DEA onto her . . ."

Don thumped his hand on the table. "McEnroe! *Never mind Margaret . . . please*, I want to know about—"

Two men at the neighboring table turned to stare.

His father cut him short. "Yes. Shut up, and you'll find out." He emptied his coffee cup. His face was strained and pale under the superficial flush of wind and bourbon. He dropped his voice lower again. "I was scared to death the media would get hold of something before I did. People know me, and a lot of people knew who she was, too."

"*Is*."

McEnroe silenced him with a furious look. "I had to find out for myself what was going on. And you wanted to know, too. So I pumped Maggie, then I went to the apartment again."

"She was there? I thought you'd been there over and over already."

"She wasn't. I waited outside—rented a car she wouldn't recognize. I waited and waited. I should've done it months ago. I'd talked to the landlord, so I knew she hadn't moved. A man brought her in. She'd gone in the door with that guy before I realized it was Ellie—she'd dyed her hair black. She looked so awful—"

"You went in after her?"

"The same man came out. I didn't get a real good look at him, but it may have been Garcia—if that's his name."

"Her boyfriend?"

"Her boss. Her lover. Probably one of the richest, smartest drug dealers in the Northeast. I found out all I could from Maggie, and the DEA will find out the rest. He'll be caught if he's up here again. But he's probably lying low. With both Margaret and Ellie gone, he'll know something's gonna fall on him sooner or later, but—" he exhaled harshly, "you want to know about Ellie. The landlord let me in. I went right up to the apartment. I insisted on him giving me a key and then told him, 'Leave me alone, don't ask questions, and don't call the police.' Flashed him my Bar card and he cleared off quickly. She was high and giddy when I got in, but then it wore off. She was abusive; she threatened me. She may have been hallucinating—I don't know. The sweat was running off her." He paused, remembering.

Don searched his father's face and saw on it the same misery he felt.

"I told her, 'Ellie, you're gonna get help. You're going with me now.' She fought me, but I told her, 'It's that or I'll call in the police.' She tried to make a call, but I stopped her. I got her out."

"You took her down to Connecticut?"

"Drove like a demon. She seemed to fall apart in the car, and they gave her something to help her sleep. Ran

tests on her—liver tests, tests for VD . . . and she'll have
more . . . psychological tests . . ."

Don groaned again. "Oh, Ellie, Ellie."

"When she woke up I was still there. She said she
felt sick—had pains in her stomach, like a cramp she
said. And her head ached. And she talked wildly, went
on and on. It didn't make sense. She frightened me."

"I would have helped you. I wish I'd been there.
What a terrible thing to go through. Why didn't you tell
me all this when it happened?"

"I'm glad you weren't there. It was too much. And I
wanted to take care of her myself, before I came out
here so I could tell you." His voice broke.

"McEnroe." Don put out a hand. "It's all right. You
did fine. She'll be okay after a while." He said it to comfort his father, but inwardly he doubted it.

But his father retreated further into morbid spec-
ulation. "If I hadn't always had alcohol in the house
when you kids were growing up, maybe . . ."

Don rounded on him. "What good's it to get down
on yourself? That's rubbish you're talking. Ellie's always made her own choices."

"I didn't guide her enough."

"Was she *ever* tractable?"

His father was shaking his head. "I don't know. I
don't know."

For a moment Don pictured Ellie as he'd always
liked to think of her: a wild rabbit tracing exhilarated
circles in the hay, jumping and somersaulting in the
sun, the dew; high on the thrum of her own blood, the
pulse of her own life. But now she was caged in some
institution they euphemistically called a "haven" or a
"farm." "The funny farms," Ellie used to call them. Now
she was trembling, enclosed, alone. Poisoned by the
sweet, choking scent of the hay, she'd run too far from
her home field. The hideous rakes and balers were flail-
ing through the grain around her, driving her in circles

more and more frantic. Killing her.

"Exactly where is she? Can I go see her? Did you go back?" He knew those were questions McEnroe could deal with: empirical facts. No probing or real thinking was required.

He handed Don a white card. "Keep this. That's the place. I've been back once. I didn't want to get your mother suspicious. And they don't want me back for a while anyhow."

"And what about me? Would they let me in to see her?"

"They said they didn't advise it. They want to get her stabilized first. Maybe at Christmas we could do something special. They said she might be in better shape then. You could go then."

"Mother will know by then."

"I suppose she will. I was hoping to keep it quiet as long as I could."

"She'll be appalled. She'll be angry."

"She won't even believe it," McEnroe said.

"No? She'll worry about scandal," Don stated bitterly.

McEnroe straightened his back. "Naturally. We're in the public eye. I've worried about it myself."

Don wanted to shout, *Yes, more than you're worried about Ellie.* But he knew that was unjust. He knew—just looking at his father's face. "Will she be liable for prosecution when she's . . . 'cured'?" He gestured in distaste. "Sounds like a piece of bacon or something."

"No. It wasn't a court commitment. That's why I took her in. She'll never come back for counseling or medical help—if the law enforcement is dragged into this."

"No one need know about it, then, right?"

His father looked back with characteristic directness. "Precisely."

"But Margaret knows quite a bit."

"And won't talk."

"How d'you know?"

"I have her word. And I believe it."

Don turned his head and stared out of a steamy window on the other side of the room. Wind whirled an eddy of powdery snow off the roof. "I'm inclined to believe it, too," he said softly.

McEnroe paid the bill, and they went out to the jeep again. Neither spoke for several moments. Then in a changed tone that Don recognized from years of acquaintance as typical of his father's mercurial mind, typical even of his courtroom habits, McEnroe pursued the last tangent. "If you do make it home at Christmas, I think Maggie'd like to come and see you."

Keeping his eyes on the road, Don asked, "How much d'you weigh, McEnroe?"

"Two-ten," he answered, looking surprised. "What kind of a dumb question is that?"

"A smart lawyer's question. Don't you think, gentlemen of the jury, that the witness is too old and heavy to play Cupid?"

"Jury *and* witness? A bit confused, aren't you?"

"No more than you. For heaven's sake, when will you give up hassling me about that woman? She's sweet. I like her." He lifted a hand from the wheel. "But I've never loved her."

"Too bad. She's still crazy for you."

"She's a manipulator. Got you twisted around her finger. I bet she put you up to this question. But it makes me more sure than ever—"

McEnroe made a noise of contempt, "Of course she didn't. She's got too much pride. You'd think she was a classic goddess of five-eleven, not a cute little gal of five foot three—or whatever."

"Well, I'm sick of hearing about her. She's mooned over me since she was in high school—that weekend her father walked out. But she's immature, don't you think? What does she even know about me? A few weekends in Bedford—years ago. A couple of summers in Vermont with Ellie . . . Love?" he snapped. "She's in love with an *idea* of me. Not me. It's tough on her, I guess, with no father to take an interest in her, but she's a dreamer. I'm tired of dreamers . . ." He heard the sound of his own voice—savage, full of rage against Ellie, not Margaret.

"Oh, get off your high horse! What a stubborn idiot you are. She's not mooning over you. Don't flatter yourself. She's got other men after her—"

"Yeah, there's some wild story about her shacking up with a guy in Cambridge," Don drawled.

McEnroe laughed, "You believe that?"

"No. Interesting story, though. Just testing your reflexes . . ."

"She *loves* you, Don."

"Keep out of it, McEnroe. I don't need you for a go-between. I can pick my own women."

"Then do it."

"Oh, but I do," he joked. "Sarah and Teresa in Vermont. Lovely girls. Roommates in Mount Holyoke College at one time. Smart. Beautiful. And Laurel, and Mary Pat—" He grinned. "Good Christian girls. You'd have loved 'em all. But one reason I came out here was to start over."

"And *did* you?"

"Mind your own business."

"It is my own business."

"No, it's mine," he said off-handedly. "I'm sorry for Margaret, honest. But I shan't be running after her. I want someone strong. This isn't pioneers' land—" He looked out at the dead, brown weeds poking up through the snow, the empty, plowed fields, the slashed cornstubble. "But it's isolated here. Tougher than Vermont in some ways. No real cities for miles—which is okay with me. But Margaret's just a wisp. A little frail thing."

McEnroe gave a short laugh. "And you think she doesn't know who *you* are! That's funny Don. You don't know a thing about her, either."

"Marry her yourself if she's so wonderful."

"Good idea. But your mother's still my ideal woman."

"You're as bad as Margaret is," Don sneered. "A dreamer, yourself. A canny old world-hardened politician who still has dreams!"

"That's how I stay alive."

"It's *not* how I stay alive. I keep my feet on the ground. The woman I marry has to do the same."

In the afternoon they made a stand on the verge of an orchard that adjoined a sloping field.

"They'll come along the edge of the hill. Out of the brush around the other side," Don told him when they first settled.

He didn't notice the cold as the afternoon moved into early twilight. Again he went over and over what his father had told him. The words were harsh, the mental images they conjured up more harsh yet. They kept him from seeing the snowflakes sifting out of the sky onto his jacket, even from paying much attention to the semi-circular panorama their stand afforded. He was glad they couldn't talk. He drank a little more coffee, took a bite of chocolate, and idly let his eyes roam over the furrows of the bare field. Irrelevantly, he thought, *I wouldn't plow it that way myself. Wrong angle for that elevation.*

A soft movement beside him made his eyes dart to where his father was staring. *Yes. Three, no, four. One with antlers. They're coming down to the orchard. A big boy!*

Without a sound both men crouched still and waited. The wind was right, and so was the light. The deer were approaching without fear. They could afford to wait for a closer range. More accurate. No mistakes. *But there's only one male*, Don noted.

The click of their safety catches startled the deer. The male paused, uncertain, only fifty yards off. His wide, sensitive ears twitched. Then in a panic he plunged forward, the females following. The orchard might mean death; but it might mean safety. Don sighted carefully. He didn't stop to count the points. He saw only the wide mouth, the lithe gold of the animal's body, the flight: terrible and beautiful. Then the buck in his sights metamorphosed suddenly into the rabbit in the field—wide, frightened eyes like Ellie's.

He raised his gun and shot wide of the mark into the crooked furrows.

His father's gun fired simultaneously, and the buck dropped into the thin covering of snow. The females scattered, and McEnroe, whooping, ran out.

Why did I do that? Don thought, stupefied.

McEnroe didn't notice anything amiss. In his excitement, he'd forgotten Ellie, Don saw. "Life in an old hunter yet!" he bellowed. "He's a beaut. Ten points. Got him right in the lungs. Where's the knife?" His father looked at him briefly and said, "Okay, I can wait for the bourbon. Want to fill out the tag for me?" And, as full of eagerness and pride as a small boy, he rushed back to the dead animal.

Don watched him; he watched but did not fully see it all. Dark shadows seemed to obscure peripheral things from him: blinkers again—though what he could see, even that seemed blurred; not blinkers, after all. Was he looking through a poor television screen at distance? Himself the passive viewer seeing only what the camera allowed? McEnroe became the active one, ankle deep in clay mixed with snow, stooping down to wield the knife with surgical efficiency. He carved off the scent glands and gutted the animal. A younger hunter would have shrunk from the red mess of blood and entrails, but McEnroe worked fast and cleanly. He had everything scooped out within a few minutes. Then he straightened up and walked over to clean his hands in an unsullied patch of snow.

Still dazed, Don stared. *Hot red blood. A warm, honey-colored pelt on frigid snow. Has there ever been pleasure in such horror? What, squeamish, all of a sudden?*

"Where's the tag?" his father was asking.

He frowned. *The tag.* Then he came to, pulled out the non-resident's license, and tore off the tag. He filled it out for his father, but his hand was shaking.

Turning away, his father found the string and rope and pulled them out of his sack. Then he attached the tag to one leg of the deer and tied the rope around its neck.

Just a carcass, Don said to himself. But he couldn't look away from the round, dark wells of the deer's eyes, from the fear, the bewilderment.

They hauled the deer over the ground. There was just enough snow to make the job easier, but not enough to fill the cavity of the carcass—to cool it. But it didn't matter, anyway; the temperature had barely risen since the early morning. Then, gathering remaining belongings from their stand among the trees, they plodded back over the uneven ground toward the jeep. All Don could think of was the crooked furrows. *Plowed it all wrong*, his mind repeated to him.

He went through the next couple of hours almost numb, longing for the time when he could legitimately leave McEnroe, shut the door of his room, and figure everything out: Ellie, the hunt, the sudden change in himself. Mechanically he worked with McEnroe to hose down and hang the deer on the block-and-tackle in the

barn. Mechanically he changed his clothes, showered
and made supper. Mechanically he listened to his father's familiar anecdotes about poachers with flash-
lights taped to their gun barrels who dazzled the deer
and shot for their eyes in the dark but hit horses instead.

But when McEnroe, yawning, went up to fall asleep
and dream about the ten-pointed antlers hanging top
down in the barn, Don wrapped himself tightly in an
afghan and sat in the comfortable front room by the
fire. *Dreams . . . that's how I stay alive*, his father had
said. And, *I keep my feet on the ground*, he had said
to himself. But it was McEnroe who had shot the deer
and waded in the mud to clean it.

Why had he flinched and shot over the deer's head?
And if he hadn't done that to give his father a chance
at the buck, then why had he done it?

December

Outside the den window, sleet fell on the parked cars and the already slick pavement. Margaret felt glad not to be going out, but that was as far as her contentment extended. The furnace purred warmly in the basement below, and on the floor above, Cindy and Walt were calling back and forth to each other over the din of Saturday morning cartoons. Familiar, comfortable sounds, but she couldn't settle, couldn't focus her mind. The pile of spelling and history workbooks she had brought home for the weekend loomed in front of her—still untouched.

Pouring a cup of coffee, she wondered why she felt so tired. Tonight would be her late night, not last night, and only two more weeks remained until Christmas. Absently, she turned her radio to a station that was playing Christmas music. Why couldn't she just work steadily until she finished, then reward herself with a happy evening with Michael?

She'd met him in late October at the racquet club. He'd approached her right away, mistaking her for someone else. It was a corny enough introduction, Margaret decided, to make her like him. They discovered that they made a competent doubles team, that they both liked the same old movies and Italian food. Over antipasto, tortellini, and braciuole di vitello alla Veronese they told each other their stories. She told him about Don, and he told her about Carol, the girl he'd been engaged to.

"We're just a couple of old misfits," she had joked

once. "That's why we like each other so much." He had laughed then, as he always laughed at her humor. But by Thanksgiving, he had turned intense and possessive, not wanting her to see another man she had dated from time to time. Flattered at first, she had gone on with the relationship. Lately, though, his questioning her about her movements and activities day and night had begun to irk her. She had told him just this week, *Mike, back off a little. I'm in no hurry.* Still, he wanted to take her to his office Christmas party tonight, and she saw no reason not to go. *It'll be fun,* she reminded herself. *So get on with it, Margaret.*

She pulled the first spelling book off the pile—the brightest child's; she felt as if she were easing into the job at last; it required no mark but an "A" in red ink at the top. She moved on to the second, the third, but then a burst of choral music from the radio sliced through her concentration. "God rest you, merry gentlemen" . . . "It came upon a midnight clear . . ." Carol followed carol in quick succession from the soaring nave and choir of some unseen British cathedral three or four thousand miles away. The voices sounded pure and young, and she stared out the window again, remembering Ellie in the choir at Bishop O'Rourke's. "Fallen angel," the choral director had called her as Ellie gestured, pantomimed, laughed, and distracted the rest of the girls.

Another carol began:

"The angel Gabriel from heaven came
His wings were drifted snow; his eyes were
    flame.
'All hail,' said he, 'Thou Holy Maiden Mary,
Most highly favored Lady'—*Gloria.*

"For lo," a blessed mother thou shalt be,
All generations laud and honor thee,

Thy son shall be Emmanuel by seers foretold,
Most highly favored Lady"—*Gloria*.

Margaret put down her pencil, laughing aloud and reminiscing. Looking down from the choir seats to where Margaret had sat once, Ellie had mouthed other words—"Most highly flavored gravy, euphoria"—over and over again, until the choir had hiccuped to a stop and the choral director had turned on Ellie in a fury, her baton snapping like a whip through the air by Ellie's head.

Now she couldn't hear the music without thinking of Ellie's irreverence.

Irritated soon by her own procrastination, she drove herself to continue with the books. The English choir faded into a perfectly architectured reverberation in the fan vaulting and was replaced by Bing Crosby crooning "White Christmas." A sentimental anticlimax, perhaps, but one that suited her mood as she realized that she simply wouldn't tackle the books today after all. She'd rather daydream now about her family.

David and Martha would be coming over from Nantucket with the children. They would all meet at her mother's home in Dedham, and once again her brother would have a new baby to show off to the grandparents. Born a few days after Thanksgiving, Matthew would certainly attract the most attention. She'd have time to spoil Rebecca, now almost four, and Jonathan, two and a half. David and Martha hadn't left the island at this time of year for several years now, she reflected; so even without her father Christmas would be a gala occasion again. No, no chestnuts would be roasting on an open fire: her mother's house had no fireplace; no one would listen for sleighbells in the snow; probably no white Christmas, either, judging by the icy mess outside as the temperature seemed to be moderating again. The songs had it all wrong . . . except the atmosphere: the joyful gaiety of her mother rocking grandchildren and making fudge, of David stuffing the turkey and pouring eggnog, of the children discovering new toys under the tree. Magic of a different kind, which would depend less on the presence of white snow, sleighbells and chestnuts than on the nearness of people who loved each other; less on television and radio reviews of traditional nativity narratives than on David and Martha's narrative of Matthew's nativity. A *Fuller* Christmas, she had called it once to Ellie: the blend of the familiar and the novel, the commonplace and the exotic.

As she sipped her coffee, she realized that behind the music of "Silent Night" and the flow of her conscious thought she had seen, unconsciously, a taxi pull away from the curb; had also heard, unconsciously, the sound of someone thumping on the front door. She leaned over to look into the street but could see no one outside. The thumping continued, nevertheless, until Walt came downstairs. Not curious to hear what happened, she took her coffee back to the kitchen and began to make herself a sandwich for a late lunch.

A knock at her own door arrested her. She went to open it, absently carrying a soft drink in one hand and expecting Walt to hand in her mail. Instead, he was hovering uncertainly at the bottom of the stairs, and in front of him—thin, pale, but impeccably dressed in a tweed coat with a lavender scarf around her neck and an overnight bag in her hand—stood Ellie.

The glass slipped in Margaret's hand, but she caught it again. "Ellie!" She stretched out her free hand, starting but not finishing several sentences of surprise and welcome.

Characteristically, Ellie grinned. "Aren't you gonna let me in?" But then her manner abruptly changed, and she shot a frightened look over her shoulder at Walt.

Picking up the cue, Margaret said, "It's all right, Walt."

They went inside; Ellie banged the door after her. "Who is that creep, anyhow? Rude as hell."

"My landlord. You rang his bell, not mine, I guess." She watched her friend, frowning. Ellie's movements were clumsy. She was shuffling, not walking, to the chair by the window.

"I need a drink." She shrugged off her coat and Margaret saw in horror that without it she looked even more emaciated. Her dress hung off her body in loose folds, and the dark purple and black swirls of its design only heightened the pallor of her skin and accentuated the enormity of her pupils.

"Juice? A Coke?"

Ellie looked at her oddly. "No. I mean a *drink*. Anything."

Margaret hesitated, afraid of the consequences. "I don't have any alcohol in the house right now," she lied.

Ellie threw back her head. "You *are* getting weird and old-fashioned. Never mind." She screwed up her mouth. "Give me a Coke. No ice."

Margaret was glad of the moment alone in the kitchen; she needed time to think. *Why is Ellie here? How did she find me? Does McEnroe know she's out? Should I call him? Is she through with drugs?*

She came back quickly and gave Ellie a tall drink of Coke, all the time watching her in surprise. Ellie slumped forward over the untidy table, zombie-like, looking out of the window at middle distance. She did not blink; her eyes didn't move as cars passed just below. To Margaret's "How about a sandwich?" she only shook her head. Margaret sat down near her and picked at her lunch.

"What time is it?" Ellie asked unexpectedly. She looked around as if unsure suddenly of where she was.

"Around two, I think," Margaret said, eyes searching for the clock.

On the radio, someone was singing "Lo, How a Rose

E'er Blooming." Margaret gradually regained her courage. "Ellie, why did you come? What are you doing in Boston? I thought—"

Ellie stopped her with a piercingly cold stare. She narrowed her eyes. "Can you be trusted?" The words came slowly, as if she had trouble articulating anything at all.

Margaret returned her stare, feeling bewildered. "Of course you can trust me."

"You lied before, though, when you moved out."

Margaret waved her hands in helpless dismissal. "Yes, I lied. I was afraid of what you were getting into. I've felt terrible ever since—for me as well as you."

A flicker of a smile crossed Ellie's face. "So you had it all figured out. And I thought you were the prim, innocent one." She wiped away beads of sweat that had formed on her forehead.

Margaret didn't reply. She looked out at the sleet and waited.

Ellie twisted her silver ring around and around on her finger. She seemed agitated, and her face—the face Margaret remembered as bright and alive—was blank with despair and frustration. "Well, I came here because I didn't know if I could trust anyone else. I still don't even know if I can trust you. But I need some help. I had to find someone."

"I don't know how you found me, either, Ellie," Margaret said quietly.

"I'd thought of doing it before. My mind is so mellowed out, screwed up by that lousy Thorazine they gave me—I haven't been able to think clearly—but it'll wear off eventually."

"You thought of doing what before?" Margaret prompted.

"Finding you after you left. That was a low trick to play on your best friend, but I remembered somewhere in my fuzzy mind that I was going to call your brother.

That he's in Nantucket. I don't know how I could re- member even that much after what they put me through in Connecticut." She shuddered. "So much for modern treatment. They lock you up with a bunch of crazies, dose you till you're sick, then tell you you're sick in the head, tell you you need help. But I didn't need their kind of help. So I got out."

She was rambling, Margaret saw, and perhaps had forgotten to whom she was talking. "You were going to call my brother?" she suggested.

"It was amazing I could remember my own name, let alone his. But there were only two Fullers on Nan- tucket, and I got your brother first."

Margaret leaned forward. "He gave you my ad- dress?"

Ellie looked back at her steadily. "Yes. But don't worry. I won't hang out here any longer than I have to."

"You—er—just walked out?"

"They couldn't stop me. I'd agreed to be committed, myself. I was sick when I let McEnroe do it to me, but it won't happen again." She shrugged. "I had enough money to take a bus up here, and a cab. But I'm not going to sponge off you for long."

"Don't keep saying that. You can stay as long as you want."

"No thanks. The rehab staff won't be after me, but McEnroe will. And this might be one of the first places he looks."

"They'll tell him you left?"

"Sure they will."

Dread was growing inside her. Margaret frowned. The sight of her sandwich nauseated her. "So what will you do, Ellie?"

"I've been trying to figure that out myself. That med- ication—it's so hard to think. I wish I could just go out and score right now . . ."

Margaret groaned. "Oh, don't say that. Don't con- sider it—at all."

"Then I could think, at least. I'd know what to do."

"Are you so sure of that?"

Again, Ellie gave her a cold stare. "Yes. It always helped me think. It solved a lot of my problems. Those nuts down in Connecticut boast about their slick drug treatment program—all that stuff about behavior modification and withdrawal on Thorazine . . . they're sicker than I am." She stopped. "But I can't cop now, I guess. I've gotta get enough cash to get down to Miami."

Margaret's heart sank. "You mean you're going back to Steve?"

"Did you think I wouldn't?"

"Ellie, he's probably gone by now."

"But I know where to find him."

"The FBI and the DEA are looking for him. He won't—"

Ellie swore angrily and demanded, "How is it you know so much?" Her eyes glittered with hostility. "I shouldn't have trusted you after all. I should have just got myself to the airport, instead."

On what? Margaret wondered, fearing the answer and so not asking the question aloud.

"I suppose you'll call McEnroe the minute I leave."

"Maybe I will, Ellie," Margaret snapped. She stood up, flushed, but then sat down again and tried to regain control.

Ellie gritted her teeth and leaned forward with her pale hands outstretched in the gesture of a strangler. "You try anything of the kind, and you'll feel it. You hear me?" She held Margaret with those crystal blue eyes of hers in an absurd attempt at hypnosis.

Feigning confidence, Margaret answered her, eye to eye. "I've known you too long to be afraid of you. And I know you want help. Cut out the threats, okay?"

Ellie laughed hollowly. "Getting awfully cool in your old age, aren't you?"

"I wish I was," Margaret said, looking down. "Why

don't you just tell me why you came?" She knew why, of course, desperately hoping she was wrong.

Ellie was sweating again; she had emptied her glass. "First give me another drink. And I need a Kleenex."

Trembling still, Margaret waited on her and sat down again. She tried to remain calm but the forced sound of her own voice was hardly reassuring. "I don't know if I'll be able to help you much."

"You might, though. All I need is enough to get to Miami and pay for a night in a hotel. And I'll need to change my clothes." She moved her hands restlessly. "I'm hot, and I got up early so I could leave. These clothes stink."

Margaret took up a corner of the woven runner that stretched across the table and began to twist it idly. "I probably have enough money for you." She almost smiled. "But clothes—"

"I don't care how I look, not today. This coat'll do. Just give me a couple shirts and—"

"Jeans? I doubt it." She laughed nervously.

"I don't appreciate the funnies right now. A wraparound skirt would make it okay." She began to look anxious again.

Margaret gave her a long look. "You seem able to work things out just fine. I thought you said you couldn't think."

"Maybe that garbage they gave me's wearing off a bit—" She jumped up suddenly. "Say, where's your bathroom? And where's your closet? I'll find something." She headed toward the back of the apartment but then stopped and turned with a desperate expression on her face. Upstairs Peter was banging a toy on the floor. "Maggie—is anyone else here?"

She blinked. "No, no—of course not."

The relief on Ellie's face was visible. "Good." She turned away again, then hesitated for the second time.

"You think I'm going to shoot up right in your bathroom, don't you?" Her face had curled into a sneer.

Margaret swallowed. She had wondered about it.

"Well, I'm not. I don't have even a fraction of a spoonbag on me. If I had, I would, like I said. But I guess I need a plane ticket more just now." She snapped the bathroom door shut.

Shaking, Margaret ran to her bedroom, jerked open a drawer, and pulled out her purse. She emptied the bills onto the unmade bed and counted out all she had drawn from the bank the previous day. She had intended it for last-minute shopping for her family. Could she give this money to Ellie—for a ticket back to Steve—for a few grams of street cocaine and a high that would leave her more emotionally bankrupt than she had been before McEnroe took her to New Haven? Could she do it? She pitied Ellie, wanted to help her, but feared for her if she flew to Miami.

Still undecided, she started to put the money away again. Ellie shuffled into the room, glanced at the money, set down her overnight bag, then sat on the other side of the bed, looking into the mirror. "Well, can you let me have some of that?" Her voice was high and tight, and she didn't turn around to Margaret as she asked the question.

"I think so," Margaret said slowly. "I'll give you all but a few singles . . ." She stopped. "On one condition."

Now Ellie swung around sharply. "What?" she demanded.

"That it goes on what you said it would—a ticket and a hotel—and that you let me call Logan Airport and make the reservation for you."

Ellie stared at her angrily. The she looked back at the mirror and made a show of rearranging her hair. Finally, she gave an exaggerated shrug, "I might have known you'd say that. Sure, go ahead. Do it now. I'll take the first empty seat I can get."

Margaret went to the door. Ellie's compliance brought small relief. "All right," she said. "I'll do it. Take a look in the closet . . . you're welcome to anything that fits." She closed the door and went to the kitchen again. *I'll call the airline*, she thought, *then I'll call McEnroe*.

She dialed the numbers fast. A busy signal. She dialed again. Now she could hear the sound of Ellie rattling metal hangers in the closet, opening drawers. The line was still busy, and in a few moments Ellie would come out. Frantically she dialed again, but again the piercing, bleeping noise told her the line was busy. *Christmas rush*, she thought incoherently, checking the number again. At last the call went through.

"What flights do you have to Miami? . . . as soon as possible . . . No, we couldn't make it for that one, how about the next . . . Yes, one seat . . . Eleanor McEnroe . . . Sure—she'll pay at the desk . . . Yes, thanks." She scrawled down the times, then held down the cradle with one hand and fumbled with the other through the Bedford directory; she hadn't dialed McEnroe's number in months. Pulling the cord to its limit, she walked away from the back of the apartment and hoped Ellie would not hurry out of the closed bedroom.

The housekeeper answered as usual during the day. "McEnroes' residence."

She dropped her voice to barely above a whisper. "Is Julius McEnroe there?"

"I can't hear you."

Grimacing, she repeated her question slightly louder.

"I'll see. Who's calling?"

"Margaret—Margaret Fuller."

"Oh, let me see for you. Just hold the line please." She bit her lip and waited. She could still hear Ellie moving around in her room.

He did not hurry to the telephone, and the minutes dragged so slowly that she broke into a cold sweat. At last the familiar voice came on the line.

"Maggie—what's going on?" He sounded afraid.

She twirled the cord around and around her fingers in frantic anxiety. "Did the rehab center call you?"

"About an hour ago. Is she with you?"

"Yes, but I can't talk."

"Keep her there. I'll drive down as fast as I can. Where are you? You never told me."

"Ludlow at Broadway—the third house on the right, going south. But what'll you do?" she begged, forgetting to lower her voice.

Then she heard Ellie's step behind her.

Simultaneously, McEnroe hung up and Ellie came forward. She wore no mask now, only menacing hatred. "You bitch!" she spat out.

Margaret dodged to the other side of the counter. Half of her wanted to laugh at Ellie's motley appearance in her own clothes, but the other half panicked. "I had to do it. You're sick."

"No sicker than you. You're crazy. You called the airlines—yes, I heard it all. Then you called McEnroe. Whose side are you on? You can't decide, can you?" Sneering, she leaned forward and snatched up the pad on which Margaret had written plane times. "Give me that. I won't trust you to call me a cab, and you certainly won't take me to Logan, either. I'll be gone in ten minutes."

"I didn't give you the money," Margaret said coolly, thinking she could buy time that way.

Just as coolly, Ellie answered, "Don't worry, dearest, I took it." She smiled without humor. "All of it, even the ones."

"But I said—"

"Don't quibble. I didn't think you'd call him. I should have known better. Your word's worth nothing. Why should I scruple over a few ones, then?"

"I need them tonight."

"So do I. More than you do." Ellie's face had become dark, ugly, unrecognizable to Margaret. She reached for the Boston and Cambridge phone book, but her movements were still slower than usual, and Margaret intercepted her.

"I'm not letting you go," she said, but the words came out without conviction.

Fury filled Ellie's face. She lunged forward and missed. Clutching the phone book to herself, Margaret ran to the front window. Ellie came after her, screaming obscenities, her hands raised like talons.

Margaret saw her intent. Then she noticed almost dispassionately her nails had been cut short. Smaller, but stronger than Ellie, she knew that she could outwit and even outwrestle her now; she was both enervated and debilitated. Again Ellie tried to wrest the phone book from her, and again she ducked past her and ran back to the kitchen. But she began to pant and sob with anguish. What if she couldn't keep this up until McEnroe came?

She turned and saw Ellie coming back to her. The demonic anger had gone, replaced by hopeless desperation. She looked driven, so insanely bent on getting what she wanted—getting high, getting Steve—that Margaret suddenly began to weep. Ellie could defeat her after all; pity won over. She passed the phone book to her.

Ellie looked at her dully, then struck it away as violently as if it had been a snake. "I'll go out and call a cab myself," she said. Without looking at Margaret, she went back to the bedroom for her overnight bag.

"No," Margaret cried after her. "I'll—I'll call one for you."

"Don't bother. I don't want the cops."

Margaret's voice choked. "Ellie, I want to help. I do." She staggered forward, holding the counter for support.

Ellie came back into the kitchen. "You have," she said coldly.

"Then let me do that much for you. Please."

Ellie shook her head doubtfully. "I have no idea of time anymore. How long since you called—?"

"Maybe five—seven minutes." The words came out singly.

"It's more than that."

"No, it isn't." *It'll take him fifteen—maybe even thirty minutes from Bedford.*

Nervously Ellie stepped to the window. Between her teeth, she said, "Then do it fast. No tricks, or so help me—"

Margaret felt for a moment as if Ellie were right. She was going crazy. Everything seemed to cave in around her. Her body shook; her hands shook; she could hardly dial the numbers. Instead of the dial, she saw in front of her over and over again the face of the friend she had loved turn black and stone-hard against her. Instead of the cab company, she heard over and over again the ringing accusation of the friend she had loved. "Bitch! Bitch!"

The telephone rang and rang. Ellie moved restlessly by the window. Margaret's throat seemed to close; when at last someone picked up the phone, she sobbed uncontrollably for a few seconds before she could manage to give him the address.

"You sound all in, miss. I'll have one up there in five."

"You're . . . sure."

"Promise. Hang in there, okay? It can't be that bad."

She replaced the receiver and burst into tears.

"Get ahold of yourself, Maggie," Ellie said bitterly. "Don't blubber."

She couldn't answer.

The cab came immediately. Still crying, Margaret stood up and followed Ellie to the outside door.

On the top step, Ellie turned. "You're mixed up, but you're a good kid, Margaret."

Margaret reached to hold her for the last time, but Ellie stepped down quickly. Over her shoulder, she threw back, "Your things will be handy. Thanks for everything."

"Take care," Margaret called. It was inadequate. She wanted to say, "I love you, Ellie."

The cab driver didn't bother to open the door for Ellie. She stooped clumsily and almost fell into the back seat. For a moment his back wheels spun on a patch of ice, then the cab disappeared into traffic.

Margaret stood at the door, crying without any attempt to stop. Then, stumbling back inside, she went blindly back to her room. Misery fell on her: hard and bitter and cold as the sleet outside. Worse than all the sadness in May, this grief sapped everything from her. Sitting on the bed, without any consciousness of her surroundings, she let the burning tears keep coming until her eyes and throat—her whole head—ached.

In a few minutes, McEnroe will come, she thought at last. She must collect herself. She switched on a lamp and saw what she had not noticed before: Ellie had pulled out almost every drawer in the room. Puzzled, she wiped her face and distractedly began to put back the clothes and trinkets. Ellie had even searched through her jewelry box. Not that there wasn't anything she wouldn't have given her . . . and not that there was anything valuable. . . .

Gramma's ring, she thought. *It's missing*. She tumbled out the box again. *Wait, I wore it yesterday . . . and I put it away last night . . . five emeralds in a cluster, around a diamond . . . the only thing . . . and she knew about it.*

The ring had gone. Ellie would get her ticket. Ellie would get her high, too.

The doorbell buzzed. *McEnroe, too late.*

————

When he put out the light in his old room in his parent's home, Don saw in his mind's eye with painful clarity all the fragmented pictures his father had been able to glean. Ellie, frantic, taking Margaret's money, her ring. And next a cab to the airport. Grateful for its anonymity, she would have slumped back against the padded comfort of the seat, not feeling it, twisting her own ring and Margaret's, too, around and around in frenzied impatience at the snarled downtown traffic. Then the sterile tiled cloakrooms at Logan, where she would have waited, deliberately missing the flight Margaret had booked and changing clothes before getting a stand-by flight; changing things so that it would be harder for someone to identify and catch her. That was what she must have feared most: to be caught by the very people who would have saved her. She had paid cash for her ticket and flown under the name of Elizabeth McKenzie, his father found out later. No one had questioned her. It was a domestic flight, after all, and she only a thin passenger escaping from Boston's frigidity to the balm of Miami. "I'm going to Florida for Christmas," she might have told the stewardess, with her enormous, brittle smile. No one would have questioned her.

Not there, nor at the ocean-front hotel desk where she used the same name. She'd been to the pawnbroker by now, perhaps, trembling as she handed over the ring and stuffed the notes into her purse. Now she had plenty of money, and credit as well; it would be enough, she might have thought, until she found Steve.

She would have lost herself in the sprawl of Miami the next day. Did some of Garcia's contacts see her and pretend not to know her? Did she feel, even in the mildness of Florida's December, a chill of fear, a shiver of anxiety? And when did it come, how did it come—the definitive, ice-cold knowledge that her lover had gone and wouldn't risk returning, even for her sake? That she was powerless to find him, to have him again? Did that realization drive her, or was it all just a fatal mistake, the measuring of white powder done carelessly in the bleak aloneness of the hotel room? A small white heap of the stuff, perhaps more or stronger than she generally used, shaken in a cotton-plugged vial, drawn out into the syringe. A tight pair of stockings tied quickly above the skin where the needle would slide in. The police had related the details with dull precision.

What would she have seen, those last moments? What would she have heard? Her own hands, shaking perhaps, pushing the plunger down for the high she thought she had to have. The ringing in her ears, the jolt of energy that sent her thrashing then let her drop down the black chute into unconsciousness, let her drift out in her snow-white boat onto the dark, coma-tose river of nullity, the whispering cessation of breath.

His mind shut down. They had found her in the hotel room with the needle still in her body, the empty vial on the floor, the stockings still tied round her arm, and her face convulsed, frozen in terror and despair. He could not bear to see or feel any more.

Shivering, he turned on the light again, reached for a robe and sank into it. In the pocket he found a crushed pack of Benson and Hedges and lit one. Leaning forward, he sat on the edge of the bed with the smoke curling up from his cupped hand over his forehead, but he didn't smoke the stale cigarette. He stared blindly at the Persian rug on the floor. *Dead. What does it mean? Gone? But to where?* And if it wasn't Ellie who had lain so white and fragile in that mound of ridiculous flowers at the wake, then who was it? If she had gone, how could she be there? But if she was there, why wasn't she the Ellie he knew?

He looked down at his hands, seeing them: the first

things he had actually observed since the afternoon. Wide, calloused, tough, with dirt ground into the quicks of his nails. But they were long-boned like his sister's—like those hands that were dead now: bloodless, immobile, alien. Why could his hands move while Ellie's couldn't? Why had he remained alive when she lay dead? *Dead . . . What does it mean?*

He went to the window and opened the curtains. Below, on the snow-covered lawn, floodlights turned everything orange except where small splashes of color from the Christmas lights blinked green and red, green, red. Who'd had the nerve to turn them on? Orange snow had swallowed up everything—the patio, the pool, the long green expanse where he'd learned to pitch a curved ball and a glider—swallowed everything except those irrelevant little lights.

He stubbed out his cigarette in the ashtray by the bed. His faded old Braves and Red Sox pennants hung in the corners; the desk at which he'd done homework was still marked, scarred with ballpoint pens, bent paper clips and stapled papers. Except for the warm richness of the Persian rug, the room looked drab, colorless; he disliked it as much as ever. It seemed to confine, to close him in.

He took off the robe and reaching to turn off the light, lay back on the bed again. New when he entered high school, it now molded to his body as it used to, sagging under his weight in the middle. He turned on his side, facing the window. Outside in the orange darkness the Christmas lights still winked. He swore ineffectually at them. He shut his eyes, but he knew he wouldn't sleep. He hated the lights, the snow, the deathliness of winter, and the finality of Ellie's death. Faces from the wake swam past his eyes. His mother's: drawn, mask-like, the make-up unnatural and ghastly, furrowed by tears, more corpse-like even than Ellie's. His father's: heavy, bowed, confused, and yes, angry.

His cousins': curiosity and disgust barely concealed; he knew their intolerance; he knew they were ashamed of Ellie, embarrassed. Margaret's . . . Maggie's . . . hardly recognizable: washed pale from all the crying, her mouth turned down at the corners, her quiet eyes catching his from time to time between heads that talked and turned. He saw that she agonized for him, and he imagined that she shared the same black hopelessness. Why didn't that annoy him, as usual? No, he was glad to find her there, after all.

McEnroe had driven her to Bedford, unannounced, from the funeral home. "Won't you stay the night, honey?" Don had heard him press her as she prepared to leave. "We'll find you a nightgown and a toothbrush, okay? Please say yes. It would be easy for you to get to work from here in the morning."

He'd heard the pleading in his father's voice. How terrible to be a father. She represented his last living link with Ellie and Ellie's lost childhood. And she must have understood, for she agreed immediately; no demur, no foolish self-consciousness flung in his direction. She knew the need, and she'd met it. She was consistent, for sure. Or did she feel guilty, responsible somehow because of the money she'd given Ellie? *Guilt.* It would corrode someone like Maggie. He wondered, *How does she really feel?* As usual, he couldn't completely interpret her expression. The sadness, the ache—they were obvious. But what else lay behind them? He hadn't spoken directly to her since they'd returned to the house; he'd left that to McEnroe. In fact they'd hardly spoken to each other all day. And if she felt weighed down by it, she wouldn't be sleeping either.

He snapped on the light again, pushed his feet into a pair of broken slippers, and pulled the robe around himself for the second time. Opening the door, he went out softly onto the long mezzanine. He wasn't certain what he wanted to do or say, but perhaps he could say something to make her feel better. *I owe her that, I guess*, he thought. A foreign thought. Where had it come from? He almost smiled.

The dry heat of the forced air ducts wafted past his bare ankles and seemed to rise in thick waves from downstairs. The house lay in blue twilight, quiet, the roof creaking slightly in the frost. His parents' room was dark; he stood in the shaded light of a table lamp by the telephone and heard his father's snoring and his mother's lighter, shorter breaths; both were even. *Whisky and tranquilizers*, he said to himself. *No wonder Ellie . . . no, I denied that when McEnroe blamed himself before; it's not their fault Ellie did what she did. . . .*

He went a few steps farther, then stood still and listened again; he did not know which room the housekeeper had given Margaret. Nothing. But then he found one of the guest room doors partly open. He hesitated on the threshold. *I have no right to disturb her if she's asleep—*

No light came through the crack. No light and no sound: neither weeping nor breathing. Cautiously, he moved the door a little and remained by the door frame, adjusting his eyes to the faint light that fell inside from behind him. Gradually he could discern the lines of her body, shoulders to feet under the quilt, but he couldn't see her face or her thick hair. Under his own shadow, which fell across the foot of the bed among the other shadows, she lay unmoving: a small woman, asleep. *So little and fragile . . . or is she?* His mouth twisted. *How should I know?*

Dismissing her from his mind, he backed away and pulled the door to where it had stood before. Soundlessly he went down the stairs; even in the semi-dark he knew every variation of the thickly carpeted treads, all the way down. In the kitchen he stood with hands in pockets waiting for a kettle to boil.

A few minutes later he passed Margaret's room again but did not stop this time, going instead right to the end of the mezzanine and turning into a part of the house rarely used by the family. There the housekeeper occupied a suite; and in the junk room his mother stored old toys, pictures, books, shoes, mattresses, and a slide projector.

Leaving the door ajar, he turned on the light. The room smelled musty, the air so stagnant and chilled that he shivered. He stood and sipped the tea and ran his eyes over the piles of junk. The limpid eyes of a life-sized china doll stared unblinkingly at him from a Dresden complexion. Dust tarnished its gold hair now; still, it looked new, not in the least offended by Ellie's childish rejection. The doll sat on a pile of boxes stacked three high; the name *McEnroe*, scrawled in Ellie's careless red handwriting, covered most of one side of each box. *College texts*, he thought with a reluctant smile of recognition. *Probably never opened*. He pulled a couple out of the top box; perhaps these were the ones she had bought only three years ago, for her last semester. Her *last* semester.

I'm Okay—You're Okay came out first. *For a psychology course, or just her own reading?* he wondered. He found Marshall McLuhan's *Understanding Media* in his other hand and flipped through its pages. "The Photograph" . . . "Press" . . . "Ads" . . . "Movies" . . . the titles, if not the contents, would have drawn her. But what did it all mean to her now? Had she entered McLuhan's reel world, or had she flown free and finally from the shackles of Dr. Harris's real world and found herself perfectly okay in a hereafter neither she nor he had ever believed in?

Shrugging, beyond grieving for the moment, he replaced the books and rummaged through a few other boxes until he found what he was looking for. The black file-boxes were marked with white jam-jar stickers typical of his mother's laborious labeling system: "Film strips, slides: Bedford, 1938–47." "Slides, Bedford: 1947–63." "Slides, Bedford: 1964—"

Leaving the oldest box on the floor, he opened the others and searched for slides of Ellie; each was dated and meticulously identified in tiny writing. "Donny with Baby, 1947." "Ellie with Daddy, 1949." "Ellie's first day at school, 1952." "Ellie outside State House with Daddy, 1955." "Ellie with Don, 1959." "Ellie with friend (Margaret)." "Summer 1964, Ellie, Don, and Margaret in Vermont." "Summer 1965, Ellie with Don . . ."

He felt no urge to sleep; so, unhurrying, he pulled out the slides he wanted one by one, and piled them in the lid of the box. He set the slide projector on a wooden crate and with the light off again directed the empty white rectangle against a blank wall; he then fed the slides into the carousel. They would come in no particular order, but he didn't care. For a few minutes in the glaring heat of the projector's bulb he wanted to resurrect her picture for himself.

He clicked the first picture across. The fan whirred on, and the room, now smelling of hot celluloid, was illuminated by Ellie's widest smile. Ellie at ten: her red curls, slender, flat-chested body and long arms fixed themselves on the wall. He looked up, horrified. The picture was as dead as she was. No movement, no life, no warmth: just the lies of two-dimensional color, line, and an incandescent bulb.

Quickly he snapped a second slide into its place. *Myself at Hammonds'. The wind's holding my hair at an angle from my head, and my two arms grip Ellie's thin shoulders—on one side and, lower down the wall, Margaret's more rounded shoulders. It's my birthday,* he realized. That photograph shocked him, too. *Ellie doesn't smile at the camera. She's looking somewhere else. Margaret's eyes are direct, as calm as the doll's. Disquieting, as if she sees more than you think.* He slid the frame across without looking up at the wall again and pulled the picture from the carousel to look at it in the blaze of the projector light. His mother had labelled it "Don's birthday party, 1964; Ellie and Margaret." *The year Ellie graduated from Bishop O'Rourke's,* he thought. *Maggie would have been a college freshman.*

Growing inexplicably impatient, he dropped the slide back in and reversed the carousel. He compared the two girls deliberately, critically, as if they meant nothing to him. Then he thought, *I'm getting obsessive. This picture's dead. The past is dead. Ellie's dead. There's no more to be done about her.* He pressed the projector's "off" button and, without bothering to refile the slides, turned to go out.

A slight movement in the hallway startled him. Draped in an ugly floral housecoat that obviously didn't belong to her, Margaret was coming toward the open door. He wondered fleetingly if she had been standing watching in the doorway before; but no, he would have seen her shadow, and her eyes would not be as light-dazed as they were now, meeting his.

"You made me jump," he accused.

"I'm sorry. I couldn't sleep. I heard someone moving around . . ."

She had been awake, then, pretending to be asleep when he had stood at her door. He pushed his hands into his pockets and felt a sudden awkwardness he couldn't remember in her presence. "Did I wake you?"

"No, I was trying to sleep . . . it didn't work."

"My parents seem to have no problem that way."

"Tonight, maybe. But the last few must have been hell." She spoke levelly, with a self-possession he didn't associate with her. Was she intimating to him that he wasn't the only one who was grieving, telling him in her own way not to wallow in sorrow?

"You're right, I'm sure," he said curtly. Then he

added unnecessarily, "I'm drinking tea. Do you want some?" He expected an assent; she always deferred that way.

"No, but maybe something else."

"Fine." Passing her, he led the way downstairs again. *This is what I wanted*, he told himself. *To let herself unburden on me for a change. But I don't know . . . maybe it'll be the other way around.* He hesitated briefly halfway down the stairs, trying to remember something McEnroe had once said about Margaret. She was right behind him, struggling with the housecoat so that it wouldn't trip her, and she almost fell against him. "Be careful!" he snapped. And he went the rest of the way down without looking back.

"Be careful yourself," she retorted. "You shouldn't stop that way."

Surprised, he shot back, "You certainly are wide awake. How about a soporific? A hot toddy?"

"No thanks."

"What, then?"

"Hot milk'll do fine. I can get it myself, anyway."

"Hot milk! You're old-fashioned. That's what Granny McEnroe used to drink nights. Said it put her to sleep."

"Smart lady. Don't knock it—tryptophan, you know. Anyhow, you of all people ought to know how good hot milk is at night."

His mouth cracked into an unaccustomed smile. "Okay, okay. You do your thing, and I'll do mine—we could sit in the family room for a while, if you want." He waited, watching the response, but her eyes revealed nothing to him.

"Yes," she said finally. "D'you mind if we talk about Ellie?" She sounded too casual.

He couldn't look at her then. The dead photographs upstairs had unnerved him, and pressure began to build behind his eyeballs. He kept his voice carefully under control, though, as he answered her, "She's all I can think about as it is."

She turned her back to him to open the fridge. "Me too." It annoyed him that he couldn't see her face, and for a moment he almost suspected that she might scorn him. But she wouldn't, he realized equally quickly; her looks of compassion all day denied scorn; she was grieving as much as he was.

They sat on opposite sides of the empty fireplace in the hushed comfort of the family room, keeping silence at first. *What was it McEnroe said?* he kept thinking, expecting her to weep. Then he remembered. *Something about how strong she was. But she's just a wisp, a little frail thing*, he himself had claimed. And McEnroe had said, *You don't know a blasted thing about her. She loves you, Don.* He glanced at her. *She's not hard, either*, he thought. She puzzled him.

She caught his eyes probing and smiled very slightly. "It's a big hole in your life. Isn't it?"

He looked at his tea, then back at her, forcing himself to say, "And yours, too." His throat began to ache. He himself, not Margaret, would soon be crying. She didn't seem to want to voice her own grief, not yet, and only nodded.

"I hadn't seen her since last Christmas, you know. She was going to come out and see me in March . . . I'm sure you remember."

Her lips twitched. "Very clearly. The weekend that wasn't."

He frowned at her wry smile. Was he supposed to apologize? No, she was often blunt like that, he recalled. Letting it pass, he only said, "We were close. You may not have seen that, even though you lived with her all that time. She drove me mad sometimes—I'll never elevate the dead to sanctity as long as I've got a memory. But she was beautiful, no matter what."

"She talked about you often," Margaret put in. "And

not just for my sake, either."

Again that directness. She had reckoned with her feelings, then, and grown up. Perhaps the other men she knew had helped. There she sat, assured, almost serene in that hideous housecoat. She had changed, he decided.

"She used to want to know what you thought of everything. You always mattered, not . . ." She hesitated.

He exhaled quickly. "Not my parents, you were going to say.

"Right." She looked uncomfortable.

"That's all right. They knew that as well as you do. It made no difference. The prodigal daughter could always come home."

"That's what she used to call herself."

"It's apt." He stared at the tea again, conscious that he didn't want it after all. He leaned forward to set the mug on the raised hearth, found the Benson and Hedges in the top pocket of his robe, and lit another cigarette. For the second time that night he thought, *There's no more to be done about her . . . and no more to be said, I guess. Closure. Life has to move forward. Tomorrow I go back to my cows. And Margaret—?*

She was watching him again when he looked up. "What?" she queried.

"I—I don't know what else to say about her, honest to God. I still can't grasp what's happened. Maybe I will in a few weeks, but not now. I wish I could think of something else." He shook his head slightly. "Like . . . where do you go from here, Maggie?"

Her eyebrows went up.

"I mean—you're going back to Cambridge?"

"After work tomorrow, sure. We have one more week of school left."

"Then what?"

"Home for Christmas for a couple of weeks, then back to Cambridge again."

He looked at her blankly. *Of course . . . back to Cambridge, she just said.* Then it struck him that he probably wouldn't see her again. With Ellie gone, there would be no connection between them. He had wanted to let her talk, but he hadn't, after all. He tried to think what to say to give her a chance for release, but what he said wasn't what he'd planned. Instead of some facile phrase like, "I'll miss her, too" or "We'll feel empty for a while," he found himself saying something quite different. "You've been a fantastic friend to Ellie. She didn't deserve you. You had a lot to put up with."

Her eyes widened and filled suddenly.

He was caught off guard by the tears he had previously anticipated but which hadn't come until now. He said cautiously, "And I've been a creep myself, around you. I should have given you better than you got last spring." The words spilled out; unplanned, as if someone else had said them.

She gripped the milk stiffly and pressed back in her chair. "Don't hassle yourself. I'm no martyr, Don. I love whom I want to love, and censure or rejection hasn't made a whole lot of difference." Her voice was steady, but the tears kept coming and she didn't trouble to wipe them away.

Panic welled up in him. If any other woman but Margaret had sat weeping those tears—not baby tears, not sentiment, not manipulation but deep grief—he'd have gathered her in his arms. Instead, he sat paralyzed, terrified. The girl had metamorphosed to a woman! A woman who loved him. Blindly, perhaps. Without basis, perhaps. But also without condition. And if she loved him still, it followed that she wanted him still—that it would be easy for him to console her. *Easy,* he thought, *but cheap. Compromise for her. Exploitation for me.*

Helpless, he leaned forward again and gestured in despair. "Maggie, I don't—"

She put her cup down. She didn't leave the chair, but she bridged the distance between them with her words. "All day—all day, Don McEnroe, I've wanted to hold you. I couldn't bear to see all that sadness. I couldn't bear it."

"Then for God's sake do it," he rasped back.

She stared at him, and for a long time neither of them said anything. "I will. But it's because I love you," she said. "Not because you love me. I don't have any illusions about that."

He stood up, hardly knowing what was happening. He was afraid of her suddenly, as she crossed the small space between them and wrapped her arms around him. Strong arms, warm, soft. He bent to put his face in her hair. "You're good, Maggie. I don't want to hurt you." She smelled vaguely of soap, and her body was shaking. He tightened his arms around her so that her head rested against his chest. They stood still together for a long time, both of them crying.

"Why did she do it? Why?" he said at last.

"I don't know . . . you mean you think she did it deliberately?" Neither of them could use the phrase "killed herself."

"That's one reason I can't get it out of my mind," he said.

"If she'd meant to do it, she would have left a note. She always left notes, whatever she did. She used to leave notes taped on the floor, or on my door . . ." Her voice trailed off.

"I want to believe it was an accident," he said slowly. "But we all protected her too much—my parents did; I did, but I didn't know it. I used to want to push her away. She bugged me a lot of the time. Now all I can think about—I dreamed about it last night—is her making that choice to do what she did. And I want to jump in and say, 'Stop it! Don't do it! Your life's worth more than that, whoever that man was.' " His voice rose in anguish. "But I can't jump in and save her. No one can. No one could." He stopped. Quiet hung between them again.

Eventually she said, "I meant it—I think it was an accident. It happens, I heard, from overdose . . ."

"I wondered that, too. The police said so."

"Or the cocaine might have been cut with—something else—something that would hurt her. She'd always bought from Steve before, so she knew the source—till this time." Her voice fell lower.

Unconsciously he pressed her tighter against him, wanting to press the thoughts out of his mind. But then he said, "But even if it was an accident, it was the stupidest accident that ever happened."

"Aren't they all?"

"No," he said. "I mean . . . the waste. She was beautiful, smart, successful—or she might've been. I was so proud when I saw her photographs in town last Christmas. 'My sister!' I thought. 'That's *my sister*,' I wanted to tell everybody! But she snuffed it all out." He sighed heavily, realizing Margaret was letting him talk on and on. "And where is she now? Do you know anything about that?" he urged.

"No. I don't."

"I didn't think so. I could see after the wake that it was hopeless for you, too."

She moved her head back in surprise for a minute and looked up, as if she couldn't believe that he'd even registered her presence all day. "I don't know anything about those things," she said flatly. "I left the church a long time ago."

"Why?"

"It had nothing to offer me. And that's how it seemed today, as well." Her voice wavered a little. "What can the church say when people have died that way? It's people who have to comfort each other. The church can't do a thing." She dropped her head on his chest again.

Without thinking, he rested his hand on her hair and pushed his fingers through it. Her hair was warm, almost alive. He screwed up his eyes. *She's alive. But Ellie's dead. Why? Why? She's alive, but Ellie's no more than a picture on a cold wall. She can't move. She can't even breathe.* Under his hand, Margaret shivered.

"I'm sorry," he said again, "I don't want to hurt you."

They stayed as they were.

Now, though, he wondered with dread, did she want something from him? He had said before, *She's a manipulator*, though he doubted it. But did she want something from him? Did she want him to take her upstairs to hold her in his arms on the narrow bed and comfort her in her turn? She had as much grief to carry as he, and he had meant to comfort her.

He drew back from her a little. "You don't blame yourself, do you?" The whole conversation began to seem unreal: their physical and emotional intimacy; the strangeness of it all.

"Blame myself?" she repeated dully. "It's crossed my mind, I guess. You can always look back and say, 'If this', and 'If that,' and 'Had I done this, or that—' But the past won't change. No, I don't blame myself. I do wish . . . just wish . . ." She clenched her teeth—"that I hadn't let her go when she came that day."

Not missing the contradiction, he snatched at the chance he'd waited for. "It wouldn't have made any difference what you did."

She shook her head. "No, I do know that." She gave him a pale smile. "But it was nice of you to ask."

Panic welled up in him again, and unwillingly he whispered, "What do you want, Maggie?"

She suddenly wrenched convulsively from him. "Nothing," she flashed back. "You should know that."

The words stung him, and he saw that she hadn't finished.

"Is that what you thought?" Her voice rose in a high, reckless laugh. "That all I'm out for is to get you at 2 A.M. when we're both feeling so *awful*? Don't worry about that." Angrily, she wiped away the tears with her sleeve and turned away.

Frustrated by the sudden change in her, he held up his hand. "Now wait a minute. Cool off. I only said—" He caught at her sleeve, so that she couldn't move.

She rounded on him. "I was only trying to console you."

He wanted to pacify her. "I know that." But then he dug himself deeper. "But we're giving each other a pretty dangerous kind of consolation."

"It's a risk, I suppose," she answered coldly. "For a silly, childish girl. But, then, I'm not a silly, childish girl."

He adapted her ironic tone. "So I hear."

"No, don't misinterpret me," she said quickly. "I'm not playing foolish little girls' games—that's not what I mean. But—" She hesitated for several minutes, and he waited for her. "I'm not propositioning you . . . I'll wait till I'm married for that, thanks . . ." Then she went on more confidently, "And you're too old, too smart for games yourself, for that matter." She shook herself free and moved back to her chair, though she didn't sit down again.

"I've insulted you," he said. "I'm sorry." He shrugged, pushing his hands in his pockets again. "Who's going to marry you? You didn't tell me." Then a shadow of a smile crossed his eyes. "What would he say, whoever he is, if he saw what's gone on here now?"

"I don't know," she shot back immediately. Her chin went up, and he could see the indignation in her eyes.

"You must have a strange relationship with him," he said with sarcasm, "if you don't know what he'd think about it."

Enigmatically, she said, "It *is* strange, I grant you."

"So you aren't living with some guy, after all."

She stared at him from the safety of the distance between them. "What difference would it make to you? But no, obviously, I'm not. I told you that, months ago."

Wanting to give her a chance to say more and thinking that he might seem less threatening, he dropped back into his chair. "Would you like to tell me? Who is this man?"

A slightly puckish grin changed her face. "Curious?"

He leaned back. "Oh, mildly."

"Well, I haven't been sitting home knitting at night. Or writing letters, either."

"Ouch. You've got claws all of a sudden."

As if ignoring him, she went on, "I've been seeing several men." Holding up her hands, she jokingly made a show of counting off on her fingers. "There's Robert, and Michael." She laughed and paused, not looking at him. Her laughter sounded fragile, still bordering on tears. "And Donald."

"Three potential husbands?" he quipped, forgetting Ellie for just a moment. "Er—by the way, Donald. . . ?"

She nodded, but her face had paled.

"Donald *who*?"

"McEnroe. Who else? I do have a strange relationship with him, admittedly. Haven't talked to him since May—by choice—haven't seen him since March— though that's not by choice." Her eyes were drying. She was poking fun at him.

"What makes you think he'd have you?" he asked. She was provoking him. He didn't want to be cruel, but she was asking for it.

"Oh, I have plenty of doubts about it," she said, as matter-of-factly as if she were mentioning the likelihood of cutting hay on an overcast August morning. "The doubts allow for the Roberts and Michaels of the world." She stood six feet away from him and took a deep breath. "But I think Don McEnroe might change his mind about me, one day, nevertheless."

"Why?" He shifted uncomfortably.

"Because in spite of Bob and Mike, I believe in faithfulness. Because I know I need you. And because in the end I think you'll find you need me—and love me, too."

Had she prepared that speech, thought it out years ahead of time? It was almost too dramatic. But it had come out naturally, as if she'd thought of it on the spot. And her dark eyes were wide, direct; expecting nothing except the same honesty.

He was silenced. Unpredictable, unafraid, she'd said what he couldn't have expected. Unpredictable . . . but unwavering, too, toward him. A complete contradiction! He inhaled to speak, then shut his mouth again.

She moved to the door without looking back again.

He moved one hand across his forehead. "You make me feel worse than ever. You thought too highly of Ellie. You think too highly of me. I wish I could love you, honest to God. You of all women ought to be the one. But I just don't feel what you feel." He was confused by the desperation in his voice.

She turned suddenly. "I'm beginning to wonder what love has to do with feelings. Very little, perhaps. I think love is an act of the will, a decision we make and then follow. It means doing something, not feeling some vague emotion. I used to think love was all about feelings. Now I don't."

He stared at her, trying to grasp what she'd said. "You're quite a rhetorician," he said lightly, hoping to defuse the highly charged flow of their talk but knowing he was risking her anger again. "I didn't know that."

"There are lots of things you don't know about me," she replied just as lightly. "If you ever made up your mind to learn, you'd have some surprises."

"So would you about me, I'm afraid." Now he sounded bitter. "You developed some grand ideas about me years ago, and you haven't let them go. I'm wed to my farming. That'll always be first. Ellie drove you crazy in the end. I would, too. You're capable of giving yourself to another human being. I'm not. I've never done it. I don't expect to."

"Ellie never drove me crazy," she countered.

"That's why you moved out, I thought."

"No. It was Garcia, the drugs, the squalor—not Ellie. I never stopped loving her."

"Or being hurt by her," he added soberly.

She winced. "It was the chance I took. My choice."

He appraised her. She met his eyes steadily. Hers were still red. He saw a different Margaret from the one he thought he knew. Emotion didn't rule her, after all. She was waiting for him to change, to grow up enough to keep up with her. *Little Maggie.* Younger than himself, stronger than himself, with a stronger will.

"You've freaked me out, tonight," he said as he looked away at the fireplace. "And you've helped me. I'm grateful. Now . . . I want to sleep." He held out his hand to her: again, a gesture he hadn't planned.

She assessed the look on his face, then stepped forward slowly and took his hand.

He raised himself from the chair to stand beside her. "You need to sleep, too." He released her hand.

PART IV

Wedding Photographs
Easter – Christmas 1972

No, let it not lull you, my dear, my dear,
But walk the water of the music in your hands.
Dance your heart to heaven's harbour
Through Jordan's darkness
To the blinding light of Galilee.
This sea becalmed will turn again
And you will ride the surf
From numbness into knowledge.

As always at holiday time, Margaret was thrilled to be at home for Easter. David and Martha had come over from Nantucket, and she loved to watch her mother's happy face as they all sat down at the table together for the first supper in a long time. Memories of her father were losing their edge after nine years, and she felt—especially with David's children there—as if things were almost complete. Almost.

The next morning, when she had come downstairs to make coffee, David handed her a letter without comment. In embossed script, the Massachusetts return address read *Julius McEnroe*; but she knew the writing immediately, and it wasn't McEnroe's.

Her heart knocking, she took the letter and shut herself in her old bedroom. Downstairs someone had turned up the television too loud, and Rebecca and Jonathan squabbled in her mother's livingroom. She hardly noticed.

He had written to her from Arcade. She saw the address first as she tore the envelope away. She remained where she had stopped when she first came in, by the bed, shut her eyes briefly, and inhaled deeply. *What if he's written about Ellie, as before? I don't want to go on thinking of her forever.* It was Easter; she had made a studied effort to free herself from the painful past, to immerse herself in the Fuller household, to identify herself with her family again. She wanted once and for all to put behind her the ache that flooded through her every time she thought of the McEnroes, every time they entered her life.

Or did she? She had thought so in the summer, too; if only the past had no way of shadowing the present, of consuming it. And the letter—here it lay in her hand. Manna: did she eat it, or toss it away? Did she want to begin again the whole wracking cycle of hope that fell through disappointment to grinding regret? No. But she had no choice, not if she believed her own dictum, *Love is an act of the will, a decision we make to follow.* She had in fact made a decision ten years before to read this letter.

> Margaret, I expect to be at home over Easter weekend. I couldn't get away at New Year's even though I wanted to and the clan would have liked me to. I thought you might be at Dedham, so I'm taking a chance writing you ahead of time. Could I see you Easter Day, or maybe on Saturday? I'll call you early on Saturday—around nine—to see when you're free.

She stared at his handwriting. The lines weren't straight, but the letters were firm and quite clear; her eyes ran over them easily. He had concluded the letter simply, "Don"; then below he'd added three more sentences in a lighter, more slanting hand, as if in hurried afterthought.

> If you aren't at Dedham after all, I'll try to reach you in Cambridge. I hope you can make it and aren't tied up both days.

She flopped onto her bed, rolled over and lay facedown on the rough fabric of the candlewick spread, her eyes shut and the letter still in her hand. Phrases from the letter sharpened into focus before the lens of her mind. *Could I see you . . . I'll call you . . . I hope you aren't tied up both days.* The shutter clicked across, and she saw them again: the strokes of his pen, the angle of the blue writing on the page.

I know how I want to read it, she thought. Her mind became leaden, resisting movement away from the wishful, wished-for interpretation. Her mouth curved into a smile. *Oh, if he's realized he wants me after all these years, I'll tease him to death.* Her body weakened as her mind tried to picture on an internal screen his coming for her after the decade's wait, his holding her as he had done only once—then in grief, not in love—in love, this time? But there her mental celluloid snapped off the reel; she could not see the film play itself out to a finale. She had discovered that the imagination was an inveterate liar; she couldn't trust it.

Then if he didn't want her, and he had said as much plainly enough only four months ago, what *did* he want? He had seldom replied to the letters she had written weekly until the previous summer. Why would he write now? He had driven her away when she came to him the year before. Why would he search for her now? He had said he could never give love to another human being. Would he have any to offer now? It made no sense. It made no sense at all unless he just needed a listener again, someone to whom he could air the crosscurrents of his feelings about Ellie. *And I won't do it,* she said savagely to herself, *not again. Not this time. That has to end.*

Five days. It was a long time to wait until he called. Perhaps she should call him at the farm, waiting for privacy, for a time when her mother and David and Martha would be out. She would refuse to see him, after all. If he could make no commitment in return for hers, then hers was void, meaningless, too. She needn't make him wait to find out; she could tell him before he left New York: *No, I don't want to see you. Leave me alone.*

She should make that call and have it over with.

She wouldn't, however. She was too weak, and hope

had sustained her beyond all the theoretical last chances she had set up for a relationship with him. *Just once more*, she told herself.

———

She always thought of Route 128 as a summer road: Wedgwood blue sky gleaming behind birches iridescent with fairyland greens and silvers; the steaming gray tarmac, hazy with exhaust, rising, curving around the granite bedrock, to ride too many travelers north to Gloucester, Rockport and the beaches. Now, though, there was no sign yet of the metallic birch leaves; and the April sky that spread over the empty highway, trees, and rocks was now more open, white with the crystal light of early spring. In its brittleness the trees bending in the wind looked drab: trunks and branches were merely white, not silver; brown, not brilliant. Lacking leaves, lacking the gentle blanket of snow, the woods had lost their mystery.

She turned her eyes from the woods to Don, beside her in an Oldsmobile. He sat silent, his eyes fixed on the road ahead; if he was aware of her scrutiny this time, he gave no sign of it. *Could I see you?* he had asked. He could see her, but he couldn't seem to talk to her.

She wanted to keep things light between them. She asked inconsequentially, "Where's your jeep?"

"I flew out," he said stiffly. "I thought Larry or Tony could use it."

"I somehow associate you with that jeep. This car is much more your father's style."

"Sure. It's his car . . . Is that a compliment or an insult? I can never tell with you." He lifted one hand from the wheel in an uncomfortable gesture. She smiled vaguely, wondering at his nervousness, and knowing a sense of strangeness in the situation. What were they doing together, he five hundred miles from home, and she in his father's car? Where were they going together, and why? The highway stretched out behind and before them, suspending them between past and future, known and unknown; artificially, not truly in linear time, they hung between one world and another, belonging in neither yet. The car pressed forward against the wind.

"Is that a compliment or not?" he repeated.

She tried to pinpoint her place between worlds. *Essex*, the last green road sign had said. Did that define their place, then?

"Maggie?"

She turned abruptly. "What?"

"You didn't hear a word I said."

"Sorry. I was . . ."

"Miles away. It doesn't matter. We weren't saying anything important, anyway."

They fell silent again, but this time she'd lost the unusual feeling of abstraction and found herself keenly attuned to him. He narrowed his eyes against the noon glare of the sky, and every so often he pushed back the shock of hair that habitually fell forward over his forehead. His face was drawn, less heavy than she remembered it. Presuming unhappiness and anxiety, she felt again the bittersweet impulse to put out her hand to him, to say, *I love you*. But she would deny the impulse and keep her hands inside the folds of her coat.

"It's not exactly walk-the-beach weather, is it?" he said grimly.

"No." She pictured the rattling dry grasses, the grainy sand pock-marked by the winter debris, the dunes carved by the wind, the sluggish ocean washing in and out, hundreds of feet below the boardwalk. "No, it's pretty enough . . . but still way too cold!"

"I think I said Gloucester, but how about Rockport? We could go for a walk . . ."

"If the wind doesn't blow us into the Atlantic."

"It's not that bad! C'mon, it's April, for heaven's sake. You'd rather not walk at all?" He looked slightly exasperated. "I thought you wanted to."

"Yes, I'll walk. That's why I put on all these clothes."

Most of the boutiques, galleries, stores and restaurants were still closed for the winter; the harbor was empty of boats. Scarves pulled over their mouths, and hats pulled down over their ears, they walked slowly up the narrow street and finally onto Bearskin Neck.

He strolled along with his hands pushed deep into his pockets, and she walked beside him, a few feet away, swinging her arms and feeling exhilarated by the wind and by his nearness. It seemed natural to be with him; more than that, it seemed *right* to be with him. Even though he could not relax with her, she could relax now. All the tension, the five days of anticipation—they had dissolved. He did not look at her at all, and she did not need to look at him to see him. Instead she looked at the water. It was slate-blue and turbulent, slapping the rocks, then slipping back with a long hiss.

They came toward the end of the promontory. "Let's turn back," he said over the wind.

Is this all he wants to do? Walk without talking? She flashed a quick look at him and caught him watching her. She blurted, "Did you want to talk about Ellie?"

He didn't answer immediately. "Yes—no. In a way."

She smiled at him uncertainly.

"In fact I think I wanted to talk about myself."

Her eyebrows rose. She watched him with interest, though he still wouldn't meet her eyes. The wind had heightened the color of his face; his brows were down low over his eyes in a frown. "Go ahead," she said, hoping she sounded encouraging.

He quickened his pace slightly but was apparently unaware of it. "I haven't been able to sleep well . . . since the funeral. I've been thinking of Ellie. I can't help it. I'm afraid she's really dead."

She looked at him strangely, bemused. *Really dead?* "What else is there to think?" she probed.

He shrugged.

"I don't believe in an afterlife, do you?" she asked.

"I'm not sure." He looked at her briefly, something akin to embarrassment tingeing his expression. "I've had hours awake to think about it. Hours awake at night. Hours in the barn when I don't have to think about scraping the floor or filling the mangers—I just do it. It's hard to explain, but sometimes when I'm in the middle of some routine chore like that, a real terror comes over me."

She stopped in the middle of the street. "What do you mean?" Her voice was anxious. Had his sister's death wounded him so—so deeply that he couldn't function any more?

"It's difficult to . . . I mean, I stop and ask myself, 'Why am I doing this? So I can do it again tomorrow? What's the point of it all?' "

She frowned. "You're unhappy?"

He shook his head and faced her. "No, not in the least. I love the farm. It needs a lot of work—" He threw out his hands. "It's still a mess. But that's not the problem at all."

"Then what?" she asked gently.

"I wonder why I do what I do, that's all. In those moments, and sometimes it's over in just a second— quicker than I can tell about it—life seems pointless, empty. I'm afraid I'm getting inhuman. I get scared I'll dry up, somehow."

"No, not you, Don," she said with positive urgency. All the same, she was bewildered and somewhat frightened by what he was trying to say.

He turned away and began to walk fast again, a little ahead of her so that she had to hurry to catch up.

"No, you don't know . . . you don't understand what I'm saying."

"I'm *trying* to," she pleaded.

"Life gets to be just a husk. Like sick corn with no kernels forming. I can't explain it, I guess. *Soulless.* Have you any idea what I'm talking about?"

She struggled with the weight of words. He was trying to say something that could only partly be said. "A little, I think."

He stopped again. "Do you?" he said heavily. "Do you *really*, Maggie?" His forehead had puckered.

She felt a tightening in her throat. He was far from her in a dark place. She did not believe in an afterlife, but she was far happier than he at the moment. She nodded silently, not trusting her voice.

"I think about the hideous way Ellie died, and I've gotta ask myself, '*Why?* What's the point?' And the only answer I can come up with isn't an answer at all—that I don't want my own life to be as void as hers was. If there's an afterlife, and if we have souls, then I want to find mine."

Her eyes filled, and she felt the tears push out. "Don, your life'll never be like Ellie's." She took off her gloves, reached for a tissue, and mopped at her face. The wind stung her bare hands. "You're truly alive," she murmured, "or you could never be a good farmer. Everything you do is an affirmation of life, Don."

He put his hands on her shoulders and drew her to him. The movement was as unexpected as it was sudden, and her whole being, her whole body, seemed to sigh with relief. He leaned over somewhat, holding her head against his lapels. She tilted her head slightly so that she could hear him; he had lowered his voice. "I hope you do understand," he said. "I guess I need someone to understand. Oh, Maggie."

In answer she put her arms round him. The immediate moment was everything, the past and the future nothing. Warmth began to seep into her.

"You're a sweet woman."

She did not want to move, but he eased apart from her. She wanted to see whether the light in his eyes was equal to the light that he had just lit in her, but she saw none yet; and she realized, painfully, that they were going to walk on as if nothing had happened.

"I don't want my life to be meaningless," he went on. "I guess that's all I'm trying to say. So I go back to things I remember from childhood—our youth group at the church, school, whatever—and ask, how do we find ourselves? How do we find our souls?"

She couldn't answer. She became aware now of how cold she was; inside her boots her toes had grown numb. At last she said, "I don't know. But I do know you won't ever live—or die—like Ellie."

"I'm not sure." He said it morosely, but then rushed on. "She lived for herself, and I've done the same. Maybe that's the answer. Maybe we find ourselves by taking care of others. I've always looked out for myself, always wanted to do things my way. I still do. But maybe that's the fault, right there."

She knew he was utterly serious, but some irreverent elf in her suddenly wanted to break free. "Don—let's talk about it some more. But right now I'm bitterly cold. How about taking care of *me*, at least?"

His eyes crinkled at the corners, but he didn't actually smile. "I want to," he said.

Something in the pit of her stomach turned over. She had been hungry; now she felt sick, tense, excited—all at once. She laughed nervously. "I mean, let's get out of this wind—please?"

He nodded, but she thought he still seemed absent as they found a place to get warm: a restaurant the size of a living room; draughty, with wooden floors that creaked as they went in. Half a dozen circular tables with round-seated cafe chairs, as in an old-fashioned soda fountain, filled the place. Otherwise, it was deserted; not even a cashier or waitress stood behind the counter.

"You sure this place is open?" she asked doubtfully.

"Yup. Smell the soup?"

She wrinkled her nose. "I don't know. I'm numb to the end of my nose."

He grinned back from the other side of the small table where they sat. A girl eventually waited on them, bringing coffee, clam chowder, and thick wedges of bread. Don ate fast, not looking up for a while; he seemed to withdraw again, to be thinking hard.

Usually she would have waited for him, let him start the conversation again; this time, she sensed it was different, that he wanted a cue from her. What had he said? *How do we find ourselves?* No, it was *souls*; he had started to use religious language.

"I think you're probably right," she ventured at last, "that we have to find ourselves in reference to others." She thought of Martha's kindness.

He looked up in evident surprise.

"I am sure of some ways we *can't* find ourselves," she went on.

"Expound, Margaret. I'm listening." He sat back. She looked up, expecting a smile that never came, then unconsciously turned the handle of her soup spoon around and around. She hadn't found time to think about these things for a long time. "I'm convinced we don't find ourselves the way I was taught to. Or maybe it was just the way I expected to, based on what I understood when I was a kid."

"What d'you mean?"

"I mean, I love my family and everything, but I don't define myself by my parents. Things were so unhappy between them—for my mother especially. And I don't want to follow that pattern. I haven't learned much about myself from watching them."

He stirred in his chair. "You sound a little arrogant today."

"No, it's just . . . I used to think I'd grow up a carbon

copy of my mother. And I didn't, of course." She broke off, half laughing. "Any more than you grew up a copy of your father. Though I see some similarity. So there has to be a different way of finding yourself."

Don said softly. "God help us if we grow up like our parents . . . But what are the other ways that wouldn't work or didn't work—for you?"

"The church." She looked up. Was he going to be offended? "I had the mystical idea for years that I could find out everything I needed to know—about myself, the world, God—if only I could make sense of what happened at communion, of what came out in the preaching every time my parents made me go to church, or in school."

"You'd find your soul, too, you thought?"

She was surprised again by his earnestness. She wanted to laugh it off and get out of the conversation altogether. Even talking about Ellie was better than this. But she couldn't disregard the demanding look in his eyes. He expected a genuine answer, not a flip joke in return. "I *thought* so," she said reluctantly. "But what's a soul? Who knows? I sure don't. Can't we talk about *selves* instead?"

He shrugged. "They're just words."

"And another thing—" She frowned, breaking off. "There's a fine line, I guess, between believing you find yourself in others, and believing you find yourself in friends. I don't believe I find myself in friends. That's another 'used to.'" She looked down, unwilling to reveal the depth of her hurt. She did not know whether he was looking at her or not, and at the moment she didn't dare to know.

"Bitterness gets ugly, Margaret. I understand more than you think."

She moved her head sharply. His eyes were gentle. She said, "Thanks. I don't want to talk about myself, though. Not now, anyway. I guess if I've found myself—"

She frowned and smiled at once. "It all gets a bit beyond words, doesn't it?" He nodded, so she continued, "If I've found myself—found fulfillment—whatever you want to say . . . it's in helping others who are suffering. They might be friends—or not." She moved her shoulders in self-deprecation. "Not that I've ever really sacrificed a thing. But I'll do anything I can for a child in my class who's having a rough time at home, or . . ." She stopped, thinking of Ellie. She and Don were moles, blindly groping in the dark for an understanding neither of them had, an understanding she wasn't sure she even wanted. It was all too painful.

"What about God?" Don asked abruptly.

"Oh, *He's* not here," she answered with certainty. She scrutinized his face to gauge his mood. She had talked too much; she needed to listen to him now. But why did he keep asking questions that elicited answers she couldn't toss back in a light half-sentence?

"But how can you be sure?" he persisted. Leaning forward over the table, he broke off a piece of bread and dipped it in his soup bowl. "What d'you mean, 'He's not here'? Does that mean He's somewhere else?"

"Are you kidding, Don?" she shifted uncomfortably. "Since when do you talk this way?"

He looked pained. "I need to today. Don't act like that. Everyone asks these questions sometime."

"Then you're not kidding." She sighed, mildly exasperated. "I don't think God exists."

"What if He *does*? What if He were sitting here with us now?" Don put out his big hand and rattled a vacant chair nearby. "What would He tell us?"

"About finding yourself?"

"Yes. I've decided He exists. Unless He exists, everything that exists and happens is just a cruel joke. And since I can't live with that possibility, I have to believe He exists. So next I ask, well, if God exists, He must have something to tell us about our problems. But *what*?"

"How should I know?"

"I think He'd say something like what you said the night we sat up and talked. Remember?"

She swallowed hard. "Yes, I remember very well . . . but what in particular?"

"About love being a commitment. I've thought about it ever since we talked. We're saying almost the same thing, you and I. You say you want to help people who suffer, and that's how you find yourself. You make a commitment. You love another person." He stopped. "I'm saying it, too. Only it's a new thought to me."

She could hardly bear to look at him. The blood rose into her face. She couldn't believe in God, though she could believe in Don.

His voice became soft and low. "I think if God were sitting here with us, the two of us—" He held out his arms for a moment, over the table, but then dropped his hands out of sight onto his knees. "He'd say, 'Love's a *gift*. It's something from me. So learn to love one another. That's how you find your soul.' "

She began to feel warm inside, as if light had broken and burned away some of the shadow. Was Don falling in love with her, or with God—or both? She hadn't said "love," only "help." "Love"—that was his word. His word!

Grudgingly, she said, "It sounds as if you've gone back to the church."

He shrugged again. "I've gone to church a couple of times, at least. The pastor knows I'm new—doesn't know I've been away from it for sixteen years. Anyway, it doesn't matter what he thinks."

"But you said—"

"God. *Directly*. Not the clergy. We don't need ministers or priests to find answers. You're right about that, though they can help."

She put down her spoon. She had barely tasted the chowder, and the sense of strangeness in the entire conversation, in the entire day—enveloped her again. She brooded, waiting for him to begin again, and trying from the tangle of words to recall what he had said about love a few moments before. There was something more personal in his tone then, as if he were trying to get something across that he'd never had to say before.

"You look so troubled," he said.

She smiled up quickly. "This is such a weird talk we're having."

"And I'm being clumsy, as usual."

"No, you say things I think and can't say. You're pretty articulate for a farmer."

They both laughed, and he put out his hands again, across the table toward hers.

"No, Maggie. I've bungled this from start to finish. You sit there so cool and quiet. I don't know how to say what I want to."

"You've done fine so far." Tentatively she dropped her hands into his. They were rough, larger than she realized.

"I was trying to say that when I think back over the kind of love you've offered me all this time—a rare commodity—I know I'd like to learn that kind of love, myself. For you. So I could love you—more than I do now."

She shut her eyes, then opened them. His eyes were warm and intense, frightening. "You want me, then?"

He hesitated, but only slightly. "Yes. I want you. You were right. Everybody was right. I need you. You have all the qualities I wish I had. And I'll love you more, yet, before we're through."

Joy leapt up in her, but it shriveled immediately. "All this . . . since Ellie died? Aren't you just on the rebound? No, that's not the right way to say it . . . your own sister . . ." Desperately she wanted to believe what he said.

"I don't blame you for thinking that. I've never done a thing for you. But that'll change, if you'll let me change it." He folded her hands inside his own.

"I don't know, Don. This is all . . . so strange. I don't believe in sudden changes of heart . . . religious, emotional . . . any."

"But you're forgetting something." He was still looking at her with that direct, gentle look. It was new to her; it made her dazed. "What you said yourself, and not long ago either. You might not mind having something flung back in your face for a change."

"What, then?" She frowned.

"It has little to do with feelings. *You* said it. I've turned it over and over in my mind for weeks . . . however long it's been. Commitment. You made and re-made one to me for years. At first I thought it was cute. Then I thought it was immature, childish. Even six months ago I thought so."

The words hurt her, but she knew he hadn't finished. She waited, the light burning more steadily inside her.

"Now I don't think so," he said, smiling. "To love another person—? That's the greatest act of courage on earth. It makes you vulnerable, but it makes you *human*. I know you love me. Part of it *is* feeling—right—?"

She nodded, grateful for his fresh perception, but still too dazed to answer.

He went on, smiling. "But it's an act. It's something you *do*, I mean. Something you decide to do, an act of the mind and will. You decided years ago. But I just didn't grow up that fast. Didn't know I needed to." His eyes darkened in seriousness. "All that's happened is that I've discovered what you've known for years, that I can't find my soul unless I give myself up a little. The only two ways I know are to go back to God, and to tell the woman who has loved me most of her life that I can love her, too."

Her mouth trembled. His face swam before her eyes, and she could not believe any of it. She wanted to push

away everything that stood between them—and be lost
in him, against him, though even in that impulse she
found something to mistrust. It was an impulse almost
like emotional and psychological suicide. She wanted
him, loved him as never before, but she had her own
identity to keep intact: it was what she had to give him;
it was all she had to give him; it was the most she could
give anyone. Somehow, she had to learn how to give
herself, to give love, but to give them in integrity, not
betraying her own identity.

At last, she managed an answer, but her voice
sounded strangled. "You're snowing me completely."
She laughed weakly. "This was the last thing I thought
you'd ever, ever say."

He grinned widely. "Oh, I'm glad I can still surprise
you." He released her hands.

She felt a connection between them, a new understanding they'd never shared. "So am I." She laughed
again, but her jaw felt tight with nervousness.

He shook his head. "This will sound like a reaction,
something you're afraid of . . . but I'm trying to say that
I can't sell out my soul as Ellie did; I can't short-change
myself like that. I want to find whatever's worthwhile
before it gets away from me."

She knew what he meant. "I don't think . . . I'll ever
be looking toward the church, though, the way you—"
She veered between exhilaration and doubt.

"Don't be so sure. Maggie, I want someone with me.
You're the only person I can think of who could be
there."

Warm, hungry for every word he was saying now,
she felt the pull toward him, the pull toward the con-
clusion—and the beginning—of a relationship she had
wanted all her adult life. "Oh, Don, if only—"

"Maggie, I'll never get it out in fancy words in some
romantic place with wine and roses and candlelight—
but—will you, could you marry me?"

Her hands flew up to her face.

"Another surprise. But it's more a surprise for me than for you, isn't it?" He was laughing, though his eyes looked very serious. "I mean . . ."

She laughed back. "Oh, I know exactly what you mean! Marry you? That's absurd, Don. Utterly absurd." Her voice was loud. She wanted to dance on the table tops or run on the beach.

She saw him waver between laughter and—anxiety. "Maggie? Sometimes you're so skittish I don't know how to interpret—"

"Utterly absurd!" she repeated. "But utterly, completely wonderful."

They dissolved into wild laughter and leaned across the table to each other, arms and hands reaching and touching, faces close together.

"Let's get out of here," Don said. "I want to take you home. I'll cook you a celebratory meal in my mother's kitchen, and then—"

They went out into the cold again to walk back to the car. The wind blew behind them. He kept his arm closely around her, but after a few yards stopped and bent his face to hers.

"I'm sure this is right," he said. "Do you believe me?"

"Not entirely. It's all—too sudden." She thought fleetingly of her father, who would probably never know Don well. She couldn't bear it if in the end Don rejected her as her father had rejected and abandoned her mother. But now was not the time to think of that.

His eyes were only inches away, deep blue, full of life. "I'm only sorry it took me so long—but please do believe me."

She saw his eyes half close and his mouth coming nearer to hers. Not waiting, she reached up, felt the warmth of his breath on her face, then his kiss, full on her mouth. She gave, and he gave back, so that everything seemed to drain out of her, and she was left laughing and breathless. She broke away from him.

"Took so long? It sure did. Why did I pick a slow old farmer, anyhow?"

"Not old," he said, and he moved his thumb slowly against her mouth. "Don't say that. And not slow. You'll see."

May

Pulling on an anorak, Don left his desk. He had been plotting dates for fitting and drilling, and he was hungry for the open air.

It hit him hard, a stiff breeze coming south off the Lakes. The same breeze that had brought snow only a few weeks ago. The heifers and cows would have to come in tonight. The spring was cool this year, late in coming, and though they could pasture outside in the daytime now, they would have to stay in at night a little longer yet.

Waving to Tony, who was working in the barn, he went down to the wooded end of the south pasture. One of the cows was freshening, surrounded by a crowd of curious onlookers, all of them bellowing loudly. He shoved the others away and ran his hand over the cow's side.

"C'mon, girl, push it out now. You can do it." The cow roared, lowering her head, and sweat streaked the black and white hide. He watched her. She was doing fine, wouldn't need his assistance.

He looked back over his shoulder as he drove the others toward the barn. The calf was dropping. "Go on, go on you!" He urged the lead cow forward. "Take them in, girl."

He went back to the mother, now bent over and licking a calf sprawling wet and black in the long grass. "That's it—you're all done, you brave girl." He patted and massaged her. She ignored him, nudging the calf to its tottering legs. *A bull calf. Veal by the autumn,*

251

poor so-and-so. "Never mind. I'll give you a little peace while I sort out the others. Get yourselves cleaned up and I'll come back for you both later."

He always talked to the cows. He had done that even at college, where some of the others, those destined for big agri-business, had laughed at him. A few of the cows had names; perhaps Maggie would give other names. But now he must get up to the barn.

He stalled the heifers first. Their pens were wider than the stanchions, and the young animals milled and pushed against each other, butting and lowing, competing for the manger. Then he tied the cows into their stanchions; they were docile and polite, watching him with soft eyes.

Tony and Larry had already filled the mangers with corn silage, so Don swept feed grain on top and moved the dumping station into the alleyway behind the first cow. He still hated the stanchions, but he was proud of the vacuum lines he had installed to speed up the milking, prouder still that at the last dairy cooperative inspection he had been complimented on the cleanliness of the new milking parlor and bulk tank. Except for steady munching and hooves shuffling on the concrete, the barn quieted down, so he turned on the radio; WGR55 blared across the stanchions. A few heads lifted, and a few tails swished; the cows liked music— any kind. He went to work quickly, washing down the first cow, drying her teats and attaching the milking machine. The pump surged into life, and milk flowed slowly into the lines. He looked more closely: *Daphne, the slow one, no wonder.* So he began to scrape the floor further along the barn as he waited for her to finish. That was the next project, to get an electric barn cleaner . . .

The rhythm of news and music on the radio matched the rhythm of scraping and milking in the barn. Outside the open doors the John Deere disk drill pulled up. Larry jumped down and came in. "How's it going?"

"Fine. Give me a hand, will you? I'll need some scraping done."

"Sure. Listen, I just finished the oats down by the creek."

"Thanks. Good thing, too. We're running late."

"Yes, but it's too cold this year. I don't like the feel of the weather at all. It's May already, but you wouldn't know it."

Don moved the dumping station and wiped down the next cow. He was thinking about Margaret, not really listening. Larry would talk all evening if he answered him. He grunted, leaning against the cow, and listened to the steady, throbbing suction of the pump instead. Larry shrugged and began pulling down fresh bedding to where the floor was cleaned.

Don worked steadily. It was usually a two-hour job at this time of year when part of the herd was dry, but things went faster this evening. He would call Maggie after he'd made some supper.

"Want me to get the bales down for you?" Larry shouted, this time right behind him, not to be ignored.

"No. Don't bother. Your wife'll be looking for you. Better get yourself home, hadn't you?" The job was nearly finished, and he liked the end of the day alone.

"Yeah. Guess so. Tony's gone. I'll just put the drill away. See you tomorrow, okay?"

He nodded. "Thanks, sure. I want to get started on fertilizing all the small grains tomorrow. We'll have to go up to Agway first."

"Right, then." Larry went.

Don finished the last cow and leaned against the door post, surveying the whole barn. It was good. The cows munched and shifted, flicked their tails. The heifers hung over their stall and stared at him. A few flies—heralds of more to come—flew aimlessly in and out.

Insecticide, he noted to himself, and lit a cigarette. For several minutes he remained quite still, smoking, looking round the barn, consciously letting the tight muscles relax. *Ten years*, he thought. *This was worth the wait*. Certainly, he had to get contractors in to wire and plumb the house properly before Maggie came, and to rewire the barn. Certainly he had overgrazed land to restore, and the inevitable cases of mastitis to treat— but it was all good. *If only Ellie had seen it.*

He flicked off the radio, ground the cigarette butt into the gutter and climbed up to the loft above the heifers where the bales were stored, throwing down the next day's supply. As he threw the bales he watched his own hands: ringless, knuckles whitening as he held the twine and braced to throw them. Hands Maggie had held and kissed. Hands he would hold and touch her with in a few weeks. *Ah, God, what have I done to deserve her love?* He could not fathom it.

———

The radio intoned news of the latest state primaries. McGovern was running well, but Nixon looked stronger. So much for the Democrats! *A good cook*, she had called him. *I'm glad she's not watching me now.* The spaghetti in the pan looked lukewarm, uninviting, no doubt because the stove was burning low today— deliberately so. He would let it go out soon and bring in the Allegany County gas men to install a proper cooker for the summer, but for now he must bank it up into a roaring fire.

He fed the fire with wood split down in the south pasture last year and continued stirring until the tomato sauce began to bubble up and splatter his hand. The food smelled hot, began to catch a little on the bottom of the pan; his mouth watered.

He looked down, suddenly. Were his jeans too near the fire? There was a smell of something singed. No, his legs were warm, but not toasting. He went on stirring.

The smell of heat, of smoke, irritated his nose so that he sneezed. It floated across the room but was invisible. Frowning, he bent and poked at the wood and shut the fire down slightly before pouring the spaghetti into a bowl. Now the aroma of tomatoes, ground beef and onions filled the room, and he began to eat.

He ate quickly, suddenly remembering the cow that had delivered two hours before. During autumn last year, before they came in for the winter, a cow had wandered away from the herd to give birth alone among the brushwood. Cows behaved uncharacteristically when they were freshening, and this one had impaled herself on an old roll of barbed wire among the scrub—relic of his predecessor's weariness and old age—and had almost bled to death before Don found her with the calf. He should get out there and check.

Leaving his plate on the floor, he grabbed his anorak again. Rain fell hard on his head and shoulders as soon as he pulled the door behind him and stepped into the yard, so he reached back inside for his cap. The farm kitchen was warm, smelling of supper, but once he walked outside again, the stench of smoke bit into his nostrils. He stopped, listening, fear tightening his chest, his eyes darting everywhere.

Wreaths of black smoke curled and rolled from the roof of the double barn. He started forward, then stopped again, panic seizing him, shouting with fear. But his own voice was lost in the hideous crackling of smoke, and—worst of all—the screaming of the animals.

No time to think. No time to call the firemen.

He plunged into the barn. The smoke was pouring from the hayloft, right above the heifers. But if he let them out first, they would stampede. He must risk them for now and get the cows out.

He ran for the lead cow and wrestled frantically with her chain. She rolled her eyes, lashing out with her back legs and wrenching the chain so hard that it was almost impossible to free her.

At last she was loose, cantering for the open door and bellowing in terror. The others answered as she skittered past, the smoke billowing overhead.

Moving now with his body bent, a wet towel from the sterilizing sink around his face, he crawled from one cow to the other and sent them after the lead cow with a smack on the rump. Some were too stupefied to move; others too terrified to stand still, and by the time they were all free, he was shaking, crying with the effort of pulling, shoving, fighting with the cows.

Above him the smoke rolled black and menacing, and first tiles, then timbers from the roof began to thud down around him. Where were Larry and Tony now, when he needed them?

The farm was barely his. The wedding to come. Money owed. Insurance hardly arranged. Plans and dreams: free stalls, expanding herd. The heifers—prize-winning heifers. *The heifers. Oh, God in heaven!*

He ran back into the middle of the barn, but the towel around his mouth had dried and was choking him. The smoke seared his lungs. A roof beam crashed down in front of the heifers, and they bellowed in terror. He pushed forward blindly. *Must get the catch open. The heifers. Must get the heifers out.*

Then there was a roaring sound, and for a second he thought he might be losing consciousness in the stinking, foul smoke. But no, the fire had taken hold, and the hayloft, the roof were now a blossom of fire, red and orange debris raining down around him, on him.

The raging flames licked toward him. Instinct took over, and he fled for the doors. The cows were bunched together in the corner of the yard by the silos; their heads down, some slumped in the muck, and rain pouring everywhere. They looked lost, absurd, and he flung himself down among them, weeping like a child on their broad, heaving backs, smelling their warmth, the singed hay and hide. Behind him the fire roared and the heifers were dying. He could not move. *Where are you now, God?*

He looked down at his hands again, clinging to the matted hair of one of the cows. The skin was raw and blistered, smutty from the smoke. For the first time, he was aware of pain. He tried to block it out, rubbing his palms against the warm, wet hides, but it only grew worse.

He raised his head. Sodden clouds raced overhead, and darkness was falling, but the sky was orange with the fire. Someone was shouting from far away, and he heard the sound of a truck and of boots running, sliding on the muck by the back porch.

Dazed, he focused through the smoke and saw two figures at the door, pushing in, one shouting at the other.

"Call the fire department, for God's sake. See if you can find a phone."

He didn't know the voice, but he wanted to say, "It's okay—just inside the door. On the desk."

Then another voice. "Can you see anyone? It's an inferno."

Then the first. "No way, it's going like hell in August in there."

He wanted to say, "Go. Never mind the barn. It's too late for the heifers. Look over here. These cows. I'm here. Over here." But instead he felt the cows, the smoke, the yard tilting away as the barn collapsed and raged behind him.

———

"You're very lucky," someone was saying.

The darkness and smoke had gone. His eyes were

burned not by the fire but by glaring whiteness all around him, his nose assailed not by smoke but by antiseptic. "How you got those cows out, I'll never know."

His tongue felt cracked, glued to his palate. He groaned, and everything came back with hideous clarity. *Lucky?* He had lost his heifers, his barn, and his equity. Where was he?

Had he spoken? His tongue did not seem to be moving, but a woman was answering him. "You're all right now. In the emergency room, you are. Can you move your head and see me?"

He turned toward the voice. A Filipino doctor in a white coat was bending over him, her apricot skin drawn into lines of concern, a syringe in her hand. "Keep still now. I'm going to shoot you up a bit." He lay still and felt the needle in his buttock. "Sorry about this. Not much dignity. There . . . That's good." She stepped aside and picked up a clipboard. Raising her voice she opened a white curtain and said, "You can come in now." Strangers—one in uniform with a note pad, another in filthy farm clothes.

The doctor spoke to him again, "Who are you?"

He tried to speak and found he could, though his voice was clogged and guttural. "McEnroe." He shut his eyes, his father swimming up under his eyelids briefly. "*Donald* McEnroe. Just bought the Davies place. Up by Arcade."

A voice—the farmer's perhaps—supplied the rest. "Er—yes, believe I've seen him up in the Agway. Never spoke to him, though. I knew someone new had taken the Davies farm. Poor idiot. Looks like one of these back-to-the-earth types. Doesn't know dimes' worth 'bout farming. Burns his own barn down the first spring."

Another voice, male, shocked. "Scram, buster. Getting the guy in the ambulance don't qualify you to mouth off in front of him like that. Get your backside outta here before I shove it out."

Don opened his eyes again and met the doctor's. A glass of water with a straw was being held out to him, and he tried to sit up and take it. "You're okay, you know," she said. "Very lucky, though. The smoke would have got you if they hadn't got you out when they did. It's just your hands."

He choked. The water dribbled down his chin and onto his shirt. He said slowly, "They didn't get me out. I got myself out. Not the heifers, though."

"No." What else could she say, after all?

"I'll need to ask you a bunch of questions, if you can handle them." The male voice again.

Someone else pushed pillows down behind him and cranked the bed half upright under his head. He shut his eyes again, weary beyond weariness. The clipboard and notepad rustled. Man's inhumanity to man: forms to fill in. Couldn't he be left alone? Couldn't he sleep?

"I'll try."

"First of all—what about your family? They couldn't find anyone in the house. Everyone away?"

Maggie, oh, poor Maggie. "No, I'm alone."

"No one we can call for you?"

"Yes, the woman I'm going to marry in a few weeks. My father. You'd better call them both." *And the cows. Who will milk them now, and where?*

Then the questions began in earnest. But his own questions clamored even louder than theirs, and under the white waffle-weave blanket his hands burned inside their bandages.

Margaret came out of the store weighed down with the usual pile of workbooks and a box of invitation cards. She would be making all the arrangements herself, he had warned her, and she had better get used to that. *Married to the land?* Yes, but she would be married to him.

Above her head Walt and Peter were roughhousing on the floor. The ceiling shuddered under their thumps. Cindy was singing an Italian folksong, and outside her window a car engine was idling loudly as two men shouted at each other across the street. *What a noise!*

She poured herself a cider and shed her jacket. The workbooks would have to wait, she decided. Though the invitations would not need to go out for a couple of weeks, they were far more appealing than the children's smudged printing and quaint drawings. She stood still in the kitchen and drew breath slowly, still not believing it all, shutting her eyes. Don's face, tender with love and longing for her, was inches from her own again. *I love you, Maggie. Can you arrange the wedding for July, when school's out and after the first hay cutting's done? First thing that month, if you can do it. I love you, and I want you . . .*

Then she saw McEnroe's face breaking into laughter, heard Don's acknowledgement that for once his father had been right all along. And why hadn't he listened?

All the old photographs were brought out in celebration, even the ones of Ellie, and their news acted like oil, healing the wounds of sorrow and bitterness. Somehow Ellie in her guise as a fifteen-year-old Gabriel had laughed with them, and the images of her death faded a little in the brightness of their laughter.

Margaret smiled and sat down with the invitation cards spilled out across the table. She began a list. *Mrs. Laura Fuller, Mr. Daniel Fuller . . . will he come, I wonder? Mr. and Mrs. Julius McEnroe, Dr. and Mrs. David Fuller, Rebecca, Jonathan, and Matthew, Mr. and Mrs. Ray Hammond . . .* It grew longer: Don's friends from Vermont. Her own friends from the school and the racquet club. McEnroe's friends from the State House and Bedford. Her mother's friends from Dedham. Her own friends from Bishop O'Rourke's and from college. The cards would take longer than she expected.

Then the telephone rang and stopped her.

———————

Don would not let her hold his hands. They felt like footballs at the end of his wrists: swollen, useless great lumps of seared meat. He kept them resolutely under the sheets and stared at her hungrily. Her eyes were huge, ringed with sleeplessness; she wore a cotton dress that was gathered round the shoulders and under her breasts, a dark green floral print that showed off the beginning of a faint tan on her neck and arms, and shapely legs below the hemline.

He shut his eyes briefly once his survey of her was complete and sighed. "I hope miniskirts never go out."

"Don McEnroe! I *thought* you were having a good look." She flushed, laughing.

"And why not? If a guy can't lust after his fiancee, what hope is there for the world?"

He smelled a slight waft of perfume as she leaned toward him.

"Don—?"

He opened his eyes again. He had never seen her so serious. "What?"

"What? Is that all you can say, for goodness sake? What are we going to do?"

He shut his eyes again and listened to the laziness of his own voice drawling back an answer. "Well, right now, you can take a peek out in the hallway, and if you don't see any of those cute nurses, you can get right under the sheet and give me a cuddle."

"Don! Come on! I want to *know*!" Her voice slid dangerously from cool alto to infuriated soprano, and he flicked his eyes open again. He needed her to laugh a little, play along a little. He could not face seriousness yet.

"Maggie." He knew he sounded stern. "I don't know what we're going to do. All I know is I want to get out of this hospital and home. I want to see what Larry and Tony are doing with my cows, and I want to talk to half the bureaucrats in Western New York." He stopped, seeing alarm on her face, and changed tack. "Oh, and I want to make sure you've got a wedding lined up. Have you?"

She waved one hand impatiently, and her hair flopped forward, brushing his face. He would have reached for it if his hands weren't swathed and burning. "Of course I have," she said. "I was going to tell you that last night. But somehow none of the wedding plans matter very much. I'm not leaving you. No way." She had caught the early commuter flight to Buffalo. *One-way ticket*, she'd said.

He groaned. "No, don't. Please don't."

"Then," she went on gently. "You must tell me what I have to do. Can you try? The surgeon said you'd be out by tomorrow, but you'll be an armchair farmer for a while. I'll have to learn fast."

He found his lips cracking into a grin. "You'll learn more than farming if you don't get back to your job in a few days, Maggie."

She tossed her head back, coloring, but there was nothing coy about her. "That's what *you* think, lover-boy."

"Okay, okay." He shrugged, then winced. His mind began to work fast. "You can start by getting me all the spring water and juice you can carry out of the grocery store. You can call my insurance man—the police have already been on to them. You can check on Larry and Tony. No—" He was thinking aloud now. "No, not a good idea. Not the best way for them to meet the lady of the house. You can find out, though, whether the cow that freshened last evening is doing okay—she was away from the herd. I left her—"

"*Freshened?*"

He nodded. "Yup. First word in your new farm vocabulary book. Worse than second grade it'll be. 'Delivered.' 'Calved.' All the same. Got it?"

She blinked, seemed unable to answer.

"Then you can ring the financing people. There's a folder in my desk . . . The equity's gone up in smoke, I guess, and I may not get a refinancing. It's bad news all round."

There were tears in her eyes, but he went on, more slowly now. "Oh, and you can find out if any of my heifers made it. I doubt if they did, not unless—"

She was shaking her head. "They didn't."

It was his turn to blink and stare. "How do you know?"

"When I came into the hospital lobby this morning there were some people standing around talking about it." She put her hand on his shoulder, and he turned his face and kissed it. "Apparently you could see the fire up on the hills, that's what they said."

He twisted his mouth and remembered the man in the emergency room. "Fame at last. Now everyone from here to Buffalo will know about McEnroe, failed farmer from Boston, millionaire's son, can't even keep his heifers intact for the first year, let alone his bank account."

She leaned down again and put her head next to his on the pillow, but he still couldn't bring himself to lift his hands and hold her. He lay passive and miserable.

"Don—no, you're wrong. They were all sorry for you. Please don't get bitter. I'm here now, for what that's worth."

He looked into her clouded eyes. "It's worth a lot. You'll be a tonic."

She was pushing the sheets back now.

"What's going on?"

"Your hands. I want to see your hands."

"No!" He jack-knifed his knees so that the sheets were trapped between the bandaged paws and his thighs. "No—don't."

"Yes, I will, too. I'll kiss them better." She wrenched the bedding back, and he was too tired, suddenly, to resist. "You thought your luck was changing, didn't you?"

There was a gleam in her eye, and his emotions swung again, erratic as a light meter on a spring day. "Like heck I did, you little temptress. Watch out, now. These hands are big as boxing gloves. I might crack you one on the head and have my wicked way with you."

"You should be so lucky," she laughed. "C'mon, let me see them."

Fear suddenly took hold of him. He couldn't banter or laugh any more, remembering the raw skin. What if he needed months of skin grafts before he could work again? Panic gripped him, but subsided instantly. They wouldn't be letting him go if that was the case. Dehydration and second degree burns; that was all. But how could he love Maggie if his hands were ruined? He watched her face with a sick, hollow feeling in his stomach.

Somehow she understood his mood. "It's all right. Oh, Don—you're so beautiful." She kissed his wrists and then dropped her mouth lightly in the concave of the bandages where his palms were.

Dressed only in blue hospital pajama bottoms, he found himself shivering suddenly and unexpectedly. But it wasn't just the cold. "Here, Maggie, you're killing me. Pull up those sheets, will you, and leave a guy in peace."

She eased the covers into place and moved back to the chair where she had first been sitting. They looked at each other for a long moment without words.

"Listen, will you do me a few favors?"

Her face was brighter again. "Anything you want."

"You'll need transportation while you're here. The keys of the jeep should be on my desk, and there's all those calls I asked you to make. Find out all you can. Then would you call the guy who was my adviser at tech? We'll need help, badly, and he can give it."

"He is—"

"Mark King. You'll find him in the Springfield directory. And, now, could you please pass me that cup?" He shifted. The mattress was stiff and made him numb, and he hated having to depend on someone else even for a drink through a straw.

She lifted the cup and held it. "No making eyes at those nurses while I'm out, okay?"

He had described the farmhouse often enough to her in the past few weeks, but nothing prepared her for what she found. He would have finished fixing the house before the wedding, she told herself; and concern over the holes in the walls, the nails poking out of the bare floorboards and the primitive pull-chain lights— half of them broken—seemed pettifogging and trivial of her. She hated herself even for noticing them. His barn had burned. *Burned,* she repeated again and again to herself. *The heifers, too.*

She walked round the house slowly, pushing open doors, peering into closets. *Our house. Home.* It felt chilled, damp after yesterday's rain, and even inside the air reeked of charcoal. She tried to picture herself in the kitchen or bedroom and couldn't. Why hadn't Don's father warned her when he put her on the plane? It was bigger—but much worse than his cottage in Vermont: flies buzzing in the windows, the bathroom suite stained and cracked, and in the farm office by the back porch, papers scattered everywhere, a full ashtray . . . and the keys to his jeep.

She slumped into his chair by the desk. She would see if she could make sense of the papers. Some sort of chart with rows of columns and dates lay on top. She moved it and discovered others: a list of breeding on an A. I. Cooperative print-out; plans for the next consignment auction; slips showing milk bacterial count; and bills from Agway and Wayne Feed.

If only I understood. The world of school workbooks, class and curriculum reports seemed remote. She would have to learn a new language. *Better start now.*

She studied one paper closely. Headed *Dairy Herd Improvement Co-operative, Ithaca*, it seemed to list various feeds and their chemical and calorie breakdowns. The words, "megacalorie per pound," "pelleted concentrate," "calcium and phosphorus" danced on the page, meaningless to her, with rows of percentages neatly aligned in the right column.

She pushed the paper aside and heaped all the papers into a pile. Others were strewn on shelves or under half-empty coffee cups, and all of them felt gritty to the touch. Dust. Or was it ash? Frowning, she began to sort them: feed summaries, herd information, Cuba Cheese receipts, breeding and drying-off charts . . . bank statements and bills. She would need to know about these. The insurance and farm association men would be around to discuss the farm's prospects, though they would have to wait for Don, of course, for details. She sighed. What did details matter? They were starting with *nothing.*

In the bottom drawer of the desk she found several clean, empty folders, labelled them, and began to sort the papers into them. Then she heard scuffling outside the back porch and looked up sharply.

Just under the window were two men. She had

heard no truck or car—perhaps it had been left round the front—but there they stood, their backs to her, hands in pockets, hair bristling over their collars at the back. One was tall and thin, the other more bent, stockier.

Larry and Tony? He had mentioned them, hadn't he? But when the taxi had pulled in to the driveway, neither men nor cows had been in evidence.

Cautiously, she swung the chair around and stood silently to lock the screen door from the inside. The habit of a city-dweller, she knew, but she was unsure of her ground.

The catch was broken off. She muttered under her breath, and the men turned.

"Oh, sorry, lady."

"What do you want?" She knew she sounded abrupt and defensive.

"Come to see this barn," one said. "I saw the fire last night. The papers'll be full of it."

She opened the screen door and stood uncertainly on the rotting boards outside. "You're Larry—or Tony?"

They looked at each other. "No, just passing by—sorry. We knew old Davies, though."

Her mind drew a blank. "Davies—?"

"Yes, the guy had this place before you did. Listen, we're sorry about your barn, okay?" They were backing away.

She hardly knew how to answer. "Thanks, I'll tell Don. Why—I mean—should I know your names?"

One of them pulled off his cap. His face was streaked with mud, but she was surprised to see that he was a lad of no more than eighteen. "This is my father, Jack Wilkinson, ma'am. I'm Joel. We own the next farm down the valley . . . be seeing you, then."

She watched them walk away. They moved fast, the boy red-faced, the father scowling. Wondering vaguely why they hadn't asked about Don or the cows, she went back to Don's desk.

By mid-afternoon, she felt utterly desolate. Across the yard, the barn was steaming under warm sunshine, the timbers still occasionally shifting loudly enough for her to catch the sound through the window. But there was still no sign of the hired hands. She had placed several of Don's calls for him and arranged a few appointments, but she felt useless, thwarted, and overwhelmed.

The keys of the jeep winked in the sun, and she picked them up. *Food, at least that's one thing I can organize*, she thought.

The jeep was nowhere in sight. For a sickening moment, standing in the wreck of the yard outside, she was afraid that it must be buried somewhere in the burnt-out barn. Then she remembered other sheds, beside the silos, visible from the road as the cab had pulled in.

Hardly able to bear the choking stench that hung round her, and unwilling to look anymore at the barn, she followed the track to the sheds. The jeep was parked close to a massive machine labeled *John Deere*, and she backed it out slowly, nervously watching the wing mirror. For a moment she forgot the horror of the barn and enjoyed a rush of excitement as she pressed down on the accelerator and the jeep jolted forward and around into the driveway. She knew she would be driving this jeep, with Don and without Don, for months to come. If she couldn't feel like a farmer's wife in the house, she could at least feel like a farmer's wife in the farm jeep.

Turning out of the driveway she glanced along the highway. A line of cars and trucks was pulled up against the fence as far as she could see, to the rise of a low hill, and people were hanging out of windows or leaning against front bumpers, pointing and looking.

She swallowed hard, lifted her right foot, and braked by the gateposts. Sitting still, and feeling her skin grow cold, she watched as a few drivers sheepishly started their cars and pulled away, their faces blank, eyes staring forward as they passed her. Others remained in place and watched her. How long had they been there? What did they want? Who were they— Don's farm acquaintances? Sympathetic neighbors? Or were they just idle, curious onlookers who had seen the fire and now determined to park, gossip and stare? She would find out.

She cut the engine, found the hazard light switch, and jumped down onto the wet gravel. The sun beat down on her shoulders and humidity rose from the long grasses and weeds around the gate in an almost palpable wave. She walked toward the cars and tried to take on her teacher's face, but her mouth had gone dry and, in spite of the heat, ice seemed to be forming inside her.

Just as she reached the nearest car, a red Ford pickup slowed and pulled up opposite her. A window rolled down, and a round man leaned across and shouted, "You Mrs. McEnroe?"

"No. Yes. What is it you want?" She tried to gauge the man's expression. Perhaps this was Larry. No, it couldn't be. He would know full well that Don wasn't married yet. "Who are you?"

"*Buffalo Evening News*, ma'am. Can I talk to you?"

She did not answer immediately, looking down the row of cars and faces, most neutral, others frankly inquisitive. "Yes, you'd better come around the back."

At last she looked back at him, saw the Agway cap on his head turned backwards. *Phoney agricultural reporter.* She lifted her arm. "These people from the *News* as well?"

"No," shouted the driver of the nearest car. "I heard there was a fire, that's all."

Several of the drivers banded together and walked nearer to the red pick-up. A few faces registered concern, but Margaret felt trapped. The barrage began.

"Was anyone hurt?"

"Are the cows out?"

"Lose any pigs and chickens?"

"Were the machines okay?"

"What about your house, lady?"

"Where were you and the kids?"

"Is your husband okay?"

She backed away and clenched her fists. The newspaper reporter was watching her through his window, waiting to pounce if she opened her mouth. She was helpless. "Please—please," she begged.

"Leave her alone." A voice she recognized. She looked sideways to see the Wilkinson boy standing next to her on the edge of the ditch. "Can't you see she's distressed? Go away. You're like crows on a dead coon, the whole bunch of you."

The reporter laughed, reversed the pick-up, and parked it near the gate. The others turned away, and Margaret walked past the boy, nodded, and opened the door of the jeep. "Thanks."

"Can I talk to you?" the reporter said again. His camera was slung over one shoulder, and he waited right by the jeep's hood.

She jammed the jeep into gear and shouted, "No, I don't want to talk. Can't you leave us alone?"

"But the press, lady. You said come around the back." He was edging nearer to the driver's side and she knew he'd hound her, wherever she went.

She sighed heavily. "Come on, then. But you'll have to talk to Don as well. There's a lot I don't know yet." And she reversed grim-faced into the yard again.

The reporter didn't even gasp when he saw the barn. Instead he squinted at the sun going down behind the barn, fiddled with his lens, and asked, "How'd the fire start, anyhow? I hear your husband wanted free-stall barns in here. Old Davies had stanchions, didn't he?"

Another trap. She would not fall into it. "He's not my husband yet. We're getting married in July."

The reporter aimed the camera, squatting down on thick haunches and pulling his mouth into a grimace as he set the focus. "Sure is a mess, lady."

She knew it was pointless and even dangerous to let this reporter question her. She would go inside and wait until he went away.

Snap. The blackened wreck froze on the camera's eye. This was one photograph she would not pin on her wall.

July

From below the window, in the darkness, came the first click, scratch and scrape of an early cicada. Soon there would be hundreds of them, the males whirring and shrilling for the females. Even by day they were invisible in the mimosa branches, lost among the ferny leaves and pink blossoms. But at night they were almost visible in the rising currents of sound that whined to a crescendo through the open screens.

The sound rose, then fell to silence so that he could hear instead the tree frogs down by the pond, the occasional car swishing along the highway in front of the house, headlights dipped so that they barely reached the bedroom. And Maggie's breathing: steady, even, quiet.

He rolled over toward her but did not touch her, could not even see her. Three nights together, that was all, and he could not imagine how he had ever slept without her.

He ran his scarred hand over her arm, and she stirred, muttered something, and turned away. He put his arms around her and began to drift away himself. The cicadas whirred and whined, rose and fell outside the window.

How strange everything was. It was exactly a year since he had slept for the first time in this bedroom—alone then—and listened to the cicadas. A year of chaos, loneliness, bewilderment, grief, and very little hope. It wasn't just Ellie who had died. He had gone through his own death then, as had Margaret, he supposed. But now, after only three days and three nights, a kind of resurrection.

If the fire had taught him anything, it was that he couldn't manage alone anymore. Maggie gave him the intimacy he needed: the laughter, trust, encouragement. And God—that token acknowledgement of His presence in Bedford with a prayer after supper and his mother murmuring quick prayers whenever there was a cut knee or broken glass—God was like Maggie: a box to be opened, explored, overflowing with all he needed. A God who listened when he complained about the fire, about the pain in his hands, about the legal and financial problems that dogged and threatened to overwhelm them. A God who had given him Maggie. The aching void inside had dwindled.

Images of the last three days shuttered across his mind's eye in the darkness: the crowd of well-wishers outside the church in Dedham—pastels and hot pinks, whites and cherry reds. Hands throwing confetti and rice. Maggie on their first night in a Boston hotel, the night paid for by her father and given them courtesy of Larry, who kept things going for two days in Arcade. Her face hungry and anxious all at once, but her body soft, her arms reaching for him.

David, Margaret's brother, huddled with the Fuller clan, his three children swarming round them, loping across the foyer with a serious face. "Martha and I are leaving the kids with my parents. We've agreed—if you'll have us—I know it's kind of odd—that we'll go back to New York with you and Maggie and work on the house and the farm for a week." David felt sorry for them, he'd said then, because apart from the first night, there would be no honeymoon. "Will you let us do that, Don?"

Stupefied with surprise, he only said, "Well, sure, why not?" And laughed.

And now David and Martha were no doubt struggling to fall asleep in the other bedroom on two cots they had bought from Agway this morning. What a bizarre honeymoon!

He rolled over again, facing the window, his back to Maggie, but feeling her warmth. It must be late; the cicadas had almost stopped. If only he could sleep.

The insurance men had been there again the week before. "Bad wiring," they had said laconically. "It was bound to go sooner or later."

Only a breathful of words, but it had brought immense relief. No questions now of arson. No careless cigarettes falling into the hay, though that possibility had dogged him for the first sleepless nights in the hospital and at home. He remembered lighting a cigarette in the barn (never again—could not remember putting it out afterward). But if it was the wiring, then so be it. One less grief to carry around.

The new barn would be free-stall, he imagined—as long as the refinancing came through. "Go for it," his adviser at the tech had urged them when Maggie telephoned him. "You've got everything to lose if you don't."

But how? He would have to take out unthinkable loans, comb the cattle auctions to increase the size of the herd so that he could begin the crippling job of paying it all back. And meanwhile he would have to go on renting milking time on a neighbor's farm. Even that was grudged. "Better off selling up," the neighbor had advised sourly. "Why, even old Davies wasn't makin' a livin' and got out. Cows'll suffer if you don't."

The words echoed in his head until he wanted to shout out and plug his ears. But Mark King's were louder still. "Go for it. Go for it."

This new barn must be red, Maggie had said. A traditional New England barn with red siding. "Only on the outside," he had told her. "Inside, it'll be the space age."

"And let's plant maples and white oaks outside," she had said.

"And I suppose you want a dog, as well, huh?"

They were standing then in front of a John Coffin painting David and Martha had given them as a wedding present—evidently one Maggie had seen before, for she was clapping her hands in glee, her eyes shining from under the white gauze of her veil.

"A dog? Yes, by all means let's have a dog. A mutt, from the dog shelter, okay?"

"What a sucker! Next you'll be asking for chickens. I knew it. I always knew you'd want chickens." He chuckled, remembering.

"Chickens? Sure. Why not?"

He pulled the veil back from her face. "Enough, Margaret, enough."

The painting drew him in; he could see why she loved it. The trees washed up against the barn in a foam of green, white and burned scarlet. White oak and red maple. Red maple and white oak. Yes, they would grow well in that corner of the yard, especially as there was little summer shade there except from the silos.

White oak and red maple. Syrup from the maple in the spring, and acorns from the oak in the autumn. Acorns for their children, one day when they could plan for children . . .

Maples and oaks heaved and seethed, cresting toward him. Red boards on the side of the barn began to ripple, warp, and stretch out—hideous bands of red elastic. Then flames burst from between slats and knotholes, curving and caving over him, branching and bending like great orange trees.

The little dog stopped bounding beside him and barked a silent bark of anguish, its wet mouth opening, but no sound coming out. Then, with lifted muzzle, it howled a siren as flaming fire trees rolled closer. The red barn spewed waves and rivers and forests of fire but was not itself consumed and, from inside, the cry of calves pierced him.

His hands went out: ringless, white-knuckled hands sliced by the twine of bales, grazed by the rust of the stanchion chains. Hands useless against flood-tides of fire, too blistered to shield or to save him. Staggering, tottering backward, he crossed forearms over his face, cried out as loud as the heifers, as loud as the branches and breakers of fire. Before he could fell them, they would fall on him, pitch him into their orange leaves, snatch him and burn him. Only water would save him. *Water.*

"*Water!* For God's sake!" Don was screaming in a terrible voice beside her.

Dazed, she sat up. In the dusky half-light she saw that he was on his back with his arms thrown over his face. He cried out, legs thrashing, the sweat gleaming on his neck, and his hair was plastered with it. She hesitated. Ellie had had nightmares, especially when the hay fever reached its zenith, and after Woodstock. She had never known whether to wake her or wait it out, and she hardly knew now.

Careful not to brush against him, she slid off the bed and risked the broken floorboards and David and Martha in the room next door to walk barefoot into the bathroom. Quickly she ran cold water, steeped and wrung out a facecloth, and went back to him.

He had scarcely changed position, but his breaths came in fractured gasps and gulps.

She almost fell on him. "Don, Don, *please.*" She ran the cloth lightly over his sore hands first, then his arms. Moved them, and washed his forehead, bending to kiss him.

His breathing slowed, and his eyes popped open, staring, blank with horror.

"It's all right, Don. You were dreaming, just dreaming. It's all right, sweetheart." She cradled him frantically, muttering and whispering to him as he woke fully.

He began to moan. "Oh—Maggie. Oh—Maggie." He touched her face.

"You were just having a nightmare." She tried to make her voice sound down-to-earth and ordinary; Margaret the school teacher, used to the terrors of children. *But what about the terrors of men?* "A nightmare. That's all. You want some water?"

"Yes. Yeah, that's what I want." He sat up and took the cool cloth from her, wiping himself slowly. "Maggie, was I shouting? What time is it, anyway?"

"Yes, you sure were, and I don't know. Does it matter?"

He pushed a hand through his hair, passed the face-cloth back to her and inspected his hands closely. "No. But my hands do. They're hurting again. I dreamed—no, I can't tell you."

"Can't?"

"Won't, then."

She took his hands, pressed them together between her own palms, and kissed them. "You don't have to, love. I'm sorry they hurt, but they're healing up fine—honest they are." She snapped on a light. "See for yourself, Don."

He didn't answer but hunched forward and dropped his head on his knees, nodding slightly. "Yeah. Sorry I woke you."

She looked at her watch. "Five-thirty. Is there any point—?"

"No. I'd rather get up. Can you get back to sleep, d'you reckon?" His voice was muffled, sad.

She shook her head. "No. I'll get up as well. Maybe David and Martha can sleep longer if we creep down now." She doubted it, even though the walls were thick. Trying to make her voice light, she said, "But they'll probably be up, too. You were making enough noise to wake the Wilkinsons."

His head came up, the shock of hair hanging in one

eye so that she wanted to flip it back gaily and tickle him, jump on him. "Who?"

"People on one of the neighboring farms. Don't look so bemused. I met him the first day when half of Allegany County came to stare at the mess. Fire groupies. Joel Wilkinson—he was about the only thoughtful person there."

He grunted. "Huh. Good to know someone's okay around here. Old what's-his-face where the cows are milking—he's bitter as gall. Guess I assumed they were all like that. Strong, silent and bitter. Like all the guys I see at Agway or Wayne Feed or the auctions."

"Kind of like you, too, Don. Bitter. Please don't." She tried to woo him away from the darkness of his dream. "I'd rather play a little."

He grinned for the first time. "I thought you wanted to get up."

"Only if you do."

"Later, I will. I'll get over and see to the cows." His smile faded, and he mused, "Almost like being back at Hammonds'. I have to haul myself out of bed and drive to my cows again."

She winked at him, coming closer to him. "Ah, but you've got a much cozier bed nowadays."

———

Frank Gray watched Don finishing the last cow, and Margaret, dressed in shorts, T-shirt and boots watched the older man watch him.

"One thing I'll grant you," Gray muttered between chews on a plug of tobacco. "One thing, lady. That man of yours likes his animals. He's a proper cow man."

"At least that's *one* thing he's got going for him," she said pertly.

He missed the irony of her tone, took her literally. "Yup. But nothing else. I told him before, I did. Those cows'll suffer if he can't get himself set up again before the autumn. Not so bad now with the weather nice and them pasturing outside day and night."

While he shifted the tobacco and leaned against a barn desk right behind him, she wondered how he had time to stand and talk so long. His desk was a landslide of magazines, print-outs, and letters—opened and sealed. Far worse than Don's had been.

"But I can't keep 'em here forever, you know. No room in the winter, and I've got a big batch of calves due in September. That means more milking, less dry ones. Hubby'll have to go elsewhere, then."

She hated the word "hubby," hated his indifference and air of patronizing experience. She could not answer him.

He slid his eyes insolently up and down her T-shirt and pale legs in answer to her angry stare. He stopped chewing. "Well, how about some coffee, if you're just standing till he's done?"

She screwed up her mouth. "No thanks. I'll wait, thanks."

"You just got hitched, didn't you?" Gray's eyes were narrowed, and she wanted to swing at him and knock his tobacco out of his cheek.

"Yes." It was all she could manage.

"Funny kind of honeymoon, ain't it?"

She couldn't bear him any more. "Don!" she called above the sucking and pumping of the machine.

He was bent over, releasing the hose, but turned and smiled.

"I'll wait for you in the jeep, okay?"

"Sure." He wheeled the dumping station away. "We'll go in a minute."

She fled from the barn and out into Grays' feedlot. It had been hosed clean, almost bleaching under the July heat, but a few free-range chickens pecked and picked at straws and seeds on the concrete. A lean cat was stretched under the overhang suckling a pile of squirming tortoiseshell kittens.

She looked back into the barn, but Gray was saying something to Don and would not follow her, so she stooped and touched the cat. It snarled and raised a front paw with claws unsheathed.

Sighing, she waited by the jeep. The back sported a luminous sticker, custom-made by McEnroe's campaign manager for the wedding. JUST MARRIED. It made her smile every time.

Then Don came out, hands in overall pockets and visor crooked over his eyes.

"Frank Gray—what an old so-and-so," she said to him.

"Maybe." He started the engine. "But he didn't need to let me use his stanchions, you know."

"He's getting a good cut of your milk, though, isn't he?"

"Of course. Look, never mind Gray. I'm taking you for coffee."

"We haven't got time, have we? Martha and David'll be looking for us. They don't know what you wanted done in the kitchen, do they?"

"Maggie, they're smart. They'll get on fine for half an hour. The barley and corn won't stop growing while we're gone, either."

They turned out onto the highway, and he took his eyes briefly off the road to catch hers.

"What is it?" She loved the way he looked at her nowadays.

"Your shorts, they're cute. You look good in them.

"Thanks."

"Bet Gray thought so, too."

She resisted this. "I thought we weren't talking about Gray any more."

He shrugged. "We won't, but the shorts are at your own risk, then. These guys don't know this is the twentieth century. He's an old lecher. I don't think you ought to come over there with me again."

She laughed. "Believe me, I won't."

They took a table right beside the window in the diner. The air conditioner hummed and dripped beside them, and the place was cool and quiet, only a white-frocked waitress going back and forth, wiping tables with a dishrag, a notepad sticking out of her apron pocket.

Don looked over his coffee at Margaret. Strands of hair stuck to her forehead and cheeks; she was flushed and bright. Something inside him quaked, melted. Her freshness dazzled him.

"What?" She was looking at him, catching him as he stared.

He sipped the coffee. "Just thinking how lovely you are."

She smiled. "What took you so long, then?"

"Can't imagine."

"Then I guess I'd better cash in on your awareness now, before you don't notice anymore."

He shoved out his boots until they touched hers. "Cash in? That's hardly appropriate. We'll be lucky if we can even afford coffee at The Ranch next week."

"Don't be gloomy. Someone in this family has to be the optimist, and that's your job. You're the faithful believer." She twitched her boots against his. "But I'll be the clown. The last of the late great agricultural lovers, Don McEnroe—my boots seem to like yours."

There was no need to answer. They drank coffee, savored the coolness, and watched cars and trucks cruising by on Route 39. Then a pick-up truck pulled in and parked by the jeep: a clapped out Chevy, the body rusted all around the wheel rims. He watched a boy and an old man jump out of the front, heard Margaret's exclamation. "Oh! That's the Wilkinsons."

He examined them as they came toward the glass door of the diner. The boy was tall and thin. He moved ahead of the old man to hold the door, his face slightly worried. The old man was sturdy, wide-shouldered and walking with deliberate but slow feet, vaguely familiar somehow. "Which is which?" he asked quickly. "I ought to know, I guess, by now."

"Joel's the boy; Jack's his father."

The old man hesitated, about to pass their table. He peered at Don and cast a glance at Margaret as well. "You're the guy that's got Davies's place, ain't you?"

Don nodded. "Yes, why?"

"I thought so. Mind if we join you?"

Don pulled out two chairs, and Margaret beamed.

"No, of course you can."

Don noticed Joel's color darken as the two of them sat down. While the old man's cap remained firmly in place, Joel's came off and lay on the table next to his place mat. They all shook hands, and the old man lit a pipe, his hands going as slowly as his boots, his lips pursed in concentration.

At last he looked up, straight at Don. "We met your wife just before you and she got hitched. The day after the fire, it was."

The boy was anxiously looking back and forth between his father and Don. He seemed to want to say something but didn't.

"I remember," Margaret said. "Joel, you were nice that afternoon when all those people were hanging around."

The boy flushed even darker and muttered, "Well, gosh, ma'am."

Don felt irritated. Neither man nor boy looked like "aw shucks" hicks. What did they want? He caught the waitress's eye. "Two more coffees, please."

"No you don't, mister. I'll take tea, thanks," old man Wilkinson growled. "And I'll pick up the tab as well."

Don felt hot again all of a sudden, ready to spar with

this cantankerous old man. "I don't want your charity," he said sharply.

Coffee halfway to her mouth, Margaret looked up in alarm. Her eyes told him he had been rude. "Don—"

"Sorry. Listen, Mr. Wilkinson—"

Joel leaned forward. "Don't take offense, sir. Dad's always quick that way."

Don caught the glare that father sent son and relaxed suddenly. This odd pair was better company than Gray any day. He leaned back. "Maybe we should start again. Why don't you tell me what I can do for you, now you're here."

The old man fixed him with a speculative gaze and puffed blue clouds around the table. He bit the pipe stem in his teeth at one corner of his mouth, then said, "It's more I had in mind what we could do for you, son."

Don took a breath, then bit back another sharp retort. He resented the word "son"—as if he were an overgrown farm boy. But, once again, Maggie was warning him with her eyes. *Don't, don't.* "Well," he began, "I don't know."

Tea and coffee came, and Joel asked for doughnuts as well. Maggie began to smile, and none of them spoke for several minutes. His mind pushed ahead. Was Wilkinson going to offer milking time? He knew they were neighbors and after the first mutual and wary assessment decided they might be better co-workers than Gray.

"I've been farming these hills just shy of forty years," Wilkinson said at last. "Suppose I learned a thing or two in that time. I've seen some down in the valley flooded out, and some up here burned out, and even some poisoned out, once, by chemicals in the river. But that barn of yours—that's one of the worst fires I've ever seen. Still, Davies kept up that place pretty good, and I'd say you ought to think, being quite high up as you are, of going to sheep instead. Cheaper'n cattle up here."

He glanced at Margaret. Her lips were twitching.

"You really think so, Mr. Wilkinson?" She said, not looking at him.

He didn't trust her goody-two-shoes voice, her deadpan face.

"Don and I were wondering about chickens, you know." How could she keep a straight face? He nudged her hard with his boot, but she didn't even blink.

"No way. Not here," Wilkinson said severely. "You wouldn't want batteries, would you?"

Don frowned at Maggie and then looked back at Wilkinson. "No."

"Then what about sheep?"

He thought about it for a moment: the smell and stupidity of sheep, the pungent taste of their meat, the greasy thickness of their fleeces, and the ugly sound of their bleating. Only for a moment. "No, I'm not interested in sheep. Worked all my life with cows, Mr. Wilkinson. Like yourself, no doubt." He looked hard into the old man's eyes, testing and gauging him. "Listen, I still dream about those heifers. I keep hearing them crying. It happened again last night. Sheep?" He shuddered. "I couldn't."

"Then how you gonna raise the capital?"

"I don't know. I'd welcome your ideas." He caught Maggie's eyes. They were wet.

Wilkinson said, "I'll give it some thought."

"Me too, Mr. McEnroe," Joel added.

Don looked out of the window. Others were coming in now. "Thanks. Thanks for the coffee, too. C'mon, Maggie. We'd better get going."

"They just don't understand, do they?" she said on the way back.

He found he was suddenly too tired to want to answer in the way he knew she expected. He shook his head, glanced at his watch, and accelerated. "No, and

I've just remembered the testing supervisor's due this afternoon. He'll be staying overnight, and getting up with me for the morning milking, too." He pushed his hand around his neck where sweat prickled under the hairline. "I forgot all about him. And we've got David and Martha *as well.*"

She groaned. "Look, I'll find a bed somewhere. There's plenty of groceries in the fridge right now. We'll manage. You've got a wife now."

"Not an unpaid skivvy."

"Right. Not my style." She touched his arm, her face pleading. "Please, I know everything looks black. But you're the optimist, remember. Please don't despair, Don. If you do, I'll despair, too." She meant what she said.

"All right, I'll try to get myself together. No making eyes at the dairy cooperative guy, okay?"

"Oh, I won't promise, not if he's—"

He reached and covered her mouth with his hand, so that the jeep swerved slightly. "Shut up, minx."

Martha was painting the kitchen cupboards when they came in. Her hair was drawn back under an Indian headscarf, and her face was streaked with grease.

"You've been scrubbing since dawn, and now you're painting, right?" Margaret accused.

The brush went back and forth over the woodwork, and the paint gleamed.

"Looks a whole lot better, Martha," Don said.

She smiled at him, and he felt proud of Margaret's eccentric little sister-in-law. So kind.

"You're quite welcome." She waved the brush vaguely. "You want David? He's doing the upstairs floorboards. Says you'll all have tetanus if someone doesn't."

Don groaned. Margaret put a hand out to him. "We can't do it all, Don. You just milked the cows, remember? And now you want to get ready for the tester, right?"

He smiled slowly. "Maggie, would you do something for me?"

She smiled back guilelessly. "No."

"*What?*"

"I *am* doing something for you!"

He threw his hands out. "It's okay, I don't mean painting or floorboards. Looks like they're doing fine without us. No, would you mind sorting out my desk for me?"

From upstairs came the bang and clack of a hammer and the sound of David whistling.

She was already at the door to the office. "That's exactly what I had planned, honey. Can't have this guy seeing the mess, and I've gotta find him a bed as well."

He lifted his hand to signify approval, but she had already turned away. "Alone, Maggie," he called after her, and heard her laughter back at him.

———

Aware that Frank Gray was standing watching again, Don felt his skin prickle in irritation. *Can't he ever leave me alone?*

The testing supervisor went ahead of him down the stalls. The cows shifted restlessly in the stanchions, their chains clanging against the rails, uneasy with the delay as the men went slowly from one to the other with the dump station, filling sample vials, weighing the milk, and marking clipboards. Don wanted to keep close to the tester, though he also wanted to get on with the milking; the man had already indicated disapproval over the appearance of some of the cows.

"They're healthy," Don had assured him. "You can see that for yourself. But the fire would have traumatized anyone."

"Butter fat'll be down, no doubt," the tester replied sourly.

Don knew he was right. All the figures on the print-outs this month would be lower, but that didn't stop him wanting to argue with the tester every time he bent forward with a vial or weighed some of the milk on the scale. Later he thought of Maggie's certainty, *Someone in this family has to be the optimist, and that's your job.* And he made himself whistle until, in revenge, Gray switched on WGR55. After that he resigned himself, turned away, and went on milking while the tester scrubbed up and went down to the scale.

"What you gonna do then with the insurance money, Mr. McEnroe?" At the supper table the tester eyed him over a forkful of Martha's chicken pie.

Martha and Maggie looked up in chorus and stopped chewing, but David kept his eyes and mouth busy on the food.

"Rebuild the herd, of course." He shrugged. "Raise enough from my animals to start again."

"But your equity's gone, ain't it?"

"Yup." His shoulder muscles felt tight, suddenly.

"What—fifty, maybe sixty thousand?"

"Something like that. Why?"

The tester put down his fork. "Don't mean to be nosey, you understand. But you don't make sense. Any guy I know'd've given up long ago. Sold out." He moved the side of his hand across his throat in a cutting motion. "Cut and run."

Don thought of Gray. They were all saying the same: Gray, Wilkinson, and now this man from the Cooperative. "No, I don't think so."

"If anyone can do it," Margaret volunteered, "Don can." She caught his eye. "Batteries and sheep—we're not interested. It's cows." She grinned at him. "Holsteins."

He knew she was doing the wifely bit and supporting him. "Yeah, and a few Jerseys."

"And Jerseys."

David and Martha exchanged smiles, but the tester's mouth twisted. "Well, good luck to you. I'd go for pigs, myself."

"*Pigs?*" Maggie laughed, and some of her tea spilled onto the table. "You must be kidding."

"No. Not so hard to feed."

"But harder to house—especially with no proper barns."

"And the smell—!" Martha murmured.

"Why not horses, Don?" David asked mildly.

"Or donkeys, huh? I always wanted donkeys—did I tell you?" Maggie asked.

They were both deadpan, and Don shook his head, "You're crazy. The whole bunch of you."

"What about ducks?" Martha asked. "Or geese?"

"Or turkeys?" That was Maggie.

Everyone except the tester laughed; then the telephone rang.

Don got up to answer it.

"Don, buddy. It's me—Mark."

He let out a sigh of relief and pushed a hand through his hair. "One friendly voice, anyway." He pictured his one-time adviser's big grin and untidy mop of hair.

"What's the matter? Your wife give you the boot already?"

He laughed, looking across at her. She was watching him, smiling at him over her cup. "No, on the contrary. Though I don't know why . . . Listen, didn't anyone ever tell you that you don't call a guy on his honeymoon?"

Mark clicked his tongue. "Call that a honeymoon, man?"

"Yeah, I do. So what d'you want, Mark?"

"Look, it's okay. I'll call you back if—"

"No, go ahead now you're on the line."

There was a pause. "Well, I just wondered if you'd

decided what to do. I've been thinking about you lots and wondering."

"Raise turkeys." He shot another look at Maggie, then at the tester, whose face was grim.

"*What?* Oh, very good, McEnroe. Your own, or the feathered variety?"

"Score one to you, too, Mark. The feathered kind. Enough of the other kind in this kitchen already, and we're not exactly ready for kids yet, either. No, hey, you already know what I'm going to do."

Mark's voice came back more quietly this time. "You're going for it after all? Loans, refinancing? Auctions? The whole bit, Don?"

"The whole bit."

"That's great news!"

Don laughed. "Sure it is. Now, write me some good advice, okay?" He leered at Maggie. "Listen, you'd better just write to me. My wife's looking jealous."

"Fine. I'll comb the library and talk to some guys here, and write you."

Don sat down at the table again. He felt suddenly happier. "You'd like Mark, Maggie. I know you would."

"Your adviser?"

"Yes. That's the one. You've got a good memory."

"Not really. You had me call him once, remember?"

"He's a nice guy." He looked across at the tight-lipped tester and thought with resentment of the neatly labeled trays of milk vials in the fridge.

———

"*To church?*" Margaret looked up sharply at David. "Why on earth are you going with Don?"

Martha blinked from behind her glasses but said nothing.

David only shrugged, leaning back in his chair and abandoning a piece of cold toast on his plate. "Why not, Maggie?"

She gripped her knife harder and watched the butter melt under it into her muffin. "You're not in our church anymore, so far as I know."

"Yes he is, Maggie," Martha said gently. "You don't turn your back on your Catholic background just because you worship with other Christians."

Maggie shuddered, piqued by Martha's restraint. "I suppose you're going too?" she needled, knowing she was on sure ground. Martha the Mennonite would never set foot in a liturgical church.

"Matter of fact, she is," David answered for her. "Don was telling me about the church and the priest there while we were finishing the boards upstairs last night. I guess we'll all go. What about you?"

She recoiled, resenting David's persistence. Don was finishing up over at Grays' barn, and they were breakfasting without him. But she didn't want to sound defensive or ungracious. Not now. They would be leaving to go back to Boston within a few hours.

She thought quickly. "Not me, thanks. I think I'll run over to Wilkinsons'. Joel promised me some kittens out of the barn, and I want to see if they're weaned yet."

"Suit yourself, Maggie," David grinned. "You will, anyway."

She watched his back as he stood up to lift the plates and coffee cups onto the counter. *My brother:* lean, brown from working with Don on the fencing for a couple of days. He looked different after a week on the farm: more like a cow man, and less like a doctor. She wished they weren't going yet. Or did she? She wanted to be alone with Don, too.

"You're off to Wilkinsons' now?" Martha asked.

"No. Don'll be back any minute. He'll be hungry."

"Didn't he eat already?"

"Sure. Before he started milking. But he's up so early—you know that—he needs at least two breakfasts. And if Larry and Tony come up mid-morning, he sometimes has three."

Wrist deep in soap-suds, David chinked cups and laughed. "Oh, no wonder he's so big."

Maggie made more coffee and put muffins in the toaster for him. Then the back porch screen door slammed and Don came in smelling of manure and with hay in his hair.

"Mmm—breakfast."

"Not in that state, man!"

"Yes in this state, woman. This is a farm kitchen. You'd better get used to it." He kissed her hotly and scrubbed down in the second sink, shoulder to shoulder with David.

Buttering muffins, her mind full of church, kittens and kitchen floors on one level, Margaret mentally compared the two men. Looking at Don, she felt a rush of desire so strong that the knife clattered out of her hand, and Don turned to look at her. But she heard herself bantering back. "No. This is my kitchen now. You'd better get used to that."

"Okay, okay, Maggie. I'll go back outside if you don't want me." He leered at her, not missing the heat in her face.

"Oh, I want you all right." She set the plate in front of him. "Your coffee. Muffins. Eat."

"What time did you say church begins?" David asked.

"Eleven. Plenty of time. I'll shower and be down in no time." Don looked thoughtfully from David to Martha and back again, and Maggie devoured the blue of his eyes. "You know, we'll miss you two. It's been great—this week. I think I'll tell everyone I know—the best honeymoon's with your brother-in-law and sister-in-law along."

Maggie laughed uncertainly. "Wait a minute . . ."

"Don't you worry, Maggie." David was watching her face. "We won't stay longer than we planned."

Don smiled ingenuously at Martha. "You should bring the kids next time."

For a moment Maggie saw McEnroe's face in Don's. She had rarely seen it before, and was surprised.

"This place'll be a bit safer the next time you come."

"We'd love to bring them," Martha said simply. "Margaret's their favorite aunt. And you'll have to come to Nantucket."

Don laughed. "Farmers don't have honeymoons, didn't you figure that out? No holidays, either."

Margaret looked at him quickly. They would have a real honeymoon later, when they had enough money. *Wouldn't they? Would they?*

Martha caught the look and returned another of sympathy, but that only irritated her more. She pushed David away from the sink so that she could turn her back on them all and went on washing dishes, furiously clattering last night's pots. *Church? No holidays? Was that it?* Or was it that she was afraid of being alone with Don when David and Martha had gone. *Surely not. Don't think about it,* she told herself.

But all her joy was eclipsed, and when the others drove away to church she felt suddenly desolate—then puzzled and angry with herself for feeling that way. After all, wasn't she just married? What more could she want?

She left the rest of the dishes in the sink, not understanding the sudden change of mood, and drove fast to Wilkinsons'. She could quite easily have walked, she knew, but she wanted to gun the engine and hear it roaring at full throttle before she pulled back and into the Wilkinsons' gate. The smell of diesel and hot rubber distracted her, and the bunched heap of multicolored kittens in the yard assuaged some of the ache, too. But she wished she had gone to church after all.

On the Wilkinsons' porch she stooped down just to watch. The mother cat was sprawled out with eyes shut, corpse-like, so thin her ribs hardly seemed to rise above the dust of the yard. Below her belly, one kitten suckled; and three others rolled, hissed, and tussled with each other. She looked closer. Claws were sharp as needles, unsheathed and shining. Tails were raised ridiculously, gray and tortoiseshell tufts that twitched as the kittens sprang, feinted and threatened each other.

She pounced, and the mother's head came up, eyes open and yellow with sudden light. "This one," she murmured. "And this one." The little bodies wriggled against her, claws pulling threads in her T-shirt. The hissing stopped, and the mewing began: frantic and thin-voiced.

Murmuring comfort, she went to the screen door and called out. No answer but the dripping of a tap over the sink. She called again, louder, and the porch steps creaked behind her.

"Oh, it's you." Joel stomped up toward her.

She turned. "Yes, I came for the kittens." She held them out, and they clawed the air, still mewing.

"Take 'em. Dad'll drown 'em if not."

Sighing, she looked back at the others. They were watching, alert now, mother and two kittens, their heads up. "All of them?"

He nodded. "Too many here already. Take the whole bunch if you want."

"Then I might as well start a cattery."

"Got some now, have you?"

"Yes, but they're raggedy old things, not up to much."

He looked at her stolidly. "They have a way of multiplying anyway." He grinned. "But if you take all four, that'll speed it up twice as fast. Get rid of twice as much vermin, too."

"Make a good salesman, you would."

He scratched his head. "So my Dad says." He went over and scooped up the other kittens. The mother cat stretched and blinked at him. "Take them all. They'll want worming." He turned one over. "See that fat belly? Not milk. Worms . . . You got a box or something?"

She moved her head toward the pick-up. A straw-filled basket was waiting within, but she couldn't bear to shut them up yet. "Are you sure they're weaned?"

"Good as. Look at the mother. She doesn't care. She'll have four more before you can say 'tomcat.' " He grinned again, "You can have those, too."

"Well—I don't know, Joel. Can't have the mice population growing too big over here. I think you'd better keep the next batch."

He opened the cab door for her and put them in the basket one by one. They squirmed and burrowed into the straw, found each other and tumbled into a heap. "Look, they know they're in for a good home."

She thought of Don. "Not a home, Joel. The barn. That's definite. Don won't put up with them inside." She leaned against the hot side of the pick-up and faced him. "But I'll look after them, I promise."

"I bet you will."

She looked away quickly from his admiration. He was just a boy, and she felt older now, much older. "Listen, Joel—I need some advice."

He waited, and a thin trail of sweat ran down his forehead under the ubiquitous Agway cap.

"Chickens, I want to keep chickens. Can you teach me—" She stopped, feeling foolish. "What'd I have to do to keep chickens?"

He looked puzzled. "What about Mr. McEnroe? Ain't he got time to teach you?"

"He would if I asked. But this is something for myself. If you can spare a bit of time, I'd like to learn. Then I can get on with them by myself."

"A bit of egg money on the side, like."

"That's right."

"Nothing to it, not really. I guess you mean a few old chickens in the barn. No batteries."

"No batteries. Free-range chickens—I just want to see if I can manage them."

He guffawed. "Oh, they'll manage themselves just fine. Manage themselves right under the pick-ups on Route 39 if you don't watch it. They're stupider than a whole field of steers, chickens are. C'mon—the kittens'll be okay. I'll show you." He led the way across the yard. "They'll need a nesting-box unless you want to go hunting night and day in the hay for eggs. You can get feed from the Agway, and all kinds of leaflets to get you started. Half the kids in the county keep them. If they can, you can."

She followed him. He was like a clockwork toy. Once he got wound up and started, he went on talking and talking, and within half an hour she felt she knew enough about chickens to start. The kittens would occupy her today, but tomorrow she would go to Agway and buy feed, then back to Wilkinsons' for some chicks Joel had promised her.

She drove home slowly, but the kittens hardly moved. In the Wilkinsons' fields the corn was knee-high, glossy in the slight breeze, green as far as she could see to the top of a slight rise in the land. *Home* she thought. *This is home now.* She wished Ellie could see it, could see them together.

––––––––––

When David and Martha had gone, hooting and waving like teenagers as they pulled out of the yard, the place seemed empty. He turned to see Maggie doing her best not to look at him, wiping tears from her face with the back of her hand. But the dirt gave her away; she had returned from Wilkinsons' with her hands streaked with mud, and now her face was dirty.

"Hey, that's not like you."

She came into his arms, shuddering and suddenly

seeming smaller. She sniffed, "No, it's not like me. Sorry."

"We'll see them soon."

"No, it's not that."

He lifted her chin and put one hand on her lovely hair. The gesture was like a priestly blessing, almost, and he withdrew it, surprised at himself, puzzled by her troubled face. "What, then?"

She shrugged. "Oh, I don't know. I just have the blues, I guess."

She looked bleak and miserable. "You need a job, Maggie," he said.

"A job?" She laughed shakily. "I just finished one, remember? And there's enough around here for a whole harem of wives." Her face cleared. "You're not shoving me out already, are you? I've got to learn how to be a farmer's wife before I go back to teaching."

" 'Course I'm not shoving you out, silly." He bent and kissed her. "How about a cup of coffee? Could you get one brewed? I need to get changed. Let's take it easy today, okay?" He wanted suddenly to cease from the round of milking, feeding and haycutting and stay inside with Maggie all day. She leaned into him, and he held her loosely against his clean shirt.

Her voice was brighter, steadier. "You want to see the kittens?" she asked.

He didn't. "Suppose I could." He let her go. "Where are they?"

"In the toolshed."

"Why?"

"Where else could I put them? They might get lost."

He sighed. "Okay, I'll see them in a bit. But let's have coffee first. You look like you need it."

He sat at the back of the house where it was cooler, and a slight breeze came in through the screen. Since David had fixed the screens, there were fewer flies in the house. He waited while she made the coffee and thought back to the time in church that morning.

A funny mixture of the solemn and the comic. Lost in the tide of words, Martha had flicked pages back and forth in the book, dropped it, and sent him a look of despair. David gave up, too, standing and kneeling a beat or two behind everyone else. But it didn't matter: when the priest lifted the bread he longed to raise his arms too and shout aloud. What if the barn had burned? He had Maggie, he had land, and he had his cows. The empty husk of last winter had fallen away, and grains of new life were forming. The land and cows mattered—they dwarfed him. He was their servant, their keeper and their feeder; they in turn taught him God's mysteries. And Maggie mattered. She healed him, gave herself to him so that he learned how to give himself to her.

At the giving of peace, Martha and David had both hugged him warmly. *Family.* He missed Ellie, but he had new family to love as well now.

Maggie put the coffee into his hand and sat opposite him. She was in her business-like mode again, and he left the church behind him for a while.

"Your desk is still a pigpen," she accused. "You were going to tidy it, I thought. I took a look at it while the coffee was perking. And look what I found." She was waving a thin piece of blue paper at him and frowning.

He leaned forward and took the paper. A check for one thousand dollars and, clipped to it, a note that simply read, "We have nothing to spend our money on at home. Please use this for the house or the new barn. Love to you both, David and Martha." Smiling in surprise, he looked up.

Maggie's eyes were narrowed. "We can't take it, Don."

"Maggie! A thousand bucks!"

"We can't."

"Why not? Your own brother."

"It's much more than they can afford."

He laid the check on one knee and sipped slowly, trying to make sense of her. "No way they can't, Maggie. Your brother's a *doctor.*"

"With three kids and a mortgage."

He decided to try another tack, "Listen, how long have you known Martha?"

She looked suspiciously at him over her mug. "Almost as long as David has. He brought her home early on, as far as I remember."

Don saw Martha's untidy hair and kind eyes, remembered her thoroughness in the scrubbing and painting. "And would you say she's given to rash, ridiculous actions?"

Maggie's mug came away from her lips with a bump that sent some of the coffee onto her overalls. "Ah—you're trying to put words into my mouth," she said irritably and rubbed at the stains with a paper napkin.

"But is she?" he pursued.

She grimaced. "You know she's not."

"And David? Is he?"

She laughed. "Yes, quite often."

"But not without quick thinking, I'll bet. No, Maggie. You won't convince me we shouldn't take it. We need every bit of money we can get—you know that. And they love you. I think they quite like me, even though I—"

"Oh, they do!"

"Then I'm taking this to the bank tomorrow. Anyway—" He stretched out his legs and shut his eyes for a moment, remembering the service again. "They both heard the same preaching I did this morning—about learning to accept what others want to do for us. The sin of self-sufficiency. A kind of pride."

He opened his eyes again and looked at her. She stared back at him and didn't answer.

He left her still sleeping and drove to Grays' for early milking. When he came back, Tony and Larry were standing in the yard staring at the picket fence and chicken wire he had just erected in one corner for Maggie's chickens. He leaned out of the jeep window and saw but ignored their amusement.

"Morning, you guys."

"Hi, Don."

When he'd parked, he swung down onto the dust beside them. Heat already rose like a wall from the ground, and the grasshoppers were shrieking and whirring in the pasture. This heat made him think of the burning barn, but he didn't want to talk about it with Larry and Tony. Not today. "You had breakfast?"

"Yup, early," Tony answered. Larry shook his head. "Not me."

"C'mon in, then, and we'll all have coffee before we get going."

The three of them stomped in through the screen door. Don put down the day's can of milk and pulled off his boots. "Boots on the mat, Tony."

"Who? Me? The little woman got you barking like a trained dog already, has she?"

Don laughed easily and winked. "She can train me all she wants."

" 'Love's young dream—beautiful dreamer—' " Larry crooned.

Their boots thudded to the porch floor. Inside, Maggie stood at the stove with her back to them. In a worn cotton dress she looked tiny, her brown hair thick and still tumbled from bed. The scrubbed table was set for two, and above her head the clock on the shelf said just after eight. She turned, flushing, her eyes dilating with a mixture of pleasure and embarrassment.

"Sorry, Don, I didn't know you were *all* coming in."

Even if he had to take his boots off, he wasn't going to ask her if he could bring in his men for breakfast. "Well, here we are."

She poured coffee and scrambled more eggs, not saying much, so he knew she was irritated. But she would have to get used to Larry and Tony.

"Sure have made this kitchen nice, ma'am," Tony said in what Don knew was his best company voice.

She moved backward and he saw the early morning shine on her cheeks.

"You don't need to 'ma'am' me, Tony."

"It does look better, though."

She nodded. "Yes. We've got Martha and David to thank for that. Now it's fit for company—you and Larry for instance."

There was a slight edge to her voice, and Don groaned mentally. She had wanted to go back to bed with him, then—was that it? She was reaching up to the shelf and then pushing two bulky envelopes into his hand. "The mailman came already."

Ithaca. He hardly stopped to look further at the postmark. "That tester was quick."

Larry took the discarded envelope. They pushed aside the cutlery and spread the computerized sheets on the table. Maggie turned her back again, her shoulders frowning in tight disapproval, and cracked two more eggs into the pan. They bubbled and hissed for a second; then he heard her stirring and scraping quickly to stop them burning. She was not yet used to the speed of the wood stove.

"What d'you think?" Tony asked uncertainly.

The first sheet of words and figures danced a jig in front of his eyes; it was always the same. *Pounds of milk, butterfat, protein, mature equivalent, somatic cell count, grain recommendation, calories . . .* He fumbled to the herd summary at the back. *RHA, 14,000 lb milk, 450 lb butterfat.* The figures were way below average for New York Holsteins, and his fingers tightened on the edge of the sheets. "Bad," he murmured.

Maggie came toward them, plates heaped and

steaming. Her face had relaxed, unfolded, and her eyes caught his. "You guys need something in your stomachs. Then we can talk herd averages, okay?" Business-like, she pushed the sheets aside. "Come on. It can't be that bad."

Don wanted to believe her, and Tony was nodding, already scooping up eggs. Hadn't he told himself all week what the results would be?

"What'd you expect, Don, after the fire?" Tony demanded. "Sixteen-five and five-fifty? Of course they're down!"

"Yeah, Don—let's look at each one separately and worry about them that way," Larry put in. "Don't make yourself ill with a bunch of figures. You know how good the print-outs were getting before the fire, and you know they'll go up again."

They ate in silence for a while, though Don noticed Maggie's eyes darting back and forth all the time. She was opposite him, next to Tony, and her hair kept brushing Tony's shoulder as she leaned forward—so that he wanted to push it away and tell Tony to move. But he didn't.

"There was another envelope, Don," she said at last. Her voice was careful, as if she wanted to placate him after the bad news.

"Couldn't be worse than the other one," he said. And it wasn't: the financing was through for the barn. "Listen to this!" He read the letter aloud, his voice shaking with the abrupt swing from gloom to euphoria.

Maggie dropped her fork, clapped her hands and leaned forward to kiss him. Larry and Tony grinned and proffered their hands. "Where's the bubbly, Don?"

Someone poured four glasses of frothing milk from the morning can, and they toasted each other and the barn—laughing, unbelieving, chattering fast about bringing the herd back from Grays' in a few weeks.

Over it all, Maggie's eyes found his again. "You were

right to hold out," she told him quietly. "Sheep, batteries, pigs—they would have done us no good at all."

Us. It was her empire as well.

————

The men had gone, Larry muttering about spraying
the alfalfa, and Tony and Don to make the second cut
of hay. She wound the windows open so that the air
came through the screens, but it was breathless, almost as stale as the air in the kitchen, and beads of
sweat formed under her dress.

She showered quickly. Don had left her a list of people to phone: the vet, the nursery, Wayne Feed and Agway, Mark King, and the contractors who would probably be building the barn. Simply making the list had
cheered him, as if plans of action stemmed the tide of
fear about the low figures on the print-out. But even
though his spirits had risen, her own had sunk almost
as soon as she found herself alone again.

Dressing, she switched on the inescapable WGR55
but tolerated it for only a few moments. The inanity of
the disc jockey, the vacuous ads needled her; and the
music jolted and pounded in her ears until she thought
her head would burst. *Is there no classical music in
this godforsaken place?*

The question pulled her up short. *I can't start thinking that way! I wanted to be here! I've got to get used
to it. This is rural New York, not Boston.*

All the same, frustration mounted. In spite of the
screens David had so carefully mended, late June bugs,
now dead, littered the floor by the side window and two
flies buzzed in slow circles overhead. She hurried with
her hair and strapped on her sandals, wanting to be
downstairs and outside with the chickens, but even so
little effort in the torpid air brought droplets of sweat
to her forehead and between her breasts, and she
longed for the hum and calm of an air-conditioner.

Don's phone calls took her longer than she expected, and her irritation continued as she struggled with the unfamiliar terminology both on Don's list and in the questions asked from the other end of the line. She replaced the telephone for the last time with a heavy sigh. Then she thought, *I must get out of here.*

She changed her clothes again, washed the dishes and went outside at last. A small breeze had come up, but still no clouds, and the charred smell of the barn tickled the back of her nose.

In the new pen the chicks clustered around her feet when she came to feed them, tumbling out of their box in haste, peeping and falling over each other like the kittens in the toolshed. She gave them fresh water and stood watching their minute beaks pecking and probing the feed. Relief flooded her. She wasn't just Don's cook and secretary after all; she had her cats and chickens to care for, and this afternoon the nursery would be delivering young trees and some shrubs for a small garden that she would dig and plant on the northwest side of the house. Her life was beginning, after all.

———————

After lunch she followed the men into the hayfield. Standing at the top as Don went down to his machine and climbed into the cab, she could forget the barn, the phone calls and the heat. With the sun on her left shoulder and the scent of conifers behind her, she turned her head this way and that and squinted into the white sky of early afternoon, saw the viridian of the cornfield and beyond it the thin ribbon of the creek in its fold between their fields and Wilkinsons'. Then she turned to the softer blue-white arc of the northern sky and the answering blue-green of the oatfields below. Beyond, Larry was throwing up a mist of dust and spray over the alfalfa heads. And from behind her, blue jays croaked and shrieked and clattered in the trees.

She felt replete, her senses almost aching from the rich fullness of it all. *Don's farm, our farm.*

Suddenly, she must remember it all. There was no way to record the hot sound and smell of birds, machines and trees, but she could surely recall the rest with a photograph.

She plunged back through the empty pasture where the cows would be grazing again in a few weeks, and across the yard. Her camera was still boxed, in an upstairs closet somewhere, and she riffled through cases, packets and bags until she found it.

In the same box were the few letters Don had written to her over the years. The pile was neatly secured with elastic bands, as she had fastened them for the move from Boston. Some time—not now when the house was so hot—she would sit and reread them all.

Outside again, she sat on a dry hummock at the top of the field and pointed the camera. Sunlight glared through the viewfinder, so she dusted off the back of her shorts and skirted the field to stand with the sun on her back. Not far from her now, Don and Tony plied back and forth cutting the hay. It lay in long waves across the field, like yellow-green waves riding toward her, foaming and cresting but never breaking. The scent of the hay entered every pore and pocket of her. Remembering Ellie's mad sneezing, she smiled to herself. This time there was no sharpness with the memory, only a soft pity. *Poor Ellie.* She could never walk through a hayfield, not now, and not even when she was alive.

With the camera she caught the two machines passing each other in the middle of the field, great wakes of hay rolling and settling behind them; two red monsters in a sea of hot colors—even the blues were hot here, she thought.

She searched the toolshed for barrow, trowel, and hoe, then trundled everything across the yard, past the chickens, and around to where the ground had been tilled for her flowers and shrubs. Not far away, cars hissed past on the highway, and she stood for several minutes looking helplessly at the overturned ridges of soil and stones. She wouldn't ask Don again what he thought she should plant next spring; he would only tease or tell her he had no time to think of such trivia. But she wished she knew more about flowers and seeds.

Tentatively at first, then with growing determination, she hacked at the clods with a hoe. Clay dust settled on her sandals and whitened her legs, and the inevitable sweat began to prick her back and glue the clothes to her hot skin. Now, however, she didn't mind. The strain of reaching, bending and raising the hoe to strike fulfilled something in her. Heavy clods broke and separated round her feet, and she piled the largest stones into the barrow. Aching, she toiled mindlessly.

At last the sun penetrated her shoulders and fore-arms. Almost in surprise, she looked to see the angry redness that stung her under the film of sweat. Sun-burn—but from sheer bodily effort? *Is this why Don loves his work? Because he can forget?*

She stopped, straightened her back and leaned on the hoe. Nearby mimosa leaves barely stirred, and the sun seemed to hang like a hawk over the house—invis-ible behind the white haze, but inexorable, missing nothing with its fierce eye. Even the cicadas and tree frogs by the pond were still, and except for herself and the mad cars careening past, the world lay limp, pow-erless, unprotesting.

I'm thirsty, she thought dully, and dropped the hoe. On the back porch the kittens blinked and stretched as she passed them. One tried to wind itself around her legs and scoot into the house, but she bent gently and pushed it back outside.

The office seemed dark after the glare, and she

paused to get her bearings as the yellow-green whorls disappeared from her retinas and left the room in its usual colors.

She telephoned the nursery to see if the shrubs would come after all. Yes, said the man patiently, as to a child, they were on their way. Then she splashed orange juice into a tall glass and cracked out some ice to top it. The temptation not to return to work outside was almost irresistible. After all, Don had only shrugged when she cajoled him to talk about the garden after the tilling was done. So she was impelled now only by her own wish to be useful, to make her own mark on the farm.

She slumped into his chair and shut her eyes briefly. No one was standing over her with deadlines and evaluations sheets now; the farm was a new world after the Boston school system. Here she could set her own goals, go at her own pace and—she hoped—find her own friends without the petty politics of the faculty lounge. But even better, here she could actually work with her body as well as her mind. In the stillness she felt her own blood flowing, her own body heat glowing. She could feel alive, and loved—and whole, after all.

Just as she was deciding to go back to work, the telephone rang, startling her. She jumped up, scattering ice cubes on the floor.

A voice she knew: deep, warm resonant, almost as full of love as Don's. "It's your old father-in-law. Listen, I know you've only been married a few weeks, but can a guy call you up now? Is the honeymoon over?"

She laughed. "No. I hope it won't be for a while. It's an odd one, McEnroe. And of course you can call, any time." She was pleased to hear from him.

"Odd? How so?" he bantered.

"You know as well as I do. My brother and sister-in-law only went a few days ago, so we're just finding out what it's like to be alone. But it's hardly alone, you

know, when there's the milk tester or the farm hands
for breakfast, and when I spend more time ringing the
Agway than talking to Don—" She stopped, knowing
she had started to sound sour. Had she worked the
morning's resentment out of her heart in the garden
this afternoon, only to be dogged by it again? She was
glad he had not telephoned in the morning. She added
hastily, "But, McEnroe, I'm loving it—honest! I think I
can even begin to understand the obsession. Don may
end up being married twice over to the land."

McEnroe grunted. "Not sure that's so good, Maggie.
Marianne and I will have to come over and see for ourselves. We were thinking—"

"You'll come and visit?"

He cleared his throat. "Yeah, well, how about a few
days in August during the recess? It'll be the last break
I get before the campaign, and I'll need all my strength
to fight off Nixon's cronies and the rest of the Republicans this year. I don't rate our chances, but—so what?
Holidays have to come first. Anyhow, Marianne wants
to see you, and I want to see the farm again." He
paused, unsure, "But you do need time on your own,
so maybe, well, what d'you think?"

She had never known him so diffident, and
laughed. "Of course you've got to come. Don'll be happy,
and if you can wait a few weeks, and if the weather
cools down any so I can work inside, I'll get the guest
room fixed up nicely for you."

"Very kind woman."

"Yeah, you wouldn't want the cots David and Martha had, I guess."

"Er—maybe not."

She knew he was thinking more of Marianne than
of himself. "No, I don't think so . . . You'd like to talk
to Don?"

"Yes, but maybe later. He'll be outside right now."

He had called because he wanted her, then, or he

would have called after dark. She was a McEnroe now.

"What's the guy up to, anyway?"

"Cutting the hay before it burns to nothing. It's hot here. Very hot."

McEnroe laughed. "I'll bet it is."

The line crackled, and Margaret waited. He had something more to add, she was certain.

"And you, Maggie? What about Labor Day or something? Could we lure you away for a few days to Boston?"

Again she was glad he hadn't telephoned in the morning. "McEnroe—thanks, that's very considerate. But not this year, I don't think. I'd rather not set a precedent for going off by myself, or I'll never get him on vacation, he's such a farmaholic. And I know he won't want to skip off in the middle of things this year. We got some good news this morning that he'll tell you about himself—I'll get him to call you. He'll need to be around for the whole summer, and I don't want to leave him."

"Not just yet, anyhow! Okay—fine, it was just a thought," McEnroe sounded easy, almost sleepy.

"But thanks—I know I'll miss Boston after a while." She looked down at the cubes she had dropped, melting at her feet.

"Then we'll see you next month, Maggie, and talk to you both before then."

August

She kept thinking the weather would break—a thunderstorm would roll in and sweep away the air hanging thick as shrouds of cobwebs over the Alleghenies. Every day the sky seemed lower and the baked ground nearer, closer. The fields, the house, the yard— sky and land—conspired to crush them together. She wondered that the earth did not crack under the weight of the lowering sky in the morning and the merciless beating of the afternoon sun—but it did not.

In between milking, spraying and feeding, Don spent more time than usual in and around the yard watching the first girders of the new barn go up. He seethed with impatience and excitement, and many times as she fed the chickens she stopped beside him to watch, too. The huge structure intersected the western sky like a great geometrical drawing: dark lines and angles against the blur of humid sunsets.

McEnroe and Marianne arrived for a few days, and McEnroe was infected by the excitement, wanted to borrow a hard hat and help with riveting and welding.

"Oh no, you don't," Don cautioned. "You can help Maggie instead. Her garden's shrivelling up like an overcooked pancake—"

"—On a hot griddle," she put in, prodding him.

McEnroe rubbed his stomach. "Talking of pancakes . . . Don't I remember some place in Arcade once—?"

Don laughed. "Junk food. Wait'll you taste Maggie's pancakes. But it's too hot. Far too hot."

They stood out in the yard on the third evening as

311

darkness fell. Marianne had gone upstairs, as she said, to dress for supper.

McEnroe sniffed. "Oh well, I guess it is too hot. I'll just have to come back in November again."

"Why not indeed?" Don mused.

She said nothing. Then it would be a year, almost, since Ellie—no, she would not think of her now. "Come on, McEnroe. You fixed up your gardens pretty nicely. You tell me what to do with this wreck of a garden."

He flapped his big hands. "Not me, girl. Always had gardeners to do my dirty work."

"Oh, but your garden—" She stopped. She should have expected his reply. "Well, come on, anyhow."

Grinning, McEnroe exchanged glances with Don, and allowed her to lead him around the side of the house to the garden. "Nice mimosa you got there, Maggie."

Above them the lacy fronds hung heavy under the humidity. Only a few of the powder-puff blossoms remained; summer would end soon.

"Yes, it's my favorite tree."

"It sure grew quick."

"What?"

"It came up quick, I said. Thought you only just planted this patch."

She punched his arm, laughing. "Patch!—it's my *garden*. The mimosa—"

"I can't see much. Apart from the tree, just a few old stalks here and there maybe."

"Stalks!" she shrieked.

"Yeah—those stick things. What are they, anyway?"

Her shoulders slumped. "They were young rhododendrons. But as soon as I got them in the ground, I looked in one of Don's college books and found they like peaty soil—acid stuff. Of course no one told me that at the nursery! There's fifty bucks down the drain before I even start. Just look at that clay, will you?"

He bent over and stared. "Looks like ordinary old dirt to me."

Behind them came Marianne's clipped steps. Even in the yard she would not surrender to sneakers but walked as usual in high heels. Now as she came around the corner of the house, she merely said, "Well, what are you two doing out here? If you want to watch the sunset you should be out past the barns."

McEnroe pulled her arm through his. "We didn't give it a thought. Talking horticulture here." He said it *haughty-culture,* with a wink at Margaret.

"Oh," said Marianne.

"Yes," Margaret confirmed. "There's a few snakes in the grass here."

"What snakes? What grass?"

"No, honey," McEnroe laughed. *"Problems.* Look, everything's drying up."

Marianne shook her head, then appealed to Margaret, her fine eyebrows drawing together, and lines gathering on her forehead. "Listen, d'you really think this farm will amount to much? Even your shrubs look sick, and the barn's burned, and I heard Don talking about some infestation in the crops, and 'mastitis' in one of his cows, whatever that is."

Margaret felt the lightness and laughter of her moments with McEnroe evaporate. She had lain awake several nights herself in the past few weeks listening to Don tossing back and forth, muttering and sometimes even grinding his teeth. She was learning that there was little that was "natural" or "easy" in farming. But she wasn't going to admit her anxiety to Marianne now. Marianne trusted nothing outside Massachusetts.

Then she remembered a conversation with Ellie long ago. *Pilgrims, fish and holy Democrats.* So long ago—but it made her laugh. The laugh broke the tension. She found herself able to say, "Of course this farm'll amount to something. I know it in my bones."

She hugged herself. "Don's a good farmer. Even old Mr. Gray—the farmer who's letting Don use his milking barn—even that grumpy old man thinks so. I believe in what he's doing. Yes, it's very hard work. But there's nowhere else on earth he'd rather be."

Marianne fixed her with a skeptical gaze but said nothing. McEnroe started whistling "On the Street Where You Live" and winked at Maggie again.

She looked away from them both to the tree. Even in the early twilight a few bees still rolled from one flower to another. Then the cicadas started. Behind the long shadows of the new barn structures; beyond the pastures, the oats, the creek, and the hawk, the sun winked out for the night.

———

McEnroe stretched and smiled around at the others. "This is a good place to be. Sure beats the stale Senate and the campaign trail. I'm not looking forward to the election one bit."

"I'm glad you're enjoying yourself." Don pushed away his plate and sat back. "Good supper, Maggie. Again!"

Marianne, too, moved her plate, but she leaned forward toward her husband, and her eyes were unhappy. "Julius—I know you'd love to stay for weeks—" Her eyes slid left to Don's face then back to her husband's. "But there are things I've got to get home for."

Margaret saw him look back, puzzled and quizzical. There was a slight pause, then he shrugged, went to the telephone, booked her a flight for the next afternoon, and offered to help her pack.

She looked relieved. "No—you wouldn't know how to fold a skirt, dear. You'd better get Maggie to pack for you when you come home, as well."

McEnroe rubbed the back of his neck wearily. "I'm sure she will. Oh, it's hot. Why the heck didn't we go out to eat at some place with air-conditioning tonight?" He wiped away the sweat.

"It's your martini mouth talking," Don mocked. "A few weeks up here without much hooch and you'd be tough and fit as we are."

"You are," Maggie moaned. "None of my clothes fit any more. I'm getting fat."

McEnroe's eyebrows quirked. "Already, Don?"

"No, and don't you rush us! We both love kids, but this just isn't the time for them."

Maggie opened her mouth to say something, but stopped, uneasy. Then, catching her eye, Marianne coughed, and said brightly, "Well, we'd better go shopping on the way tomorrow. Are there good stores by the airport some place?"

"Buffalo?" Don said through a mouthful. "Sure—lots of good places."

Marianne brightened. "We could all go, Don. That'd be nice."

"No thanks," Don insisted.

"I'll go, but only if they've got air-conditioning." McEnroe sighed. "Otherwise, Maggie can drive you herself."

Marianne turned the stem of her glass between her fingers. "Not in the jeep, please, dear."

"Nope, I'll need it myself . . . McEnroe, of course the stores are cooled. You take the women up, okay? I'll get you another car."

Dazed, she watched them fence back and forth.

Don was looking back, a smile in his eyes. "You really need new clothes, Maggie?"

Surprised by her own sudden awkwardness, she felt herself flush. "Well—I guess I can get by with—"

McEnroe seemed to read her thoughts. "No way. You're a McEnroe now. Marianne and I'll get you turned out just dandy tomorrow."

"Oh—McEnroe! You're generous." She began to

laugh. "But no one says 'dandy' any more." *McEnroe. I am really a McEnroe!*

"He does," Don said firmly, and beamed at her.

———

She knew McEnroe was watching her as she drove back from Buffalo. He pretended to have his eyes on the road, but they were on her, instead. *Something's on his mind.*

The car windows were down to cool them, but McEnroe's cigar smoke still seemed to hang in the breeze that burst past them. She wanted to say *Penny for them?* but talking was almost impossible. At last they pulled onto Route 39: the last stretch of the ride home, and she deliberately slowed the car. Beside them a white sign advertised a highway to the town of Freedom, and she laughed aloud.

"What?" he asked.

"That sign back there. It says 'Freedom.' Weird names in this state, aren't they?"

"Guess so." He puffed smoke out into the wind. "Maggie?"

Now he'll tell me. "What?" For a second her eyes flashed to his, and she felt foolish, echoing his own word.

"I just love to see you laugh and smile now. You and Don haven't got it easy, but you seem happy. Tell me, are you?"

"Happy? Oh, yes."

"Utterly, completely besotted? Yes, you can nod, and I've got to say it. Don *better* make you happy. He doesn't know how lucky he is with you." He drew on the cigar, turning slightly from the corner of her vision, then blowing out smoke again. "Look at you! You're turning farmer yourself. Marianne, now—there's a lovely, lovely woman. But when she doesn't like something, off she goes. Doesn't matter whether I go or stay—and here we are coming back from the airport, and there *she* goes, flitting off in a plane to Boston! Same thing at party caucuses. But Don—he'll have you around, thick or thin. You're good, Maggie."

She heard his voice veer from weary to maudlin, and didn't know how to answer. Marianne had a mind of her own, but because Maggie knew how solid their marriage was, what he was saying made her uncomfortable.

He went on, "Like I said, look at you. Can't get certified right away to teach in New York even if you wanted to—but do you complain? No! You hitch up the rototiller and make a garden, put up a picket and make a chicken farm."

She began to laugh again. "Not exactly, you know. Don humored me. He tilled the garden and put up the fence. He says I'm playing Mr. and Mrs. Old-MacDonald-had-a-farm, and he'll let me do that until I learn how to be a real wife."

McEnroe snorted. "Doesn't know when he's got one."

"And anyway, we've only been married a couple months."

"That all? Seems like years. Should have been."

"No—don't say that. It wouldn't have worked before. He didn't want me. I was just Ellie's appendage. He didn't really even see me, I don't think." She hesitated, feeling somewhat the outsider again. Ellie had hardly come into their conversation during the four days they had been together; Marianne resolutely would not speak or hear of her, and McEnroe only sighed heavily each time her name passed Don's lips. But Maggie had loved Ellie as much as they had and couldn't remain silent for ever.

McEnroe tapped her shoulder. "Well, if Don was blind at the time, I know for sure, Margaret McEnroe, that he didn't get his blindness from his old man!"

His eyes were crinkling again, she noticed. It was all right then—was it—to speak of Ellie? She waited.

"You know, if that was how Don saw you—and I'm not sure you're being just to your own husband—then that was how Ellie saw you, too: an appendage to Ellie. A convenient one." His voice was smooth: the courtroom or State Senate rhetorician.

"Do you *really* think so. Really?" She slowed the car more. Ahead of them, the cemetery on the edge of Arcade lay prostrate under the afternoon heat, its banks of petunias wilting. His voice had lost the professional edge, but he was serious. "Yes, really and truly and really."

Keeping her voice light, she parried, "Now who's just?" He sighed heavily again, and she took courage to go on. "I think I'll ask you a very hard question, Mr. Politician, sir."

"Ask, then."

"Statement first." She was thinking quickly, unsure even of her own conclusions. "Some things I know, McEnroe. One of them is how blind prejudiced you are about a certain daughter-in-law of yours. She knows how much you love her. You show it over and over again. Look how you came after me when I'd given up on Don and Ellie—and you say how loyal I am! You gave me the guts to keep hoping—for both of them. You did, you know."

"Okay—you've made your statement, so where's the question, Mrs. Prosecutor?"

She took a quick breath. "Yes . . . I know how much you loved me from the very first time I was in your house. But Ellie—what about Ellie? Did she know you loved *her*?"

Inwardly, she trembled. Somewhere there was a boundary, a limit to his love for her. Had she passed it, risking this question? She was driving so slowly now, not seeing the stores and clapboard houses in the town, that she even heard the flick of his cigar ash out of the side window.

"Maggie."

She wanted to stop the car and run. His voice was pained, low.

"Gentle Maggie, but sharp as well."

"Oh—McEnroe, I'm—"

"No, don't say sorry."

She wished they could start the conversation all over again. "But I *am* sorry. I was presuming too much."

"No." He shifted suddenly, pulling at the seatbelt. "No. Want a job in an aging attorney's office?"

"Ouch."

"Now I can say sorry, too."

"So we're quits."

"Not exactly. I still haven't answered you. 'Did she know?' You tell me, now."

"I'm not sure—honest." She groped for memories of holidays and weekends in Bedford. "I know she felt close to Marianne—"

"In a superficial kind of way, maybe."

She could neither agree nor disagree. "And I think— I think she probably loved you. But never stopped to say it to you or even to herself. You know?"

"But we're not talking about whether she loved Marianne and me. You asked whether she knew *we* loved *her*. And I said—you tell me."

Margaret cringed, began to falter. "I guess she loved you for what you could do for her, give her. She knew you would be there for those things." She stopped, took a breath, then tried again. "But I don't—"

"Nor do I. I'm not at all sure she knew that Marianne loved her, let alone that I loved her." He twisted the cigar in the dashboard ashtray and discarded it there, only half smoked.

In a small voice, Margaret said, "Listen, it's over

now. We can't unmake the past. We can't live in it and let it poison the present. I should never have asked what I did. It was wrong, especially . . ." She broke off, uncertain how to go on without giving offense. "But we were talking about justice a minute ago—it all seems so unfair to Ellie. She had men, clothes, media attention, fun. But she had nothing if she didn't know—"

"And you're trying to say we didn't show her love?" His voice was full of restrained bitterness.

She almost let go of the wheel on the bend she was taking. "No! Oh—no." She shook her head and tried to think more clearly. "It sounded like that, I guess. But I wouldn't dare. I don't have children. What do I know about raising kids with wills of their own? Oh, isn't love twisted and sad sometimes, McEnroe? It goes one way—parent to child, woman to man—for years and years with no return, no flicker of an answer. *Why?* It doesn't make sense. It's unjust!" They were wandering blindly in a dead-end conversation, and Maggie felt stifled, breathless, wanting light and understanding.

McEnroe made no attempt to answer her. Instead he retrieved his cigar and tried in vain to relight it. Then he laughed, suddenly. "You'll be a good mother, Margaret McEnroe."

She sighed at the release of the tension. "What makes you think so, huh?"

He elbowed her lightly. "You loved that crazy son of mine for so long. Now look what's happened. Even your own brother's under the McEnroe spell—didn't you say once he was against Don? But—back to you, I'm rambling! You'll be good. Madonna Margaret."

She gritted her teeth at the thought of paint and plaster statues in old churches. "I hope not."

McEnroe went on, unperturbed. "And since Ellie'll never give me any, you and Don have to get busy."

She groaned, felt herself grow hot, and laughed. She looked extra hard at the road ahead. They were passing the conifers that bordered the south pasture, and ahead of them the silos poked up into the haze. *Nearly home.*

"I want a nursery full of bonny bairns, you hear me?"

I do too, she thought, *but even though we're doing nothing to prevent children, Don doesn't want them. Not yet, oh, not yet.* She sighed. "We already told you," she said gently, "don't rush us."

"You got some nice loose clothes today. Could come in handy."

"Maybe. They're the style—that's all." But then she thought of the kittens burrowing into her: warm, wriggling, intimate.

"You're sure you're not expecting already, then?"

From anyone else the question would have been presumptuous. She scoffed, "'Course I'm not. I know I'm not." But inwardly, she knew her certainty sounded silly, the very opposite of what she wanted to say.

"Well, Maggie, I'll let you off for now. But I mean what I said about coming back in November. Don and I'll go hunting and I'll check on the progress then, okay?"

The broken gateposts were still broken, and they jolted between them along the baked track. She didn't look across at him. "Oh, you can check," she said blandly. "But I have no plan whatever to get pregnant." *Or not to,* she added mentally.

"What about God's plans?" The reply came back with a quick laugh.

"Oh—" She gave him a quick look and her voice was high with exasperation. "You're worse than Don!"

September

The barn building was behind schedule but would be finished soon anyway, in time for the cold weather.

Since Larry and Tony and the construction crew were off for the Labor Day holiday, Don stood by himself in the yard and allowed himself the luxury of a leisurely stare. The old barn had long gone, and in its place rose the pale green siding of the new barn. The roof was already half on, and in its shadow lay heaps of sand, discarded shingles, pieces of wire, broken blocks, and lengths of plastic pipe. Soon that rubble too would be bulldozed and hauled away, and the cows would come home for good. There would be a new batch of heifers; perhaps Margaret could learn to care for them.

He turned to look at her chickens and saw a young rooster strutting and scratching through the dust of their enclosure. The birds looked healthy and content; the hens—beady-eyed and glossy-feathered—would soon be laying. And if he knew Maggie she'd have ducks in the pond by Easter.

Something popped and whizzed past his ear. Suppressed laughter welled up behind him, followed by a hissing noise. He swung around in surprise. She was standing behind him holding a magnum of champagne. White spume erupted down the bottle and onto her hands. She stood licking them, laughing at him, her eyes very bright, and her throat catching the last of the sunlight.

"What on earth, Maggie?"

"You were celebrating the barn. Don't deny it. I saw

you from the window. So I thought I'd help you out a little." She produced two plastic cups from her pocket and started to pour.

"You amazing woman! Here, let me—it's an insult to pour that into those. . . . Where'd you get it, anyhow?"

"The wedding. Several bottles were left. I hid them."

"There are more?"

"Oh, sure."

He began to laugh, dazed and full of wonder at her. They sat down together on the porch step in the gathering dusk. "I've never drunk champagne on the back porch before."

She looked at him happily. "Me neither. But it's Labor Day as well. See—we've got *two* reasons to celebrate."

"And never out of plastic cups, either."

"Well—" She leaned toward him. Desire took hold of him, and he set down his cup to put his arms around her. She was saying into his hair, "If you don't like your drink I'll have both. Here, give me it."

He stopped her mouth with a kiss, but she was struggling, trying to reach his cup, and teasing him. He moved it out of her reach and held her very still. "This reminds me: we haven't had a real wrestling match since you broke that jar of jam—at Hammonds' last year—remember?"

Her eyebrows rose exaggeratedly. "*I* broke it? Funny, Don. No, *you* broke it."

"*You* did. It was all a ploy to get me into your arms."

"Baloney! It was *your* fault. And you started the fight, as well, that time."

"About time we had another match, I'd say. Can't have you getting out of practice."

"Oh no you don't!" She leapt up suddenly, spilling her champagne, but quickly enough to grab the bottle. The screen door slammed after her, and he heard her giggling from his office. Then the light went on in the kitchen, and he realized how quickly darkness had fallen. The evening grew quiet except for the inexorable cicadas and tree frogs and the whine of gnats. One of the cats snaked itself around his feet and tried to climb into his lap. "Oh—you'll get the better of me yet," he murmured, stroking the little ears and scratching under the cat's jaw until it purred.

He waited, expecting her to come out again. He felt warm from the champagne, and warm from the sensation of her nearness, her straightforward happiness. How had he overlooked her for so long? He held the cat up and addressed it, nose to nose. "How did I, huh?"

Then he heard footsteps again. "Out here talking to yourself already, Don McEnroe?" she laughed.

He turned lazily. Her nose was pressed against the screen, and she held two plates of food. The aroma of curry wafted over the air.

"Eat in or out, Don?"

He stretched and stood up. "Inside, I guess. But I think I'll have you for supper before I eat that curry. What d'you reckon?"

She whirled around, and he chased her through the office and into the kitchen. "Not fair! I've got plates—" She set them down quickly next to the champagne, and he reached to catch her. She dodged him and began to wail in mock dismay, "You can't do this! The recipe was for a redhot curry—supposed to cool us down ready for fall!"

"Oh, Maggie—d'you believe everything you read in cookbooks?" He lunged again, missed again, but then stood still. "Hey, not bad, Maggie. Never knew you were so agile."

"Ah—all that tennis and racquetball I played while I was pining for you."

"Racquetball?" he echoed, laughing.

"Well, I had to do something while I was waiting for

you to come to your senses."

"Oh—you're fresh!" He stepped very slowly around the table, but his tactics failed again, and still she faced him from the other side. "C'mon, I'm much hotter than any curry, and I'm hungry—"

"Then let's eat."

"—For you. Yes—let's."

"Last of the red-hot lovers—that what you think you are?"

He tried to gauge from her face whether she was being coy or sarcastic, but she dissolved into laughter again, and he made a last rush around the table to the bottom of the stairs and caught her in his arms. She leaned in to him and he held her very close, one hand on her back, the other in her warm hair. "Oh, Maggie, I hope you like cold curry."

October

She opened her eyes to full daylight. The bedclothes on Don's side were tossed back, but the sheets felt cold under her hand. Groaning, she flopped back. *He's been up for hours!* She told herself to leave the warmth of bed, but her body felt heavy and her stomach hollow and strange. She rolled over and fell asleep again.

When she awoke the second time, Don was standing by the bed with a mug of coffee in his hand. His hair was untidy, and a streak of mud ran down one side of his face, but he was smiling.

"Oh, no! What time is it?"

"Nine-thirty. I came in for breakfast, and you weren't down there." He sat down and stroked her face. "You okay?"

Flustered, she sat up and took the mug from him. Rubbing her eyes with her free hand, she murmured, "Sure. Guess I just fell asleep again. This won't do at all!" A picture of a calendar formed itself in her mind, and she saw herself as she usually was at the turn of September into October: changing bulletin boards to celebrate fall, collecting colored leaves on the playground with the children, checking that they all had gloves for the coming winter. . . . She was losing the focus and clarity and order of her life now that she did not have to be up so early every day for school.

She groaned again. "Sorry—you must be pretty hungry. Oh, and I was going down to the store this morning."

"No sweat. There's still plenty of time. I grabbed

something out of the fridge, anyhow."

She sipped the coffee, but as soon as she swallowed the first mouthful she knew she had made a mistake. Her gorge seemed to rise into her throat, and a violent cough made her splutter droplets of coffee all over the bedspread.

Don took the mug back from her as she tried to catch her breath, and she dropped her head onto her knees so that he wouldn't see her face. For a few moments her stomach felt so leaden that she was afraid to move. She heard him saying something about some machine parts he'd have to pick up in Buffalo. "So I'll be gone most of the day. You can have the jeep, if you want. I really need the pick-up for this job. And keep an eye on the guys in the yard, will you?"

"Uhuh." Tendrils of dread crept up from the pit of her stomach and twisted themselves like bindweed around her insides. She still did not dare to move or speak.

He bent and put the coffee back into one of her hands and laughed at her. "Get going, Mrs. Lazybug." He tousled her hair, kissed the top of her head; then she heard his steps on the stairs, and the slam of the screen door. He was gone.

Very deliberately she set the coffee down and moved cautiously to swing her feet over the edge of the bed. Her mind was working faster now, and her own quick breaths frightened her. *I'm going to be sick unless I do something quickly.* She dropped her head again, this time between her knees, until her breaths were steady and even, then she stood up shakily. *It can't be. Not yet, oh, please not quite yet.*

She inched down the stairs, clutching the banister, intent on getting to the kitchen. Toast, not coffee, was what she needed first. But then the calendar loomed in her mind again. She stiffened her back and marched straight past the kitchen table into Don's office.

The calendar still said "September." She fumbled with the top sheet, a thin mask of sweat breaking out on her face, and counted out the days. Then she ripped off September and went on counting.

Either she had eaten something the night before that was making her feel ill—or she was carrying their first child.

The telephone rang. The sound was so shrill to her tense body that she dropped the calendar, laughed hysterically, then felt again the warnings of nausea. Leaving the phone still pealing, she ran back into the kitchen and was sick in the sink. The phone stopped, and she remained where she was, leaning over the sink, her whole body trembling but strangely relieved.

She did not know whether to laugh or cry. *This is what I've dreamed of, isn't it? I'm married to the man I wanted and loved all my life. His child may be growing in me already. Then why not be glad? Because I'm afraid. Afraid of what? Afraid of being a mother when I'm scarcely a wife. Afraid of failing as my father must feel he's failed. Afraid of having no money to care for that child. Just plain scared, Maggie Fuller McEnroe, that's what you are.* Don's words rang in her head over and over again: *"We both love kids, but this just isn't the time for them."*

She shivered, spat out and rinsed her mouth. Then, as she cleaned up and made herself something to eat that would not make her sick again, her mind cleared. *Of course I'm not pregnant. It's a ridiculous notion. No need for Don to know. He's no more ready than I am for a new life. I can't be.*

Outside the kitchen window she heard the clang of steel on steel, then the roar of a bulldozer shifting some of the rubble beside the new barn. The rest of the world was going on as usual. *Of course I'm not pregnant. The barn's not even finished yet, and we've got the neighbors coming to see it in a few weeks. No way I'm preg-*

nant. There's simply too much else to do. And then she heard herself mocking herself, laughing at her own false reasoning.

Though she chose her food more carefully at lunchtime, she still felt hotter and heavier than usual afterward. *Imagination,* she told herself severely as she went out to feed the chickens.

The wind came up in a gust and tossed her scarf round her ears as she scattered the corn. She stood watching the birds pecking and squabbling and squawking, and the new weather-vane on the top of the barn went spinning like a mad thing in the wind. The sunlight slanted down between the silos and seemed to shift as the dust motes danced in it.

She turned to watch the workmen, but not one was in sight. The building was quieter now that the roof was on; the men seemed to be working inside most of the time this week, fitting pipes and wiring.

A construction vehicle drew up behind her. No, it wasn't a construction truck; it was a car she did not recognize. She hesitated, curious, as the hens fluttered away to the corner of the house.

A man she did not know stepped out and stood with one hand resting on the top of the car. She noticed vaguely that he was too slightly built for a farmer and too cleanly dressed for a milk tester.

"Margaret?"

She looked at him uncertainly. "Yes—" Something bitter-sweet stirred in her memory, but was lost. She frowned, looking again at his close-cut black curls and neatly trimmed beard. Then she laughed, realizing how tightly she was clutching the bowl of corn. It was a nervous laugh. "Can I help you?"

"I tried to call you before I came. There was no answer. So I thought I would just show up. I heard you were living here."

She pushed her hair out of her eyes. "Forgive me, should I—?"

"Ah, it's the beard, I guess."

Then she remembered. *That night in Boston . . . that "party" . . . Constantine.* She panicked. *What does he want? And what should I say?*

"But I thought you might remember anyhow. Well—" He must have seen the look of confusion on her face, for he suddenly broke off and moved toward her. For a moment she thought he would reach out his arms to her or kiss her, but he only took the bowl from her and dumped all the rest of the corn onto the ground. "Here, let them have a feast. Oh, look at them go, greedy beggars! Come on, Margaret, won't you ask me in for a cup of coffee at least? Or tea, maybe—I mean the right kind."

She laughed again. "Constantine," she said.

He faced her, still again. "Yes, that's me. Back from the dead."

She watched the wind make furrows in his hair, then her eyes dropped to meet his. They were dark but alive, not the eyes of a man who had suffered more than he could bear in the war. She remembered praying for him and found herself smiling. But then she shook her head. "I can't take this in! What, why, how—?"

"Listen, seriously, can you spare some tea? I've only got an hour or so this time. More another day, I hope, but I don't want you passing out with shock. I'll explain." He threw out his hands as he talked; there was something endearing about the way he spoke with his hands, but she must not think of that now.

"I'm married, Con," she blurted out. The heat came furiously into her face, and she felt gauche and foolish. She had to tell him, but what would he think now?

His eyes didn't waver. "I always figured you would be. Then I found out you were anyhow." His confidence seemed to evaporate, and the smile left his face. "But I wanted to see you for myself. I remembered you all the time I was out in the Far East—"

She noticed he did not name Vietnam. Was he after all one of the shell-shocked ones? She examined him again, more closely this time. No, he didn't look drugged or traumatized. His eyes were alert and keen. She had forgotten his face, but she remembered now how bright his eyes had been, and they were still bright.

"I wished I had your photo." He flapped his hands, and his face cleared. "Sorry, I don't mean to sound obsessive, crazy, like I'm some kind of nut. But all the other guys had photos of their girls, and before I left you were the only one who seemed to care. So I had to see you for myself."

"Oh, Con . . ." She suddenly felt very old. "Come on, I'll make you a pot of tea. We have a lot to talk about." And she led the way up the porch steps and through the office, her mind dazed as she went through the routines of filling the kettle and stoking the stove. She had seen in his face the same devotion Don must have once seen in hers and wanted to run from. But she must be kinder to him than Don had once been to her.

Over two steaming cups of tea, they faced each other across the bare table. She would not invite him into the parlor; she felt far more at ease and at home in the kitchen.

"I promised I'd explain," he began.

"Yes, please." She did not trust herself to say too much. Let him wonder where her husband was before she told him he was gone for the day.

"I'm on my way home for a few weeks—Chicago. My folks wanted to see me before I take the plunge."

"You're getting married, yourself?"

"No, no, not so fast. Hey, I thought it was Ellie who was always in a hurry, not you. No . . . it's more complicated than that. I've decided to go into the Abbey of the Genesee."

She looked blankly at him. "What's that?" The

whole day was taking on a surreal air: first she had overslept, then she had felt ill, and now a man she hadn't seen for three years had appeared—as if in the wind that still blew dust and sunbeams across the yard outside—telling her he was going to an *abbey.*

"A monastery, up the other end of the state." He rushed on, not waiting for more questions, though her brain was seething with them. "When I came back from the Far East, I got some money from the Vets and decided to take a theology course at Yale. There was a man there who talked all the time about Genesee. I went weekends with him and found a peace I'd never had. But I struggled with it, you know—if a guy can say he 'struggles' with peace. I kept thinking of you, wondering where you were, and somehow I didn't care to look out for other women at all."

She looked down, her discomfort increasing. She almost did not want to hear the rest of what he had to say.

"Wait, I don't mean to embarrass you, but you're a bigger part of my story than you know."

She stayed silent, thinking sadly, *He deceived himself, creating a memory of me that was a lie. Love— it's a kind of madness.* She sipped her tea and still did not look up.

He went on, smiling now. "It's all your fault! How well do you remember that night?"

She thought of Ellie—the sneezing and helpless hay fever, the laughter, the relative innocence of marijuana and the red-haired Santa Claus of a boyfriend. So different from cocaine and Steve.

"Yes," she said reluctantly. "Yes, I remember it very clearly."

"Then do you remember you prayed out loud for me?"

She flushed again, keeping her eyes on the rings in her mug of tea created by the movement of his hands as he talked. "Yes, why?"

"I think I told you I wasn't much of a Christian. But many of my friends were—after a fashion. And by the time I'd been in the war and back again I had questions I wanted answered. That's why I went to Yale. That's why I'm going into Genesee. And that's why I'm here to see you, today."

She shook her head again. "Con, I don't know what to—"

"You maybe don't have to say much of anything. I thought if anyone cared enough to pray, I must have some value in the scheme of things. That's something I held on to out in the jungle when I heard the Vietcong tracking us, or when the mortars were going over my head."

She looked up sharply. "You had more faith in that prayer, then, than I had myself. And I thought you were asleep! Dear God, I don't know a thing about prayer!" Now it was her own voice that was rushing on, throwing out words that would divert him off whatever trail he was following blindly in her direction. "I couldn't sleep that night, and I felt desperate. I suppose some of the habits of church education die hard, and that was one." She saw that he was shocked, but blundered on anyway, "You shouldn't have thought about me any more. I wasn't worth it. The prayer was all a sham, something that came out of fright." For a second she put her hands over her eyes, then glanced up again, her emotions swinging like the weather-vane on the barn. "Oh, but this is ironic! I'm surrounded by religious—" She was going to say "nuts," but it sounded too strong and bitter.

The hurt on his face registered, and she stopped. "My husband's a Christian. He'd be interested in your story—more than I am. And my brother, and my sister-in-law. You're wasting your time with me. I don't want God, and I'm sick of hearing about Him."

Con drank tea and stayed quiet for a moment. "Is it because of Ellie?"

"No," she said quickly. *Does he know, then?* "If anything, Ellie's dying seems to have driven people I know back to God. Don, for one. No."

"Then?" He registered no surprise.

Her mind went blank. "I don't know. Look, d'you mind if we talk about something else?"

He smiled. "Like—?"

"Like how you knew I was here, for a start." *Safe ground, at least,* she thought. And she half retreated into her body to think and wonder about the possibility of the new life within her. But she listened to him, all the same.

He took a deep breath. "I couldn't remember your last name. Maybe I never knew it then, anyhow. But I was almost done at Yale and decided I'd look you up. I remembered Ellie's surname because of her father, but I couldn't find any Ellie McEnroes in the book. I tried her father, but I found out he's unlisted, so I called his office. In the end I went to see him. A bit presumptuous, but by then I was even more curious." He caught her eye. "Margaret, he told me Ellie had died and you had married her brother. And the way he talked I knew it was right for you both. So I haven't come to interfere. If anything it's the other way around, I came to say I owe you my life—possibly physically, and certainly spiritually."

Her eyes filled. "Oh, no, you mustn't say that. You don't know. I'm a faithless person." She thought of her own reactions that morning, of how her first thoughts were for herself and Don and their finances, not for any child she might be carrying. So what she had said about herself was true.

He laughed. "Faithless? Baloney! I don't know you really, but I know that much about you."

She swallowed. "Ah, but you don't know. Here I am—married only a few months, and I think I'm already pregnant." She stopped, horrified, hearing the words out of her own mouth for the first time, and not even being spoken to Don, but to a virtual stranger. "And though I do like children, you understand, and always have, I don't even know if Don will want a baby yet, and, and . . ." She paused again, listening to her own lamenting voice and hating it. *What's the matter with me?* "Sorry . . . you were telling me how you knew I was here."

His eyes measured her. How gentle he was! "Your father-in-law told me where the farm was. And I thought, well, going west from Boston I'd not be too far out of the way. And I wanted to see you anyway." He swept one arm round the kitchen, pointing out into the yard. "You're happy, aren't you?"

A cloud seemed to lift. "Yes, yes, I am. I didn't talk to you about Don that night."

"No reason you should have."

"Except that he was always, always on my mind. And I'd loved him since ever I could remember. I wouldn't have guessed we'd be living so far from home, but here we are. Yes, I'm happy. Just scared, that's all."

He waited for her, his eyebrows curved in enquiry.

"Oh, about the baby," she said miserably.

"But why?" He raised his hands again, palms up, in amazement, and for a chilling moment she remembered Steve's gestures, almost the same. But there was kindness, not suspicion and malice, on Con's face. "Your husband—Don—won't he be excited?"

"You should meet him," she said absently. "He's in Buffalo for the day."

He was listening carefully, not missing even the words she didn't speak. "You think he won't be pleased?"

Irritation suddenly built inside her. What right did this man have to ask these questions? "Please, let's not talk about that, either. Don doesn't know. I wish I hadn't mentioned it. Please."

Constantine looked down. "I didn't mean to probe. I'd just love to know how you came to be here . . . and about Ellie, if you can bear to tell me."

A sort of dam broke inside her, and all her annoyance with his questions vanished. The words began to pour out. "I got on well with Ellie in school, you see. No one expected us to be friends—I was always the frumpy one no one expected her to notice, but she had no order, no routine, no certainty in her life. And that's what brought us together at first. I guess that's what she liked in me. Then, after I met her brother one Christmas when I went home with her, I had other reasons for sticking up for Ellie, for looking out for her. We got an apartment together not long before you came to see us that night in '69.

"I was so besotted with Don I could hardly stand to be apart even from Ellie. And she got tired of me, not surprisingly, and chose friends I couldn't stomach. One in particular, a drug pusher—" She took a deep breath. "It was about two years after you and your friend came over. In fact, it must have been in March last year, because I remember I had been to see Don for a fiasco of a weekend in Vermont, when I thought everything with him was doomed. But that relationship wasn't doomed at all—" She smiled wryly, "As you can see. It was Ellie who was doomed, from the moment she set eyes on that man. She died last Christmas—maybe McEnroe already told you—in Miami. Cocaine overdose, or suicide. They couldn't really decide, or if they did, no one told the family."

He did not speak, and somehow she felt as she used to in the confessional, years before. She wasn't quite sure why Constantine was listening or even why she was telling him so much, uncovering the past again. But the words freed her, left her lighter.

She continued, "Then, well—Don ought to tell you this part of the story really—Don began to think about

God more. Somehow, I'm not sure how, wanting God in his life again got mixed up with wanting me in his life after all. And now—" She knew her face had split into a wide grin. "Well, now, I think he loves me far more than I love him."

She went on, talking more to herself now than to him. "I used to keep photos of him on every wall. He made fun of me and said I didn't know what he was like, and that he could never love a woman the way he loves the land. But he didn't know himself any more than I did, and now he's married to the two of us." She looked out at the farmyard, and added, "And I'm half married to what's out there myself. And he was right; I didn't know him. He's a good man, a better man than I even knew. And I'm trailing along somewhere behind, trying to find out what real love is. I don't think I understand anything about it, after all."

Con threw back his head. "Oh, Margaret!" he was laughing. "Oh, that's good. That's when you know all—when you come to the place of knowing that you really know nothing."

She scratched her head. "Too much Yale University theology, Constantine, for me. Let's have another cup of tea instead."

She would not need to give him a photograph of herself. Like Don, he was miles ahead of her. And he would find what he wanted at the Abbey of the Genesee, just as Don had found what he wanted here, with her, and at the little church in Arcade. Now it was only up to her to find what she wanted. Don was what she wanted, but she had come to understand that he could not be her all.

———

Don straightened his back, dusted off his hands and sighed. Then behind him he heard the jeep swinging into the yard, engine roaring and bits of gravel flying.

Maggie jumped out, her hair awry, turned, and started pulling bags of groceries out of the front seat.

"You're in a hurry! And that exhaust system needs—" He stopped, seeing her properly as she lifted two of the brown bags onto her hips. "Maggie—what's wrong?"

She puffed out her cheeks, and her breath showed white in the crisp air. Her face was red and unhappy. "Oh—I just feel rushed, that's all. Too much to do before this afternoon."

He took two more bags out for her and followed her into the kitchen. "It's okay. I'm around to help. And you needn't overdo it. There'll only be a few locals, that's all."

She dumped the first load of groceries on the table and pushed back her hair. "But I *do* want it to be nice. We hardly know anyone yet—I want time to make the food nice and myself—" She threw out her hands. "Well—a bit less like a sack of Portageville potatoes. I feel like a wreck."

Seeing her look of anxiety—so uncharacteristic, even during the early months with bad test results and a charred barn daily reminding them of the fire—he knew he couldn't laugh her mood away, so he bent and kissed her. "Please—it'll be fine. And look, there's something I want to show you."

She flapped her hands. "Now? We don't—"

"Yes—you've got a couple more bags out in the jeep, haven't you? It's out in the yard. Come on."

Outside he pointed to the new bumper sticker he had been pasting onto the pick-up as she returned.

Her face cleared and her eyes crinkled. "My cows vote Democrat! Oh—Don. Where on earth did you get that?"

"McEnroe's campaign manager, of course. He and

my father always dream up some kind of gimmick during the campaign. And look—there are more." He opened the tailgate of the pick-up and pulled out the padded envelope that had arrived this morning while she was shopping. "See? 'Even New York State farmers vote Democrat—vote McEnroe.' Hah! That'll get everyone's goat!"

"You're not going to stick those up everywhere, are you?" She frowned.

He laughed, "You sound a bit like my mother!"

"Don! This is New York—Republicansville, New York! You're crazy."

"All the more reason to wake them up."

She shrugged, and the sparkle left her eyes. "Show me tomorrow, okay? I think we'd better get started on this reception."

Resigning himself to spending the next few hours in the kitchen with her, he moved both vehicles out of the yard, stickered the pick-up, and took a last look at the barn before he went in. It gleamed. *God—thank you!* Even if it wasn't the traditional New England barn Margaret wanted, it was new and clean, and the cows would come home tomorrow. *My cows vote Democrat.*

––––––––

"It all looks great, Maggie. Thank you so much for all you've done." Don gave her hand a slight squeeze. Her hand was damp, and he turned his head sharply to look at her more closely. Her face was mottled—white in patches, pink in others, and her eyes looked huge. "Oh, sweetheart!" He took her by the shoulders, turned her to face him, feeling a chill of unexpected anxiety. "Whatever's wrong?" She averted her face, and he followed her gaze toward the laden table. She had even remembered flowers, and a spray of chrysanthemums shone from among the food. He knew he would never have thought of them.

He waited for an answer, but she only looked troubled, and took her time replying. "Just very tired, I guess," she said at last.

They were repeating themselves, he knew. "Are you sure that's all? Is there something—this morning I thought—"

"I told you, I'm *tired*." She twisted away, straightened a row of paper napkins, and went to the doorway. "Listen, they'll all be arriving any moment. I'll run and take a quick shower. I'm sure I'll feel better then." She blew him a kiss, and he saw she was trying to sound less nervous than she felt. "You look fine as you are," she added. "Could you answer the bell if they ring?"

"Ring? No one rings around here! Probably all come over the porch and in the back door."

"But your office!"

"Is a mess as usual, and always will be. Big deal! Theirs are probably worse." He watched her, and she seemed to be struggling with something inside. He wanted to hold her and wipe away the furrows on her forehead, the wordless ache speaking from her eyes, but there wasn't time now. "Go on—Maggie. Get your shower." She was retreating down the narrow hallway now, her back to him, so he raised his voice. "And the chrysanthemums look gorgeous. Like a painting. *Thanks!*" But he wasn't sure she'd heard him, and her figure dwindled to a shadow in the dusk of the October afternoon as she turned to climb the stairs.

The visitors came in twos and threes, and none to the front door. Chevies, Fords and Plymouths jammed the yard, most of them rusted, all of them muck-splattered. Tony and Larry directed traffic, uncomfortably dressed in clean sweaters and pressed trousers.

Margaret plied back and forth between the yard and the barn doors, bringing Don neighbors and townspeople to welcome and show around. Every time their eyes met she seemed more relaxed and self-possessed. Small as she was, she stood and moved so straight-backed that she looked quite tall. Was this her teacher's part? He caught snatches of what she was saying to the wives, and her tone was confident again.

"See—the cows can roam in and out through those back doors, and we've got an automated water system. Don'll explain if you're interested."

He smiled at her proudly, and she smiled back, uncertainly at first, then more gaily. But when some of the men came to ask questions, he lost sight of her as she went back out into the yard.

"How you gonna keep your animals clean enough with this set-up?"

"You won't know much about their feed consumption this way, will you?"

"I see the cows can't drink in these new stanchions. What'll you do about that, Mr. McEnroe?"

The first voices were hard and skeptical, the hostility barely veiled. He looked around him; most of the first arrivals were older men, New York farmers for generations, who were used to the long frigid winters, thin topsoil and stifling summers of Cattaraugus and Allegany counties. Their scorn was as unsurprising and as ingrained as the dirt in their skins.

"Old Davies would have a fit! What kind of a barn d'you call this, then?"

"He's a book farmer. This looks like something out of an Ag Tech showroom. No damn use at all for the poor cattle."

"What about your old barn, Mr. McEnroe? I heard it was arson."

"Someone careless, more like."

He couldn't let that pass. "It was faulty wiring. Mr. Davies couldn't have known about it—" He swallowed hard. "—or I'm sure he would have done something. At any rate, this barn wouldn't be up now if it'd been a case of arson or negligence—we'd still be fighting a court battle somewhere . . . look, if anyone's interested in the way we're going to work the feed and water systems—I'll show you now. Feel free to look around all you want." He felt like a tour guide one moment and defendant the next. His father would have been amused, and he suddenly wished McEnroe were with them.

Patiently, he showed them the outside feed bunks and pointed out the advantages of the free-stall arrangement. He heard dissent, however, between two or three men at the back of the group who stood with hands deep in their overall pockets and faces frozen in suspicion. *Why ever have they come?* he wondered. *Envy, curiosity?* Frank Gray was among them, sourest of all, like a bad taste in his mouth as Don tried to win them all around. Even as he explained the way the building was laid out, he overheard repeated murmurs of the words "arson" and "insurance money." Then, worst of all: "His father's some hot-shot lawyer and state senator over in Massachusetts, so I heard tell. Gotta be something funny about all this."

He bit his tongue and turned out of the open parlor doors toward the pasture so that no one would see the rush of angry blood to his face. The knives would have to be put away, he thought, before they all went inside for something to eat. Surely the wives would be more interested and generous than their husbands?

Larry came and found him at last. "Listen, man. Don't get uptight. They'll accept you in the end. Keep cool, okay? Your wife says she's going to serve up some coffee and cake. Let's go, Don."

Under her light jacket and sweater, Margaret felt the sweat prick and begin to trickle. She hated the way her body seemed to be betraying her now, when she most wanted to feel assured and in command. But even her words seemed to be coming out garbled and fragmented, and she finally gave up trying to say all but the essential "In here" or "There's my husband" or "Thank you for coming" and went on mechanically pouring coffee and passing plates of food.

The women clubbed together. They all seemed to know each other from diet clubs, bridge clubs, fish fries, auctions, 4-H Club meetings and the PTA. And they all dressed in the same way: open polyester jackets hanging to their wide hips; loose-fitting pastel slacks, and low-heeled shoes. Their hair was set and curled as if by one hairdresser, stiff and high in front, flattened behind their heads; and their voices were loud and full of forced, braying jollity. She disliked them, yet, even on her own ground, felt isolated and wanted somehow to belong.

She looked at a few of the younger wives—thinner than their older sisters, their eyes wavering toward hers with a mixture of sympathy and distrust. Their husbands would have told them to steer clear of her, perhaps; she never went to church, had never stood behind a stall at the PTA rummage sales, and apparently did not play bridge. So who knew if she was a nice girl at all?

At last all the visitors were gone except old man Wilkinson and his wife. Joel was nowhere in evidence, but she felt relieved to be left with at least one family she knew a little, even if their friendship so far had been guarded and slow in showing itself.

"You didn't have anything to eat yourself, Mrs. McEnroe," Sally Wilkinson commented.

Margaret looked up in surprise. "What? Oh—I guess I didn't." Automatically, she went on, "And please, call me Maggie, or Margaret, at least."

Sally Wilkinson laughed. She was large-boned, big bosomed, and her hair was as artificial and ugly as that of all the other women. But her smile seemed genuine. "Here, take this—and this—" She pushed plates into

Margaret's hands, and Don exchanged amused glances with her from across the other side of the table.

"That's right, Mrs. Wilkinson, fatten her up, will you! She's getting thinner than she used to be."

Margaret pulled a face at him and thought of the lumbering bodies of all the other women. She had never been thin herself, but she vowed she wouldn't let herself go entirely, either, even when the first baby came.

While Don and Jack Wilkinson talked—Wilkinson as laconic and crusty as ever, and Don with an unnatural joviality she hardly recognized—she gave half her attention to them and half to Sally, who began to talk about her grandchildren and about Joel, the last son at home. Maggie picked at the food. Having smelled all morning cupcakes in the oven, vegetables and cheese on the chopping board, she felt her stomach harden to a ball. She pushed her plate aside and looked up to find Don watching her with the same concern on his face as he had shown all day.

Sally Wilkinson clucked, "There. That's right— you've done such a good job today!" and sat down next to her, offering a cup of steaming tea.

Margaret smiled fleetingly at Don as Wilkinson began to talk again in his usual staccato sentences, this time about the local Rotary club, and tried to concentrate.

"I don't think I've ever seen you at church," Sally's eyes were speculative. "Don't you ever go with your husband? I see him there every week."

She flushed guiltily.

"Or are you not a Christian?"

It was hard to resent the inquisitiveness, especially in the only woman who had treated her humanly during the day. "Well, yes, I am, but—"

Sally hardly heard, shaking her head. "My daughters are the same. Ah, never mind, when you have children—"

"Yes," she said vaguely. "Yes, perhaps." She thought about Constantine going into Genesee Abbey. How strange that faith mattered so much to these people!

"And what about barn dances, now?" Sally pursued. "Would you and your husband ever want tickets? There's one in town next Friday." Don heard her and raised his brows inquiringly. She pretended not to have noticed his response. "I'm not sure. Usually, yes, it sounds good. But not this time," she said.

Don grinned disarmingly at Sally. "Not this time? Why not, Maggie?"

She shrugged, unable to think of an excuse, then became conscious again of the hardness in her stomach, of her own weariness. "Don—next time, maybe. I'm pretty tired."

"'Course she is." Joel suddenly came through the door, and she was glad he felt at home enough to walk straight in.

Wilkinson looked up at his son in surprise. "Thought you'd gone."

"Me too," said Sally.

"Have all you can eat, Joel." Margaret stirred herself and poured another cup of coffee.

"Why 'of course,' Joel?" Don asked.

Margaret felt awkward, suddenly. From the first there had been an unspoken link between her and this gangly, open-faced boy, and she sensed Don's wariness.

Oblivious, Joel dropped into a chair next to hers. "All this work for unfriendly neighbors—*and* the chickens and cats—there's a lot to be done around here."

She knew he was joking, but knew equally that he was on her side and that he understood her.

"You've been looking around out there, have you?"

"Yup." He gestured toward Don. "And I like it, Mr. McEnroe."

Don nodded curtly. "Good. So do I!"

"And I checked on those cats of yours, and the fowl. They look mighty fine." Joel had stopped calling her "ma'am," but now called her by no name at all.

Sally bit into her third—or sixth—cupcake. "Very good, these are. You'll *have* to come to the barn dance— we all bake something. And I can tell—"

"You're coming, aren't you?" Joel looked at her first, then, with a glance at Don, added, "Both of you?"

She wanted to hug him, but she shook her head. "No thanks, Joel. Next time, maybe."

Wilkinson got up suddenly, "Well, son, we'd better get off to the milking. Mr. McEnroe has to get over to Grays' as well, I guess." It was his longest speech all afternoon.

"Yes," Don agreed. His smile lit the room, and Maggie's heart turned over. "The last time. I'll be up early to bring them home tomorrow."

Later, Don asked, "What's this with Joel? He's got a crush on you bigger than his father's pumpkins."

"I've noticed."

"And why don't you want to go dancing?"

She didn't know what to say.

"That's not my Maggie. It's not just because you still feel out of place here, is it?"

"No—oh, no, Don."

"Then what?"

"I just don't want to."

He turned away from her to lock the back door and check to make sure there was enough wood in the stove for the night. She felt miles away from him, as if he was on a movie screen and she was in a dark hall watching him. He bent with that untidy lock of hair falling over his face, and the glow of the fire caught his blue eyes. But he did not look at her. "All right, then. I guess we won't go."

She took a quick breath. "Don—? Could I—I mean,

would you mind if I borrowed the jeep again tomorrow?"

Small lines appeared between his eyes. "No—" he said doubtfully. "I'll take the pick-up to church, after the cows come back, I guess. But why the jeep? Won't you come with me? It's an important day tomorrow for us, Maggie." He sounded almost pleading, and a heaviness settled on her.

She hardened herself. "No—I'd like to get some photos tomorrow morning. The trees are so gorgeous now."

He looked hurt, came toward her with his arms open, then dropped them to his sides. "Okay—you do that. Suit yourself."

It was like a paralysis in a bad dream. Why *couldn't* she tell him? Remembering McEnroe's question, "What about *God's* plans?" she suddenly wanted to cry.

———

Sunday proved so wet that she did not go out with the camera. She kept herself busy cooking, and drying out Don's clothes until early afternoon. Then in windbreakers they toured the barns, looked in on the cows in their new home, went out to the pasture that had lain fallow until now. Holding hands in the downpour, they dodged muck and puddles, Don laughing and she licking the rain off the end of her nose, longing to know his joy, but feeling almost numb. Wet, filthy but exultant, he was all but singing as he talked to her. The ebb and flow of their conversation was outwardly the same. She was making an effort to be perfectly natural and easy with him, and his anxiety about her seemed allayed for now.

But after he had gone out to do the morning milking on Monday she could wait no longer to get away alone. Not even staying to have breakfast with him, she nosed the jeep between the gateposts, turned onto Route 39, and felt a surge of relief.

The concrete ticked away below the wheels. In the blue-gray of morning the fall landscape next to the highway blurred to a drab continuum. Only the red torches of sumac illuminated her way until she climbed one of the longest hills and at last felt the full flood of early light on her face. Even her tired, veined hands on the wheel looked softer, and her wedding ring glinted.

Well, it's what I wanted.

The road fell away again. For a few seconds she re-lived a much longer journey the year before; the rush of adrenalin came again as the film replayed in her mind. She saw again the Hammonds' red farm build-ings in the wilderness of Vermont grays and whites, and knew she was near him. He would come walking up from the pasture again, and the dogs would bark again, and the wind would toss and turn her around as she stood waiting, aching to hold him as he came toward her. But then the look of disappointment: "Where's Ellie? Where's Ellie?"

The movie became still, framed on her internal screen, and the soundtrack repeated itself madden-ingly, "Where's Ellie?" Don had asked her the same question when Ellie died—asked it hopelessly then. But that was before he trusted in God and talked to her of His kindness.

She pressed harder on the accelerator, approaching a narrow bridge at the bottom of a valley, and the next hill came up to meet her. It was like a roller-coaster: swooping, dipping, rushing her forward, then up again. She felt suddenly loosed from the bounds of earth, free of the careful order she had always imposed on everything. Free, as she had said to Constantine a few days before, to admit that she after all knew noth-ing about love. She needed to push out her boundaries more, take risks. She remembered for an instant think-ing (as she'd quizzed McEnroe about his love for Ell' that she was taking a great risk. *And now I ne take another big risk*, she thought, *to tell Don that this child is on the way. And risk his dismay—even possible rejection? No. Then end this child before it had a chance to breathe or call her, "Mama, mama." Never!* It was an evil thought, and she pushed it away. *Then what was she to do?*

Another hill, and another valley. She rose and fell, faster and faster, her foot right to the floor, exhilaration taking over.

This then was freedom. This was what Ellie had sought—the high, the rush, the risk.

A slow tractor loomed just on the far side of a rise. She sucked in her breath, lurching forward, and jammed her foot on the brake. The back of the tractor, its orange triangle gleaming, filled all her windshield. With a sickening, screeching jolt, she stopped the jeep only inches from it. Everything on the seat beside her smacked against the dashboard and crashed to the floor.

She fell forward over the wheel, gasping and sobbing.

Somewhere a woman's voice was saying, "Pull over, pull over, for pity's sake!" She looked up wildly to see a woman waving and gesturing frantically, her mouth open to shout through the glass. Numbly, automatically, she swung the jeep aside, turned off the ignition key and waited, trembling. They would come for her. The sense of freedom had vanished. She was left with horror—dull, aching horror. There was nothing real in that kind of freedom.

The engine clicked, and she smelled burning rubber and diesel, saw the tractor's exhaust, blue and straight above the cab as the tractor moved on and went clear of the narrowest part of the road.

Then the woman reappeared beside the jeep. "Are you ill? Whatever happened? You trying to kill us both? I saw you a minute ago—coming down that last hill like you'd lost your brakes."

The door beside her was wrenched open. She felt as if the hardness in her belly had hardened further, and she could not answer.

Anger melted to anxiety in the woman's face, and suddenly Maggie found herself leaping into the ditch, coughing, heaving, and retching. Her stomach soon was empty, willing itself to quit her body.

At last she slumped down on the grass, face between her hands. She felt foolish and angry with herself. "I'm sorry." She began to moan again, "So sorry." She spat, tasting bitterness.

The woman was at a loss, her booted feet planted among the dew-edged grass at the top of the ditch. She put her hands on her hips. "You got far to go?"

Maggie didn't answer right away. Then, with an effort, said, "No, not really." *And miles to go before I sleep, miles to go . . .*

The woman's head went on one side. "You need a cup of coffee and a slug of brandy. Come on, I've got both in the cab."

"No, I'll be fine. I'm very sorry. I'll just sit here, thanks."

The boots turned away, the wet grass brushing them. "For gosh sakes, don't you do anything so crazy again! You sure your brakes are okay?"

She looked up. "No, no, you're right. I won't. Yes, I'm sure the jeep's all right. Thanks—I won't do that again." She waited, and at last the tractor sputtered away. Only a thin zig-zag pattern of mud showed that it had been there at all.

The damp began to penetrate her jeans. Shaking herself, she stood up unsteadily and looked around her.

The hot smell in the jeep still sickened her, and she found as she reached to start the engine that she was still shaking too much to drive. She leaned back again, staring sightlessly out of the windshield.

What am I doing? What do I want? This wasn't

what I wanted. Her eyes refocused. She looked dully about her, still not seeing the dreary road, and then shut her eyes.

At last the sound of her own breathing comforted her, and she opened her eyes again. The wooded hills spread out before her. Why hadn't she seen them properly before? The highway was not dreary, as she had thought. Yes, the sumac blazed a brilliant contrast with the gray blocks of the highway, but beyond the ditch the field was even brighter, pierced with smoldering goldenrod. It stretched dusty yellow to other fields, and beyond these again to the tapestry of woods.

Joel had told her about a gorge not far away, where the Genesee River dropped in three waterfalls between great boulders and wooded cliffs. If the goldenrod here was beginning to catch alight, the trees there would be a conflagration. Since she had Don now and needed no photographs, she wanted those photographs instead.

Hardly thinking, she groped the seat beside her for the camera. On the next hill she would stop and take pictures of the red, yellow and crimson fire over these hills and valleys.

She looked down. The camera lay at a funny angle on the floor, and when she retrieved it the lens splintered into tiny shards in her palm. She would take no photographs today.

Don was waiting for her when she pulled up in the yard, his face full of love and anxiety. "I didn't know where you were."

"Photos—remember?" She couldn't quite trust her voice, and she didn't tell him about the camera or the tractor.

He pulled her into his arms. "Maggie—come on. What's eating you?"

"I—I will tell you. But not now. I need a cup of coffee, okay?" She struggled free, turned her back, and crossed the porch. Then she flung back casually, "Want some?"

She heard his boots thud one after the other onto the porch and knew that he would follow her in. But he did not come straight into the kitchen, and she heard him pick up the telephone in the office. The conversation was well under way before she realized its import.

"Yes, that's right. Four years, I believe . . . What? Oh, it was in the Boston school system . . . Yes, I know it." His voice was patient, almost weary. "Yes, she knows she has to get New York state certification first, but what about substituting? . . . You will? Today? That's good. Yes, thank you."

She heard him give her name and the rural delivery number the mailman used, then he came into the kitchen looking pleased.

She must have looked thunder at him, for the smile faded immediately. "*Now* what?" he demanded. His eyes darkened, and impatience sharpened his voice.

"You had no right to do that."

"No right! You've been moping about like a sick animal for days."

It was true, but she felt the heat flare up to her cheeks and slopped the coffee as she poured it. She would not look at him. "So what." Her voice came out blank and cold, and the same kind of hardness was gathering inside her as she had felt sitting by the ditch.

"So what? So *what*?" he repeated in mockery. "So what—it's that I love you. Can't stand to see you miserable. You said yourself you need plenty to do."

"Yes—I—"

"And no matter what your little boyfriend Joel thinks, the cats and chickens just aren't going to keep you busy for ever. Unlike half the women round here, Maggie, you've got a *brain*."

Dimly, she knew that even with his sarcasm he was trying to help. He truly thought this was the answer: to send her back to work in the local schools. But she needed time to become part of the farming world first, she had decided. And she resented his interference; it smacked of the same sort of patronage that McEnroe afforded and Ellie had so much hated. *If you can't do yourself a favor, I'll do you one. Why, you don't even know what's good for you.*

She glared up at him. "Yes, I've got a brain. And wits to make my own decisions. I don't need you to make them for me."

"Then make your own. You can't go on like this."

"Like what?" She dared him to name the bad temper she knew characterized her behavior now; wanted to see how far she could push him. She was behind the wheel again, pushing the jeep to its top speed on those hills—testing him to see how far she would go before he would snap. She needed to know, before she could tell him what she had to.

He sat down across from her, poured milk in his coffee, and stirred it slowly. "Just cool off, Maggie. This is silly."

Of course it was silly. "Oh, you would think so." She took a deep breath. "So—what did they—I mean, are they going to call me for a subbing job?" her voice slid up the scale. "I won't go. You can't organize me like that."

"No, they're not going to call you. They're sending you some forms to fill out—that's all."

"I'll shove them in the stove." She began to feel like a small child, pushing and beating on an immovable door and only hurting herself.

He laughed harshly. "Go ahead, if that's what you want. I can't make you out! What *do* you want, Margaret?"

Her head came up at the use of her full name. It stung her. She didn't reply.

"I said what *do* you want, then? More clothes? A trip back to Dedham—is that it? I'll book it if you want."

Some demon in her made her say, "Yes, I'm sure you would. A one-way air ticket. Then I'd be out of your way." She knew she was being impossible.

He leapt to his feet. The coffee slopped over the scrubbed wood, making an ugly brown stain. Don's face was suffused with blood, and she knew she had found his boundary. Any more and she might cross the pale beyond the reach of the love she knew he wanted to give her.

He flung out his arms. *"Out of my way?"* He was shaking as visibly as she herself had been shaking in the jeep. "But I don't *want* you 'out of my way.' Maggie—sweetheart—what is it? Just tell me what you want. I only want to love you. Do you want to go see David and Martha? Would that help? Please just tell me, honey."

She had faced his sarcasm and his anger, but the look of dazed hurt on his face was more than she could bear. She expected him to reject her, but she couldn't stand to see him feeling rejected—as if she had rejected him.

Her eyes fixed blankly on the coffee cups and the brown pool creeping into the grain of the wood. She said slowly, sadly, "Don, I don't know what I want right now." She pushed her hands up into the warmth of her hair, hardly feeling it as her own. "But please, please don't try to figure out for me what I want. Let me do it for myself. Please."

Clumsily he came around the table to put his arms around her. She stood in the circle of his arms, leaned against him smelling the familiar mixture of straw, diesel and cattle, but felt limp, lost, and still far away from him.

November

They settled into an unsatisfactory co-existence, not intruding on each other, skirting each other warily. She saw him suffering, saw that he did love her, but was herself afraid to face the love fully. His love was a consuming fire. She was as afraid of it, she realized, as he had been of her love for him all those years before. Love was a demand as well as a giving. She did not know if she could answer the demand, after all. And she certainly didn't know what she would do if, in the end, the demand turned into a rejection. Constantine's words came to her mind over and over again. *"That's when you know all—when you come to the place of knowing that you really know nothing."*

When the county board of education forms came, she did not burn them after all but put them at the back of Don's desk. Perhaps, she thought, she would do something with them later. Not now, not now when there were other things to understand, to think about, to discover.

McEnroe was coming today. Would he see through the feints she knew she was devising? Would he ask uncomfortable questions? Would he notice—he surely would—that she couldn't seem to laugh anymore?

She stood in front of the full-length mirror Don had fixed onto the bedroom wall for her. The house was empty, and weak November sunshine came obliquely through the window. It showed with deadly accuracy the curves and indentations of her naked body, and she quaked. But the mirror was merciful after all. There was nothing out of the ordinary: no tell-tale swelling of her belly yet. Or *was* there?

She turned sideways, staring so hard that for a second she could have been staring at someone else's body. Had she ever really looked at herself until now? Were those small feet hers, or the bumpy knees and strangely childish hips? The shoulders were smooth skinned— and lovely. Were they hers? And the eyes, huge and anxious, almost laughed at her, belonging to a brown-haired stranger.

Impatiently she picked her clothes off the bed and began to pull them on so that she need see no more. But what about McEnroe? Would he see that this betraying body of hers was different? Would he see all and say all, even before she had spoken to Don herself?

A sort of paralysis had settled on her. *Don will not want me with a child.* She had told herself these words repeatedly as he breathed quietly beside her, falling asleep before her every night. She tried to analyze this conviction. *Why, why do I think so?*

Her father came to mind immediately, and she knew she was beginning, perhaps for the fist time as an adult, to reckon fully with the way he had abandoned her mother, David—and herself. The pain and insecurity of the early years of his absence still made her ache sometimes, and she knew she'd be facing up to both now, as a mother herself. Also, it was too soon. Even after so many years they hardly knew each other. They needed time, he would say. Time and money. The loans on the barn, the grants—they would owe money for years unless they paid out even more capital they did not have for good breeding and milking stock. And, since the fire, every bill that came had been a source of worry. A child would be impossible: the hospital bills, pediatric bills, school bills . . . how could they possibly manage?

What would Ellie have thought? she wondered suddenly. It came to her with brutal clarity, then, that Ellie would have counseled, "Get rid of it. You can't have a squalling infant messing up your lives yet!"

Was that, after all, the answer? She pictured some of the children in her classroom: the pressing warmth of their little bodies crushing against each other and against her by the doorway at the end of the day. The strange mixture of sunshine and shadow, human and animal that was a child. The distinct school smell of soap, hot pencils, stale breakfast and baby shampoo on Monday mornings.

But those children were not her own. They did not clamor for life from *within*, and this one was her own.

Once again, cold revulsion stopped that line of thought. *No, never. Not ever.* She could not, would not do it. She knew that now, with even greater certainty than when driving the jeep on those hills where she had almost found the wrong kind of freedom.

She glanced back at the mirror before turning for the last time to prepare the guestroom for McEnroe. This time she saw unwavering eyes. She would tell Don soon. After all, he believed in God's love. And if there was a God, He must have willed this child. *So Don will want it, too. Surely he will, surely.*

Then she heard yet again McEnroe's voice, speaking to her in the summer. She had said, "I have no plan whatever to get pregnant." But he, of all people, had asked her, *"What about God's plans?"*

———

She was sleeping with her knees drawn up and the fingers of one hand splayed out over her cheek. *Like a child*, Don thought. Even the light hadn't awakened her, and he dropped down on the bed beside her again, for a moment, just to look.

Memory stirred. He had stood looking before, once, at his parents' home. Something had died in him when

Ellie died, and only Maggie had been able to give it back to him. *How blind!* He remembered watching then the rise and fall of the covers over her shoulders.

Only a year, but he had known and understood nothing about her then. That made him smile a little. He knew her more now, could make sense of the particular curves under the bedclothes, but if anything he actually understood her less. Or was it that he had in fact reached the final understanding: that he would never know or understand her fully. Was that it? Was marriage a journey, then, not a haven or end in itself, but a journey with a companion he had to learn to know, love, trust—and let go, to walk her own path?

He put out his hand to touch her shoulders, stroke her thick hair, but stopped. She was at peace, her face cloudless, as it had not been for weeks. He ached for her, wondered at her, but did not want her to stir.

Moving slowly, he rose again and turned off the light. He had been so close to her that he felt cold, as if his being apart from her were a physical loss. And in the sudden darkness the rustling of his hunting clothes made him pause. He waited to hear her breathing, the quiet drawing and releasing of breath, and tiptoed out.

The guestroom door stood open. He hesitated in the doorway but could neither see nor hear any sound. "McEnroe?" His whisper sounded loud enough to wake her, and he berated himself. *Might as well make coffee and throw some more logs on before I get him up.*

But his father was already downstairs, sitting in his stockinged feet, stuffing the L.L. Bean bag. His breath came in short gasps as, without turning, he pushed in the same bits and pieces he had insisted on carrying the year before.

"Up to your old tricks, I see," Don murmured.

McEnroe swung around and grinned. A wave of affection washed over Don. But it was affection tinged with pity, too, as last year's hunting trip suddenly unreeled almost palpably before his eyes: the way his father had cut a thumb; the vicious frost and the sound of the tires on the sub-zero road to their stand; the restaurant's smoke and smells; the agony of hearing of Ellie's addiction—and the frantic, frightened deer.

McEnroe set down the bag and reached for his boots. "Yeah—my old tricks. But I've got a new knife this year. And my malones fit better than they did."

Don opened the stove, poked at it, and pushed in a few more logs. "You getting thinner?"

"Must be. No bad thing. Hey, is she still sleeping?" McEnroe pointed to the ceiling. "I was quiet as I could be."

"I didn't even hear you myself."

"Good."

"You put some chocolate in that thing?"

His father grinned. "Sure I did. Goes well with the whisky and cheese. I changed my mind. You can teach an old dog new tricks, after all."

Don closed down the stove and dusted off his hands. "Huh! I'll believe that when you ditch the malones and wear one of these outfits."

"No way. I told you."

He shrugged. "Ready?"

"Yup." McEnroe stood and stretched. "What about the guns?"

"Out in the office. Slugs? License? Tags?"

His father patted the bag. "All present and correct. Let's go, son."

On the road to the same stand they had taken the year before, McEnroe began to talk about the election campaign, about Nixon, and about some of his colleagues in the state senate. Don listened with only half his attention. Somehow Ellie still sat between them on the seat. Ellie? No, it was Margaret. His mind followed a road of its own, pained at the thought of Maggie's distance. He could not bear it, if, after all the years she had wanted him, he now was the cause of any further pain. And in the foggy beams ahead of them on the highway he kept seeing her sleeping face. He imagined the touch of her springy hair, too, and winced inwardly.

"What's the matter?" McEnroe growled from the depths of his red coat.

"What?"

"You made a noise like you've got the toothache."

"No, I didn't."

"Yes, Don, you did. What's on your mind, anyhow?"

He took a deep breath. "Well, if you must know—Ellie—some. At least, she was when I came down and saw you in the kitchen. But then I was thinking of Maggie, if you really want to know." The words had come out clumsily, and he wished he hadn't answered at all.

His father hardly seemed to have heard. "Oh, that reminds me."

"What?"

"Your mother sent some things with me for you and Maggie. Just a few old photographs and slides. Said she thought you'd like them."

"Maggie would, I expect." He remembered the empty, sick feeling of seeing those pictures a year ago, in the junk room at home.

"No, your mother thought you'd both like them. Photos of you and Ellie going back, and quite a few of Maggie. I'd almost forgotten how much we saw of that kid growing up."

He half laughed. "Kid!"

"Yes, and yet she—" He broke off, veering back whimsically, Don thought, to their earlier conversation. "But you weren't thinking *good* thoughts about her just now—or about Ellie."

Don was glad McEnroe could see little of his face. "Why ever—?"

"Because you sucked in your breath. Toothache, as I said. So what's wrong?"

He thumped one glove on the steering wheel. "Oh, don't try the shrink on me, McEnroe."

"Why not? I love Maggie like she's my own. You're lucky."

He didn't want to reveal much, and sighed. "Yes, yes, and I know it. You needn't keep telling me. I know it for myself now. She's a lovely, lovable woman."

McEnroe didn't answer immediately. A car passed them going in the opposite direction, lights dimmed in the frozen fog. At last he said, "Yes, Don. But she's not herself just now."

"What d'you mean?" His voice came back with such a snap that he added, "Do you reckon she's not well?" He could feel his father's eyes on him now.

"You tell me," McEnroe said drily.

What was he supposed to say? If he said he knew, his father would pull a courtroom cross-examination on him. And if he said he didn't, his father would demand to know why he didn't know. So he said nothing, concentrating instead on parking the jeep.

"You don't know, I guess, Don, what's eating her." It was a statement more than a question.

Don flung himself out of the jeep and slammed the door hard before he remembered what they were doing. He stopped, annoyed with himself.

"Hey! Quiet, nit-wit," McEnroe hissed.

"All right, all right!" He opened the tailgate and pulled out their gear, this time closing it softly. His mind was moving slowly, but he knew his father would not let the subject rest. There would be more questions. *What are the answers?*

His father covered the flashlight with a rag and went ahead of him down the trail. The feeble beam picked out small rocks and roots in the path, but the ground was clear of snow this year and made easier walking.

The balance of this hunting trip seemed different, with his father somehow taking charge. *Just as well,* he thought, *when I can think of little else but Maggie.*

Increasingly uneasy, he followed McEnroe's bulky shape through the swirling fog. A slight breeze came up, and he felt the cold air burning his cheekbones. The fog made them vulnerable in the obscure darkness, especially if others with guns and licenses were out to bag the year's deer. He was far more uneasy, however, about the nagging fears within than about the fog without.

He cast about in his mind for some inkling of Maggie's change toward him. Was it because he spoke now of God as being the source of his light and life? Because he actually enjoyed worshiping God in church, he came home lifted up by it and unable to refrain from talking about the One who had given him back his soul? Was it because—when he spoke of his new joy—he often spoke of God's love and Maggie's in the same breath. He was restored by both, after all.

Perhaps she would accuse him—tongue in cheek but her eyes serious—of turning into a fanatic. *I'm not,* he thought defensively, as if she were facing him now, arguing with him. But if that were why she had withdrawn, he would not know what to do, what to say.

Or was it something to do with that Wilkinson boy who was always hanging around on pretense of discussing chickens and cats with her. What was he to her? Or—worse—perhaps it was that man she'd told him about who had stopped one day to see her on his way home or to some monastery. Was that it? A likely story. He laughed to himself. No, that story was so preposterous it must be true . . . and she wouldn't lie to him, anyway. If the guy really meant anything to her, she wouldn't have told him—would she?

Or maybe it was what he had thought before, that she was getting cabin fever stuck at home with no teaching, no children, no school politics, for the first year since her graduation. Was that the problem?

His mind went as blank as the air surrounding them. He could see nothing. Ahead of him, he heard McEnroe stumble on a root. He reached out and caught him by the arm. "Hey! Steady on. D'you want me to go first? It's not more than a few yards."

"Right. This looks familiar." His father moved the flashlight slightly, pointing downhill. "Wasn't that where we were last year?"

Don narrowed his eyes. "Could be. Close to here, certainly. It's hard to tell—the brush has grown."

"You ought to know."

"Lots of things I ought to know and don't."

"Well, what the heck." McEnroe handed him the flashlight and reached into the L.L. Bean bag. "Don't know about you, but I'm eating some of your chocolate."

"Sounds like a good idea." Glad of the diversion, he pointed the light into the bag as his father searched through it.

"I got a feeling."

"What?"

"That we'll get us a good one this year."

"Why?"

"I just do. Come on. Let's get moving—but quietly, okay?"

"Sure." The slab of smooth, sweet chocolate began to melt on his tongue.

They went forward more slowly again. At last, after deciding that the breeze was changeable and that the deer might pick up their scent wherever they went, they settled among the thornapple. He steeled himself for more discussion about Maggie, but his father said nothing at all until the first glimmer of light came hesitantly through the mist. When he did speak, the words took him utterly by surprise.

"Don—can't you *see* what's troubling her?"

He felt defensive again and couldn't even express how much he longed to know but feared to ask. He snapped. "No!"

His father's whisper came back evenly. "Well, I can. You better ask her yourself. Or take a good look at her face."

He turned his head quickly, but his father was deeply shadowed, eyes directed to the whisky he was pouring from his flask. *Deadpan*—his lawyer's face.

He said the first thing that came into his head. "No—if you know so much—*you* ask her." He hated the sound of his own sudden resentment and bitterness.

His father proffered the flask of bourbon. *Déjà vu.* He remembered the glint of it in the frosty light of last year, remembered turning it down.

This year, though, he would take it. "Thanks—what about some coffee?"

"Later." Again and again, as if he were in a bad dream, paralyzed, he found himself avoiding a confrontation with his father about Maggie. He knew now he was afraid of what he might find out, and the vagueness of his fear only exaggerated his anxiety further. It was better to say almost nothing.

The whisky slid down his throat, smooth and yet burning, then seemed to rise into his nose and choke him. He coughed hard, buried his face in his sleeve, and only coughed even louder. In the darkness the sound exploded like invisible shrapnel.

He sighed heavily. The deer hunt was over for now. "So much for hunting."

"Yeah." His father stretched, his joints cracking audibly. "So much for hunting. And you gotta talk to Maggie, son."

———

Outside the back door of the barn he stood with his

hands in his overalls and watched the cows. Light had flooded the hills as the fog burned off, and it was a bright, crisp November afternoon, the kind that drove him outside again, even though the farm was quiet at this time of year; and he could have been at his desk catching up on paperwork at last, as Maggie would have liked.

The grazing was getting thinner, he noticed, the grass stunted by frost and with patches of bare mud showing through. The ground had frozen the night before and would soon freeze solid for the winter. He shivered, despite the sunshine; desolation crept up on him. How long until the summer?

He went to the toolshed, backed out the tractor, filled two wagons—one with alfalfa and the other with corn—then pulled them one by one into the pasture. The cows stared at him, lazy in the milky sunshine, breath blowing in white clouds around broad faces. They ambled over to snort and tear greedily at the feed. He watched them abstractedly, his mind scrolling back to the hunting that morning.

His father's prophecy had not come true; they had shot no deer today. In a strange way he was relieved, unsure that he could stand to relive the moment of the deer's wild-eyed terror. He smiled to himself. *But which is worse? The terrified deer or the deflated paterfamilias?* "What'd you expect," he had said in the end to his father. "Some deer to oblige us by coolly strolling right in front of us, posing while we shoot like we're *Boston Herald* photographers?"

Photographers. What about those photographs his mother had sent?

He went back through the barn again, checked that the heifers had enough feed in their mangers, then saw Maggie out in the yard. She was muffled in a parka, her face glowing. She was scattering corn grains and calling to the hens. He hesitated; she had not seen him.

He thought of telling her about the photographs, but something held him back; McEnroe might have mentioned them already, anyway. Either he would look at them by himself, or not at all.

Then McEnroe came out on the back porch with coffee for them all. For a while Don forgot the photographs, forgot the ache and anxiety inside, and basked in the nearness to them both. His eyes kept straying, first to his father's face, then to Maggie's, but neither was giving anything away, so he let his eyes wander to the new barn.

Something in him always leaped up when he looked at it, but this time the pleasure was short-lived. Even the sun as it slid down behind the barn—now so early— was tinged with a ring of frost. Winter was slinking up on them, hunting them as remorselessly as he and his father had hunted that morning. Only, unlike themselves, winter would not miss its prey. The crystal clarity of such days would soon splinter, he knew, as winter crept on. Snow clouds, heavy and gray as wolf pelts, would come in wadded packs from the north; the ground, the sky—all would be blotted out, stiffened in the rigor mortis of winter's teeth. He longed suddenly for the heat and haze of summer, the unfurling of corn stalks and uncurling of mimosa leaves.

Steam from his coffee cup spiraled around his face, but he hardly felt it; hardly heard McEnroe talking to Margaret. They seemed a long distance away. He made himself snap awake, made himself concentrate on them. Yes, winter was deathly, but it restored and cleansed the land each year. And far worse than the winters of New York was the winter of Margaret's withdrawal—and now—the winter of his own fear and withdrawal.

Old man Wilkinson had spoken of ice jams on the Genesee and the Cattaraugus, of sudden thaws in alternating sun and downpour in spring, and these were what he needed now—a smile or other sign from Margaret. He felt alone, slightly desperate, yet at the same time dispassionate enough about his own feelings to mock them. *Wolves of winter, broken crystal—oh wouldn't Maggie tease me! This is the man who says he believes in God's warmth and love!*

Two of the cats suddenly sprang from under the porch and went rolling and tumbling over each other along the lowest step. Maggie laughed, handed Don her cup, and scooped them up. They squirmed and hissed, clawing at her parka, but she only laughed more. She turned to look directly at him, her eyes full of light, full of what he hoped was the desire to talk with him, understand him, and cross whatever barrier had come up between them.

Then he caught his father looking up at them, his mouth screwed drily to one side, his eyes shrewd. *Yes,* he must question her. *When? How?*

December

It was painful to avoid talking to her about anything that mattered, but easy. He saw the board of education forms on the back of his desk and knew she would do nothing with them, so he quietly pushed them into a drawer. He watched her doctor the cats and helped her build nesting boxes in the toolshed for the hens. He even sat down with her one evening in the parlor and discussed Christmas, making plans to fly back to Boston and leave the farm with Larry for a few days. They avoided all but the most surface discussions, however, and he still couldn't make himself ask her again what was wrong. Her eyes became worried, almost haunted. He knew he must look equally worried himself, but he remained paralyzed, not daring to ask for a name for the nameless thing that was threatening them.

While they were packing suitcases for Christmas, he remembered the photographs his mother had sent with McEnroe in November. Perhaps they would unleash whatever conversation they needed to have. So, when Maggie's back was turned in the closet, he stuffed several albums and bags of slides into the suitcases, concealing them under shirts, socks and sweaters. He suddenly felt more cheerful.

She came back with an armful of clothes. She was wearing only a thin blouse, but although the bedroom was cool, she looked hot.

"You okay?"

"Sure."

"You're all red. Here, let me get those."

She averted her eyes. "Thanks. Have you got a few minutes to spare?"

He sat down on the end of the bed and began to fold the clothes mechanically, glad she wanted him with her.

"No—not that, Don—I can do them. I was wondering, could you bag up the presents I wrapped? They're in the office—behind the door." A pixyish smile creased her face. "But no shaking and peeking into them, mind."

"Yes, boss." He stood, grinning. Perhaps these few days in Boston were what they needed.

She balled a pair of socks and threw them at him. He threw them back, and soon they were laughing like children, lobbing slippers and socks, ducking, feinting and throwing until the bedclothes were twisted off the bed, the suitcases were half empty again, and the entire bedroom was a wreck.

"Truce! Pax!" she shouted, waving a handkerchief at last and holding up a blanket as a shield. "End of the sock wars—please." She was shaking with laughter.

He collapsed on the bed and pulled her down with him. She smelled hot and alive. "Ah, Maggie, I love you so much it scares me sometimes."

Her eyes clouded immediately, and she swallowed hard. Her body became still, resting heavily on his. "Me too—oh—Don—" She skidded to the edge of saying more, then held back, levering herself out of his arms. Her mood had changed again. "Come on, honey. Larry'll be here to take us to the airport, and we're not nearly ready. Please can you get up?"

He sighed heavily, pushed the hair out of his eyes, and stood up. Another chance had passed.

———

As the plane dipped out of the low clouds over the city, she saw the familiar tree-divided suburbs, and her heart rose like a bird. "Oh, look, Don—haven't you missed it?" She laid her hand on his arm, leaned across him, and pointed out of the window. Dusk was just beginning, and the street lights flickered like chains of colored beads.

"Not much," he said evenly. "Don't forget I left home a long time ago." He looked anxious. "You wouldn't want to come back here to stay, would you? I thought you were crazier than I am about the rural idyll."

"No, I wouldn't," she said flatly, but saw that he had caught a slight hesitation in her voice; she would have to lighten things. "But not because of any rural idyll, Don. Do you call five-foot icicles, frozen pipes, chilblains, and blocked highways a rural idyll?"

He smiled. "Of course not. But you get all those things here as well."

"I know it," she answered drily. "Don't worry. I haven't forgotten. But ah, it's good to come home!"

Below them stretched the gray waters of the harbor, then the drab, scrubby wilderness that marked the perimeter of the airport, then—immediately—the concrete slabs and neat blue lights of the runway. The engine roared into reverse, and the plane bounced and taxied toward the lights of the terminal. "We're home, Don!"

"I think you're happier than I am at seeing my parents."

"My mother, too, in a couple days. And David and Martha and the kids. Oh, if it weren't for Christmas I couldn't stand winter."

She saw his jaw tighten. "I feel the same," he said slowly, and she wondered afresh at how little she really knew about him.

McEnroe was waiting in the terminal to meet them. As he hugged her to him, she smelled cigar smoke and the cold of outdoors on his coat—he must have just arrived. *Déjà vu* took over, but there was also the giddy, heady feeling that came with the knowledge of the child.

A few people stared, recognizing McEnroe and pointing, but he paid no attention, and soon they were all three piling cases and presents into the back of the car.

Crowded between Don and his father in the front seat and seeing the familiar signs of Route 95 flash past them as they drove to Bedford, Maggie felt again a rush of gladness and a deep sense of security. Surely in *this* setting there could be no difficulty telling him about the child? And surely even their financial worries would seem less important here.

"Marianne'll be gone to the six o'clock by the time we're home," McEnroe was saying. "You know how she hates crowds and how packed the church gets. But I thought we could go to the midnight, if that suits you. You don't mind the crush, do you?" He took his eyes off the road momentarily and flashed a look at Maggie. "You've got circles under your eyes, girl. Don, aren't you looking after her? Think you can stay awake until midnight?" He gave them no time to answer, firing off the questions so quickly that they both laughed. "How'd you like some eggnog? I'll get the fire going as well. We'll crack out a new bottle of something festive and admire the tree. You *will* admire it, I hope? Your mother spent hours on a stepladder. Said it was an occasion-and-a-half this year, with both of you coming home. And, Maggie, she phoned your mother and the whole clan's coming over after lunch tomorrow. How about that?"

Don groaned. "Oh, I thought this was just a quiet family Christmas."

"It is, it is!" Maggie clapped her hands. "Oh—you don't know! I can't wait."

"But what about going to church midnight, Maggie?" Don was pressing her hand, anxious again.

She tried to think fast. Had he guessed her news?

McEnroe seemed to know. Or was it just that Don wanted her to set foot inside a church with him once in a while? "I'm not sure. Your father is right. I'm flaked out—maybe I'll take a nap. I wouldn't want to miss the rest of Christmas Eve."

Everything in the house was warm and welcoming: a smell of mulled cider and the sound of the fire crackling in the family room. Don and his father heaved suitcases and bags to the bottom of the stairs and shrugged off their coats while she stood just inside the door, dazed by the lights, dazzled by the tree.

Memories crowded back. *"Kick your shoes off,"* Ellie had said, *"Kick your shoes off."* The voice echoed in her head, and her eyes filled unexpectedly. She remembered that she had felt small, an outsider. Now, except for Ellie but also because of Ellie, she felt different. The tree towered over her, bright with ribbons, glittering with lights.

Stepping forward, she was bathed in an intense joy. It lit her from outside and within. She remembered for a moment the flicker of transitory joy she had felt long ago, hearing the music of Ellie's Woodstock recordings; but this warmth was a burst of flame by comparison. It washed over her like warm oil, and she stood transfigured, as if on holy ground. All her fear melted, and she knew only an inner peace. Had she found freedom, then, after all? Not the false freedom she thought she'd found one morning in the autumn. No, this freedom ran like a great tide through and over her. She wanted to fling out her arms and sing and laugh, but instead the tears were pouring down her cheeks and she stood unmoving. Here was the ultimate risk: to give herself to the flood of unknowing, to the flood of love that engulfed her. It did not matter that her own father had never come back to her mother. She and Don had a heavenly Father who would never stop loving them—or their children.

She tottered, and suddenly Don was beside her. Looking alarmed, he came and took her coat. "Poor Maggie. Done in, are you? Come on—let's get you upstairs for a bit." He wiped her face unceremoniously with his shirtsleeves, and she let him do it, dumbly.

Part of her knew he was treating her like a child, and that all she had to do was tell him what was happening inside her—the wave of joy, the rush of light— and that he would understand. But she couldn't even speak at first. And because another part of her did want to be coddled and cuddled like a child—did want the surge of happiness to go on and on—she allowed herself to be led up the carpeted stairs.

"I don't know where we're sleeping," he was saying, "but I'll find out. Not my old bed, I hope!"

They went slowly along the mezzanine. Everything looked the same. Don pushed open one door after another, and she followed him in a daze. "Not in here, I guess." Some of the rooms were cold, including his old one, and he shut the doors again, each time. Then they came to the guest room where she had slept—or tried to the night of the wake, and found that it had been redecorated and fitted with a new double bed.

She slid onto the quilt and gasped, and he shut the door behind them. Except for the soft hiss of the forced air ducts, the room was utterly quiet. Still in a dream (or was it) she stared around at the rich blue velveteen of the drapes, the swirling colors of the quilt, and felt the thick pile of the carpet under her feet. The tears came again, irritating her, but unstoppable, and words poured out that had nothing whatever to do with her real emotions. "They did this all for us," she wailed, her mouth going askew.

He began to laugh softly. "Oh, Maggie, what a funny little woman. Come on." He bent and pulled off her boots, folded up the sides of the quilt and wrapped her in it. "You just pass out for a while, okay?" He bent and kissed her.

She felt even more weary, suddenly, and the warmth of the room was already drugging her. He stood looking down at her. "We'll make up some eggnog for you after my mother gets back. You sleep now." He turned off the light. Then the door closed behind him.

She fell off the precipice of sleep and remembered nothing more.

———

When she awoke a door was opening and someone stood in the doorway with the light behind him. She raised her head, bewildered, then remembered where she was.

Don turned on the lamp beside the bed and held out a glass. "Feel better?"

She pushed her hands into her hair, still not fully conscious. "Oh, we're here. I feel like I'm dreaming. I'll wake up and it won't be real."

The side of the bed dipped as he sat down by her. "You were more shattered than I've ever seen you. It's all real enough, Maggie. Happy Christmas, sweetheart."

Her head still felt heavy, and she struggled to sit up. "It's Christmas Day? Did I sleep all night?"

He smiled. "No, no. It's about nine-thirty, still Christmas Eve. I thought you ought to wake up now and eat something." He moved closer to her.

She lifted her arms to him and spoke into his ear, "You're being so kind and sweet." She did not want to emerge from the cocoon of happiness yet. Not yet.

He shook his head, bumping her nose slightly. "No, I'm not sure I have been. I just got a lecture from McEnroe. He says I've let you get run down. I'm sorry— guess I had no idea you were so exhausted—" he broke off, his face turning toward hers so their noses almost touched again, "—so exhausted, or why, though I'm almost ready to hazard a guess or two."

She looked down, but he raised her chin, and his

voice became soft as velvet. "Maggie—please—what's wrong?"

She leaned forward against his chest so that she would not have to meet his eyes, and was surprised to hear how fast his heart was beating as he spoke to her. He went on, "I've known something's been bothering you—for weeks and weeks—and it's bothered me, too. But I was afraid—"

She had waited far too long to tell him, and the fear had grown out of all proportion. But that was long ago, before she had stood under the tree and that wave of joy had crested and curled over her and lapped her in itself. Her heart speeded up, too, but even now she could not get the right words out. "I was scared," she mumbled at last, still avoiding his eyes.

"Maggie—for heaven's sakes! It's been months now."

She sat up straight and with a sudden resolve swung her legs off the bed. "Yes, I know it. So I promise—" She turned and looked directly into his troubled blue eyes, made bluer still by the lamplight. "So I promise I'll talk to you before Christmas is over. I do—I do feel completely different already—truly."

He took her gently by one shoulder. "Promise?"

"Yes, I promise. It's okay, I'm awake now—I won't renege on it. Listen, where's that drink you promised me?" She took the glass from him and sipped the eggnog slowly, leaning against him, still savoring the lazy sleepiness. She wanted now to say something about what had happened in the foyer. "Don—?"

"Uh-huh."

"When we first came in downstairs—when I was crying—"

"You were just overjoyed to be here." He moved his hand slowly up and down her back, comforting.

"Yes—but more than that. Oh—I can't explain. I suddenly felt, well—" She searched his face and saw only encouragement. "It sounds crazy. *Loved.*"

His arms came around her again, "You are. Of course you are."

"But it wasn't just you, or your father. The feeling was mixed up with Ellie—and with someone else."

He frowned slightly, looking puzzled. "Yes?"

But she couldn't amplify, and they fell silent.

At last, Don ventured, "Mother's been home for a while. She's made a sort of smorgasbord. You hungry?"

"I think I am."

Don stood up. "I'll bring in the luggage. No hurry. Then—what about midnight?"

She hesitated, knowing he wanted her to go. Then—suddenly there was no need to hesitate. It was Christmas; they were home, and she had been flooded by love—Don's love and God's love, too. "Yes, I'll come," she said simply.

———

The church was empty of people when they arrived, but in the side chapel thick greenery was spread over a roughly made stable. Children from the parish school had made quaint little clay shepherds and lambs, and the figure of Mary stood serenely with an enormous nose, and eyes painted green. Laughing in delight, Margaret pointed them out to Don and his father. McEnroe gave her a questioning look from under his thick eyebrows but said nothing. She stared back at the crib. Under the roof of hemlock, spruce and douglas fir, the manger held only straw, and there was no sign of the three wise men. Then she remembered: they would put the Christchild into the manger during the communion, and the wise men would not come traveling until January.

How far away it all seemed—something associated with grade school Christmas pageants, unintended comedies all, and with Ellie as a brilliant Angel Gabriel.

And yet it was real, now, for her—as real as the wave of joy that had rolled over her in McEnroes' foyer, as real as the bed where she awoke; as real as the man who had put his arms around her and held her until she was properly awake; as real as his love for her.

They turned to find a seat. People were pouring in through all three doors of the church; there was a sense of festivity, of party, that she did not usually associate with churches.

McEnroe was kneeling with his eyes closed, Don next to him, and she moved awkwardly to join them. Don's eyes were wide open, looking up at the crib but also seemingly beyond it.

She bent toward him and whispered his name. He turned immediately, and she said. "All this celebration for a baby born two thousand years ago!"

A half smile touched his mouth. "Why not?"

She trembled. Here they were, kneeling in a church painted blue and white and decorated with greenery and red and white candles. The festivity had meant something to Don for the past year, but until now not to her. For a moment she felt again as empty as the church waiting for the Christmas parishioners; as empty as the straw manger waiting for its diminutive Jesus.

Then she remembered the child she herself was carrying. The joy surged back again. *I have promised to tell him.* She looked at Don. *I have promised.* And as communion began, she saw it all through Don's eyes, this time taking part in it herself, as well.

Later, when the church was a flurry of parishioners, priests and servers all shouting "Merry Christmas" and pulling on coats and scarves against the cold outside; and when McEnroe had left them to talk to some of the others on the way out, she followed Don back to the crib. She let him walk a few steps ahead of her, wondering if she was somehow intruding, and wondering, too, what he was thinking.

He knelt by the crib and remained quite still for a moment, then smiled as he turned and looked over his right shoulder at her. "A very specific prayer, that's all, Mrs. McEnroe."

"And He will answer you," she murmured.

Around them a few children were pushing forward with the round eyes of midnight wonder to see the crib. Don and Maggie were gradually pressed aside by the crush of people standing to watch or pray by the crib. There was a babble of voices all around them, and the smell of several different perfumes. But stronger than all these impressions was the tide of love that was washing over her.

This is it. She must tell him now.

They were halfway toward the back of the church, where McEnroe was laughing and talking to a group of men she supposed must be his golfing partners, but the time and place didn't signify, and she stopped.

"Don—if you were praying for me just now—" Her throat went dry, and her voice forsook her, croaking, "Well, it's good if you were." She coughed, looking up, and his eyes burned blue into her own. "I—we—I'm carrying a child, Don. Our child."

For weeks she had imagined dismay or even rejection. Today she had expected surprise, even amazement. What she had never expected was to see him bend, laughing, to scoop her up. He swung her around dizzily and set her down again so quickly that she had to clutch his arms to steady herself.

———

After his parents had gone upstairs to bed, they sat together in the family room, facing each other across the fireplace, as they had done a year before. There was so much to say, but at first they said nothing. He stared at her, and she stared at the fire. The logs shifted, hissing, flaring, and smoking. It wasn't until he said, "Why didn't you tell me before?" that everything she wanted to say came pouring out.

He squatted by the fire to stoke it a little. She fell on her knees beside him, and they stayed there, holding each other, warm and still for a long time.

At last he went up to their room and returned with the photographs he had kept hidden since November. "My mother thinks you'll enjoy these," he said.

Pictures of the wedding. Pictures much older, too— of Ellie, of Don, of Margaret. They no longer gave her a lump in her throat. They no longer made Don feel cold and bitter inside. Instead, all the old photographs of those long summers made them laugh at themselves and even at Ellie.

The white bird of winter settled for the night over the house. Under its wings, with fire crackling and photographs scattered all around them, he was healed of sorrow, and she was made whole by joy.